MORTAL

BY TED DEKKER AND TOSCA LEE

The Books of Mortals

Forbidden
Mortal
Sovereign

The Books of Mortals

MORTAL

TED DEKkER
AND TOSCA LEE

Faith
Words

New York   Boston   Nashville

Copyright © 2012 by Ted Dekker

FaithWords
Hachette Book Group
237 Park Avenue
New York, NY 10017
www.faithwords.com

FaithWords is a division of Hachette Book Group, Inc.
The FaithWords name and logo are trademarks of Hachette Book Group, Inc.

The Hachette Speakers Bureau provides a wide range of authors for speaking events. To find out more, go to www.hachettespeakersbureau.com or call (866) 376-6591.

The publisher is not responsible for websites (or their content) that are not owned by the publisher.

Printed in the United States of America

Originally published in hardcover by Hachette Book Group

First mass market edition: February 2013

10 9 8 7 6 5 4 3 2

OPM

MORTAL

The Beginning

IN THE YEAR 2005, geneticists discovered the human gene that controlled both innate and learned forms of fear. It was called Strathmin, or Oncoprotein 18. Within fifteen years, genetic influencers for all primary emotions were similarly identified.

Nearly a decade later, in the wake of a catastrophic war that destroyed much of civilization, humanity vowed to forsake ruinous emotion and serve the way of a new Order. To this end, the first Sovereign unleashed a virus called Legion, which genetically stripped an unsuspecting world of all emotion but one: fear. As humanity forgot hope, love, and joy, it also left behind hatred, malice, and anger. For nearly five hundred years, perfect peace reigned.

But a sect called the Keepers closely guarded the terrible secret that every soul on earth, though in every appearance human, was actually dead. For centuries they tenaciously clung to a single prediction that the viral code introduced by Legion would eventually revert in the blood of a single child. Humanity's final hope for life would be found in his rise to power. Also passed down among the

Keepers: a sealed vial of ancient blood with the power to awaken five souls who would assist him.

In the year 471 a boy named Jonathan was born to a ruling family with true life running through his veins. His existence was kept secret until the day he was discovered by a lowly artisan named Rom Sebastian and four others brought to life by the Keeper's ancient blood.

Around that time, the powerful alchemist, Pravus, began to hunt the Keepers, while devising a serum to counteract the effect of Legion. But rather than grant life, it returned only the darker emotions with all their ill effects.

According to the Order's rules of succession, one woman stood before Jonathan in the line of power: heir apparent Feyn Cerelia. Through the intervention of Rom, she tasted life once, albeit briefly—even as her powerful brother, Saric, fell thrall to Pravus's alchemy and planned to seize Feyn's throne for himself.

Persuaded of the boy's power to awaken humanity, Feyn agreed to sacrifice her life and clear the path for Jonathan in exchange for the promise that her body would secretly be kept in stasis, technically dead by law, until the boy took power at the age of eighteen.

She gave her life on the day of her inauguration, and Jonathan's sovereignty was kept in the interim by his regent, Rowan. Exposed for his malicious plot, Saric vanished and was thought dead.

Surrounded by powerful warriors called Mortals sworn to protect him, Jonathan went into hiding for nine years. He now nears his eighteenth birthday, when he will return to the world capital of Byzantium to claim his rightful place as Sovereign. It is believed by all those who follow him that his blood will return life to the world and usher in a new kingdom.

But Saric is not dead. Even now, he gathers his forces to stand against Jonathan before he can take his seat of power and return life to a dead world.

CHAPTER ONE

Roland akara, Prince of the Nomads and second only to Rom Sebastian among all Mortals, sat unflinching upon his mount, scanning the valley below with the eyes of one who'd seen far too much to be either easily disturbed or easily satisfied. He was a warrior, loved desperately by all who followed him, a leader descended from generations of rulers, a man given to purpose without an ounce of compromise.

And that purpose had never been clearer: to usher in the reign of Jonathan at any cost in utter defiance of death.

On the dark stallion next to his own sat his sister Michael, twenty-seven—younger than Roland by three years. A composite bow was slung across her back in the same manner as his. The long drape of her coat covered the curved sword that rode her hip. They were two Mortals, clad in black, overlooking their kingdom.

But this was not their kingdom. This was a valley of death. It spread out to the west and east, a vast waste only intermittently broken by a patch of twisting scrub. Whatever had once flowed through this dry riverbed had all but poisoned it. Even now, hundreds of years after the wars that had ruined massive stretches of countryside—including the vineyards that had once characterized this region—only the staunchest new growth survived.

Michael spoke in a low voice, jaw tight. "He's there." A slight breeze lifted a dark wisp of hair free from the torrent of braids that fell down past her shoulders, each of them tied in darkly colored cords, each of them telling a tale of rank, victory, or conquest so that one might read the entire volume with a glance. Only her brother's plaits, shot through with feathers, onyx, and lapis beads, were more elaborate.

Roland's stallion snorted, tugged at the bit, shifting on the rocky cliff. With a twitch of the reins, Roland commanded stillness. The stallion quieted, his black coat quivering once. They had tracked death to this valley, pushing their mounts to the breaking point through the waning night and the better part of the day. No creature had the same acute sense of smell as a Mortal, and they had picked up the scent from a distance.

Death. The smell of Corpse. The scent was common, particularly near the cities and towns in which the world's millions lived—human in appearance...dead in reality.

But the odor Roland and his ranking second, Michael, had chased through the night was different than the scent of mere Corpse. Deeper. Pungent and metallic. The fragrance of Hades itself. The putrid odor rose from the lone outpost on the crusted valley floor half a mile before them, an affront to every breath they took.

Whatever had seized Maro, that impetuous Nomad who'd taken up with the zealots as of late, was either not a Corpse or a new kind of Corpse altogether.

And that was what Roland needed to know.

There had been rumors. Of a new kind of death gathering to crush Jonathan, the Maker of all Mortals, before his inauguration in nine days. Roland had heard far too many rumors to give them much attention. They were as prevalent as lore of the Maker's Hand—the mystical involvement of a divine Maker. But Roland had seen no evidence of the angry god of Order that Corpses clamored to appease by following their ludicrous rules.

But now, with the new odor thick in his nostrils, the reality of an opposing force gained credence in the company of several other pungent tells: horses. Four in front of the canteen. Two more out back. Fresh earth churned up by hooves, stale water in the trough. The pine wood of the building itself. Maro. Roland had not smelled his death, which could only mean he was alive.

"How did the scouts miss this?" Roland said.

"It's beyond our usual perimeter," Michael said. She studied the valley for a few moments. "Thoughts?"

"Many," Roland said grimly.

"Any you'd care to share?"

"Only the one that matters."

"And that is?"

"He lives or we die."

She nodded. "How then should we help that insolent zealot we call cousin live?"

Roland had gone after Maro after hearing that he'd let his drunken mouth flap about bringing the scalp of a Corpse home to the Seyala Valley, home for the last year to all twelve hundred Mortals awaiting Jonathan's rule. Michael had caught up to him in the middle of the night and Roland had agreed to her company, expecting no real trouble—other than his annoyance—in retrieving him.

Until they'd found Maro's horse five miles south of the valley, dead, covered in the new scent of death they'd tracked here.

He would have returned for more fighters but he couldn't afford to lose the new scent—or the chance to learn if the rumored new death was real. With Jonathan's inauguration days away they couldn't afford to take chances.

Beyond that, Roland felt a personal responsibility for the hotheaded zealot. If they did salvage his cousin's life, Roland would personally see that he spent the rest of his days painfully aware of his folly.

"We kill the rest," Roland said.

"How?"

"I'll know once I'm inside."

"You mean 'we.' Once *we* get inside."

"No, Michael. Not 'we.' "

Michael was in her prime as a fighter, vastly skilled in the blade and bow arts. Last year he'd watched her take on four men at the games and bring each to his knees—three with nicks from her blade just deep enough along their throats to remove any vestige of doubt as to her dominance and precision.

He'd promoted her to his second then, not because she was his sister and bore the same ancient blood of the rulers, but because she could not be matched in battle. And every one of them knew that battle would come.

She turned hazel eyes to him. They had been brown before her Mortality, as had his. Mortals couldn't smell the emotions and natures of other Mortals—but if he could, Roland was sure, the aroma of loyalty would be seeping from her every pore. She would die for him—

not as her brother, but as her prince—as all Nomads had sworn to do.

Which was why he must not give her the opportunity.

"May I ask why?"

"Because I need you to burn that shack to the ground if I fail."

"Rom is the leader of the Mortals. Over the Keepers and Nomads both."

He leveled his gaze at her. "Rom's strong and we serve him, but we serve Jonathan and our people first. Never forget that. One of us must live."

"Then let me go in first," she said.

He had to fight the quirk of a smile at the corner of his mouth. "When has any Nomad leader not been the first one in? No. I go first. Alone."

She acquiesced with a tilt of her head. "My prince."

"Put up your hood. When I go in, slit the throats of all their horses except one. If things go wrong, return to Rom, give him a full report and lead our people. Am I clear?"

Her jaw was as stiff as her nod.

Roland pulled the horse round and started down the steep embankment, acutely aware of Michael a horse-length behind him.

It was true, what he'd said. The only thought that mattered now was whether they lived or died trying to preserve the life Jonathan had given all Mortals. Jonathan was nine days from his inauguration. And then everything would change.

It was also true that his thoughts were far more complex than he cared to voice, even to Michael.

For twelve years he'd led the Nomads—since the death

of his and Michael's father. He had led them in their rebellion against the Order, living in the wilderness of Europa, north of Byzantium, that city once called Rome in the age of Chaos centuries before.

His people had tenaciously clung to resistance out of a fear of being controlled by the statutes of state religion—a religion that still claimed vast casualties among the Nomads as most caved in to the greater fear of Order's Maker. And of rules with eternal consequences.

Those Nomads who remained true were the purest of humanity, a fiercely independent people who carried their fighting and survival skills like a badge of unsurpassed honor. They kept to themselves, vagabonds with a long heritage of carving out harsh livings in the hinterlands, dreaming of a day when they would overthrow Order.

Two years after Roland had become ruling prince, word had come that a child once known to them—briefly sheltered among them as a baby—had been confirmed rightful heir to the Sovereign throne. His name was Jonathan.

Jonathan, the prince of life. He had returned to them with Rom Sebastian and the warrior Triphon—two men altered by a vial of blood obtained by the ancient sect of Keepers in anticipation of the day when Jonathan's blood would ignite a new kingdom.

Mortals, they called themselves.

Roland had offered his full support. Not because he necessarily believed in the sayings about the boy or the Keepers' history of friendship with the Nomads, but because any rebel who stood against Order was a friend. And so he had welcomed the Mortals and taught them the Nomadic ways of survival and fighting.

Rom Sebastian demonstrated superior skills as a leader. He spoke with strange fire about new emotions unlocked by the blood he'd taken, and of a coming age when all would taste the life he had tasted.

And then the day had come when, five years later, the boy's blood had changed. The old man who had come with Rom—the last surviving member of the Keepers— had proclaimed it ready to bring others to life. The world of Nomads was in an uproar. Could it be? To be certain his people were not being deceived, Roland had accepted the boy's blood himself.

That day, injected with a stent directly from Jonathan's vein, his world had forever changed. Life had come like a tidal wave, sweeping away a death he did not know existed. For the first time he'd felt the arcane emotions of joy and rapture and love. He had raged through camp, delirious. He'd also found the darker emotions—jealousy, sorrow, ambition—and wept as he never had, clawing at his face and cursing his very existence. Whatever challenges this mix of emotions brought, they made him feel utterly beautiful and deplorable in ways he had never fathomed.

Teeming with new, uncaged life, Roland had called for all Nomads to take Jonathan's blood and serve him in a new mission as the last hope for a dead world. Over the next weeks and months, roughly nine hundred Nomads came to life. In subsequent years, another three hundred common Corpses joined them, each approved by council quorum, before the council called for a moratorium until the full maturing of Jonathan's blood.

Within a year the first Mortals born of Jonathan's blood began to note new changes to their senses. They could smell the faintest scents with greater sensitivity than animals. They could perceive swift motion in such detail, all at once, so that the world seemed to slow about them, giving them great advantage in combat. Their senses of touch, taste, and hearing were all heightened—and continued to heighten—to the point of near insatiability.

But perhaps the greatest physical change for any Mortal was the promise of extended life. When the alchemists among them—most notably the old Keeper himself—first noted the change to their metabolism, he calculated a new minimal Mortal lifetime of hundreds of years.

They were a new race, fully deserving of the name *Mortal*. They were a chosen and powerful people waiting in wild abandon and terrible anticipation for the day when Jonathan would claim the Mortal kingdom for good.

A new era was upon them. Nothing else mattered.

But today there was Maro's foolishness and this new scent to contend with, this death emanating from the cantina on the ancient riverbed not two hundred paces ahead.

Roland and Michael walked their horses abreast of one another, eyes fixed, arms relaxed. The odor was by now so repulsive it was all he could do not to cover his nose.

"Break right, to the back," Roland said. "Slowly. All the horses but one. And listen for me."

"I refuse to lose my prince today, brother."

"Your prince will live a thousand years."

"What if this is more than you bargained for?"

"If it is, Rom will need to know. Listen for me. Do as I ask. Go."

She pressed her horse forward, cutting across his path, angling toward the back of the cantina.

The wood structure was little better than a shack,

hastily and poorly built. Roland could see gaps between the wallboards even from here. He drew the hood over his head as the wind kicked up, sending dusty eddies up from the stallion's hooves. Mortals who rode beyond their home in the Seyala Valley weren't always immediately recognized by Corpses who didn't know to look for the unique hazel of their eyes. But Roland sensed that whoever had captured Maro knew exactly what they'd taken.

He could feel the weight of the throwing knives beneath his coat, strapped two to a side to his belt, as he stopped at the cantina and slid from the saddle. He wound the reins around the rail with a secure tug and glanced at the other horses.

Straight-edged swords hung sheathed from the saddles. They were short, each blade perhaps only two feet in length, a weapon for cutting and thrusting—not slashing from horseback. He had not seen weapons like this before, and yet the hilts were worn and obviously used. At least the fact that they were here meant that the Corpses within weren't expecting any trouble.

Roland turned his eyes to the door, inhaled.

Someone was talking inside. A chuckle. Another voice. Drink flowing into a cup. Wine. Beer. Bread. Salt. Sweat. The faint, acidic scent of fear. Too faint. Far less than the fear that stank upon most Corpses, spawned by the sole remaining emotion that deceived them into thinking they were human.

He'd just set his boot on the first step when another scent assailed his lungs, seeping into his consciousness. A new one he'd never smelled before. Tangy. Sharp, but not offensive. On the contrary, quite agreeable.

Something other than death or fear.

His heart surged and he willed it to calm. Mortals couldn't smell the emotions of other living Mortals the way they could the fear of Corpses. If he couldn't smell Mortals, then the scent wasn't Maro's. And yet it stirred something new in him, so that his heart started again, like a breakaway colt.

He briefly considered retreating to consider the situation, but this was a matter that would be learned only from experience.

Roland mounted the steps, stopped on the landing. He shoved his jacket behind his blades, hitching the side of it into his belt, clearing the path for his knives. He flipped out two, one in each hand. Held them firm by his waist. Tipped his head down, eyes on the dark seam at the bottom of the door, and collected himself. Not merely his thoughts or his courage—these any man or woman do before engaging an enemy. Now there was far more to gather.

Mortals called it *seeing* and technically it was. But by *seeing* they meant fully understanding every component of that vision so that the world seemed to slow, filling each instant, breath, heartbeat, with information. A superior advantage, a great gift of the extraordinary blood flowing through their veins.

The wind rifled through his braids, swept across his nape. He felt that, and far more. His heart beat like the hide-covered drums of the Nomads. Beyond the odor swilling in his nostrils there was more...than the textures and scent and sound of the world immediately before him.

Time seemed to slow around him. There was the door lever, scratched and prematurely weathered. Latched, through the thickness of the wooden door itself. There was the distance between him and that door, the wind, funneling between them, the particles of dust gusting by.

He held that posture, that vision, the scent in his nostrils, for an elongated second until, like a man stepping into another world, he became a part of it.

And then he moved, fully committed, knowing he held a supreme advantage to whatever waited inside.

His shoulder slammed into the door, splintering the wood around its latch. It flew wide with a crash and the details of the room snapped into place all at once.

Bar: across the back of the room, topped with an array of bottles. Three were open, one of them reeking of hundred-proof alcohol. Twelve mugs. Three were dirty. Stools: nine, aligned in front of the bar, no backrests. To the right and left: seven tables. Round. Dark wood, treated with creosote. Side wall: closed door. A back room, then.

Four large warriors dressed in strange, paneled leather armor, large knives on their belts, leaning on the bar. Two with mugs of beer in their fists. They were larger and stronger than any Corpse he'd seen—muscled necks and quick black eyes, already jerking toward his disturbance.

One common Corpse in a smock behind the bar. No sign of Maro.

Roland saw all of this at once before his boot landed on the floorboards.

The room seemed to stall, the scent of freshly poured beer in his nostrils. One heartbeat. Half of another— theirs. Not his.

And then his hands flashed with the speed of vipers. He flung the knives underhanded with enough force to send them straight and true for thirty paces.

The blades flashed toward their targets, one at each end

of the bar. End over killing end, through the air. Turning heads, too slow, eyes bleary with drink. Facial muscles flinching, too late.

His blades took one in the right eye and the other in his forehead, slamming home to their hilts in rapid succession.

The scent hit him then, like a wall. An odor of emotions he'd never encountered before in any Corpse. The realization sliced into his mind like a spear.

But it wasn't life. Not possible.

His hands were already on the second set of knives, committed to the certainty that these men were *not* alive. That they were enemies who would kill him without a second thought. He spun to his right, gaining momentum for a second salvo.

When he rounded again he saw how quickly the other two had turned. As fast as any fighter he'd seen. Perhaps faster.

One had his knife drawn and was halfway through the throw. The other was shoving away his slumping neighbor.

Roland took the one who had launched the knife first— in the face, not certain if his own blade would penetrate the heavy leather armor over their hearts. Without waiting to watch his blade find its target, he plunged forward and catapulted his full weight toward the last man.

Head lowered, three sprinting strides, up under the man's jaw like a battering ram.

It was customary for Nomads to sew leather into the crowns of their hoods for such a purpose. There were few parts of the body that could not be used in combat if properly protected, the head chief among them. No wasted movement, no wasted weapon, no wasted moment.

He felt the crown of his head crash into the man's jaw. He heard the shattering of teeth and the crack of jawbone. The man arched wildly over the bar, instantly oblivious, limp.

Even as the body collapsed on the bar Roland saw that his third knife had found its mark, leaving only the server behind the bar, wild-eyed and scrambling for a sword propped against the wall behind him.

Patience spent, Roland sent his last knife into the back of the man's neck. The Corpse dropped like a bag of feed.

Roland stepped back and ripped off his hood. The air was still, filled with rot. Four were very dead and would never feel again. The fifth was unconscious, unable to feel anything for the moment.

He would soon learn everything that one knew.

But first—Roland strode to the door leading into the back room and pulled it wide. Inside a small storeroom lay the hogtied body of his cousin, Maro, mouth covered by a thick gag, eyes wide.

Roland took one long look at him and slammed the door shut again. A muffled cry sounded from within.

"Michael!"

She was already at the door, studying his handiwork as one reads the page of a book. Her eyes flicked up at him.

"Maro?"

"In the storeroom."

"Alive?"

"Until I get to him."

Her eyes settled on the form slumped backward over the bar. She flipped out a knife and started forward to finish him.

"He stays alive," Roland said.

She halted in midstride, shot him a glance.

"Untie Maro. Use the rope to secure this man to his horse. We take him with us."

He strode for the door.

"And the others?" she asked.

"The rest remain in their funeral pyre," he said without looking back. "We burn this box to the ground and piss on the ashes."

CHAPTER TWO

THE FORTRESS SPRAWLED along the edge of the forest, her turrets rooted deep into the earth like industrial claws. Like the talons of a steel-footed throne.

From the highest lookout among the twisted pines, one might monitor the hills of Byzantium twenty miles away and gaze at the roiling sky's ominous poetry, diffusing the sun's light as those beneath lived under the guise of death.

The thin strain of violins filled Saric's master chamber, pumped in through the vents like air. Not the soulless stuff composed in the last half millennium, but the music of Chaos as it had been five centuries earlier, resurrected—a melody to tear at the soul. The minor key saturated the darkened chamber, the heavy silk hangings, the very candlelight, until it ruined the air for anything else. Saric had ordered it played throughout the fortress every evening at the same time for the benefit of those dwelling within these walls.

So much had changed.

Nine. It was the number of years since the Master Alchemist Pravus had first injected him with the serum that awakened him to a semblance of dark life. His entire being had seethed with new emotion. It had been a tortured birth that nearly destroyed him. And yet today he celebrated that first awakening because it had ultimately led to a far greater life—the same one that now allowed him to relish the ancient paintings of lush landscapes that lined the walls of the room in which he sat.

The master chamber was twenty paces to a side. An expansive, thick rug woven from the hides of lions lay before a long ebony desk that doubled as a dining table when Saric felt so inclined. And he was inclined often. Gold silk panels gathered in each corner, hanging from the ceiling to pool on the marble floor like sunlight fallen to his feet. On the far side of the room, a tall cylindrical glass sarcophagus stood against the wall.

Eight. It was the number of years he had spent in stasis in that very sarcophagus, here, in his former master's fortress. He had little memory of those years except for the nightmares of his time before stasis—dreams of sweaty ambition. Of clawing and desperate jealousy. Of anger like poison in the veins.

Seven. It was the number of months since he'd woken from those dark visions to find himself a man reborn. Something more than he had been, a masterwork of his maker, Pravus.

He was evolved, perfected from those first violent days of a lesser life years ago. The base sentiments of anger and greed and raw ambition had been joined by a capacity for joy and love, peace and wonder. It was then that he became aware of his true purpose: to fully embrace true life at any cost. And for this hunger he would be eternally grateful to his maker.

Saric sat behind the carved ebony table and considered the steak topped with the tiny raw quail egg. The egg was smattered with caviar, the salty aroma of which he had inhaled now for a full ten minutes. His eyes fluttered closed. The ecstasy he felt at the thought of eating life into his very cells was only the beginning. Soon he would taste life in a way that exalted him to the heavens.

He touched the silver knife with a fingertip, slid it across the damask tablecloth before gently picking it up. He lifted the fork with similar reverence and then, with deliberate leisure, slipped tines and tip at once into the steak. The egg trembled and spilled yolk onto the plate as he lifted the first salty bite to his mouth. He chewed slowly, the caviar popping, briny as life, against his tongue.

Six. It was the number of months since he had first discovered that out of this reborn life there were two things he could no longer abide: death, and any power that threatened his mastery of life, which equated to any power greater than his own. He had found true life at last in this dead world, and nothing could be allowed to compromise or supplant the unquestioned power that came with it.

He slid his gaze down the table past the glow of the candelabra to the glass sarcophagus. Pravus stared back with sightless eyes.

Five. It was the number of months since he'd killed Pravus. The memory of that day was stamped into his mind like a birthmark. His master had been bent low over a microscope in Corban's lab, analyzing a new sample of flesh quickened by a strengthening serum, when Saric had quietly stepped in behind him, axe behind his back, trembling with the thought of what he was about to do.

He'd hesitated only a moment, considering the profanity of killing the one who'd given him life so abundantly. But Pravus could not become Sovereign of the world as he, a royal in the line of Sovereigns, could. Though he loved the man as a father, he would always stand in the path of Saric's discovery of all this new existence could offer him. Raw power was an expression of life, and Saric's destiny lay in unrestrained consumption of both.

Pravus had turned as Saric rushed forward, but the rage he felt as he buried the axe in his master's face had been directed at himself. The slaying had been a deeply distasteful experience. He'd fallen to his knees and wept as Pravus slumped in the chair, dead, bleeding onto the floor.

And yet, in his death Pravus had given him a great, final gift brimming with power. And so he would revere him forever.

Saric set down the knife and fork, slid back his carved chair and rose. He rounded the end of the table and walked to the sarcophagus, napkin still in hand. Tilting his head, he wiped the barest bit of a smudge off the front of the glass, resisting the urge to weep at the sudden loneliness that seized him.

Tubes fed into the back of the sarcophagus, twitching ever so slightly at the pulse of the fluid within them. For an instant he thought of ripping them away. Instead, he touched one thoughtfully, knowing it sent nutrients even now to the layer of living flesh he'd ordered Corban to graft over the long wound that had forever separated Pravus's eyes an inch too far—that gash that had opened under Saric's ax, spilling blood and brains so that he could fulfill his calling.

He stepped back, his faint reflection transposed over the soulless face of his former master. Saric could not count the times he'd stood before this sarcophagus and wept. But there was new life yet to be found. And power greater than any yet understood. He leaned forward and placed a light kiss on the glass.

"Forgive me."

And he knew his master did.

Four. It was the number of days ago he'd first learned that Byzantium's Citadel, home to the world's highest administrative offices, housed a terrible and beautiful secret.

A knock at the door. Saric slowly turned his gaze from the sarcophagus and glanced at the delicacies on his plate. He didn't like to be interrupted at times like this. He considered ignoring the intrusion. Instead, he folded the napkin between his fingers.

"Come."

The carved double doors swung open on their hinges, revealing the robed form of Corban, his chief alchemist.

His head was bowed, his long hair bound into a braid wrapped tight with black silk that fell down over his chest. It was a preference the alchemist had adopted since waking to the life that he had once been denied by Pravus. It was Saric who had given it to him.

Two others stood behind him, taller, broader of shoulder than Corban—products of the same chambers from which Saric himself had emerged like a butterfly from a cocoon. They knelt in reverence, one in the shadow of each door, twin images of sinister beauty, perfectly muscled with inky veins beneath their pale skin so similar to his own. As Pravus was his maker, he was theirs—a better maker, having seen to it that they were stripped of all ability to countermand him. They would never know the disquiet or anguish of killing their creator as he had. He was their father, and they were his children, whom he loved as much as his own life. To a point.

"Yes?"

The black eyes of all three lifted to him with devotion. So much had changed.

"We've found her," Corban said.

"Where is she?" Saric was careful that his words not bely the acceleration of his heart.

"Here, liege."

"You brought her?" His heart drummed to a thundering crescendo within his chest.

"Yes."

"Alive?"

"In stasis."

For a moment he could not move. Could hardly fathom the good fortune that had found him with these words. But this was his destiny, and the day of that glorious fulfillment had finally come.

Breathing deliberately against the terrible new hunger that flooded his veins, he strode forward, barely aware now of the floor underfoot, the walls that hid his legion from an unwitting world, the air he breathed.

He swept past Corban and walked down the stone corridor, quickly now. Silks—red, the color of life—billowed out from the wall in his wake like lungs, lifting with crimson breath.

He did not ask where they had brought her. He knew.

Violins assaulted his nerves, ricocheting off the basalt stone of the corridor. He passed several of his brood—

Dark Bloods as evolved, nearly, as he. They knelt the instant they saw him, their heads swiveling as he passed to descend the vast stair at the far end of the fortress into the subterranean chamber below. Dimly lit, it reeked eternally of chemicals and formaldehyde. Of death—one of the two things so offensive to Saric.

But he hardly noticed that now. There, on the great steel table in the center: a body sheathed in cloth, one arm dangling off the edge, snaked through with tubes. The skin, where he could see it, still perfect...

He willed his breath to slow again. Inhaled.

"Leave."

He waited until the test tubes along the far wall, neatly stored in their racks, untouched in years, ceased their jittering shudder after the great doors slammed closed.

Only then did he notice the silence—the music did not reach this chamber. But in this moment, silence was the only appropriate sound.

With reverent fingertips he peeled back the cloth from that face. From the long line of that neck, shoulders, and torso, unblemished all this time except for the red marks where the tubes had been sewn in to keep her alive. From the seam of a great scar where metal sutures had once held it closed.

He lifted the hand, righting the pale moonstone ring that had twisted on Feyn's slender finger. He lifted it to his lips.

"My love," he whispered, turning his cheek against the delicate backs of those fingers. "Now we will embrace the full power of life... together."

CHAPTER THREE

HIDDEN DEEP IN THE SEYALA VALLEY, twelve hundred Mortals began their routines after a late night of revelry. A daily rhythm of gathering, hunting, grazing horses, and consuming life with eagerness bound up in the imminent promise of the boy's coming reign. After five hundred years of oppression and death, the entire world would soon be ruled not by the statutes of Order, but by life.

By Jonathan.

But those twelve hundred living souls were oblivious to the turn of events that had brought strange new death among them in the dead of night.

Roland and Michael had returned to camp before dawn. Now, six hours later, the Council of Twelve convened in the temple ruins built into the craggy cliff. Here, in the temple's inner sanctum, the ancient windows still boasted an array of stained glass, the only ones still intact.

Roughly thirty paces deep, the chamber lay beyond the outer courtyard. Richly woven rugs covered the pocked marble floor and ran past the stone benches up three steps to a small platform. An ancient altar stood at its center, draped in burgundy silk embroidered with the emblem of Avra's heart. Avra, the first Mortal martyr. Atop the altar lay a simple volume propped on a wooden stand. The Book of Mortals. Within it were recorded the names of every Mortal and the date of his or her rebirth as well as an exact translation of the Keeper's ancient vellum that had put every event in motion to make such life possible.

Torches lit against the overcast morning threw warm light on the exposed stone of the chamber's six pillars standing like sentries down the length of the room. But they did little to lend color to the ghastly pale Corpse gagged and bound to a chair at the foot of the platform.

Rom Sebastian, Keeper, First Born Leader of the Mortals and protector of Jonathan, stood before the Corpse, carefully considering what this turn could mean.

Nine years had passed since Rom had drunk from the ancient vial of blood that had brought him to life and sent him on a quest to find the boy foretold by Talus.

Talus, the man who had created Legion, the virus that had stripped the world of its humanity five centuries ago, who had sworn to undo his grave offense.

Talus, the geneticist who'd calculated the coming of a child in whose blood that same virus would revert.

Talus, the prophet who'd established the order of Keepers to protect a single vial of blood—enough for five to wake from death and protect the boy from those forces that would seek to kill him.

Talus, who had penned the ancient vellum by which Rom had found the boy.

Rom glanced up once at the gathered council. Jonathan was conspicuously absent, as always, preferring to be with the people rather than deciding protocol. No amount of persuasion had changed that in him. And so the Council of Twelve was truly a council of eleven—seven Nomads, including Roland and Michael, who refused to sit, and four Keepers, including the first Corpse convert, a woman named Resia, and those two who had first joined Rom nine years ago: Triphon and the Book.

The Book, as the aging Keeper was called, kept his long white beard unbound in ways that mystified the Nomads, who braided everything, including the manes and tails of their horses. He had, however, adopted the long, dark leathers of the Nomads, which lent him a surprising air of youth despite the snowy white of every hair on his head and chin. In fact, the man had seemed to thrive in the wilderness, though Rom knew it had less to do with the Nomadic lifestyle and more to do with the new blood flowing through his veins since having experienced, at last, the thing he had hoped for all his life: the true life of Jonathan's blood.

Triphon, sitting next to him, had grown his beard in recent years along with his hair. Both were braided, tied with the threads of the warrior. Red, for the Corpse kill. Black, for prowess in the games. He rarely wore the long coats of the Nomads, having never learned the patience for the elaborate beading and time-consuming needle and leatherwork with which each fighter distinguished him- or herself, but had adopted the simple leggings and hooded tunics that served all Nomads well—particularly in a fight.

Michael bore signs of fatigue, if only in the scowl that curled the corner of her mouth. Council proceedings were well known to try Michael's patience. As did Triphon's stares.

Rom turned his attention to Roland. The Nomad stood, arms crossed, beside his sister. No one would have guessed by the set of his jaw that he had gone nearly three days on so little sleep. Or that the prince with the wealth of beads in his hair and such an eye for artistry was as brutal a warrior as any Rom had ever seen.

The Nomadic Prince slid him an unwavering gaze.

"You say there were four of them?" Rom said.

"Five."

"All as strong?"

"Except for the one behind the bar."

"And they're now dead."

"They were always dead. Now they're ash."

So he'd burned them in Nomadic custom. If the Nomads had their way, every Corpse on earth would be better turned to ash than turned to life—a sentiment Rom could only barely understand.

"Weapons?"

"Swords, axes, knives. Heavy steel." Roland withdrew a twelve-inch bowie knife from behind his back and tossed it at Rom, who deftly plucked it from the air. The butt was black steel, as was the blade, polished so that it glistened like oil in the torchlight.

He ran his finger along the razor edge. It was a beautiful weapon. "Have you ever seen a knife like this?"

"I've seen too many blades to count. But never one like this."

Rom studied the Corpse. It glared back with coal-dark eyes, unflinching. Armor covered his torso, thighs, and arms with overlapping flaps that allowed for movement. Black leather, a quarter-inch thick, crafted to stop a blade. His boots rose to his knees, steel tipped with soles an inch thick. His hair was long and coarse, twisted in dread-locks; his jaw was obviously swollen, but otherwise his features were quite refined despite his size. This was no mere thug.

Mortals had encountered elite guard before—splinter groups whose roots they'd never been able to properly trace to a single source. They'd known that forces would rise against them to challenge Jonathan's sovereignty. But while the warrior before them was obviously battle trained and as fine a specimen of power and strength as any Rom had seen, Roland had only encountered five of them. Where were the rest?

And then there was the question of *what* the warrior was. The strange scent the man emitted brought a slight shudder to Rom's nerves.

"What do you make of it?" Rom asked, glancing at Roland.

They all knew what he was talking about.

"I can't be sure."

"It's emotion," Triphon said.

"Impossible," one of the ranking Nomads, named Seriph, said. "If he were Mortal, we wouldn't be able to smell him."

"He may not be Mortal, but he doesn't smell like any Corpse I've met," Triphon said. "How can he be Corpse with that scent?"

"He's either Corpse or Mortal. There's nothing between."

"We know what Corpses smell like. We don't know what Mortals smell like."

"You're suggesting that we smell like that? Death and these other odors mixed into that...*nasty bouquet*?"

"I'm saying we don't know."

Rom lifted his hand. "Enough." He turned to Roland. "What's your best guess, Roland?"

"Ask the alchemist. This is a wizard's doing."

Roland had never been keen on alchemy, preferring instead nature's way of distilling purity through the generations. Nomads, once homogenous by necessity, considered themselves especially pure-blooded now that they were bound by Jonathan's blood. This in contrast to the Keepers, who were all of varied descent except for the one thing they had in common: that they were changed from Corpse to Mortal by the same blood.

"I'm asking you," Rom pressed. "You saw them, fought them, killed them. You have the sharpest instincts here."

Roland turned an icy gaze on the prisoner and said in a low tone: "This is what I know. He is an enemy who took one of my men. His stench of death is far deeper than any Corpse. If this new scent is life, then it's the work of an alchemist wizard. The real question is how many of them exist and under what authority."

Rom nodded. "What do you say, Book?"

The ancient Keeper turned his eyes from the prisoner to Roland. He dipped his head. "I would say you are right. Roland has good instincts."

The man had grown quite stoic this past year as Jonathan approached his maturity, keeping mostly to the task of monitoring the steady change in the boy's blood and advising the council like a father of few words. All that mattered to him was that Jonathan fulfill the promise of the Keepers who came before him. That his blood change the world. It was the boy's destiny, and seeing it fulfilled was his.

Rom shared the old Keeper's resolve to the end.

He nodded at Roland. "Remove his gag."

The Nomad stepped behind the prisoner, slid the knotted cloth up, and jerked the gag free.

The Corpse spat blood onto the ground, not in apparent disgust so much as to clear his mouth. A tooth skittered across the dusty stone, landing near Triphon's foot.

His friend glanced at Rom, then bent and picked it up. Sniffed it. Flipped it back toward the prisoner with a flick of his thumb.

"Vanilla," he said.

"Vanilla?"

Triphon shrugged. "That's what it smells like to me. Vanilla pudding. There's plenty of death mixed in there, but I'm thinking vanilla."

Rom suppressed the slight turn of a smile. Triphon, the man of bold words and no guile, loved by all. Except maybe Michael.

"It's from a vanilla plug," the prisoner said.

His words robbed the room of sound. It was amazing the man could speak so well past his swollen jaw—obviously broken. Rom wasn't sure how to follow such a statement. Vanilla plugs were common in these parts, chewed to clean teeth and freshen stale breath. But to hear a Corpse with dark eyes who carried a knife the length of Rom's forearm make this his first confession struck him as strange.

"What's your name?" he said.

The prisoner stared without answering.

Mortals could be quite persuasive and seductive, a trait that had grown with their abilities to perceive others in unique ways. Seduction began with understanding the needs, fears, and longings of another. Jonathan's blood had afforded them heightened perception of all of these.

New scents drifted off the prisoner, mitigated by one far more familiar: fear. Respect motivated by fear. Honor, bound to that same fear. The prisoner was obviously loyal. Breaking him would be difficult.

"You're in a tough position," Rom said gently. "I recognize that there are many things you're not free to tell me. But some things you are, and I would know them. You should know that we have no intention of torturing you because we already know you won't break."

Immediately the thin scent of fear began to ebb. The stench of death did not.

"We know you are dead. Do you know that, my friend?"

The man swallowed once, opened his mouth as if to speak, closed it, and then did speak.

"Corpses are dead," he said. "I am not a Corpse."

Rom paused. "Are you saying you're Mortal? Because you smell like death."

"I'm not Mortal. And I'm not a Corpse."

"Then what are you?"

"I'm human, made by my master. Alive."

"Really. And who is your master?"

"Saric."

The name hung in the air.

"Saric's dead," Triphon said, his voice hard.

"Saric . . . is alive," the Corpse said. "A Dark Blood. My maker. Fully alive, as I am fully alive."

Cold prickled along Rom's arms. *Impossible*. He glanced at the old Keeper, whose eyes had widened in shock.

He rounded on the Corpse. "Saric *made* you? No. You mean he changed you with his alchemy."

"Wizards," Roland muttered.

"Saric gave me life, as he has given all Dark Bloods life."

"Dark Bloods."

"Those made in his image, resurrected from death to know full life."

"Sacrilege!" Zara, one of the Nomadic elders, cried. "Only Jonathan can give life."

Even Mortals who brought Corpses to life with the blood from their veins—a discovery of the last six months—could do so only because their own blood came from Jonathan. Unless Saric had taken Jonathan's blood…But that wasn't possible. This was a different kind of life entirely.

"How many has Saric given 'life' to?" Rom said carefully.

The Dark Blood nodded once, eyes steady. "Three thousand."

A faint but distinct collective gasp filled the ruined chamber.

"Three thousand?" Triphon said. "All like him?"

"Roughly," the Dark Blood said. "And others who are not warriors like me."

Triphon was on his feet. "He's lying!"

"Sit!" Rom ordered. Roland's hand fell on Michael's wrist where it had reached toward her sword.

Triphon slowly lowered back down to his seat.

So the threat they had always feared had finally surfaced. But Rom refused to allow fear to gain a foothold among his council. For nine years they had protected Jonathan with regular communication from Rowan, Jonathan's Regent and acting Sovereign. Never once had Rowan spoken of any true threat. And Rom would not abide any threat to him now. In eight days, Jonathan would claim the Sovereign office.

Anything else was unthinkable.

He turned to Roland. "Three thousand. Is that a problem?"

The Nomadic Prince answered deliberately. "It would be far less of a problem if we had known and acted sooner."

"That doesn't answer my question."

"If you're asking if we can handle three thousand of these in direct confrontation, the answer is yes. But it would be foolish of us to think the threat doesn't go deeper into the Order."

"If there was a threat in the Order, Rowan would know."

"Perhaps."

Rom let it go. To the Dark Blood, he said: "Where is Saric now?"

"Where he can't be found."

"What is your name?"

"I can't tell you."

"Do you feel fear?"

The Corpse shrugged.

"And hatred?"

"All men hate their enemies."

And yet Corpses did not feel hatred, only fear.

"Sorrow?"

"When it is fitting."

"Is it fitting now?"

The man slowly dipped his head. "My mate will weep when I fail to return."

Rom felt a strange prick of pity for the man. Hatred and sorrow, then. These were two of the new scents they smelled. Which was which, he wasn't sure.

"Joy?" the Book said from across the room.

"None today."

"It's a lie," Seriph said. "Only Mortals feel these emotions he's mimicking."

"Hold your tongue, Seriph."

Could it be possible Saric brought these emotions to life?

"What are your orders?"

"To seek any who threaten our Maker."

"To what end?"

"To destroy," the Dark Blood said.

"And now that you've seen us in action, do you think you can?"

A pause. "Yes."

"Do you know how many we are?"

"No."

"And yet you believe you can destroy us. Why?"

"Because only Saric can prevail."

"Jonathan has *already* prevailed!" Zara snapped.

Without warning, Roland strode to the prisoner and slammed his fist into the man's temple. The Dark Blood slumped in his seat, unconscious.

Silence.

He shot Zara an angry glare and turned to face Rom. "He's heard far too much."

"Removing him from the room might have been easier," Rom said.

"Killing him would have been easier."

"We don't kill Corpses out of hand."

"We kill any enemy who stand in Jonathan's way. And this enemy has given us all the information he can."

"I haven't agreed to kill him."

"He's unclean, full of death. We have no choice *but*

to kill him rather than risk any harm to Jonathan. No unclean thing among us, isn't that your own edict?"

"It is, but that doesn't mean we just kill him!"

"And what would you propose? That we keep him in chains forever?"

Rom had already considered the issue and not landed on an answer. They had never allowed a Corpse to dwell among them except those who came to be brought to life. Separation from Corpses at all costs was a hard and fast law that he himself had argued for as the time of Jonathan's ascension drew near.

"Kill him or not," Triphon said, standing, "we have to acknowledge that if Saric's really alive and managed to make three thousand of these, we have a problem."

Rom turned away, picked up the wineskin sitting upon the altar step, uncorked it, drank deep.

Saric...alive. *Was it even possible?* And if it was, could he have fashioned a force of Corpses to some kind of life—and enough of them to take the Citadel by force?

Eight days. He would not be pulled into direct conflict with Saric with the end so close.

He handed the skin to Triphon and faced the council.

"This changes nothing. We do not alter course. We remain sequestered here and deliver Jonathan to the Citadel on the day of his inauguration. If we are challenged we will accept that challenge, but we won't go seeking it. We can't risk exposure before Jonathan assumes power."

"What about after?"

"Then he'll decide how to deal with Saric."

"Jonathan decide?" Seriph muttered. "The boy's a carrier of life and rightful Sovereign, but let's make no mistake. He's not a leader."

"Silence!" Rom thundered. His voice echoed through the chamber. "Speak one more word and I will personally put you in chains for a week!"

Seriph shifted his gaze away in deference.

"Seriph misspoke," Roland said, pacing to his right. "But we can't ignore the popular call for a more proactive way to bring Jonathan—and Mortals—to power."

"If you mean your zealots, I want nothing of it," Rom said.

"You need to know their number is growing. And they grow more convinced."

"Of what?"

"That Jonathan was always meant as a figurehead, not a leader. That he will begin the new kingdom as foretold, but that he need not necessarily rule it."

"He will be Sovereign," Rom gritted out. "And Sovereigns rule."

"Yes, I know."

"Don't tell me you give them any credence."

"I serve the Mortal life with my own, and Jonathan with the life of every Nomad. But to dismiss the sentiments of other Mortals who have sworn to protect Jonathan is dangerous. Jonathan has brought us life and we must protect it at all costs."

"We will protect him. As our Sovereign."

"Yes, of course. Meanwhile, a more proactive approach to eliminating any threat presented by Saric and these Dark Bloods"—he jutted his chin in the direction of the slumped prisoner—"might be the best way to ensure that he does become Sovereign. We should at least consider the option now, while we have it."

"What? Ride into Byzantium and take the Citadel by force?"

Roland shrugged. "Whatever is required to ensure Jonathan's ascension."

"We will not bathe his rise to power in blood unless our hand is forced," Rom said.

"No, of course not," Roland said with a slight dip of his head. Ever the warrior, ever the statesman. "In the meantime, I expect that we kill this Dark Blood."

Rom considered him, then glanced at each of the council members in turn, landing, at last, on his truest friend.

"Triphon," he said. "Find Jonathan. He's our Sovereign. Let him decide."

Chapter Four

THE CITADEL. Heart of Byzantium. Throne room of the Sovereign. Seat of world power.

Place of whispers. Place of secrets.

A day had passed since Saric's world had changed once more. Now he strode into the outer foyer of the senate chamber, footsteps on the marble floor echoing through the hall's vaulted ceiling. He was only vaguely aware of the two Citadel guards flanking him on either side, cowering in his wake.

He breathed deep.

It all rushed back in an instant: the Chaos of these ancient chambers. It seeped from her very stones like sweat from her subterranean walls. It flitted through her hallways like the ghosts of a former age, whispering songs of passion. Anger. Love.

Power.

Did those sitting within the Senate Hall have any idea how very wrong they were? How weak and flawed was the foundation on which they'd built their staid and stoic laws?

No.

Today they would learn. Today he would teach them.

He smoothed the dark sleeve of his robe and angled toward the great doors leading into the senate chamber. He had owned many fine robes in his life before, but none of them could equal the one he wore now, glittering with faceted onyx and garnet at neck and cuff, snug across shoulders that had emerged from the years of his metamorphosis more broad and muscled than before. Corban himself had drawn back his hair, wrapping it in a length of the finest silk he owned. An adoring tribute to his maker, one Saric had accepted with full love in the face of such worship.

Two guards stood at the twin doors as he approached. One of them paled, the color in his face replaced by recognition. As it should be—Saric was a veritable ghost come back from the dead. A reaper come to take what was his.

"My Lord," the one whispered, drifting aside.

The other one glanced sharply at his partner, but stood his ground, the ceremonial pike at his side not wavering once.

"Senate is in session," he said. "Entrance is not permitted."

Saric slowly closed the distance between them until, an arm's reach away, he towered a full head over him. The man's eyes darted to the two guards behind Saric and then back to Saric and down his neck, where the inky line of his veins disappeared beneath his neckline.

"Do you know who I am?" Saric said.

"No." His hand trembled once on the pike.

"Then it's time you do."

Saric leaned in, as though to whisper between them.

The guard's eyes darted up and after a moment's

hesitation, he tilted his head toward him. Saric lifted his long, pale fingers to the man's head and drew him close, so that his lips touched the man's ear.

"You may call me death," he whispered.

He twisted the guard's head. A sick pop, half of a gasp...and then silence.

The young man slumped to the marble floor as his spike clattered beside him.

The guard on the other side of the door took one more step back and then stood frozen, ghostly white.

Without a word, Saric stepped past him, black hem of his robe sliding over the dead man's boot. And then he laid his hands against the heavy double doors, pushed them slowly wide, and stepped into the great senate chamber.

The hall had not changed in nine years. Very little did among the dead. The great torch burned above the dais, constantly fed by a supply of gas—the flame of Order, gathered from all corners of the world, never to be extinguished. Its smoke had all but obscured the ancient painting on the ceiling, blacking it out.

A debate was in progress—about what, Saric did not care. None of their paltry concerns now mattered. Only he did.

The cacophony of voices began to die as those sitting nearest the door of the chamber theater reacted to the sight of him standing in the open maw of the great doorway. Swiveling necks. Gasps, sibilant as prayer to his ears. One or two of the senators half-rose from their seats, papers falling from their laps.

Saric released the doors and walked down the great center aisle, through the middle of the tiered seats, not seeing so much as sensing the hundred gaping faces on either side of him. He took in the astonished silence as one does the sun, or the power of a coming storm. In the back of the chamber, the heavy doors fell closed with a dull and hollow thud.

There, on the rounded platform protruding into the chamber, was Rowan, the Sovereign Regent. For the first time in his life, Saric regarded the man he had known so long ago with new curiosity.

The dark-skinned man who had once served Saric's father as senate leader was as seemingly unchanged as Order itself. He wore the same dark robes as before, his hair bound back in the same manner Saric so vividly remembered. Only the slightest streak of gray in his hair and scant lines beneath his eyes betrayed his aging. Otherwise, he was exactly as he had been. Saric found this disappointing.

The Regent stood near a marble table, the Sovereign's seat neatly tucked behind it, signifying the symbolic presence of the rightful Sovereign, not yet of age. On the other side of the table sat another man with gray hair, his nose hawklike, hands grasping the arms of his chair, eyes fastened on Saric. This then, must be Dominic, the new senate leader.

"Order!" Rowan said, reaching for the gavel, pounding it twice on the thick travertine. The old fool hadn't yet recognized him. "What is the meaning of this interrupt—"

And then Saric saw the recognition in his eyes, the collision of the impossible and inexplicable at once. The way his eyes coursed over him, lingering at his changed frame, returning to his too-pale face.

The gavel slipped from his fingers and came to rest on the table. Rowan staggered back a step.

Saric slowly mounted the steps to the platform. Crossed to the table, not once removing his gaze from the man.

"Saric ... We thought you dead ..."

Behind Saric, the theater was utterly still.

"Please sit."

The Regent glanced at Dominic then toward the greater senate chamber. He dipped his head slightly and returned to his seat. He sat as one not sure of his own movement.

Saric lifted the gavel, tapped it once against his palm, and turned to face the senate theater. One hundred senators stared at him with varied expressions of confusion. Little did they know just how appropriate that sentiment would soon be.

"Esteemed senators. I have returned to you. I, Saric, who was once your Sovereign."

Murmurs from those in the chamber.

"I have been gone from you for many years. Perhaps you, like your Regent, thought me ... dead." He paused, allowing himself the barest smile. "As you can see, I am very much alive."

He faced the senate leader, seated to the left. "Dominic, I assume?"

The leader held his stare, steady. "That is correct."

The man was strong. Unwavering. Good.

"You serve Order. You serve it faithfully as a way of sustaining life, given as the gift of Sirin after the Age of Chaos. Tell me if this is true."

"We have pledged our lives to it."

"Indeed. Your lives." He turned back to the assembly and spoke the words with clear, perfect authority.

"It was Sirin who first preached the denial of emotions in a new philosophy designed to prevent the great passions that led to the wars five centuries ago. And so humanity learned to control its passion and baser sentiments. Old things passed away and we became new, evolving beyond those baser instincts that once guided us only to death and destruction."

He twisted his head and addressed the senate leader. "This, too, is true, is it not?"

"Yes," Dominic agreed. A murmur of assent from the chamber.

Saric nodded and smiled. "Yes." He paced to his right, scanning the auditorium, holding them in silence for an extended moment.

"Unfortunately, it's *not* true."

Glances between the senators. In his periphery, Rowan sat forward. Saric stayed him with a glance.

"You have been fed a lie. You are the products not of philosophy, but of treason . . . and Alchemy."

A confused ripple of voices throughout the chamber.

"The truth is, you are not evolved. You have, rather, been stripped of those emotions not required for control. Namely, every emotion but fear. All through a virus called Legion."

"Madness!" Dominic said, leaping up from his chair, face white.

"The truth is, Megas assassinated Sirin when he refused to infect the world with Legion, knowing it would strip mankind of its humanity. The truth is that after killing Sirin, Megas released Legion on the world, killing it to all but the fear required to create puppets of Order. The truth is, you have not evolved—you have, in fact, devolved."

"Preposterous! Absolute heresy!"

"Is it? Ask yourself: is it loyalty that compels you to your feet in this instant? Love, for Order?"

"Yes," Dominic said, straightening.

"Are you so certain? Or is it only that you fear losing Bliss in the next life if you do not leap to your feet and defend the way of Order? Just as you function from day to day caring only that you're not caught in transgression and that your offenses do not multiply so that on the day when life arbitrarily cuts you off from the world, you do not end up in fear eternal?"

The senate leader stood absolutely still—not angry, as Corpses were incapable of such emotion—but terrified. Rowan had risen to his feet as well.

"Fear guides us as it should," Dominic said.

"Should? The truth is, you are incapable of anything *but* fear because you've been genetically stripped of those sentiments. Of that which makes you human. The truth is, my dear Dominic, Rowan...esteemed members of the senate...all of you are in fact, quite *dead*."

They stared at him as if he were a madman. By these words he'd just killed all credibility in their eyes, naturally. But this was expected. Who, being told they were dead, could possibly believe the bearer of such news sane?

Saric waited for a moment, briefly considering the gavel in his hands, before laying it aside on the marble tabletop, just so, and moving again to the edge of the dais, where he faced Rowan.

"Am I not your former Sovereign? The last acting Sovereign to stand in this chamber?"

"Yes," the Regent said, "but—"

"Have I not had access to every archive in the chambers beneath this very one?" He glanced toward the door beyond the dais. It was quite obviously sealed around the edges, without doorknob or handle. But anyone who knew the Citadel had at least heard rumors of its subterranean maze of secrets.

"Yes."

"Do I not come from the royal line of alchemists?"

"Yes," Rowan said, his mouth a flat line.

"And am I dead, as you and everyone else here, once presumed?"

He hesitated. "Clearly not."

"Tell me," Saric said, pacing along the dais, pulling wide the top of his robe where it fastened at the neck. He turned to face the assembled senate.

They stared at the black treelike skeleton of veins beneath his pale skin, far darker than the coveted blue of royal Brahmin veins—so praised that royals had for years highlighted their color with blue powder. His body was chorded with muscle, stronger than any other body they could have possibly seen.

"This is life! I know so because I was once dead." He released his robe. "Tell me, when is the last time you wept at the sight of the sky? At the devotion of your constituents? That you looked forward to a meal with anything more than duty to your body…when you did not crave every experience if only for the sake of taking each ounce of life into yourself?"

They stared, unfathoming. That, too, was expected.

"But you cannot possibly do any of these things. Do you know why? Because you lack the capacity for any of it!"

This time there was the beginning of an outcry, but he threw up his hand for silence.

"Nine years ago, the Master Alchemist Pravus injected

me with a serum that fired my veins with emotion the likes of which you have never even imagined. Anger. Lust! Jealousy. I was a thing turned feral. Chaos ruled my heart. Yes, I know it is blasphemy against Order. But I tell you today, your Order is a blasphemy against life itself!"

Off to the side, Rowan was staring at him strangely, as though with a new revelation of his own.

"Those days . . . ," Rowan said quietly. "Before the inauguration . . . when you wanted to become senate leader . . ."

"Yes. And so now you know. I could not contain such virulent emotion, and Pravus reclaimed me. Eight years I spent in stasis. Until the day that he drew me out as one reemerging from the womb. This time, perfected. He spent months with me, teaching me. Schooling me in this new, reclaimed humanity." His voice broke. "I was his child. He was my father."

"This is . . . this is abomination," Rowan whispered.

For that, the man would die.

Saric ignored him and spread his arms as if he were their father. "Today there is only one living man in this chamber. See now and know that I am he!"

For an extended moment, no one spoke. The dead could not stoop to challenge such an absurd claim. So it had been, and so it would be . . .

At least for a few minutes more. And then their entire world would change before their very eyes.

"My Lord," Dominic said, in a practiced, conciliatory tone. "We will most certainly investigate the veracity of all that you claim. This is quite a . . . revelation."

It was not the word he wanted to use. It was blasphemy to him, Saric knew. As Order was blasphemy to him.

"We revere you for your service to the world—in such

a time as your father's abrupt passing, no less. And while Order is given by the Maker, law is not the Maker. It is not perfect. But we must follow the dictates of the law until it is changed. These are serious claims, and to make them known would throw the world into nothing short of raw panic. We cannot afford such uproar, and if such claims are proven true, we must proceed with utmost care."

Rage rose up within Saric like bile. Did the man really believe he would be placated by such patronizing foolishness?

Dominic continued: "Until such a day that your claims are proven and the senate dictates otherwise, Order must be upheld. Our Book of Orders is infallible, created not by Sirin or by Megas who wrote that holy book, but by the Maker who inspired its writing. And until such a day it may be proven wrong, we serve Order and the Maker both by obedience to its statutes."

Murmurs of assent.

Saric inclined his head. So very predictable. Somehow he had hoped for more from this one.

Overhead, the senate flame burned straight and even, throwing her faint smoke onto the black of the ceiling. Dominic would look quite handsome, he thought, in a glass sarcophagus.

"Yes. Forgive me," he said, tilting his head. "Your memory is infallible. These items, you have said, will be investigated by the senate. The veracity of them will be checked, and the senate will act accordingly—even if it means altering the history of Order itself, which is the history of the world, and of the Maker."

Dominic hesitated, obviously uncertain about this last bit. "Yes. If such a revelation may be proven true."

"Until then, I bow to your wisdom."

"Thank you, my Lord. Now, if we may—"

"As you bow to the authority of the senate. As only the senate may decide these matters under the Sovereign."

"Yes. Such is the way." Dominic inclined his head.

"And to the authority of the Sovereign, who holds all sway over the senate."

"Yes, of the Sovereign. That is true."

"But the Sovereign is not here...?" Saric turned, looked around him.

"He will soon come of age. Until then, there is Rowan—"

"And if your Sovereign were here...the one chosen by the cycle, as dictated by Order...born on the seventh day of the seventh month, closest to the seventh hour, would you bow?"

"My Lord?"

Rowan was sitting forward, frowning. Out in the senate chamber, the senators had returned to their seats, most of them, the alarm of earlier having smoothed into a strange calm—except for those few, still white-faced, obviously undone by Saric's claims.

"You would serve your Sovereign first, before the senate," Saric said, brows raised.

"Of course. I serve the Sovereign first in all things. As do we all."

Saric glanced at him sidelong. "And you would have it no other way."

"Of course not."

"Good. I, too, bow to the full authority of the Sovereign."

Saric looked at the cloaked man who'd slipped in the back after him to wait his orders. Corban. Saric lazily lifted a hand to motion to his chief alchemist.

Corban turned, grasped the large doors by the handles, and pulled them wide, stepping to one side.

Two Dark Bloods walked through the double doors with the unmistakable shape of a body draped in white silk on a pall between them. The sight of his Dark Bloods towering so majestically over the frail bodies of those assembled flooded Saric with a father's pride. Now they would see.

Soon they would bow.

But first, the senators closest to the door bolted to their feet and backed away, skittering like crabs. When was the last time any one of them had seen a lifeless body?

The caustic reminders of death weren't allowed, even at funerals.

Near him on the dais, Rowan stood. "What is the meaning of this?"

The Dark Bloods carried the pall down the aisle, up the dais steps, and laid the draped body on the top of the stone table.

Not a soul moved. Breath had fled the room. A dead body in the senate chamber—by that alone, Order had been shattered today.

On either end of the altar, the Dark Bloods faced him, sunk to one knee, and bowed their heads.

Saric moved to the side of the body, hip brushing against the Sovereign chair. He traced one finger along the edge of the still form, his touch trailing toward the head. He grasped the silk cloth with the tips of four fingers, and, with a quick yank, flicked off the cloth, revealing the naked body of a woman, staring with dead eyes at the ceiling.

Rowan stood frozen, eyes wide with recognition,

face as white as the silk on the floor. The room was utterly
still.

And then that one name, whispered by Rowan for all to
hear in the perfect silence.

"Feyn!"

CHAPTER FIVE

JORDIN SIRANA PASSED THROUGH CAMP like One Who Is Not Seen. It was the name her companions had given her, growing up, for her uncanny ability to go practically unnoticed.

She was smaller framed than the other fighters. In a camp full of ornately adorned Nomads, the eye did not notice the simple russet of her tunic and brown leggings...until they saw the braids bound with so much red as to appear dipped in blood.

Her father had been a deserter of the Nomadic camp in northern Europa, one who left the wilderness for Order— a stigma passed on to her and her mother, who had died on a hunt less than a year later. The tribe no longer wanted the motherless child of a deserter and had offered her up at the Gathering that year. Had Roland not approved of her adoption, she would have been left to survive on her own or die. Thin chances for a child of six.

What had once been seen as shortcomings made her who she was today: a fierce warrior recognized as such by all the elders, including Roland himself. A young woman of uncompromising character, whose many days hunting

alone and sparring larger opponents had gained her a rep-
utation for speed and deadly accuracy.

She didn't speak much. She didn't tell stories about
the hunt or show off her kill the way the others did. She
wasn't the first to challenge an opponent at the games, nor
did she quickly raise her fists in victory.

A warrior without pretension was unencumbered
by distraction. Little escaped her observation. Like the
fact that Roland's and Michael's horses were not only
back before dawn, but lathered with sweat. Like the fact
that four hours later, the smoke of the fire of Adah, who
cooked for Rom, still coiled in wisps thin enough only to
keep the fire alive before cooking the hot first meal of the
day.

Whatever news Roland had returned with in such a
hurry had stolen Rom's appetite.

And now they were frantically calling for Jonathan.
She could hear their voices sounding through the camp.
They needed him urgently.

Why?

Triphon, meanwhile, had come directly to her instead.

"Will you find him?"

"Yes."

She was the unspoken guardian of his side, the one who
knew, always, where to find the Sovereign of the world.

Jordin strode on silent feet through the camp, past
Rhoda the blacksmith's yurt—the dwelling of the Nomad.

Here, the broad Seyala Valley narrowed between the
cliff and the rising foothills. She glanced up, just making
out the familiar sight of the scout on the hill above the
camp. From there, the watch could see any sign of movement in the valley below and the plateau beyond.

She jogged down toward the smaller river branch that passed on the far side of camp. Several men and women were washing clothes, utensils, children, themselves—their songs carrying downstream like soapsuds. She waded across and hurried up the hill opposite the ruins, only pausing when she'd reached the top of the scrubby knoll. From here she had perfect vantage to make out the bullish form of Triphon passing through camp in his own search for the young Sovereign. Wasted effort, she thought, but then, you could never be absolutely certain with Jonathan.

She knew this: Jonathan was rarely where many thought he was supposed to be. And where they assumed he would not be, he usually was.

Beyond the rocky knoll there was a place where the hill leveled out against the rising cliff face, where children often went to play out of sight of their parents and lovers met far beyond the reach of campfires at night.

Jordin crested the edge of the hill and saw them. Five children, playing knuckle-sticks. And with them was Jonathan, as she'd guessed, having overheard the children's plans for the game earlier.

He was sitting cross-legged on the scrubby grass, dust on his pants and boots. He had changed so much from the boy with the limp who had come to them nine years ago when Jordin herself was nearly ten, just after her mother had died. He was now a rangy young man two heads taller than she, with a strong neck and broadening shoulders, and hands that played the Nomadic lyre as easily as they wielded a sword. He had his knife out and was just blowing the dust off a new carved game piece when he saw her and smiled.

She returned his smile with her own and quickened her stride, easily concealing her gladness at having found him. Again.

Jonathan. The man who gazed at her differently than the way he looked at other women. The man who bowed his head when they came to tap his blood as if he was a well. She wanted to take him away every time the Keeper came looking for him.

"Jordin, come play!" one of the children said. "Jonathan's making a second set!"

"Oh?" she said, dropping down to the ground beside them.

"What do you think?" Jonathan said, handing her the piece. It was the length of a man's hand, cylindrical in shape.

"I think it looks like…" She paused, taking in the rough carving of the hair, pulled back. The figure was standing on a stone to make her the same height as the others. She glanced up at Jonathan. "Like me."

"It *is* you!" one of the children crowed. "And here are Michael and Roland!"

She let out a soft laugh as she glanced at Jonathan, whose braids had fallen into his face.

"I'm surprised you didn't make Triphon."

"The piece would be too tall," Jonathan said with a wry smile.

"He's calling for you. The council needs you. It seems to be urgent."

"Urgent? Isn't it always?"

"I think this is different."

Jonathan looked down at the knife in his hand, nodded once, and got to his feet, extending his hand to help her up.

"Don't go!" one of the boys said.

"I'll be back. Promise."

Jonathan took her hand and led her from the children, then released it and helped her down a short drop. He'd never been reserved about showing affection, but there was something more to the way his hand had held hers of late. She had wondered each time, afraid to ask his intentions, afraid that what she dared hope might be crushed with a simple word that he was only showing her friendship. Could he feel the surge of her pulse when he touched her fingers? Hear the shortening of her breath?

They didn't speak as they descended toward camp. There was no need to fill the comfortable silence between them; in this way they were much alike.

Those bathing and washing clothes got to their feet as they crossed the river, several of them coming to greet him, reaching for his hand.

"Jonathan," they murmured, lowering their heads.

He let them. He always let them, as they took his hand, their fingers touching the vein along his wrist—an acknowledgment of the life that flowed through it. A few, an older woman among them, reached up with aging fingers, to touch his neck.

And then they went on, along the edge of camp—passing through it would take far too much time. They slowed again as those working out behind their yurts came to touch him, to murmur his name. Even then some, seeing him, hurried into their tents and came out with bits of meat, a cup of wine, mare's milk. He took them all, drinking the milk, tearing into the meat with a gusto that made those watching nod approval, tossing back the wine as expected.

It had never been a mystery to Jordin why he kept to the fringe of camp when he could. It wasn't just for his sake—because he wouldn't do anything other than accept each of their gifts with grace, no matter how tedious—but for their sake, because they could not see him without feeling compelled to thank him for the vast gifts of Mortal life. For the acute perception that served them so well in every hunt. For the wild existence they celebrated in everything they did from the riot of color in their clothes to the beat of their drums and strength of their wine at night. All of which they craved and consumed with abandon.

All of which Jonathan—and Jordin, too—enjoyed as much outside camp as within it. More.

They came to the temple ruins from the side. Above the stone stairs, the ancient pillars opened to the sky. The vaulted ceiling that had once covered them had long ago caved in and been carted away by scavengers. It had been a basilica at one time, before the time of Order, when men knew the Maker as another name: God.

In the face of the lone stone beam that bridged the two columns at the front of the courtyard, Rom had chiseled the creed by which all Mortals lived: *The Glory of the Maker Is Man Fully Alive*. They said it had first been spoken by an ancient saint named Irenaeus during the second century of Chaos, twenty-three hundred years ago.

Today, the stone corners were broken away and tiny plants grew in the cracks between each step, but every time Jordin mounted these stairs her skin prickled. In the sanctum of this temple called Bahar—a name she was once told meant "Spring of Life"—she had come into Mortality on the high platform without mother or father to clasp her afterward.

It had been Jonathan who'd kissed her and welcomed her to life with the stent still in his arm.

They passed through the long corridor of pillars to the inner sanctum at the back, pulling open the double doors together and entering without a word.

The smell assaulted her without warning and she jerked back. Jonathan, too, hesitated.

Stench of Corpse.

Of something more...

Ten heads had turned, Roland, Michael, Rom, and the strange old Keeper among them. On the wide aisle before the altar, a large and very pale man slumped in a chair. Was that what she smelled? He looked like a Corpse. He was half again as tall as she, his tangled and unkempt hair hanging like ropes from his head. Her hackles raised at the sight of him.

Rom hurried forward to meet them as the others got to their feet. Roland and Michael were already standing.

"Jonathan," Rom said. He lowered his head.

"Who do I smell?" Jonathan said.

"That's the Corpse Roland and Michael brought back last night." His jaw was tight. "We need a decision from you."

Jonathan stared at the Corpse, the Adam's apple in his throat bobbing slightly as he swallowed.

"Please."

Rom led Jonathan to the front of the chamber.

Jordin faded back toward the last row of stone benches, to stand on the edge of a fringed rug. Something was wrong about the Corpse, obvious by the sidelong glance of Siphus, the dart of Zara's eyes from Roland to Rom and back. The set of Roland's jaw.

Behind her, the doors opened and Triphon burst into the room. One of the doors slammed on the ancient hinges. The stained glass shuddered in the nearby window. The Corpse in the chair stirred at the commotion.

"I can't find h—" Triphon stopped. "Ah, Jonathan." He wrinkled his nose, apparently readjusting to the smell in the chamber, and then strode down the aisle to the front, giving Jordin a slight nod as he passed and went to take his seat.

"This...Corpse that Roland and Michael brought back," Rom said, gesturing to the man stirring in the chair, "is new."

Jonathan nodded, gazing at the man. His tunic was still dusty from where he had been sitting on the knoll.

"He claims to be alive. To have been given life..." Rom paused, as though unsure about what he would say next. "By Saric."

"Saric?" Jonathan said, more sharply than Jordin had ever heard him speak.

"Yes. He claims Saric is alive. And that he has made three thousand other warriors—Dark Bloods, he calls them—like him. But there's something else. This one..."

"He feels," Jonathan said.

"Yes I think so."

"He feels emotion."

"That's what we think."

"Impossible," Seriph murmured.

"Yes, impossible," Rom said, his voice hard-edged. "But apparently the impossible has come to us here, today."

Jonathan looked quietly from Seriph, to Rom, and then at the Corpse.

"He's seen us here," Roland said. "He's heard too much. I would advise we kill him."

Jonathan seemed to consider Roland before slowly turning his gaze back to the Corpse in the chair. He had just lifted his head and was blinking at them, slowly working his jaw, a heavy bruise along the pale skin of his face—a fresher one near his temple.

Jonathan walked past Roland, stopped just before the Corpse and reached out his hand.

Roland stepped forward. "Jonathan..."

Rom threw out his arm, staying the prince. The two of them stood back, posture taut, as Jonathan slowly touched the man's head, his fingers coming to rest on the unruly dreads of his hair.

It was one thing for a warrior to touch a Corpse, but the council had agreed no unclean thing should touch Jonathan unless it be to bring life to that Corpse—a rare occurrence this past year so close to his reign. The risk was simply too great. Jonathan had to be protected at all costs.

The Corpse lifted his head to look at him, and Jordin shuddered at the cold glint of his black eyes.

"My master will see all of you dead," the Corpse said.

"Silence!" Rom hissed. "That is your Sovereign you speak to!"

"My Sovereign is my Maker. And my Maker is Saric," the man said.

Jonathan regarded him a moment longer and then slowly turned away.

"What do you say in this, Jonathan?" Rom said, the line of his mouth tight. "Should he go free, stay our prisoner, or die?"

"You're asking for my advice or a decision?"

Rom hesitated, glanced warily at Roland. Anyone close to Jonathan knew that he had never expressed an interest in exercising explicit authority to make specific decisions that affected the safety of Mortals.

"Your decision," Rom said.

Jonathan looked from him to Roland. "None of those. Make him Mortal."

For a moment, no one could respond. Not a sound, not a movement.

Then Triphon and Seriph were their feet. Roland's glare fell on Rom, its meaning unmistakable. *Make him understand.* The old Keeper slowly got to his feet but said nothing.

"Jonathan . . . are you sure?" Rom said.

"Yes. Make him Mortal. Give him my blood."

"We can't waste your blood on new Corpses," the Book said, voice wavering. "We put a moratorium on it for a reason."

Rom lifted his hand. "Jonathan is our Sovereign. He has spoken. We do as he wishes."

The man in the chair was looking from one of them to the other in confusion. "I don't want your blood."

"Because you don't deserve it," Seriph said, spitting at him.

"Do it!" Rom snapped. "Now!"

The Keeper moved to the altar, lifted up the edge of the silk draping it. There, in the altar, was a heavy iron ring. He pulled on it and an entire portion of the stone slid open with a grinding scrape. Reaching inside the stone drawer, he drew out several implements: a stent nearly eight inches long, hollow and tapered to needle sharpness on

either end, and a piece of cloth. Brown, Jordin thought—
but then she smelled it, even from here.

No. Stained in blood. Jonathan's blood.

Jonathan knelt on one knee next to the Corpse, rolled
up his sleeve, and propped his forearm on the chair arm
as if it was just another day of bleeding. The Corpse in the
chair looked wildly around.

"What are you doing? You will kill me! Please, you
can't do this!"

No one answered.

The Keeper knelt down in front of them, took out his
knife, and cut away the sleeve of the tunic the Corpse was
wearing beneath his armored vest and quickly disinfected
his arm and Jonathan's wrist. Dropping the sleeve to the
floor, he leaned over Jonathan first, blocking Jordin's
view, but she didn't need to see to know what was happening now: one end of the stent sliding home into the
short, permanent sleeve inserted into the vein in the crook
of his arm. Jonathan turned slightly, as the old alchemist
guided the other end into the vein in the Corpse's arm.
The Corpse grimaced.

Silence in the chamber, except for the breathing of
the Corpse. As it grew heavier and more labored, Jordin
could not help but remember the day of her own rebirth—
the fiery pain of it, like acid through her veins. The way
it had subsided into a warmth like that of drink, but more
languid, more exuberant, so that she could feel the drumming of her heart too loudly in her ears, as though it had
begun to beat for the first time.

The elation. The gratitude. The overwhelming sense
of strange loss. Her sudden urge—need—to weep. The
way she had collapsed in the old Keeper's arms, her eyes

unable to look away from Jonathan. To see anything but him. Her need to cling to some vision like an anchor against the wave that threatened to overtake her.

The Corpse suddenly gasped. Strained against his bonds. The Keeper was swiftly removing the stent, first from him, and then from Jonathan, taking care to wipe the blood from his skin with the cloth. She could smell it, even from here, well beyond the reek of the Corpse, that was rapidly...changing.

The Keeper stepped away, but Jonathan remained kneeling, looking at the man as he began to breathe deeply, and then to pant, as though in great pain. With a sudden grimace, he arched his back. And then his expression stretched and then fixed into wide-eyed horror.

He stopped there, frozen.

Jonathan looked quickly at the Keeper, who rushed forward, obscuring Jordin's vision of that hideous face, as the Keeper slapped him, lightly at first, and then with a ringing blow. The man's head fell to the side.

The Keeper turned around. The look on his face was stunned.

"He's dead."

Jonathan was looking between them, at the man's arm and then his own. The council members were getting to their feet, rising in slow shock.

"Impossible," Rom said faintly.

"He's dead," the Keeper said again.

"How can that be?"

"I don't know."

Jonathan staggered to his feet, pale.

Jordin had just moved out of the row of seats to go to him when one of the double doors flew open.

Smell of Corpse—true, mundane Corpse—blew in with the sudden gust of air through the columns outside. A man, dressed in the clothes of the city.

This was Alban, a Corpse spy loyal to Rowan and paid heavily by the Mortals to watch events at the Citadel and ordered to report as needed. As such, he was loyal to the Regent of Order as well as determined to remain Corpse until such time that Order permitted his Mortality.

Which would be never.

"Forgive me," Alban said, striding down the aisle, right for Rom.

"What is this?" Triphon said, moving to stand in front of him.

"I've brought a message from the Citadel," the Corpse said, staring around himself nervously. He positively reeked of fear.

"Yes?" Rom stepped past Triphon. "What is it?"

"Feyn's body." He cleared his throat. "It's missing."

CHAPTER SIX

SARIC DRILLED ROWAN'S ASHEN face with an uncompromising stare, fully aware that the Regent knew about Feyn already. That she'd been hidden deep in stasis, dead by law. That her body had not decomposed.

None of these disturbed Rowan as they did the rest of the senate, now bursting out in cries of alarm and horror. No, Rowan's terror was in seeing Feyn's body *here*, in the senate, rather than in the crypt that had housed her for the last nine years, her body fed by nutrients. Now the old pillar of Order wavered in his regal robe, threatening to collapse along with the power he'd protected for so long.

Saric ignored the uproar echoing through the great hall, his eyes lingering on the Regent as he savored the onset of crushing victory.

One voice roared above them all. "What is the meaning of this?"

He broke the gaze reluctantly. Turned to Dominic, who stood trembling to his right, hands balled to fists, face blanched with fear. The outrage settled on the floor, all eyes on the scene before them: Rowan on the right, standing like a dead man; Dominic on the left, possessed by terror. Two Legion coated in armor, each on one knee, their heads bowed, undisturbed by the chaos.

Feyn. Nude body supine on the altar of Saric's making, dead to the world, veins dark with dormant blood beneath pale Brahmin flesh.

Saric, towering over them all, Maker of their destiny, seizing unmitigated power before their eyes.

"What sickness compels a man to exhume a body from the grave?" Dominic thundered. "She has passed to Bliss!"

Saric brushed a thumb over one of her cold eyelids. Saric himself had lovingly braided her hair, washed and perfumed her body, working gently around the long scar in her chest where the Keeper's blade had cut her down. It had faded some, from what had to have been an angry and grotesque thing to a beautiful seam. The musky scent of her filled his nostrils with promise.

"Has she?" Saric asked softly.

"Yes! How dare you violate the sanctity of this chamber with the dead!"

"She's no more dead than you who breathe and bleed and piss."

"This is your purpose?" the man cried. "To use the dead as a lesson? To defile the Maker with profanity?"

He lowered his hand, glanced up at the speechless man, this defender of Order... who would now watch its demise. "And a powerful lesson indeed, wouldn't you say?"

He turned, considered the senators, many of whom he knew by name. There, Nargus, from the Sumerian house, robed in blue as was their custom. And there, Colena, the aged bat with powdered skin to hide the deep wrinkles that whispered death. Stefan Marsana from northern

Europa, Malchus Compalla from Russe, Clament Bishon from Abyssinia—all leaders who served in the senate when he himself had been their Sovereign for a few days. Only a handful were new to him.

Today he would be new to them all.

"Guard!" Dominic ordered. "Remove this body!"

Saric didn't bother to acknowledge the demand. His Dark Bloods had already handled the Citadel guard.

He stepped to the front of the platform, aware of every eye upon him.

"Tell me, Rowan, Regent of Jonathan...Is Feyn, who was rightful Sovereign before her cruel and unwarranted death, in Bliss at this moment? Or is she here with us?"

The Regent's mind was either too preoccupied with the tragedy unfolding before him or not occupied at all, having shut down.

"Answer. Now."

The Regent's eyes flicked to Dominic. "I...It is unknown."

"Isn't it appointed for all to live once? Once for them to die? Isn't that what your book claims?"

"Yes."

"And when you die that death, your soul goes either to Bliss or Hades, is that not written?"

"Yes."

"And yet our own ancient texts record accounts of those brought back to life. Were they truly dead? Had they gone on to Bliss when their hearts stopped?"

"I...I don't know," Rowan said.

"No, you don't. Because you don't really know the powers that make life and death. Only the Maker can know these things, isn't it so?"

"Yes."

"Then Feyn might not be in either Bliss or Hades at this moment, but here with us. We cannot know. We can only know if she is dead or alive as we understand life and death. Tell me this is true."

His brows relaxed slightly. "It is."

"And so, according to your understanding, is Feyn now alive or dead?"

He hesitated, choosing his words. "Dead. By law."

"Not by flesh?"

No response.

"Did you not aid the alchemists in keeping her body in stasis in a crypt below this very Citadel since the day she was slain?"

He blinked. He could not hide the truth etched on his face.

"Yes."

Saric spoke before the floor could react. "And you did it in anticipation of the day when that *boy*, Jonathan, had safely risen to sovereignty and you might bring her back without compromising his reign."

They all stared at Rowan—Dominic, the senate leaders, Corban, Saric—all but his two children, who bowed their heads in submission still.

"Rowan," Dominic hissed. "Surely not!"

Rowan gave a shallow nod. "What he says is true."

"*Why?*"

"The reason no longer matters," Saric said. "The truth is this: that if Feyn were alive today, she would be Sovereign, as succession fell to her before Jonathan. Tell me, Lord Regent, is that not true?"

He nodded, his face a hollow mask.

"And you would not be Regent, because Jonathan would have no claim to Sovereign office."

"None of this matters now!" Dominic said, stepping forward with sudden urgency. "Feyn's fate is sealed. She is dead. Jonathan is Sovereign and will take his seat in eight days."

Saric rounded on him.

"Only the Maker decides if Feyn is dead! *And today you will see her Maker.*"

His statement put the senate leader back on his heels.

Saric spun to Corban: "Bring it."

The alchemist withdrew a black velvet pouch from beneath his gown and crossed the dais. Saric shrugged out of his cloak and draped it over Feyn's lifeless legs. Without any explanation, he took his right sleeve cuff in his fingers and folded it back four times, exposing his forearm.

"Rise."

The two Dark Bloods rose and stepped to one side, ominous. Out in the senate, no one moved.

To Corban: "Proceed."

The alchemist set the pouch on the table beside Feyn's head and pulled out a pair of black medical gloves. After slipping them on, he withdrew a clear rubber tube roughly two feet in length from the pouch, stainless steel needles on both ends.

Before him, Feyn's lifeless body reclined not in death, he knew, but in defiance of it. The jugular there, just beneath her translucent skin, begged to pulse once again. For his absolute mastery over her. For the gift given him by Pravus, now perfected by him so that he could bestow it as he wished. As he did now. He could not suppress the slight tremble that spread through his torso at the thought.

This was his destiny: to consume and give life as he alone chose.

Master and Maker.

His eyes closed. His mind raged with beautiful darkness. "Sire?"

His eyes opened. Corban stood ready, stent in one hand. Saric silently presented his forearm.

"I beg you do not do this!"

Dominic's protest was cut short by the dark glance of one of Saric's children. Saric hardly noticed. His attention was on the stent in Corban's hand. The bite of its razor edge in his vein. He gasped, softly, as it slid home.

Black blood spilled into the tube. Filled it to the clamp halfway along its length.

He held the device in place as Corban slipped the other stent into Feyn's jugular. The alchemist lifted his eyes to him.

Saric nodded.

Corban removed the clamp from the tube.

For a fleeting moment, Saric became aware of how perfectly still the chamber had become. Fear ruled the hearts of those within Order. But he was the Maker now. They would remember this day. His supremacy. The glittering eyes of the Dark Bloods upon them so that none dared utter a sound.

His blood entered Feyn's jugular slowly, pumped by his heart in a transfusion of life. He let it flow, curling his fingers into a fist, willing it to flood her. It would not be a making like his at the hands of Pravus, but one perfected, both more potent and refined. He'd brought only six to life in this way.

They called elected Sovereigns to-be "sevenths."

Feyn, his half sister, Sovereign of the world, would be *his* seventh. The one he, not the dictates of Order, chose for the throne.

"Sire?"

Saric ignored Corban, eyes fixed on his arm.

"Sire, it is enough."

"No."

Corban would only inform, never protest. He'd been Saric's first and could never betray him. As with all of Saric's children, his heart was not his own, but solely owned by his Maker.

He waited until he felt the first hint of depletion and then went a moment longer, his heart surging, tenaciously pressing blood into her lifeless body. Dominic backed away, lips moving in prayer.

To the wrong Maker.

"Now."

Corban moved to reclamp the stent, but before he could, Feyn's eyes snapped wide. Her body arched, the small of her back jerking a full foot off of the stone table.

Corban swiftly slipped the stent out of her neck.

For a full beat, her contracting muscles held her in contortion, impossibly bent. And then her mouth suddenly spread wide and she sucked in a thick lungful of oxygen. Her ragged gasp echoed through the hall.

She collapsed on the table, eyes wide. And then she clenched them tight and screamed.

It was a raw scream of birthing in excruciating pain that Saric himself so longed to feel. He had not been made in this way, but how he wished he had been!

A second scream chased the first, joined now by a hundred cries from the assembled dead on the senate floor.

Saric tore the stent from his arm and stepped back. Blood dripped down his arm. He did not gloat, he did not smile, he did not offer any sign of satisfaction. All were beneath him.

He simply was. Maker.

Feyn collapsed against the table, panting, clawing at her neck, legs stiff. The solution that had kept her in stasis had preserved most of her muscle, but it would take hours to recover any semblance of her former mobility.

And a few days for the pain to leave entirely.

Saric stepped to her and gently lowered his hand to her heart. It throbbed beneath his palm, beneath the sudden flush of her skin. Of his life, become hers. She absently tore his hand away, oblivious, twisting in panic.

He slapped her face. "Hold!"

She stared with wide, dark eyes, seeing him for the first time.

"Hold," he said, with tenderness this time. "The pain will pass."

She whimpered once and settled.

"Better."

He leaned forward, kissed her lightly on her forehead, and whispered his will into her very soul. "My love, my Sovereign...Rule for me."

Tears slid from the corners of her eyes, toward the table beneath her.

Saric snapped to Corban: "See to her."

And then he turned to address the senate chamber, now roaring with fear and dissonant confusion. Many were out of their seats, some crowding the aisle, some close to the doors. All in horrified shock.

He held up his hands.

"Esteemed members of the senate, leaders of Order, I

have but one question to put to your leader before your witness, here, in these hallowed halls. He will speak truth for all to hear on pain of death."

They expected him to turn to Rowan, the Regent. Instead, he faced Dominic, who immediately glanced at Rowan with questioning eyes.

"Feyn is alive," Saric said, done with mincing words. "Chosen at birth by the laws of succession as our rightful Sovereign. Does she or does she not retain full claim to the Sovereign office?"

His mouth opened but he didn't seem capable of speaking. His eyes darted to the stone table where Corban and one of his children were easing Feyn up by the shoulders.

He blinked. "If she—"

"She breathes. She bleeds. The same as you. No. Better than you, now. Was she not designated by birth rightful Seventh in line for Office?"

"Yes."

"Louder. Speak the truth for all to hear!"

"She was—she is."

"I will permit you to live."

He walked over to Rowan, who was now only a frail mirror image of his former self. "Forgive me, old friend, but there can only be one Sovereign," he said quietly.

His hand flashed with a speed they would soon come to know all too well. The knife beneath his vest filled his fist. Before any could see, much less react, the blade slashed through the Regent's neck, four inches deep.

Blood spurted from the man's jugular onto the dais floor. Rowan grabbed at his head in an attempt to keep it, eyes already fading. He toppled with a loud crash as Saric turned his back.

Corban and one of the Dark Bloods had eased Feyn's feet to the ground. They stood her upright, facing the Senate Hall. She trembled, leaning to one side, weak as a fawn staring out at the world for the first time. Such terrible beauty. Heart of his heart. Blood of his blood.

"Now," he said to those on the chamber floor. "I present your Sovereign. You may kneel before her."

The senators looked from one to another, only the barest rustle of turning heads and bodies shifting in seats filling in the oppressive silence of the chamber.

And then one man moved.

Dominic.

He stepped slowly forward. A motion born of obedience— not to the man on the dais, but of a lifetime of Order. The Sovereign stood, alive. And so he knelt.

The rest of the chamber followed.

CHAPTER SEVEN

THE CORPSE SPY might as well have walked into the council chamber and told Rom that the Citadel had fallen into the ground. No. That news would have been far better received.

Rom felt the blood drain from his face. Surely, he hadn't heard the words correctly.

"Feyn? What do you mean *missing*?"

"I mean her body is gone."

"Gone? It can't just be gone."

"I'm sorry, sir. It was there just three days ago."

"That's not possible!" His voice rang through the stone sanctum. "She's been in stasis. She can't just disappear!"

"Everything in her chamber is as it should be, but her lines have been cut and her body is gone."

Rom felt the hot prickle of panic against his nape. Lines cut. Feyn gone. There had to be a mistake.

"You went to the wrong crypt, then. Did you *see* her body being taken?"

Alban's fear-filled eyes darted to Roland, searching for help.

None would be forthcoming.

"There are no other crypts like it below the Citadel. I've been checking the same room for five years now, sir. It's no mistake. She was taken in the last two days. I came as soon as I could."

"Then Rowan took her." Rom spun to the Book, who'd ensured and monitored all of the arrangements for her stasis. "You knew of this?"

His eyes were locked on the spy. "No. Did you go to Rowan with this?"

The spy shook his head. "You yourself instructed me not to. In the case of any tampering with her no one but you was to know. But I spoke to him about some other matters and am certain he knows nothing of her disappearance. He would have said something."

"If not Rowan, then who?" Rom demanded.

"Saric," Roland said.

Rom stared at the prince. Just behind him, Saric's Dark Blood slumped in the interrogation chair, dead from Jonathan's blood.

"Who else knows?" he demanded of the spy. "How long has she been missing?"

"As I said, two days at most. I swear to you, I came as soon as I discovered the empty chamber."

There was no deceit in his scent.

"You know nothing else?"

"Nothing." His voice wavered. His eyes were on the Dark Blood.

"There are no other changes in the Citadel?"

"None that I know of."

Rom raked at his hair. "Leave us. Wait at the edge of our camp for orders. Speak to no one and be sure to stay downwind."

The Corpse dipped his head and hurried out. For several long seconds, no one spoke.

Feyn, the once Sovereign to-be.

The sudden swell of emotion coursing through his body surprised him.

"Book?" His voice was raw.

Behind him, the Keeper remained silent.

Rom turned and faced him. "Tell me something, man!"

"We may have a problem," the old man said softly.

"If what Roland says is true..."

"How would Saric know to look for her?" Triphon asked, rising. "No one but Rowan knew!"

"And that Corpse," Michael snapped. "We're fools to trust any of them."

"*We* knew," Seriph said.

They looked at her. "You're suggesting one of us told Saric?" Triphon demanded.

Seriph shook his head. "I'm only saying what needs to be said. That we were foolish for allowing a dead Sovereign to be kept in stasis to begin with."

"*We?*" Rom said, glaring at the Nomad. "Say what you mean. Accuse me. Accuse Book." He flung his arm out to Jonathan, who stood in the grip of his own distress over the dead Dark Blood. "She gave her life for Jonathan under the express agreement that we would keep her in stasis for nine years until Jonathan took his seat. Once he became Sovereign we were to bring her back to serve under him. But *we* were the ones saving the woman who died for Jonathan while you were still a *desert Corpse!*"

"She died to see him to power, not to come back and undo it all!"

"Silence!" the Book snapped, stepping out onto the

floor. His eyes were fired, his face cut with an urgency Rom hadn't seen in many years. "*I* made the promise with Jonathan's full agreement." He stared Seriph down. "Only a fool would question what was done long after it was done. No more of this!"

Rom nodded once. "Roland's right. We have to assume that this was Saric's doing."

Triphon wasn't ready to assume anything. "But how could he have known—"

"That's not important now!" Rom said. "No one else in Order would have the same incentive as Saric to take her body. Even if they did, they'd present no threat to Jonathan. But if Feyn is resurrected before Jonathan comes into power, *she*, not he, will be rightful Sovereign."

Silence.

"Tell me I'm not right, Book."

"Yes. The laws of succession are clear. Her claim precedes his. If Feyn is brought back to life before Jonathan takes office, she is Sovereign by right."

"Then we find her and kill her," Roland said. "Now. Before Jonathan comes to power."

"No!" the Book cried. "If Feyn is alive, she is Sovereign already! And if a Sovereign dies, power passes to the last living former Sovereign, not to Jonathan."

A beat of silence passed between them all.

"Saric," Rom said.

"Saric?" Roland glanced between them. "I heard nothing of Saric being—"

"Few knew." Rom paced, one hand digging at the back of his head. "He became Sovereign for a few days when his father died. As Sovereign, he changed the laws of succession. It doesn't matter. What does matter is that if Feyn is alive now, Jonathan will never be Sovereign. And her death would only put Saric in power."

"As I said," Seriph murmured. "Keeping her in stasis—"

"Leave us!" Roland thundered.

Seriph blanched.

Roland shoved a finger at the door. "Now."

The Nomad got up, slowly dipped his head, and strode for the door, jaw tight.

"Your zealots are fools," Rom said, after the door closed behind him.

"They aren't my zealots," Roland corrected. "And they're not all fools."

And yet, all of those who'd argued for a more forceful approach to ensuring Jonathan's coming to power would have to be watched, Rom thought. But for this moment, at least, they had far more immediate issues to deal with.

"You have to find her."

The voice came from the back, from Jordin. He looked at the young fighter who'd taken up the unspoken role of Jonathan's second—and perhaps, of late, his closest—protector. Her face was set and her hazel eyes blazed with surety.

"Jonathan owes her his life," she said.

Rom turned from the girl. "Book? How long can her body survive disconnected from the machines that kept her in stasis?"

The Keeper shook his head. "Forty-eight hours. At most. We must assume Saric has her."

He had to force himself to say his next words:

"If he has her, he's killed her already and become Sovereign."

"No. He will need to establish her as ruling Sovereign

first to prove that she is alive. He will need her in power. If Saric has her, he will install her."

"Or has already."

"It's possible."

"Then we'll hope so," Rom murmured.

Michael stepped in front of what had been Seriph's seat. "How can you say that?"

"No, he's right," Roland said, frowning, deep furrows across his forehead. The Nomadic ruler rarely betrayed concern, but he had to be as unnerved as the rest of them, Rom knew. There was no better man to have at his side.

"If Saric has Feyn in hiding, we have as little chance of finding her as we do of finding these other Dark Bloods. But if he installs her as Sovereign we know where she'll be. It's our best hope."

"To what end?" Triphon demanded. "If she's Sovereign already, Jonathan is finished!"

"Hold your tongue!" Rom snapped.

Triphon stared at him and then looked away.

In all of this, Jonathan hadn't moved once from the side of the dead Dark Blood. He watched them now with silent eyes. His was not the look of a world leader on the cusp of losing his reign, but neither was it the reaction of a naïve boy. There was far more happening in that mind, Rom was sure, than perhaps even Jordin knew.

To date, everything predicted by the first Keeper, Talus, four hundred and eighty-nine years earlier, had come to pass. There could be no doubt about the veracity of the first Keeper's claims. The fate of humanity rested on Jonathan's shoulders, and Rom was prepared to give his life to see that fate fulfilled.

Never mind that Mortals could now make other Mortals

with their own blood, rendering Jonathan's blood redundant, as some had recently begun to whisper.

Never mind that no one knew just *how* Jonathan would bring life to the world. Or that the zealots in particular were far more interested in protecting Mortals as an elite race than seeing any more Corpses come to life.

Never mind that Jonathan had shown neither defining desire nor expected aptitude for ruling the world as Sovereign.

Everything Rom and the Keepers had done had been with one purpose in mind: to bring Jonathan to power as required by the sacred vellum written by Talus. Nothing else mattered now.

Nothing.

A single tear broke from Jonathan's eye and snaked down his right cheek.

"Jonathan?" Even in the midst of sick unease about Feyn's disappearance, Rom felt a tug of empathy for the boy chosen to carry the world's burdens. "Forgive us. No harm will come to you, I swear it on my life."

Jonathan dipped his head, barely. "You have a good heart, Rom. It's Feyn I worry for."

Of course Jonathan's heart was drawn first to the woman who'd paid a terrible price for him. The woman Rom himself had led into life once, if only for a short time.

Desperation thickened in his chest.

As he turned to the others, his mind was already set, but he would at least act in deference to the Nomadic way.

"Roland. Your recommendation."

The prince spoke after only brief consideration: "If we knew where these Dark Bloods gathered and the full nature of their defenses, we could take them and Saric with them. They're very strong and we're outnumbered, but we have seven hundred fighters with unequaled skills and Mortal perception. We would destroy them."

"Even if we knew where," Rom said, "slaughtering them would go against everything Jonathan stands for."

Roland gave a nod. "You asked. I speak my mind. Either way, we don't know where they are. So we go for Feyn."

Rom faced the old Keeper. "Book?"

"You must find Feyn…" He rubbed at his head, shaking it. "Saric will have moved quickly. If she isn't Sovereign already, she will be soon."

Michael said flatly: "So we find her and do what?"

"She has the ancient blood in her," the Book said. "She'll hear you, Rom. That's our one hope."

Yes. It was.

"Roland, you're with me."

The Nomad nodded.

"We ride for Byzantium." Rom stepped toward the door.

He had taken two steps when Jonathan's voice sounded from behind him.

"I will go."

Rom stopped. Turned around. "No."

Jonathan was on his feet. "I must go. She loved you, Rom, but she died for me. My blood is stronger than any other Mortal. I'll go to Feyn."

He had never been beyond the perimeter of protection. He'd never stepped foot in any town or city since the day he had entered Byzantium as a boy to make claim to the Sovereign throne. He'd never even seen a Corpse beyond those who came to camp.

"I can't allow that."

"He goes," the Book said, crossing to the altar, retrieving the stent where he had left it. "We may not have a second chance."

"Then I go as well," Jordin said, stepping toward Rom.

"Out of the question."

"She goes," Jonathan said, eyes on the olive-skinned girl.

Michael flung up her hands and began to protest, but Roland stopped her with a raised palm. "Jonathan's right. Jordin goes. She's one of the best fighters we have." To Michael: "You will stay with our people."

Rom looked from one to the other, then to Jonathan, whose arm was already in the Book's grasp, the stent going into the vein.

Blood? Now?

"What are you doing? We don't have time!"

"I need to know what happened." The Book glanced at the dead Dark Blood. "You'll be gone for a day. And I need to know now."

CHAPTER EIGHT

DOMINIC PACED BEHIND the heavy desk in his office, staring at the bookshelves. Staring without seeing. He needed to consult the texts. The commentaries on the Book of Orders. He needed counsel. He needed Rowan.

Rowan, whose head had all but toppled off his neck, blood spurting into the air...

What abomination, what profane act, had he just witnessed?

He shook his head, suppressing terrible fear. Not for Rowan, but for himself at the spectacle of death.

Saric's claim that they were all dead still rang in his ears. Perhaps the most blasphemous words ever spoken in the senate chamber.

Dominic stared out the window and willed himself to feel something other. *Other* than horror. *Other* than abject fear at what he had just witnessed.

But he could not. Gone were the sentiments of a baser age called Chaos. Humanity had risen above them and peace had reigned.

It simply wasn't possible that a virus had changed them genetically as claimed by Saric.

We know the Maker exists by his Order. It was the first line of the liturgy. The most basic statute of Order. Order was the hand of the Maker. To question Order was to question the Maker. By that alone, he knew Saric's claims from the dais for sacrilege. That whatever dark blood flowed in Saric's veins was anathema.

And yet . . . he had brought his sister back.

So then . . . it was possible to bring a body back from stasis. There was no end to Alchemy. Megas had been an alchemist—was it possible that he'd crafted this virus called Legion?

The thought stung Dominic's mind. No. There was only one truth, given by the Maker in the way of Order as written by their prophets. The fear Dominic felt now was borne of righteousness. He knew without investigating any of Saric's claims that the man was more than twisted.

He was evil.

Born once into life, we are blessed. And if we please, let us be born into the afterlife, into Bliss everlasting.

Dominic's greatest fear now wasn't for his own life. It was that in failing to act today he might have somehow left his fate unsecured. Or that in failing to act in the future, he might achieve the same. He dare not risk Bliss. He feared Hades.

He straightened, his purpose clear. Adjusting his robe, he strode for his office door, yanked it open.

The anteroom of his office was filled with senators. They were only slightly less pale than when they'd witnessed the horrors of just an hour ago.

He dipped his head. "Senators."

"What would you say?" Senator Compalla of Russe said.

He strode forward, heart set. "Isn't it obvious? Feyn is our Sovereign. We will serve her without question as we serve the Maker."

"And what about Saric?"

"Saric," Dominic said, facing her, "is a blasphemer."

"And his claims?"

"You dare ask?"

"Not to question." She faltered. "Only to know where you stand."

"False! All of them."

They were in the grips of fear, practically wavering where they stood. A nation could not be ruled like this. A world could not be ruled by the weak.

"I have consulted the archive. He fills your ear with lies. Guard your mind, lest you compromise your hereafter."

It wasn't the truth—he hadn't gone to the archive, he'd spent the last hour pacing. But it *was* the truth. Order was infallible. It was far better to lie once than to display such lack of obedience as to go looking for proof that it was not.

The prudence of his decision—of his own obedience— was immediately evidenced in the slight, but very real, settling on the faces before him.

"We know the Maker exists by his Order," he said. "And for that reason, hear what I say now. Saric must be stopped. At all costs." He spun and walked past them.

"And how will you stop him?"

He stopped at the outer door and faced them.

"I won't. The Sovereign will."

CHAPTER NINE

EIGHT HOURS HAD PASSED since Feyn had woken to find her world completely changed. And although she knew precisely who she was, in some ways she didn't know herself at all.

The face looking back at her was not her own. Familiar, yes. So pale. Skin to set the standard of beauty for the world. And right there—the dark vein beneath her temple. So dark. It had been blue before. And her eyes had been palest gray. They glittered now, like faceted onyx.

Feyn turned her head, considered the inky veins spreading up over her cheek like the branches of a winter tree...the tributaries of a black river. A river with a single headwater.

A face appeared beside hers in the mirror.

"You're beautiful, my love."

Saric.

Feyn considered him in the glass. The strong line of his jaw, broader than she remembered it. The neatly trimmed hair beneath his lower lip, precise as she remembered it.

"Am I?"

"Yes."

His voice filled her with strange warmth.

He reached around her and unfastened the top of her gown. Pulled wide the broad neck, bearing the scar that crossed from her sternum almost to her waist on the other side.

She flinched—not at the sight of it, but at the sudden memory of the sword. Flashing down, light glinting off the blade. A scream in her ears—her scream as she held her arms wide. She had opened herself to the slashing blade. Given herself to it.

She had died that day.

Feyn clasped the front of the gown, pulled it closed. And then his hands were on hers and pushing them gently away, fastening the hooks up the front.

"Don't worry, my love. I will remove the scar. I'll see it gone from you. Nothing will mar your beauty or remind you of that day. Nothing except the fact that it brought you to me. That would please you, wouldn't it?"

She lifted her gaze to his in the mirror. "Yes." And then: "Thank you."

He smiled. "Wait here."

Her brother stepped away, and she turned to watch as he moved toward the chest in the corner. Her jewelry chest. Here, in her chamber.

She glanced out toward the broad windows at the tumultuous sky, churning beyond the curtain of heavy velvet drawn back on each side. At the dressing table with the large, round mirror. At the bed, too big for one person, or even three. Up, to the vaulted ceiling overhead.

Saric was back, holding up a pair of dangling sapphire earrings.

"You never wore these before. A state gift, I believe, of

Asiana on the occasion of your inauguration the day you were taken from me. You always insisted on such simple baubles. But the time for those childish days is over, isn't it?"

"I suppose it is," she said, as he slipped them through her earlobes.

The old Keeper had said she would not die. That she would sleep for a time...and would live again. And he had been right, in a manner of speaking.

He had been wrong, too.

It had not been sleep.

And now there was Saric, the face she remembered, peering at her distantly, as though from another life.

She didn't remember him being so muscled, or even quite so tall. She didn't remember the curve of his mouth when he smiled as he did now.

There had been pain. Pain, worse than the wound that had killed her. She had no doubt now that she had been dead.

Had she been in Bliss, then? She had no memory of fear. Of the eternal torment of Hades that one goes to when one fails the known bar of Order, wherever it might be set, that day, and for that person. And on the day she'd died, she had renounced Order and changed the course of its succession.

How strangely it had all worked out.

"Tell me, sister, did you dream?"

He wanted to hear that she had. She saw it in his eyes.

She smiled slightly.

"But of course you did," he said in a low, soothing voice. "Of me, I'm sure."

Her mind drifted to the scene at the senate. Like a dream, but real, alive. Every eye, staring at her. She had been naked, but it hadn't mattered at first because she was still in the dream, and in dreams fear always manifested as nakedness. A fear that the world would see the dreamer as they really were. That they were never what they pretended to be.

"Of course," she said, smiling again. She wanted to see him smile. Had Saric been quite so gentle with her before? Or as beautiful? Had he changed as much as it seemed?

Or was it her, only now seeing him for who he was?

The flush of warmth again, this time, as he took her hand. He had chosen her rings, her gown, even put her shoes on her feet. With great care, he had drawn back the sides of her hair into a sparkling diamond clasp.

"You smile, sister," he said. "For love, yes? For me. For your master."

"Yes," she said. And her confession brought her more comfort.

The door to her suite opened. Several of Saric's servants came in, the ones he called Children and sometimes Dark Bloods. They were setting the table there in the dining room.

"Do you think you can eat? You must make yourself take normal food, not only what I feed you."

"Why do I feel this way?" she said, looking up into his eyes.

"What way, my love?"

"I...I don't feel myself. Something has changed."

He tilted his head. "How do you feel?"

"I don't feel the same fear I once did."

"Tell me more."

"I...feel pleasure. At the way you look at me now. At the way you smile. Seeing it. I want very much to see you pleased."

"The thought of my pleasure pleases you, then."

"Very much," she said with some wonder. "And there's more. I feel..." She couldn't fully express the emotions flooding her mind and heart. She wasn't sure where they lived in her, only that they had somehow come from Saric.

"Joy?" he said. "Love? Peace?"

She nodded. "Yes. Yes, I think so."

She'd felt this way once before. One beautiful day in a meadow where she had learned a truth that had changed the course of her dead life...

And brought her, ultimately, here.

"Why?" she asked.

"Because. You are alive."

"Alive." Her heart tripped once in her chest. So he'd found the serum and come to the life she herself had once known? Had the Keeper fulfilled his promise?

She felt herself weaken at the beauty of the thought. Saric's hand was instantly under her elbow.

"Yes. Alive." He turned her toward him. "Full life. My life."

Her heart stuttered. "Yours?"

Why did that set her instantly on edge, as though she had bitten down on metal?

"Not like I had before. Forgive me for my former indiscretions, my love." He took her hands. "I was weak then. A lost soul desperate to find truth. I have realized it is my destiny to know and experience the purest kind of life—and now, at last, I have found it. There is no life greater than that which now flows through my veins. Now I truly love as I could not before. And now you serve me as you've wanted to, often without knowing it yourself. I have liberated you from the Order of death and all of its rules."

She tilted her head. "You have?"

One of the Dark Bloods appeared in the doorway and Saric glanced up. "Ah, good. Come, my dear. You will eat now."

He slid her arm through his and led her into the front room. She studied the Dark Blood as he held out a chair for her at the table. He was broad and well-muscled like the two exquisite creatures she'd seen earlier in the senate. His eyes were black, his skin like marble veined with ink—like hers—but a warrior like the others.

"Janus, how is your mate?"

The Dark Blood glanced up as he came to the side of the table to pour wine into the goblets before them.

"She's very well, my Lord. Thank you."

The table was filled with an entire array of food so delicately and painstakingly prepared that Feyn couldn't remember seeing a meal quite as inviting. Fish. Roast. Quivering eggs, poached across the top of the filet. Color everywhere—from the vegetables to the flowers on the sides of the plates. And in the middle of their two settings, a bowl of pale rock salt. She glanced at Saric. His eating habits had changed.

He took his place, adjacent to her at the table, reaching over to shake out Feyn's napkin and drop it into her lap before doing the same with his. "I envy you, Janus. She's lovely."

Janus hesitated, the pitcher of wine in hand.

"She could be yours if you so desired, my Lord."

Saric glanced up at him. "No, no," he said with a slight smile. "I only want to see you happy."

"Thank you, my Lord," Janus said.

Saric touched the knife with a forefinger before lifting

it from the table. He looked at Feyn deliberately, seeing into her in a way that unnerved her, if only every so slightly.

"If she ever displeases you, Janus, you'll be certain to tell me," he said, eyes fixed on Feyn.

"Of course, my Lord."

"On that day I wouldn't hesitate to have her killed."

Feyn glanced up.

Janus paused. "Thank you, my Lord."

"Leave us now."

The Dark Blood dipped his head and left the room.

Feyn studied Saric as he cut into a piece of meat, laid it onto the center of her plate. The smell of it briefly threatened to turn her stomach, unaccustomed to food for nearly a decade as it was.

"You would kill his mate?"

"Yes."

"Is she also one of your children?"

"Yes."

"But you say you love your children."

Saric glanced at her sidelong, thoughtfully licked off the edge of the knife, and then delicately, precisely, set it down parallel to the fork on the edge of his plate.

"I would kill Janus, too, if he failed to serve me," he said simply.

"You would kill your children? Those you call your own?" she said very carefully.

She could not tear her gaze from his face. The simple tilt of his head. His lips, without tension. The cast of his gaze, as quiet and as heavy upon her as a vise.

"You don't understand the power of the Maker? Does he not torture and send to Hades even those he once loved because they failed to love him the way he wished? Is that not the way of the highest power?"

She blinked.

Bliss. Hades. The two destinies of the deceased. Eternal freedom from fear. Eternal fear, bound in wailing and the gnashing of teeth. It was taught from birth. It was the way.

"Yes," she said.

Should she tell him that in her death, she had seen nothing of Bliss or Hades? That it had been filled only with nothingness?

Again, she was aware of her strange desire to please him.

Was this love, then, as she had known it once?

Perhaps.

Loyalty?

Yes.

Freely given?

Given.

"And so you see," he said with a slight smile, "I, too, am like that one. That Maker."

"Yes, you are."

"I am. And you will serve me, my love, as my Sovereign."

"As your Sovereign," she said.

"You will rule the world as I say."

She dipped her head. "As you say."

He held out his hand.

"You will obey me as your Maker."

She lifted the napkin from her lap and laid it on the table. Slipped from her chair, to a knee between them. Lifted his hand, turned it over.

"As my Maker," she said, laying a kiss against his palm.

CHAPTER TEN

THEY RODE ALL AFTERNOON. Rom, Roland, Jordin, and Jonathan. South from the limestone canyon lands of the Seyala, through rough terrain, sweeping three miles east of the most direct route, far from the train tracks and the primary road into the city.

South, to Byzantium.

Two miles outside the city they paused to water and rest their horses. Jonathan and Jordin ate a simple meal of cheese and dried meat in silence. Neither spoke much in the company of others—Roland had wondered aloud once whether they actually communicated with each other some other way. Did the boy *see* beyond normal Mortal perception? Could he, with a glance, discern another's thoughts?

They were both uncanny, even for Mortals. Jordin, with her undemonstrative nature among a class of warriors from whom a certain amount of swagger was expected. Jonathan, with the burden of the world on his shoulders.

And then there was this new threat of Saric and his Dark Bloods.

The prisoner's death confirmed one thing in Roland's

understanding: Dark Bloods were an abomination. A defiled race.

And yet, somehow, the Dark Blood's death had disturbed the boy greatly.

"The boy." It was funny how they all still thought of Jonathan that way despite all of the evidence to the contrary. He was as strong as most warriors his age and faster than all but a few among all Mortals.

Roland glanced at Rom, offered him a piece of dried jerky, and ate it himself when the man refused it. He knew there was only one thing other than Jonathan on their leader's mind.

Feyn.

Rom had spoken less of her as the time for her waking had neared—clear indication that there was far more weltering beneath the surface. He spoke even less now.

Roland admitted his own concern about her potential ascension, but only insofar as it affected their mission to see Jonathan into power. To protect the Mortal bloodline. To see their superior race thrive. This was Jonathan's true purpose—nothing else mattered. For the sake of the Nomads, he would die to serve that cause.

The sun was just nodding toward the horizon when they started the last miles into the city. Rom, riding in the front. Jordin, always at Jonathan's side. Roland, flanking them all.

Within a half hour the muted lights of Byzantium appeared—not the bright orange Nomadic fires they were accustomed to, but a glow dimly reflected by the opaque sky. He watched Jonathan lean forward in his saddle as the spires of the city came into view.

That's when it came to him, faint as smoke on the wind, but far less pleasant.

Corpse scent.

Rom stopped, hand up. It was coming from just west of them, too near to be the population of the city itself—not yet, at least. Too near, and too weak to be so many.

Roland nudged his mount forward, past Jordin and Jonathan.

"There," Rom said, lifting his chin toward a copse of trees that hid a small lean-to, about a hundred and fifty yards off. It was barely more than a piece of siding propped against the gnarled trunks of two trees.

Scavengers, escapees of Order. Two, from the look of it—a woman, her arm bound in a heavy bandage, and a teenage girl, black-haired, perhaps fifteen, with a noticeable limp. Victims of an accident, then, fleeing the city and the wellness center with it, and with good cause. Many who went in as victims of sickness or accidents often did not return. The Order did not permit reminders of Mortality, of the thing all Corpses feared most: death.

It was said that those who left did so in secretive fear, knowing that spouses and family members were obligated under Order to report them to the authorities. Which they did, because there was only duty to the laws of Order.

These two didn't stand a chance. They'd be found by the authorities that regularly roamed the city outskirts for just their kind within days.

Jonathan pulled up between Roland and Rom, rapt, staring from the saddle. Why the keen interest? A Corpse was a Corpse. Dead. Diseased. Worthy of Mortality only through council approval.

"They've fled the city," Rom said to Jonathan. "In an effort to live."

Roland glanced west. The sun was dropping below the horizon.

"We need to go."

He threw one last look toward the lean-to and moved on. Jordin waited for Jonathan who, after a long moment, finally turned around.

Bringing him had been an unnecessary risk in Roland's judgment. It was true, his blood was much more potent than their own and could not survive more than an hour outside his body. But their blood might just as easily be given to Feyn to turn her Mortal. Still, Jonathan was Sovereign.

Ignoring the Corpses completely, Roland rode after the three of them.

The Mortals had long ceased to enter Byzantium by conventional means. Nine years ago, Rowan had undertaken a new project in Jonathan's name to fortify portions of Byzantium's sewer system, beginning beneath the Citadel itself and extending to the northern edge of the city. The ancient sewers that had weathered millennia would have easily weathered a thousand years more, but thanks to Rowan, a portion of them had been conveniently connected to form an underground route into the city.

It was by this route that the Keeper would meet with Rowan regarding Feyn's care. The same way that Rom's spies had come and gone unseen from the capital.

They reached a hill just outside the city. There, a metal culvert the height of a man opened into a stony bed that had once been a shallow drainage river.

They dismounted in a sparse grove of trees, tying their horses, retrieving torches from saddles in the dark.

"Jordin," Rom said. "You'll bring yours and Roland's

horses to the back of the northeast basilica—the Basilica of Spires. Leave the other two here."

Jordin gave him a sharp look and then glanced at Jonathan. Her skin appeared dusky in twilight, emanating its own kind of glow.

"We take no chances with Jonathan," Rom said, seeing her reluctance. "We need two escape routes. Wait behind the basilica with the horses. If we're not there in three hours, return and meet us here."

Her gaze flicked from Jonathan to Rom. She nodded.

It was the right choice. She was the most likely to find her way out as swiftly and inconspicuously as possible.

Rom pulled up his hood. Roland had his up already and was tying a dark scarf over his nose and mouth. It wasn't to mask the smell of the sewer, but something far more offensive: the reek of five hundred thousand Corpses walking, breathing, and dwelling in fear.

Jonathan glanced back at Jordin once without speaking, and then pulled his hood up over his head.

And then they crossed the rocky drainage bed to the culvert, lit the torches, and went in as darkness settled over the city.

Rom hadn't entered these tunnels in six months—since the last time he'd met Rowan in Feyn's stasis chamber as he had twice a year for nearly a decade.

He moved quickly through the culvert, pushing back the smell of rat feces, the refuse of the city, the rot and mildew seeping through the thick weave of the scarf over his mouth and nose. The image of Feyn's body hung in his mind.

Still. Pale. Her lashes so distinctive in the fluid-filled

tank that he expected her to open them. Her hand with nails so meticulously trimmed. The finger with the moonstone ring.

She'd been in stasis so long that the few days he'd once known her seemed less like a memory than some vestige of a dream.

A dream that had brought them to this moment, here. Now.

He picked up the pace, boots splashing through the sediment that had settled at the bottom of the culvert. He glanced back at Jonathan, who moved with all the stealth of the Nomads, head down, Roland a shadow behind him.

Just ahead, the culvert opened into the brick sewer tunnel. The opening was new, reinforced with rebar, but the brick was ancient. They stepped into the tunnel, which was slightly lower than the edge of the culvert and filled with half a foot of water.

The tunnels belled out beneath the edge of the city, near the northern underground terminus. A grate in the side of the tunnel emitted soft light—and then a distant squeal of brakes on wheels.

"Hold," Rom said. "It's just the underground. The public transport."

A gust of air came through the grate after another distant squeal.

Stink of Corpse.

Rom heard the boy stop behind him. "Keep moving."

Past the terminus, the squeal of wheel brakes faded as they made their way deeper into the city. After another ten minutes the tunnel opened into a vast chamber with thick columns that rose nearly two stories to a vaulted ceiling. An electrical box took up half the wall, wires running from it in all directions. It was covered with a padlocked metal cage and emitted a faint hum. Metal stairs led to a second-story transom that hugged the circumference of the upper level; four arched passageways opened out of it in the brick, each in a different direction.

"We go up," Rom said, nodding to the stair spiraling up the side of the wall. The three of them ascended, boots ringing on metal steps, then moved across the transom above to the arch of the northern passage.

Rom could hear the breath of the boy behind him, the skitter of a rodent, the crumble of mortar, here, where the bricks were the most ancient of all. He tasted the stagnant air.

Place of secrets.

They emerged from the tunnel and approached a door, the stone frame of which looked as old as the history of the city itself except for the obvious new addition of electrical wires running along its edge. The lock in the door was also modern.

Only three people had a key to this door: Rowan, the Keeper, and the Corpse who tended to Feyn. Rom had retrieved the key before leaving camp, but now he saw that it would be entirely unnecessary—the door was not only unlocked, but slightly ajar.

Rom pushed past it and stepped inside, torch held aloft.

Dark niches, the size to cradle a body, were hollowed out in the walls like the eye sockets of a skull.

He strode through the first chamber to the bell-shaped crypt beyond. To the great sarcophagus in the middle of the room, with its ancient carvings and metal tubes worming through holes drilled straight through the stone.

The heavy lid had been pushed aside and onto its edge

on the stone floor between the sarcophagus and the crypt wall.

Rom hurried forward, his torch throwing light into the glass lining.

Empty. Severed tubes dangled motionless in the fluid-filled chamber. So it was true. He'd held out a bare hope that the spy's story had been wrong.

He turned to find Jonathan staring around the chamber with wide eyes.

"As expected," Roland said.

Rom took a slow breath. "We'll find her."

"You're sure you know the way? The Citadel is three square miles."

He nodded. "Let's hope so."

He led them out of the room and down the underground passage. It had been nine years since he'd passed through these halls of death and prison cages. The majority of them had been sealed off immediately after the commencement of Rowan's regency. Up, near the service entrance, with its back corridor…

A corridor he remembered from one surreal night when he had abducted Feyn herself. A lifetime ago.

If he had done it before, he could do it again.

"Where will this take us?" Roland said.

"To the Sovereign's chamber."

"You know the way to the Sovereign's chamber?" the Nomad said in a strange tone. "I should have known."

Rom didn't respond.

It took them another fifteen minutes to reach the hidden passage that led into Feyn's chambers.

He led them down the corridor, his free hand held up for silence, and then to the top of a narrow flight of darkened stairs. Faint light seeped past the edge of a heavy velvet curtain below. He signaled them to extinguish their torches and wait.

The scent of Corpse was unmistakable. With it, burning candles. The lingering scent of a meal—meat. Wine.

And a deeper odor.

Dark Bloods.

Rom's pulse quickened. He padded down the stairs and eased aside the edge of the curtain.

Faint glow of candlelight throughout the dimly lit chamber. Faint strain of...violin? The meal was gone; the smell came from the front room, adjacent to her bedchamber here.

The smell of Corpse was stronger. Of Dark Blood.

Saric had to be nearby.

A figure near the expansive window. A woman, in a gown of blue velvet, a diamond clasp in her hair. She sat at a desk piled high with newspapers.

Feyn?

He willed his breath to calm, slipped past the curtain with only a whisper of a rustle, glanced to his left, toward the dressing area, and once up at the ceiling, noting the faint mismatched edge of plaster where it had been repaired.

His heart was hammering, too loud.

He took several steps to the middle of the chamber and stopped.

"Feyn."

The woman at the desk paused, newspaper in hand. She lowered the paper, very slowly, and then turned in her chair.

It was Feyn, and she was alive.

It came back to him then, all at once: the day he had taken her out of the city, the way she had come to life when he had given her the blood. The ways she had laughed, and then kissed him. Had asked him to run away with her.

How different it all might have been then. But there had been Jonathan.

And Avra...

His last sight of Feyn had been on the day of her inauguration. She had fallen to her knees, arms out, a terrified scream coming from those lips so beautifully set together now. Her blood had spilled to the platform as she had crumpled, sliced open by the Keeper's sword...

A horrible image that had haunted his sleep for years.

Now, with the light of the candelabra illuminating her hair like a halo, he felt his breathing still. He'd forgotten just how regal, and absolutely beautiful, she was.

"It's Rom," he said, when she said nothing.

She was the picture of composure, her hands folded in her lap. Blue gemstones dangled from her earlobes.

"Rom," she said.

He took two steps and stopped, staring. She wasn't rising. Or hurrying to meet him. Or crying out how Saric had taken her. He had expected anything but this calm self-possession. But of course he should have known. She was a Corpse again, schooled to carry herself as one without fear, no matter how acutely she felt it...

"It's true then," he said. "Saric took you."

Nothing.

"How?"

She rose from her chair.

"Once again you invade my chambers, Rom Sebastian. History repeats itself, after all."

She folded her hands, placing her left hand over her right. There was no mistaking the heavy ring of office on her finger. Sovereign.

He'd come expecting nothing less, but seeing it so vividly confirmed...

Nine years flashed before his eyes. The lives of Avra. Of his mother. His father. The old first Keeper he had met.

Every memory now at her mercy.

He strode to her, half-expecting her to take a startled step back. But she didn't. Instead, she allowed him to drop to one knee and take her hand.

Rom had been so distracted by the sight of her alive that he'd pushed aside the scents in the room, but now so close to her they registered again, demanding to be noted.

Dark Blood. Heavy as tar in his nostrils.

He looked up at her eyes. Black.

For a moment he froze. Now he saw the black sprawl of vein up her cheek.

Her gaze held no fear. She seemed to be taking him in, as though his sudden proximity had ignited strange fascination. Memory, perhaps—a tumult of emotions passing through those eyes like a confused mosaic.

"Feyn," Rom said, pushing down his panic. "We'll find a way to fix this. Where's Saric now?"

Her gaze flicked to his left, over his shoulder. Rom spun around, expecting to see Saric himself. Instead he found himself staring at Jonathan and Roland. Their hoods were off, their scarves pulled down from their faces.

"Who is this?" Feyn said. But something in her tone told him she already knew.

Rom stepped to the side.

"This is Jonathan. The boy you gave your life for." He

fell silent as the two considered one another in the dimly lit chamber.

"Jonathan . . . ," Feyn said faintly.

"Yes."

She glanced at Rom and then walked past him, stopping just short of Jonathan who continued to take her in without a word.

"I remember you," she said. "The boy on the horse. Coming to take the seat I gave up. And now here we are. What are we to do? Two Sovereigns. But only one now." Her gaze left his eyes to trail over his braids. She reached out, took several of them between her fingers, thumb brushing over them thoughtfully. They were all tied with black cords for skill in the games and adorned with feathers—gifts from children.

"I remember you as well," he said softly.

"They said you were crippled."

"I was. But my leg healed."

"It's his blood," Rom said. "Like the blood you tasted once, but much more. We've all taken it. We see differently now. We feel emotion, but we sense in ways that we never did before. There many of us now. We call ourselves Mortals."

"Indeed?"

"You died for me," Jonathan said. "I owe my life to you."

Feyn was silent. A tear slid out the corner of her eye. Jonathan lifted his hand, as though to touch it, but before he could she had dropped his braid and brushed it quickly away.

She turned to Roland.

"And who is this?"

"This is Roland."

"A Nomad," she said in a musing voice, seeming to take in not only his appearance but his very stature. She tilted her head. "Not just a Nomad, but a prince, I think. And so the stories are true. You still exist."

"Indeed we do," Roland said, inclining his head. He showed her respect, but Rom knew he would not bow before Order—or any other Corpse, for that matter. Only another Mortal would have noticed the barely perceptible way that he stiffened when she stepped toward him. The way his nostrils flared slightly at the smell of Dark Blood. And it was strong. Strong, but different from that of the Dark Blood that Roland had brought back to camp.

"I take it you've taken the office of your ring," Roland said. "Before the senate?"

"Yes."

He glanced at Rom. "We must hurry."

Rom pushed aside the questions flooding his mind and nodded.

"Feyn...you remember why you gave your life for the boy?"

She looked at him, eyes dark, expressionless. "I remember."

"Then you know how critical it is that he rule this world..."

He waited for her answer, breath stilled.

She gave none. But that was good enough for now.

"He must bring the world back to life from this office, either as Sovereign or through you." He flipped his hand. "We can figure it all out later. For now we act on what we know, which is this: Saric wants to rule. How he managed to stay alive and find you, we don't know, but he can only have one purpose. Surely you know his intentions."

He couldn't tell if she was at a loss or just allowing him to make his plea.

He continued, picking his words carefully. "Nine years ago as Sovereign, he changed the laws of succession. You do realize that if you were to die now, *he* would become Sovereign. Not Jonathan."

She hesitated and then offered a single, shallow nod.

"At any moment he could reach out and kill you and rise to power."

"Saric will not kill me," she said.

"And what would stop him?"

"Love."

"Love? Evil knows no love!"

"Then I am evil?" she asked with a raised brow. It was a soft-spoken challenge, not a question.

"No. But we can't take any chances. You must remember Jonathan's destiny to rule and save the world!"

She shifted her gaze to the boy who seemed to return her rapt interest.

"Is that how you feel?" she asked him.

"My blood brings life," he said. "Not death. You died for me once...I don't want you to die again."

They faced off like two lost souls meeting for the first time. Two unsure Sovereigns at a critical crossing. Jonathan was only being crafty, he thought. Feyn...

The Sovereign was critically confused.

"How did Saric bring you back to life?" Rom asked.

"With his blood," she said. "Isn't that how you showed me life once? Through blood?"

"His?" How was it possible? "Saric's?"

"This surprises you?"

"You're saying blood from his *body*?"

"From his veins," she said.

The revelation felt like a blow.

Roland moved closer, glancing at the door. "We don't have time."

Rom held up his hand. "There can be no comparison between whatever alchemy Saric has conjured up and Jonathan's blood. Surely you know that."

No response.

Roland was right. They had little time. "We need to reverse whatever Saric has done. You must take Jonathan's blood." Even as Rom said it, the image of the Dark Blood, slumped in the chair, tugged at the back of his mind.

He glanced at Jonathan. "Will it work?"

The boy nodded slowly. "It might."

"It has to. We have to make her Mortal and figure out this problem of succession."

"There's something different about her," Jonathan said quietly.

And it was true. She reeked of Dark Blood, but not in the same way as the Dark Blood earlier that morning. And Rom was suddenly certain he knew the source of the scent.

He turned to Jonathan, eyes wide with hope. "She drank the blood. The ancient blood. Not enough, but she tasted life once before."

"Maybe that's it," Jonathan said, biting his lip.

"Roland." He reached out to his second. "Stent."

Roland withdrew the Keeper's black bundle from under his cloak and handed it to Rom.

"Feyn—" Rom glanced up to find her looking through the great window at the dark sky outside. She turned at the sound of her name.

"We'll begin with only a drop," he said, laying the bundle on the bed. He released the ties and rolled it open, lifted out the gloves the Keeper insisted he use.

"You'll need to sit still for a moment."

"So much talk," she said, folding her hands. "As though I weren't truly here."

"I'm sorry. Actually, you could take my blood—it has that property now. Any one of us can bring another to life."

"Like Saric."

"Yes. No. Not the same at all. There's no blood as pure as Jonathan's. If there's one blood that can save you, it's his. That's why he insisted on coming."

Feyn regarded Rom with a slight smile and a tilt of her head.

"Save your blood, Jonathan, for those who need saving."

"*You* need saving!" Rom snapped.

"Do I? Do I look wounded to you? Like one who is sick? One near death in the Authority of Passing?"

"Authority of Passing?" Jonathan said.

She turned from Rom to Jonathan.

"Where the diseased and defective go to die, away from a fearful public. Where all who offend by their very Mortality are sent."

Rom stared at her, struck by her choice of words. *Mortality?*

"Where is this center?" Jonathan said.

"You don't know? On the southeast edge of the city outskirts. It's where you would have been taken, born with a crooked leg as you were."

"We didn't come for them." Rom fought a sudden surge of panic. "We came to help you."

"Help me what, Rom? Give up my life again? I did that once."

"This isn't life you feel!"

"Isn't it? I feel pain. I feel remorse. I feel pleasure…" She slid her gaze to Roland and back. "Ambition. Great purpose. And yes. Love. I've found a beautiful life, Rom Sebastian. How can you know that it is less than yours? That my love is less than the love you feel? The answer is: you can't. I feel every bit as much beauty and joy to find myself alive now, tonight, as I ever felt once with you."

"That can't be," he heard himself saying. "You're confused. Nine years in stasis have left you weak."

"But I'm not confused. I'm the Sovereign of the world. I am alive because of my Maker. I don't need your help."

"Your Maker?" Rom said, his voice rising.

She stared at him for a long time, expressing neither frustration nor hope. Perhaps her head was spinning in the pangs of rebirth.

And yet…she had experienced no rebirth. It couldn't be.

"You should leave now," Feyn said.

"Saric will kill you if you don't let us help you, Feyn. You must see that. All hope will be lost!"

"You should leave. Now."

"Please, Feyn!"

"Guard!"

CHAPTER ELEVEN

NINE YEARS BEFORE, the world had found hope through the death of one woman. Today that hope was shattered by her return from the grave.

Feyn, the Sovereign of the world, once pure of heart, remade by a dark force bent on crushing Jonathan. Feyn, whom he had loved.

And now she betrayed her intention to make it permanent with a single order.

These thoughts skipped through Rom Sebastian's mind as his reality collapsed around him, threatening to weaken him in the face of the sole task that rendered all others moot.

Save Jonathan.

The cry was still in her throat when he moved, *seeing* it all at a rate familiar only to Mortals, the breakneck world slowing around him.

"Roland!"

He was across the chamber in three giant strides, slamming the door shut. The Nomad was there, shoving Feyn's elaborate dressing table—the closest piece of furniture—in front of it.

Knuckles rapped on the bedroom door. "My Lady?"

Feyn took all of this in with wide eyes, but did not cry out again.

"My Lady!" More urgent.

Rom snapped his fingers at Jonathan and waved him toward the curtained stair. "Hurry!"

Rapping knuckles became a beating fist.

Rom gestured Roland after Jonathan and was halfway across the room himself when the fist on the door struck again, this time splintering the paneled wood. The ease with which the guard broke through the door stopped Rom for a split second. He knew Dark Bloods were strong, but what strength shattered a thick door so easily?

He could hear Roland and Jonathan running up the narrow stair. With a last glance back at Feyn, still rooted to the floor, he shoved the curtain aside and bounded up after them.

"Left," he ordered, slipping past them. "Stay to his back."

They ran down the hall, slipped through a door at the end, and flew down another staircase that spilled into a dark room.

Rom spun back, breathing thickly. He could hear footsteps running down the corridor—cutting them off from the direction they had come in. He glanced at Roland. He had heard them, too.

He spoke low, quickly. "We go out on the surface. Through the streets." He flipped his hood up.

To Jonathan: "Stay on my heels, stop for nothing. Ten blocks to the basilica—you can't miss the spires in this moonlight. The tallest you can see. If anything happens, keep going."

To Roland: "Any threat, take them out. If we get separated, we meet there."

Rom hurried to the door that exited into the outer hall, cracked it open. He glanced out for a moment before slipping through it and then sprinted for the palace's main entrance, around the next corner. He'd been in the Citadel under duress too often for his liking, but was now thankful for his memory of its layout.

Jonathan was close behind him. Like all Mortals, he'd learned to maximize his ability to *see* in a fight, which put him at great advantage against a Corpse. The Dark Bloods were a different matter, but Roland had killed four of them easily enough. If the worst found them, Jonathan should be able to defend himself until Rom or Roland could step in.

Yet the worst *had* found them. As they ran, Rom cringed at the folly of risking so much by putting him in danger.

He stopped at the corner, snatched a look into the atrium and, finding it vacant, led them forward. They walked in even strides, straight for the main entrance.

Pounding feet and a shout of alarm echoed down a side passage from the direction of Feyn's apartment.

Rom pulled up at the doors with his hand on the lever and turned quickly to Jonathan. "Don't leave our backs. For any reason."

The Sovereign yet-to-be returned a curt nod. Sovereign, because there had to be a way.

Rom glanced at Roland. *Protect him with your life.* The words didn't need voicing.

He pushed the door open. Slipping out into the night, his eyes scanned the darkness.

Six broad marble steps descended before them to the concrete walkway, white in the moonlight. Beyond that, manicured lawns, tall shrubs against the thirty-foot-high Citadel wall, and the ornate ironwork of the Citadel's side gate. Two guards in the gatehouse.

The wide street beyond the iron gate ran perpendicular to the Citadel perimeter. At the end of the street an alley cut north before entering a maze of roads that would lead them to the Basilica of Spires, where Jordin waited with two horses.

He heard Roland slip his knives from their sheaths. Rom motioned the fighter forward with a jerk of his head and grabbed Jonathan's sleeve. "Stay close!" he whispered.

Before Rom took his first step, Roland was past him. Two long bounds to the bottom of the steps. He flew across the lawn, straight for the gatehouse. No room for temperance; he would do what he must, given the stakes.

Behind them, the sounds of chase grew louder. Fast. Heavy. Close—far too close. He could *smell* them.

Dark Bloods.

Rom grabbed Jonathan by the arm, urging him forward, faster. To the bottom of the steps, across the lawn in Roland's footsteps.

But then Roland suddenly changed course, his hand up, signaling warning and now Rom knew why: the pervasive stench of a city full of Corpses had momentarily masked the smell of Dark Blood.

They veered toward the gate, committed, thirty-foot walls on either side. It was either through the gate or not at all.

With a single glance over his shoulder, Rom released

Jonathan and flipped out both of his throwing knives. Roland slid up against the wall of the gatehouse, facing them, paused a beat, then spun through the door.

A grunt. Two. Nothing more.

They paused against the gatehouse as Roland slipped out, blades dripping red in his fists. In another place and time Rom would have demanded to spare innocent Corpses, but this was not there or then. No time for second-guessing now.

The fighter shoved a key in the lock, twisted hard, kicked the iron grate wide, and stood firm, heels planted, to face the Dark Bloods rushing him from the outside perimeter.

Stealth was no longer their luxury or advantage.

Seeing was.

Rom saw every move with intense precision, impossibly slow as the suspended beat of a bat's wings.

The rush of both Dark Bloods converging on his second, who stood with his legs spread, muscled taut, blades by his hips, head tilted down, unflinching.

They came at him. One running stride…

Two…

Three…

Every movement protracted in Rom's sight happened faster than with any Corpse or Mortal he had ever seen.

They drew their swords back.

It was then, with their flanks exposed, that Roland's arms flashed, like striking serpents.

But he was too slow.

Rom saw it all in an elongated instant: Roland committed, both knives releasing off the tips of his fingers. Flying.

Roland's first knife took one of Dark Bloods in his throat, slicing deep.

But the Dark Blood to Roland's right shifted just in time to avoid the weapon flying toward him. He'd moved far faster than he should have been able. Speed to match their incredible strength!

The second knife sliced through the Dark Blood's clavicle instead—a searing slash that would slow a weaker man, but that did nothing to stop this man's sword, arcing toward Roland's head.

Roland threw himself back, just avoiding the Dark Blood's blade, his advantage gone along with his knives. The Dark Blood didn't allow the momentum of his swing to compromise his balance, but used it, spinning for another strike.

Rom, still taking in the implications of the speed of Saric's dark warriors, didn't react in time.

Neither did he think to stop Jonathan, who flung himself past Rom and crashed into Roland's legs from behind so that they buckled, the Dark Blood's sword hissing harmlessly over his head.

Rom's hands flashed, palmed the carved handles of his knives. He surged forward, throwing his upper body into the uncoiling of his wrists as he whipped both forward from his hips, underhanded, not bothering to steady his aim. The target was hard to miss.

It happened in slowing ticks, the spring of time having forgotten its tensile strength: Jonathan, landing on his shoulder as Roland started to rise, lips stretched back in a snarl.

Rom's blades slamming into the Dark Blood's chest, a single hand span apart.

Jonathan, rolling to his feet.

In one smooth motion, the boy swept low, fingers curling around the hilt of the dead Dark Blood's sword just as the man's companion, stunned by Rom's knives, started impossibly forward again, weapon drawn back.

With a feral cry, Jonathan whirled 360 degrees, sword extended in a deadly arc. The heavy blade severed the Dark Blood's arm just above its wrist, flipping hand and sword end over end, overhead.

Roland stretched for the weapon, snagged it from the air with both hands—one on its hilt, one on the fingers that still grasped it—and swung the blade with a roar that smothered the echo of Jonathan's cry.

The sword sliced cleanly through the Dark Blood's neck. The headless body faltered for a long count, then toppled back onto the cement.

Rom, Roland, and Jonathan remained crouched for a suspended instant longer.

More Dark Bloods were coming, running heavily down the stone steps of the palace. Alarm spread through Rom like fire.

"Jonathan! Blade!"

Jonathan flung his sword at him. It was good to see that their future Sovereign could handle himself in real fight, but the look on his face betrayed a horror that Rom feared would compromise him next time. Violence beyond the games wasn't in his nature.

Or was it?

"Hurry!" He rushed by Jonathan, tugging at him as he passed. "Roland, rear!"

Roland spun just in time to engage the two Dark Bloods sprinting to the gate, three others behind them.

Rom pushed to keep up with his charge, who had proven himself among the three fastest runners in the camp numerous times. "Ahead—the alley to the left."

Jonathan threw a glance over his shoulder. "Roland?"

"Can handle himself. He buys us time."

Rom twisted back to see Roland's blade in full swing, cutting down one of the Dark Bloods with the precision Rom had come to count on. Having miscalculated their speed once—with nearly fatal results—Rom knew Roland wouldn't be taken off guard again. No one of Saric's making could match the fighter's skill. He was sure of it.

But Rom had another problem; that darker smell of death, so obscured by the Corpses of the city, came to him from farther ahead.

They had nearly reached the alley when a dark shape stepped into their path, blocking their way. Beyond him, two more Dark Bloods ran across the street. The place was crawling with them!

Ignoring a stab of panic, Rom turned to Jonathan, who he knew to be unarmed. His escape was the only thing that mattered now.

"Through that alley to the Basilica of Spires. Get to Jordin. Stop for nothing. We'll meet you outside the city."

Without waiting for a response, Rom veered to his right, straight toward the first Dark Blood. "Roland!" His cry rang down the street. "More!"

He swung his sword as the closest one moved to block Jonathan. With a single blow, he buried the heavy blade into the man's chest.

"Run!" he shouted. "Now!"

Jonathan dodged the falling body and ran, sprinting around the corner. Alone and running. Gone.

Maker help him.

Rom was so distracted by the thought of this newest risk to him that he only narrowly avoided an oncoming blade. He blocked it at the very last instant, dancing out into the street, away from the alley. Away from the path of Jonathan's flight.

There would be blood on this street tonight, but at least it would not be Jonathan's.

The two Dark Bloods converged on him at once.

"Roland!"

CHAPTER TWELVE

AN HOUR HAD PASSED since the others had entered this city of death. An hour that Jordin had spent fighting her own battle—namely, the terrible fear that harm might find Jonathan.

What if the Dark Bloods were already in the Citadel? What if they were more formidable than Roland said? What if there were hundreds of them?

What if, what if, what if?

She had reminded herself that he was with Rom and Roland, who could maneuver and fight their way through the thickest spot. That Jonathan himself was fast and surprisingly skilled. But the truth was that if it came down to it, she wasn't sure he had the heart to kill.

What if Jonathan was wounded or taken? Or simply unwilling to use his blade?

She should have gone!

Nerves raw, Jordin had hurried through the city, her hood pulled low over her forehead, taking as many back alleys as she could find with the two horses, avoiding the pungent odor of death wherever it was strongest. But any concern for her own discovery had been wholly overshadowed an hour ago by her sheer need to see Jonathan at her side again, unharmed and beautiful.

She had tied the horses to a utility pole tucked behind the basilica and then climbed up the fire escape to the roof. From there it had been an easy matter to climb up the exterior ladder of the tallest spire and swing beneath the rail of the narrow walk near the top.

Byzantium, city of the dead, stretched out before her, its stone-and-brick buildings looking to her eye like nothing so much as a mausoleum. From here she could see the Citadel just to the south, the broad wall around it, the rare, dim outdoor electrical lights of its grounds. For half an hour she'd searched the gates, the streets leading to the far entrance, for any sight of them, looking for any Mortal movement beyond the occasional truck or cart or dead pedestrian ambling by. With each passing minute her anxiety twisted her gut tighter.

The sound of hooves drew her attention to a closer side street intersecting the main way. There a horse-drawn covered cart wobbled in the moonlight, alone. She could smell the human contents from here.

Corpses, Corpses, everywhere.

Too strange, to think that but for the blood she might be oblivious to the odor of death. That she might see in Byzantium a world as alive as the Nomad camp. To think that apart from the external factors of custom and dress, there had once been no difference between Nomads and those of the Order.

That was before Jonathan's coming, when they had celebrated life without having it.

Without knowing it.

She studied the streets for sight of the others. Her

vision had grown more acute the last few years as Jonathan's blood had matured in her veins. But no amount of Mortal vision could conjure him from the shadows.

She willed herself to be still and to master the cold creeping into her fingertips, to relengthen her breath.

Until tonight, her greatest concern for Jonathan had been that he'd be misunderstood. That the uncertainty and gentleness in his eyes would be seen as weakness by a people who lived by a code of vigilant strength and wild life.

She knew better than perhaps even the old Keeper that Jonathan carried a terrible burden—one she doubted he could carry alone indefinitely.

The blood in his veins had chosen him, not the other way around. He hadn't asked to take on humanity's redemption from death, to bleed out for the world, one portion of blood at a time.

Did the others see the torture in his eyes? The questions that followed him like carrion birds? Did they lay awake at night and beg the Maker to ease the way of their savior, as she did? Did they care as much for his life as his blood?

Or was Jonathan only that vessel selected by the centuries to do the Maker's bidding?

Jonathan, where are you?

She would be the one by his side—not someone who cared only about the promise of what he could bring—but a woman who knew and loved him for the secrets in his heart.

The instant she thought it, she chided herself. He was the Sovereign and savior of the world. She was an orphan who had been saved by his blood. Her role was to protect and love him. His was to right the world.

From here on out, she would vow to keep her mind in its proper—

Her train of thought broke with movement at the edge of her vision: a man, tearing from an alley into a street two hundred paces west of here.

Her heart hammered against her ribs, adrenaline flooding her veins. She would know that running form anywhere—that head lowered into the night, the length of that stride, his braids streaming behind him.

Jonathan, alone, headed for the front of the basilica.

And then not alone. A tall form sprinted around the corner, thirty paces behind him. A Dark Blood. On the side street, the horse-drawn cart meandered on, on a direct path to intersect Jonathan's flight.

There was no sign of Rom or Roland.

Something had gone wrong.

Jordin reached around for the bow on her shoulder and then stopped. The distance was too great, a low-percentage attempt that would only delay her getting to him. She had to get closer.

She sprang, catlike, over the short railing, bounded across the ceramic roof tiles, seven paces to the fire escape along the back of the basilica. She swung onto the ladder's guide rails and slid down, palms burning from the friction of rusted steel on skin.

Down two stories. Three. She shoved away from the fire escape, dropped fifteen feet to the ground on light feet. And then she was running before her thoughts had time to catch her, focused on one thing only: reaching Jonathan before the Dark Blood did.

She ran along the basilica's eastern wall, sprinting on her toes, demanding her legs fly faster.

Around the corner, grabbing for the drain pipe on the turn.

Hand over her shoulder, slipping her bow free.

The main street careened into view.

Jordin pulled up hard, arrow notched, *seeing* the scene before her: Jonathan running full bore, still a hundred paces off. The Dark Blood closing, not quickly, but too fast for her to reach him in time.

She dropped to one knee, gauged the distance and sighted two feet over the warrior's head. She drew the compound bow's string to her ear, held her breath to steady her aim, and loosed the arrow.

It flew nearly two seconds before striking the man in his breast armor. He jerked, caught off guard by the blow from nowhere. But the strike only slowed him a pace before he continued his charge.

Jordin had already notched her second arrow. Pulled back, let fly.

This time the Dark Blood was ready for the projectile, saw it coming, and jerked out of the way with stunning speed. Still running. Fast.

Too fast.

She'd never reach Jonathan in time!

The clip-clop of the horse-drawn cart edged into the street directly ahead of her, driver perched lazily on the cab, reins in hand.

Flinging her bow over her shoulder, Jordin bolted up and tore for the horse. There was only one way to reach Jonathan before the Dark Blood did.

A single strong horse pulled that cart. She needed it. Without warning to driver or animal, she launched herself at the horse, landing on its back like a black-clad wraith.

Grabbing it by the neck, she jerked the reins from the driver.

The startled horse snorted and bucked, but she had ridden horses far stronger and wilder than this domestic dog and she hung on, heels digging into flank.

The horse bolted, terrified. She sent a vicious lash of the reins to its right hindquarter. Hooves pounded the cobblestone street as the horse picked up speed, the covered cart a forgotten distraction.

The driver cried out but when she glanced back he was gone, having fallen from his perch or jumped.

Thirty yards.

"Run, Jonathan!" Her scream echoed down the street. "Run!"

He ran directly toward her, face glistening from the dead sprint.

The Dark Blood had somehow picked up his pace. His sword was in his hand. He was going to throw it!

Jordin smashed her heels into the horse's flanks, pulling it to the right to avoid Jonathan.

"Run!"

But the moment she passed him, Jonathan slowed, following her with wide eyes.

"To the back!" she screamed. She jerked the horse hard to the left, directly toward the oncoming Dark Blood.

She saw it all in a mosaic flash: The alarm on the Dark Blood's face. The careening cart breaking free of its hitch. The horse jerking its head back at the sight and scent of the looming Dark Blood.

The cart veered to the left and slammed into a darkened light pole.

Then they were on top of the warrior.

He was far too agile, avoiding them again at the last instant, but he'd been thrown off guard.

Keep him off balance.

The simple thought broke into her consciousness even as she acted out of instinct.

The horse was already galloping by the Dark Blood, whose back was now to her. She threw herself backward off the horse, feet over head, snatching her knife from the sheath in midair, twisting so that she would land facing the Dark Blood from behind.

She landed on the run, sprinting silently for his exposed back—four long paces. She was half his size and he was quick, but she now held full advantage, and she couldn't afford to waste it.

He had just begun to turn back when she launched herself at him.

Landed on his back.

Wrapped both legs around his belly.

Jerked his dreadlocks back with her left hand.

Ripped the blade in her right hand across his exposed throat with a shrill cry.

No one would threaten Jonathan.

Blood gushed to the ground as the Dark Blood staggered forward. She rode him to the ground, breathing hard. His body twitched once under her, and then lay dead.

Her rage caught her off guard. But of course it was rage. She would take a hundred like him if they dared touch the Sovereign. Her Sovereign.

Her head snapped up. He stood twenty paces away, staring not at her, but through the bars at the back of the covered cart that had crashed into the light post. The lettering on the side of the cart finally arranged itself into three cohesive words for the first time.

Authority of Passing.

This, then, was one of the transports that took frail or flawed Corpses to their living graves—Corpses like the ones they had seen on the way in to the city a few hours earlier.

The thought skittered through her mind like a piece of refuse blown by the wind, here, and then gone in the face of far more pressing matters. Where there was one Dark Blood there might be more. They had to get out of the city. And where were Rom and Roland?

She glanced behind her. Clear…except for two shadowed silhouettes running toward them, still nearly a quarter mile away. Mortals. Rom and Roland.

Relief flooded her. They would make it. Jonathan was safe, and she had been the one to save him.

She would harbor a quiet and small amount of pride, knowing that.

Jonathan, however, was fixated on the cart.

"Jonathan?" she said, striding toward him. "Are you hurt? What happened?"

He stepped closer to the cart, peering through the barred door at the back. Not only peering. He was absolutely fascinated. Wholly consumed by what he saw. She hurried to him, mentally steeling herself against the smell of Corpse.

She drew up against his side and looked inside. Two benches, one on either side. Chained to one of the benches sat a young girl, perhaps ten or eleven years of age wearing a torn gray dress that hung on her thin body like a sack. Her long dark hair looked as though it hadn't been touched by a comb for a week; her face was smudged as though it hadn't seen soap for a month. Even so, she was a beautiful girl, Jordin thought, even dirty and staring at both of them with large, unblinking eyes. Eyes so resigned as to be nearly absent of fear.

Nearly.

Jordin saw the reason she had been taken: her right arm was wrong, crooked at the elbow. The hand below it only had three fingers. How long had she hidden that condition? How many years had she been kept confined, away from the others who would report her out of fear for their own lives... and afterlives?

"What's your name?" Jonathan asked in soft voice.

Jordin glanced over. "Jonathan? We don't have time..."

He stepped forward, ignoring her. The girl pulled back a few inches, face round with worry.

"No..." He reached for the bars. "Don't be afraid." His voice strained. "I'm not going to hurt you. Please... what's your name?"

The girl still didn't answer. The stench of fear was so strong that Jordin felt compelled to lift her arm to cover her nose, but then immediately took offense at her own weakness. This young girl could have been her not so long ago...

"My name's Jonathan," he said quietly. "I was born with a crooked leg. I was also born to give life and hope to the dead. They take my blood." He paused. "It hurts me."

Jordin glanced at him. There were tears on his cheeks, but that wasn't what caused her breath to stifle in her lungs. She'd never heard such a bold statement of pain from him, and hearing it now, spoken to a Corpse who couldn't possibly understand, somehow crushed her.

She told herself that he could only confess it to one he couldn't hurt. That he cared too much to burden the recipients of his blood with the truth of his suffering. And yet...

Jonathan had said this, knowing that she, Jordin, would hear and understand.

She stood rooted to the street, fixed by a deep and terrible love for him. Suddenly desperate to repay him for his love with her life.

For his life... with her love.

"You're a beautiful girl," he said, "Please, tell me your name so I can remember you always."

The girl could only feel fear, but the stench of it softened. Rom and Roland were almost here, two blocks from the fallen Dark Blood. Behind them, just entering the street from alley, four others came at them at full sprint.

Jordin touched Jonathan's shoulder. "There's more coming."

He ignored her. "Please tell me your name."

"Kaya," the girl whispered.

"Kaya," Jonathan repeated. "A beautiful name. Where are they taking you, Kaya?"

Tears flooded the girl's eyes and broke down her face. "To die," she whispered.

Jonathan's hands began to shake on the cold metal bars. "My blood can bring you to life."

"I have to be brave," she said.

Jonathan glanced down at the heavy lock on the door. There would be no breaking it.

He looked up again. "Then we have to be brave together, Kaya. I'm afraid too." He reached a hand toward her through the bars. "We have to be brave together. Take my hand."

His tears snaked down his mouth to his jaw.

Rom was yelling now, racing toward them. "To the horses! Hurry, Jordin!"

"Jonathan, we have to go!"

"Take my hand. Please!" And in that moment, Jordin wasn't sure who he did it for—the girl . . . or for himself.

The girl looked from Jonathan to his outstretched hand and then slowly reached out, touching the tips of her fingers to his. He reached in, took her frail fingers in his, and held her hand.

The world seemed to stall. Her vision swam, distorted—whether by the tears blurring it or the vivid sight of her Mortality as danger approached, she didn't know. Only that something changed in that moment as she watched the exchange between Jonathan and the doomed girl.

"Run!" Rom cried, running past the fallen Dark Blood now. "Move, now!"

"I'll find you, Kaya," Jonathan said. "Remember me, when I bring my new kingdom!"

The girl nodded, holding tight to his hand with both of hers.

"Now!" Roland shouted.

Jordin took his elbow. "Jonathan, please!"

He let go of the girl's hands like one tearing himself away. He turned to Jordin. "Don't tell anyone what you saw."

"I—"

"No one."

"I won't," she whispered.

"Where are the horses?"

She swallowed the knot of thick emotion in her throat. "Follow me."

Then they were running for the back of the basilica, and Rom and Roland were with them.

Jonathan was safe for now.

But Jordin also knew that Jonathan would never be truly safe.

CHAPTER THIRTEEN

FEYN HEARD THE FOOTFALL on the same stair by which Rom had fled an hour earlier. The sound of a boot that made no effort to mute itself, heavy as it landed on the flagstone of the chamber.

She spun, half-expecting to see Rom returned. But it was Saric, now tying the curtain to one side with the heavy bullion cord tied to a ring in the ancient stone wall. He had shed his long velvet coat and wore only a simple pair of black trousers, his boots, and a dark shirt with sleeves rolled away from forearms far stronger than she remembered them.

"My Lord," she said.

Silence.

She paused, still unacquainted with this new Saric. He was so different from the impetuous half brother who had pushed for power with seething indignation. This man was far more controlled, far more affectionate, and far more strangely alluring. Her Maker.

She wasn't a concubine to come bounding after him, to come begging for his approval, though there was indeed the strange compulsion to go to him, if only to win that approval and hear again his words of love.

When he turned and looked at her at last, she smiled.

He did not.

"I understand you had visitors," he said, walking toward her.

"Yes. The guard told you, then?"

"Yes. The guard told me."

He stood over her, less than an arm's length away, nostrils flaring slightly as he released a measured breath. His lips twitched—a slight smile.

"Did you think?" Saric asked, gently drawing back a strand of hair from her cheek with tender fingers. "To tell me?"

"I didn't want to trouble you."

"And so you let them come . . . and you let them go."

"I thought your guard would stop them. Surely—they have, haven't they?"

His eyes, so startlingly dark, searched hers.

"Tell me about them."

She glanced away, trying to subdue the strange sense of need—to clasp his hand to ask forgiveness for something, to thank him, to ask him to stay. Strange reactions to this man, her brother. But oddly beautiful.

This new life was disconcerting. No wonder they had called it Chaos . . .

"Rom Sebastian came to see me," she said.

"And was he alone?"

Surely he knew the answers already.

"No. He came with the Nomadic Prince, a man named Roland. And . . ."

Why did she feel the urge to hesitate?

"And?"

"And the boy. Jonathan."

Saric stepped past her and walked to the large arching window to stare out at the night beyond.

"And how is Rom Sebastian?"

"He's changed."

"In what way?"

"He's their leader—the ones who've come to find life through Jonathan's blood."

"To find life," he echoed softly.

She hesitated. "They call themselves Mortals."

"Mortals. How quaint." Saric turned around to face her. "Tell me about Jonathan. What did he say?"

"That he was sorry for what I did. They tried to give me his blood."

Saric stood as though carved of stone. "And?"

"And I refused it. They thought I needed saving."

"And?"

"And I said those at the Authority of Passing would be better served than me."

"Why would you say that?"

"Because they're dead. I am not."

He dipped his head slowly, his first gesture of any approval. She found herself instantly eager for more.

"The boy's blood . . . Did they say anything about it?"

"Only that it brings them to life."

"So the boy is a Maker. He tried to make you?"

"They wanted me to take the boy's blood. Or any of theirs."

"What do you mean?"

"Rom said that they can make others from their own blood. But that Jonathan's is still the strongest."

Saric's eyes narrowed a fraction. "You're certain of

this? I need you to be precise. They claim they can make other Mortals from their own blood."

"They claim to, yes. They looked at me strangely, as if offended by my presence. It was very strange, as though—"

"This boy you once died for...Do you realize what he is asking of you?"

"Please tell me, my Lord."

"He would ask you to die for him again. You must understand this. Not a physical death, perhaps, but they would destroy you under the guise of saving you. Don't you see? They have no place for you, Feyn. You are a pawn to them."

"They put me in stasis—"

"Yes, to calm their weak consciences so that they could claim they did not kill. The letter of the law, isn't it? Or perhaps they really meant to bring you back again at some point for some self-serving purpose before discarding you permanently, and no doubt more effectively than before."

"They say that if I die you will be Sovereign, so they have no desire to kill me."

"Yes, of course. This is common knowledge. But they will not stop until you are destroyed or a puppet in their hands."

She glanced down at her own hands. At the moonstone—the reminder of a nonlife far simpler than truly living... and at the ring of power on her other hand that was her fate. Why did it feel to her as though she were winding her way through a carefully engineered maze?

"Knowing that, what do you think of them?"

She hesitated. Something within her said, *Saric, too, wanted to kill you once.*

But Saric had brought her to life. True life, and true purpose. And she loved and served him for it.

"I'm glad."

"Glad."

"Glad that I did it. And grateful to the Keeper who killed me. If I hadn't died then, I would not serve you now."

The need, by now, for a look, a touch, a word from him was overwhelming. It rose up in her chest, an urge far more powerful than the need to eat.

"So," he said, as though to himself. "The boy is a Maker."

"They say so."

To this, Saric did not respond. He seemed to have stopped breathing.

Terrified that she had hurt him, Feyn stepped forward. "Saric...My Lord..." She stood before him, desperate for his love. "I hope I pleased you."

She didn't have the chance to react before his fist slammed into her face. She crashed to the floor onto her chest, unable to break her fall. For an awful moment her lungs felt like iron, refusing to expand. Sticky warmth filled her mouth and ran out to the floor.

"There can be only *one* Maker!" Saric said.

With a heavy gasp she hauled in a breath, then coughed up blood along with a bloody tooth.

A heavy step sounded near her head. She braced herself. But instead of another blow, he crouched down onto a knee beside her.

His was strangely gentle. "Didn't you understand when I told you the first time? Only one. Anyone who stands in my way will die. Do you understand me, my love?"

She pushed herself up and slowly nodded, head still ringing.

"Please answer me."

"Yes," she said thickly.

He sighed. "My poor love." He leaned forward and wrapped muscled arms around her. "Please don't force me to do it again."

She reached a hand up toward her lip, to feel the place just beneath it where the tooth had been.

"You've lost a tooth?"

She nodded.

"Please don't cry—it's beneath a Sovereign."

Hot tears coursed down her face.

"You must understand, Feyn . . . All that I do, I do for destiny. For true life. For love. Until you submit fully to the life I have given you, you will never know its true beauty. Correcting my children is no easier for me than for them. It pains me to see your confusion." He kissed the top of her head. "There is no greater love than mine. You will see."

Saric rose to his feet, cradling her against his chest. Through the pounding in her head she was vaguely aware that he had bypassed her bed and strode to the open archway leading to the stair. He carried her up the stair and down the dark corridor to his own chamber above.

She hadn't set foot in this chamber in far more than nine years. It had changed. It was flooded with candlelight. The hard clip of his boots muted the instant he entered, cushioned by thick rugs and animal pelts. Heavy silks hung everywhere, reflecting rich, crimson hues.

He settled her among the thick pillows of his bed, arranging the comforter over her, smoothing back a tendril of her hair

A Dark Blood appeared in the archway to the anteroom.

"Bring Corban," Saric said. "The Sovereign has been hurt. Hurry."

"Yes, my Lord."

"Take a team and seal off the crypts. Close the tunnels. All of them."

Time seemed out of place. Darkness threatened to steal her thoughts. She was only aware of Saric's caring hand lightly stroking her cheek.

Corban came in, took a knee in the chamber, but only for an instant before hurrying to the bed.

"See to your Sovereign," Saric said.

He bent and kissed her gently on the forehead before straightening. "She is far too precious to be hurt. Tend to her as if she were me. Not a bruise by morning."

Chapter Fourteen

Below the vista of the high limestone cliff over-looking the Seyala Valley, revelry had finally given way to sleep. The beating of the great Nomad drums in time to the hearts straining at full gallop around the fire had slowed to a nodding pulse and then quieted at last. The songs had landed on their final strains, and the echoes of ululating calls had died. Lovers had slipped away from camp and returned to darkened yurts to lie down in one another's arms.

The Seyala Valley held the very promise of life preparing to burst onto the world's stage. Or so they all believed. What would happen if they knew that another kind of life had taken to that stage with its own alien roar?

Panic would run through the camp like a wildfire. And so they must not know.

In four days' time the annual Gathering would sweep the camp into a night of unrestrained revelry in anticipation of Jonathan's coming reign. Nothing could be allowed to dampen the hopes and dreams that would be celebrated that night.

Rom glanced at the sky. His eyes were gritty from

riding and sore with fatigue. In four short hours, dawn would illuminate this plateau, but it would be an hour more before the same light made its way into the sleeping valley below.

Beside him, Roland pulled a flask from his saddle. Neither one of them had spoken of the previous night's disaster on the ride home. Rom had sent Jonathan and Jordin back to camp ahead of them and then ridden with his second to the vista, a place they often came to discuss matters alone, away from the too-seeing Mortal eyes and ears of the others. The Nomad took a long pull and held the flask out to Rom, who ignored it. He'd lost his appetite for food or drink.

"Take some," Roland said. "You need it."

Rom accepted the flask and took a swig. It was wine, not water. For a moment he thought about spitting it out, but then swallowed it instead.

For nine years their path had been so clear: bring Jonathan back to Byzantium to claim his office as Sovereign of the world on the day that he reached eighteen. It had been simple, though he had never been naïve enough to think they might not encounter at least some resistance. But now . . .

He couldn't get over the sight of Feyn, the ring of office on her hand. The strange turn of her lip when she'd told them to save those who need saving. The way she had yelled for the guard.

She had given her life for this very cause—for the cause of life itself! How could she refuse to accept it from Jonathan's veins?

And how long would she refuse him his place on the throne?

He took another pull from the flask and set it on the rock beside him. Roland stood to his right, thumb hooked in the belt that held his scabbard, staring at the valley.

"Jonathan turns eighteen in six days," Rom said at last. "This changes nothing."

"Jonathan can't succeed her now."

"He has to. He was born to rule."

"And so begins the last struggle for power," Roland said.

"There will be no struggle for power," Rom snapped. "Not the way you think of it."

"I think of it only one way—either we win or we lose."

Rom turned from the valley and raked a hand through his hair, which he wore free except for a few braids designating his rank among the the Nomads.

"If Jonathan can't rule we've already lost. And I can't accept that."

Roland eyed him stoically. "I didn't say Jonathan can't rule. I said he can't succeed Feyn. Her rule changes the succession. Even if she dies now, Saric becomes Sovereign. Saric has assured his own power. Or am I missing something?"

Rom scrubbed at his face with a hand.

No. He hadn't missed anything. Saric had effectively snatched supremacy out from under them without warning or recourse.

"All I know is that Jonathan *must* come to power."

"Must he?"

Rom jerked his head around and stared at him. "What are you saying?"

"How do we know that Jonathan 'must' come to power?"

"What do you mean how do we know Jonathan must

come to power?" Rom demanded. "You question this now? After all these years?"

Roland turned his face to the dark valley. "No. But I'm not always certain what that power will look like. Mortal blood will rule this world, I know that much. And in that sense, Jonathan's already ascended—in us. We're alive, and the rest of the world is dead. We will live a very long time while generations of Corpses come and go. Our power is *supreme*. Meanwhile, Jonathan's blood grows stronger—there's no telling how powerful Mortals will become. In that way, Jonathan already rules through our blood. And perhaps it's our privilege to rule with him."

"Sovereignty is *his* right, not ours. Maker, what are you suggesting?"

"Only that we may be placing a burden on the boy that isn't his to carry." Roland squatted to his heels and squinted over at Rom. "Do you honestly see a ruler in that boy?"

Rom paused.

The Nomad picked up a pebble and flicked it over the lip of the cliff with his thumb. "You heard what happened by the Basilica of Spires."

The boy hadn't spoken a word, but Rom had quietly questioned Jordin on the ride back to the valley. He'd seen Jonathan peering into the Authority of Passing transport, the way he'd been rooted to the spot, unhearing, risking himself. Risking all. Jordin, ever-protective of Jonathan, offered no more detail other than his empathy for some girl being taken to the Authority of Passing.

"He's got an unnatural fascination with Corpses," Roland said.

The bluntness of his words grated. Grated, because they were true.

Rom himself had known a girl like the one in the cart once, who might easily have ended up in her same place. A girl destined for far greater things than to disappear behind institutional doors.

Thinking of Avra no longer hurt, but it did bolster his resolve. She, too, had given her life to this cause, the first among them to do so. Her death would not be—would never be as long as Rom lived—in vain.

The boy had to come to power.

"He's the Giver of Life. What do you expect? Maybe we should all be as fascinated."

"It's self-destructive. There's far more at stake here than a few Corpses, Rom. He jeopardized his own safety and by extension the future Mortal kingdom. Do you see a leader in that?"

"I see a Sovereign who understands love more than any of us. I can't believe I'm hearing this from you—you, of all people. Nomads rule by bloodline. So will Jonathan. The only reason Feyn is Sovereign now is because of Saric's interference. You vowed Jonathan your life. It's not your place to question."

Roland rose, jaw set. "You dare question my loyalty? I will defend his legacy to my death! But there's more than one way to rule, Rom. Jonathan made us Mortal. We have his blood in our veins. *We* are his legacy. If anything happens to him, we are bound to honor and defend that legacy. *That* is how we win. Anything less than that— anything that brings death to Mortals—is defeat to us."

"And what of Jonathan?"

"Jonathan—"

"Will you defend him or not?"

"Yes! Do not insult me by questioning my loyalty."

Rom exhaled a single long breath, through his nostrils. "Forgive me. I don't mean to direct my frustration at you."

"Your frustration's warranted. But the fact of the matter is I'm right. Everything *has* changed. A great struggle for power has begun. This won't go down smoothly. And so we must consider all options, including the possibility that Jonathan may not be Sovereign in six days. There are other ways to win this war."

"Now you call it a war?"

Roland shrugged. "Is it anything else?"

He had a point.

"We won't be spilling any blood just yet," Rom said. "You saw how strong the Dark Bloods were. How quick."

"They only have a few thousand."

"*Only*? We *only* have seven hundred warriors."

Roland eyed him, brow arched. "Most of them Nomads and superb fighters. My men can defeat three thousand Dark Bloods, you have my word on it."

"We don't even know where they are."

"No, but we can get to Saric."

"How."

"Via his puppet at the Citadel," Roland said. "Let me take twenty men and I'll bring you his head in two days' time."

"Kill Saric and his hive will come after us in a swarm." Rom shook his head. "We can't risk all-out war—not now."

Roland seemed prepared for this answer. "At the very least I insist we send out scouts beyond our perimeter in search of the rest of his Dark Bloods. It's a risk, but we can't sit back and wait."

"Fine. But we risk nothing more. Not so close to our goal."

"But our goal just changed. Saric has to die."

"That's your only suggestion? To assassinate Saric and engage his army?"

The Nomadic Prince studied him. "You have another?"

"Yes."

"And?"

Here it was, then. "We take her."

Roland stared at him for a moment. "Take who?"

"Feyn."

"Take Feyn. Just like that. You think Saric is going to just hand her over? She's the Sovereign of the world!"

"Yes. I think he will."

"And assuming Saric would do something so fool-hardy, what do you plan to do with her? Seduce her?"

Rom reached for the flask. "I'm going to talk sense to her."

A twitch at the corner of Roland's mouth. "I know you had something with her once and I can't say I blame you. But whatever it was, it's gone. You saw her."

"I didn't have something with her before. But she has the ancient blood in her. Maker knows—I gave it to her! Give me a few hours with her and I'll make her remember who she is and why she died."

"You saw her eyes. She's not going to help us."

"She will." But even as he said it, Rom felt again that vague sense of encroaching panic.

Feyn's eyes, once the celebrated Brahmin gray, haunted his memory. They had been her trademark to the world before the black of Saric's alchemy had obscured them. The true Feyn had to exist somewhere beneath those inky depths.

"She's Saric's pawn. He's her Maker now," Roland insisted.

"No. She has the ancient blood in her."

"She has her *Maker's* blood in her now."

"*I* was her Maker!" Rom thundered.

Roland held his gaze steady but said nothing.

Rom turned away, relaxed his balled fists. He'd gone over and over it for hours on the ride back—the way she'd looked at Jonathan. The tear from her eye. Something had moved in her. The way she'd hesitated before calling for the guard. She was loyal to Saric, but she was also confused. Disoriented. In a freer context, she would surely see the truth. There was no other way without risking all-out war.

"She's our best play."

"Our best play is to act now. Come down on Saric like a hammer. Slaughter him. Wait for his Dark Bloods to come raging and crush them in one blow."

"I won't commit our destiny to a single campaign that could backfire and invite military hostility toward Jonathan—not while we have other options."

"Taking Feyn from Saric, assuming it's even possible, will have exactly that effect!"

"We aren't going to take her from Saric."

Roland lifted his brows.

"Saric's going to give her to us."

"He's going to give her to us. Of course. Now why didn't I think of that?"

"Maybe because your mind is on blood. Maybe because you haven't tangled with that monster before the way I have. Maybe because you don't know Feyn as I do."

"As you *did*, you mean," Roland said. He sighed, squinting at the rising sun and then back at Rom. "So just how do you get Saric to hand over the Sovereign of the world to his enemies? Enlighten me."

Rom paced, hands on his hips. "I don't. You do."

"Me."

"Yes. You alone."

"I see. And I do this how?"

"You offer him what he wants."

"Which is?"

Rom hesitated a beat, gripped by a sense of betrayal at the mere thought of what he was about to voice.

"Jonathan," he said.

Roland's unblinking gaze held his own. For a moment neither of them spoke.

"He'll never believe it."

"He would never believe *me*. But you, the wild Nomad prince with ambition and blood in his veins..."

"He'd suspect a trap. Saric's no idiot."

"Of course he'll suspect a trap," Rom said.

"How would I even approach—"

"By doing exactly as I say," Rom said. "I know the Order. I know the Brahmins and I know Saric. I'll lay it all out for you and you can judge the plan as you like. All I ask is that you put thoughts of war from your mind. Follow me in this, Roland. I could command it, but I'm asking. For Jonathan's sake."

Roland crossed his arms and then said slowly: "For the sake of Mortals. All right. Feyn it is. Assuming you've thought of everything."

"I have."

The sound of a hoof scattering pebbles clattered behind them, and Rom spun, hand already on his knife.

"Easy." The old Keeper's voice grated through the night.

Rom stepped forward as the Keeper's horse ambled toward them in the early dawn. "Book. What is it?"

The old Keeper stopped his horse and slid cautiously to the ground without answering.

"Who told you we were here?" Roland said.

The man looked up, adjusted his tunic where it had bunched around his hips. "You don't think I know where to look?"

Rom exchanged a quick look with Roland and then addressed the Keeper.

"So?"

"I have news."

"What news."

"About Jonathan's blood."

They waited as the Keeper seemed to search the still-dark western sky.

"Well?" Rom said at last. "What about Jonathan's blood?"

"I tested it with the Dark Blood's own and there's no doubt about it."

"About what, man?"

The old man shook his grizzled head. "That his blood is poisonous to these Dark Bloods. Even a drop of Jonathan's blood would kill one."

The poisonous aspect was obvious, if the quantity that it would take was not. So why the urgency?

The image of Jonathan offering Feyn his blood suddenly flashed before Rom's mind with a prickle of panic.

No. She had the ancient blood in her veins.

"You came here to tell us what we witnessed with our own eyes," Roland said.

"No. There's something else."

"Well?"

"Mortal blood, any Mortal blood—not only Jonathan's— would kill these Dark Bloods as well."

Roland arched a brow. "So I could kill them all with only my own blood. We have a new weapon."

"Yes. And in fact your blood, Nomad, would kill them more quickly than Jonathan's."

Roland narrowed his eyes, and Rom could all but hear the thoughts whirling through his mind like a desert dervish.

"What do you mean would kill them more quickly? How is that possible?"

The Keeper turned his eyes to Rom.

"Because his blood and your blood—all of our blood—is now stronger than Jonathan's."

Rom blinked. "Stronger? That's impossible..."

"No, my friend. I've checked and rechecked. Jonathan's blood is weaker now than it was two weeks ago when I last drew a sample. The effects of his blood are lessening. At a rapid pace. All the key indicators are reversing."

Rom stared at the old man. How was this possible? It had to be a mistake! But the Keeper did not make mistakes and then ride to the cliffs to announce them in secrecy.

"What I'm saying," the old Keeper said, "is that any who would take Jonathan's blood today would not live as long as those who took it a month ago. Their emotions would not be as vibrant, their sight will not be as bright as it would be if they took blood from one of us."

"So Jonathan's blood is becoming obsolete," Roland said.

"No! Impossible!"

"No," the Keeper said. "Not obsolete. But certainly less potent."

Roland stepped forward. "Then—"

"Then nothing! It only increases our urgency to get him to power. He is Sovereign and he will reign as Sovereign. Until then, *no one* learns of this. Do you understand? Not a soul!" Rom paced, frantic, mind washed with impossible questions. He stopped dead in front of the Keeper.

"Draw another sample at first light," he said, before turning to Roland. "Feyn. You will get her. Immediately."

Roland looked from Rom to Keeper then back.

He nodded. "Tell me how."

CHAPTER FIFTEEN

SLEEP CAME WITH DIFFICULTY for Roland that night. When his dreams finally shut out the world they were filled with images of death. Of Corpses and Dark Bloods swarming the earth in search of those few remaining Mortals left in the wake of a misguided promise of dominion.

Before returning to camp, he'd spent another half hour with Rom, stepping through the path that might lead to Feyn's acquisition. The plan was fraught with madness, but no more than going directly after Saric or staging a coup of the Order itself—notions that had surfaced in Roland's mind in his most far-reaching moments.

Which was more often than he cared to admit.

But a conflict with Saric would cost many Mortal lives. And though a coup might secure power in the Citadel, that power would require force to maintain.

In the end, Rom was right: the best—if not the most likely—path for Jonathan's ascension to power would be through Feyn's resignation of her seat. Or, failing that, some kind of irrevocable agreement granting Jonathan power in her stead. In either case they would still have to contend with Saric and his Dark Bloods, but doing so from a seat of political power would be much easier than as outcasts.

How exactly Rom planned to maneuver Feyn into agreement once she was in his grasp Roland wasn't sure, but his insistence that they had nothing to lose held merit. If the ploy failed they could resort to more hostile measures.

But none of these thoughts were what kept him from sleep for a full hour as he lay alone in his personal quarters. He owned three yurts—one for his two concubines who'd been chosen for their fertility and health to bear heirs; one for his wife, Amile, who had given him two girls and wore her status as the sole wife of Roland with supreme pride; and one for his position as ruler of all Nomads.

He'd retired to this last yurt and reclined on a mat in the early morning, mind still circling this revelation from the Keeper about Jonathan's blood.

Around him the rest of the camp was bedded down, oblivious to the truth—as they must be for now. If word leaked...

No.

The greatest strength of any Nomad was his resolve to independence. Generations of separatism had bred deep loyalty to their own. Now, having woken to raging passion and ambition, their desire to consume the world knew no bounds.

Life—as Mortals fully alive—was the cornerstone of their existence, and his people were determined to experience it as none else on earth could. As a race of humans who would live for many hundreds of years without subjugation. And now the Keeper seemed to be suggesting that the very source of that life was slowly waning.

Roland still couldn't fathom the full implications of the Keeper's news. What bearing it might have on Jonathan's rule. How it might affect the rise of Mortals or the overthrow of Order's oppressive regime that had squashed the world with fear. Fear of failing Order in this life. Fear of questioning truth. Of breaking from the status quo. Of veering from perfect obedience. Fear of death because in death all who failed in any way found only Hades. And everyone knew that everyone failed.

Many things were unclear to Roland, but the destiny of Mortals was not among them. Their race would throw down Order and live free from fear. Free of restraint. And he knew, too, that the task of ensuring that destiny fell on his own shoulders more than anyone else's—including Jonathan, the vessel who'd brought them life.

All these thoughts circled relentlessly through Roland's mind even as he slept. When he woke with the first sounds of a stirring camp outside, he ordered Maland, the long-time servant who kept guard outside his yurt, to find the Keeper and bring him immediately. Under any other circumstance he might go to the Keeper himself, but the chance of running into Rom or any other council member might undermine his intentions. He had to speak to the man without anyone's knowledge.

An hour passed. Roland glanced over at the door flap. Heavy and set into a frame, it was made to withstand severe weather so that even in the midst of a storm, it only seemed to breathe like a diaphragm with the wind. This morning it was utterly still, a faint ray of sunlight filtering down to the yurt floor from the small wheel-like opening at the top. The yurt was furnished with a couple thick rugs and the mat he had tossed and turned on the night before. A goblet and plate of dried meat and wild plums sat atop a trunk that held several items of clothing—those that were not hung on the inside lattice of the yurt itself: several hand-beaded coats and tunics made by his wives and decorated by Roland himself. Three compound bows, including one more than three hundred years old. Several curved swords and knives, including three swords from the Age of Chaos—relics carefully preserved as reminders of the tenacious Nomadic heritage passed down over the centuries for this day.

Roland would not fail his race.

Knuckles tapped the door's wooden frame.

Finally.

"Come."

The door swung wide and the Keeper stepped in wearing the same robe he'd worn last night, hood over his head. It was easy enough to guess by the circles under his eyes and the sagging at the corner of his mouth that he had slept far less than Roland—if at all. But it wasn't so much the fatigue in his eyes as the tortured questions in them that told Roland all he needed to know.

He closed the door, threw off his hood, and regarded Roland for a long moment without offering any greeting.

Roland nodded at a chair by the trunk. "Please, sit."

The Book looked at the chair but shook his head.

"I can't stay. I have to get back," he said.

"To what? More testing? To be certain that our world is crumbling as we speak?"

The man said nothing.

"Did you?"

"Did I what?"

"Test his blood again with your magic vials."

"It's not magic. The darker the blood turns the solution, the more potent the life within it. But yes."

"And?"

"The color grows lighter every day."

But of course. The Keeper was meticulous and sober—more so as of late, only rarely venturing out to join the celebrations around the fires at night as he used to. He had laughed often when he had first become Mortal, but that mirth had since been replaced by the growing burden of securing the same Mortal destiny Roland was committed to. Roland had always respected the old man; as with Nomads, the Keepers had clung to their own way of preserving the promise of life through the centuries. Two orders, Keepers and Nomads, now one: Mortal.

"Nothing else?" Roland asked.

"I tested my own blood as well."

"And?"

"It hasn't deteriorated."

Roland stepped to the trunk and picked up a plum, offered it to him. When the old man refused, he bit deeply into it himself. The tart juice pricked his taste buds, firing awareness of the new life in his veins. It never failed. He closed his eyes. The senses had always been celebrated among Nomads, even without emotion, but Jonathan's blood had turned sensory experience into a wildly extravagant and life-affirming affair. Next to the pale sensory comforts they had known as Corpses, these vibrant pleasures threatened at times to be almost *too much*. A sensory experience speculated to be far greater than any known even in the Age of Chaos, before death came to the world.

The first time Roland made love after coming to life it had so fired his nerves that he'd begun to panic, sure that he was in the throes of death rather than quaking pleasure. But he hadn't died. He'd lived and been pulled into the hot sun of raw, living bliss. When his wife had welcomed new life into the world nine months later, he'd named the boy Johnny in honor of the life that had facilitated his conception.

"Tell me something, old man," Roland said. "What would your founder, Talus, the one who first predicted that life would come again in the blood of one child, say your chief charge is?"

The man replied with marked hesitation. "To ensure that life is not suppressed."

"And where is that life now?"

"In Jonathan. But you know this as well as I do."

"Humor me. I'm a Nomad, not a Keeper. We may share the same resolve and blood, but our roles in this world are different."

The aged eyes beneath the Keeper's wrinkled brow did not offer agreement or disapproval. Roland pressed.

"There are twelve hundred Mortals now. Would Talus demand we preserve life in all twelve hundred, or would he suggest we sacrifice some to ensure Jonathan comes to power?"

"Both."

"I agree. And I remain fully committed to this end. But now my question is this: how many should we be willing to sacrifice to ensure Jonathan's ascension to power?"

The Book's response came slower than the last. "That isn't for me to say."

"Yet you recognize the question that falls on my shoulders. And so I'm seeking your advice. How much bloodshed is acceptable to this end? Ten of my men? A hundred? A thousand? Tell me."

"As you said, this falls on your—"

"Please don't patronize me." Roland realized he was squeezing the plum in his hand; juice dripped from his fingers onto the floor. "I want to know how you feel about the shedding of this precious blood that now flows through our veins. How much should be spilled?"

"As much as necessary."

"To the last man if necessary?"

The Keeper's left eyelid twitched. "I don't think—"

"Just answer. Please."

The Keeper's frown deepened. "As much as is needed."

"So you disagree with Rom on this matter?"

"No. Rom would agree, I'm sure."

Rom might indeed agree. But not to the same extent as many Nomads. The zealots, he knew, would go to any measure to protect that life—including a preemptive strike of any magnitude that best facilitated victory. He let the matter slide.

"Then tell me this: the life foretold by Talus...In whom does it now reside?"

"In Jonathan."

"Not in you?"

The old man stared him down for several long moments. Then he began to turn, as if intending to leave.

"My loyalty to Jonathan is unshakable, Keeper. I would cut any throat to save him—don't mistake me. He must come to power for the sake of all Mortals. But I need to understand that path."

A slight tremor shook the Keeper's old fingers. He was sleep deprived, but there was more here.

"Please. Where does that life reside?"

The old man glanced back at him. "In all of us. To be protected at all costs. How is not my concern. I'm a Keeper of truth, not a maker of history. That responsibility rests on other shoulders, as you said."

"But the rest of what you said is also true, no? That your blood—my blood—is now stronger than Jonathan's. And as such you are a maker, if not of history then of life. As am I. A maker of life perhaps more powerful today than Jonathan. Is this not now a part of the truth you keep?"

"There's more to the boy than his blood," the Keeper said, warning in his voice.

"I'm no longer talking about Jonathan. I'm talking about a race of Mortal makers full of life-giving blood. Is this not the blood that will save the world?"

The Keeper was silent.

"And if it is, then we must take whatever steps necessary to protect not only Jonathan, but the Mortals who will become the makers of the world."

"Perhaps."

"And if it comes down to a choice between Jonathan's blood and your blood? His blood and mine?"

"Pray it doesn't."

"I do. I will."

The Keeper turned to go.

"Does Jonathan know?"

"No," the Book said, his back to the Nomad.

"You took another sample this morning."

"I did."

"How fast is his blood reverting? I need to know how much time we have."

The Keeper's voice held a tremor. "At this rate, his blood may be that of a common Corpse by the time he ascends to power."

Roland blinked, mind vacant. So fast! He had no idea. Still reeling, he spoke the first words that rushed to fill it.

"What power? How can that happen now?"

"He has already given us his power," he said. "Use it wisely."

Without another word, the old man left the yurt, shaking his head like a prophet who has lost the voice of his god.

Roland stared at the door after it had fallen back into place. So then the matter became clear. He would do as Rom asked and make the play to acquire Feyn. But he wouldn't trust the fate of all Mortals to a single course of action.

They had to dispatch fighters far beyond the perimeter immediately with orders to take captive any Dark Blood they encountered. They had to find Saric's stronghold.

They had to prepare for the worst.

Roland strode to the door, threw it open where Maland waited outside.

"Get me Michael. Now!"

CHAPTER SIXTEEN

DOMINIC STRODE DOWN the grand hallway of the palace, boot heels clacking against the marble floor in time with the cudgeling of his heart.

A day had passed since the senate leader had witnessed the most horrific, profane act of his life in the slaughter of the Regent. And he'd heard the most unfathomable profanity from the man who had committed the act, right there on the senate dais, where Saric had effectively revived and then installed his sister as Sovereign.

That first night, he'd suffered nightmares. Nightmares of the Regent's neck opening in that yawning gash. Of the naked Sovereign screaming from the great table, as if it were an altar and she the sacrifice. Nightmares of blood flowing from the stent in Saric's arm into hers. Of the unmistakable scar that cut across her torso, clear evidence of the savage slash that had ended her life nine years earlier on the cusp of her own inauguration.

Of Feyn standing and speaking, not with her own voice, but with Saric's.

You are dead. All of you. Dead.

He'd woken in a sweat. Paced his Citadel apartments.

Come to stand at the window and look out at the dark night in the direction of the palace and the apartment of the Sovereign. Candlelight had burned there throughout the evening.

And then, the most terrible voice of all seeped into his mind.

His own.

You are dead.

Was it possible?

Chills had crept across his nape, had prickled the tips of his fingers and set his ears ringing. Fear, at its most visceral.

He'd passed the next day in sleep-deprived vigilance, his hands cold and numb, already anticipating more nightmares in the night to come. He had gone to evening basilica to settle his spirit. It wasn't the customary day, but such services were performed throughout the week to allay the fears of those needing comfort, and to stave off dread of the eternal with one more proper act in deference to the only thing that would be reckoned at the end of one's life.

Order.

We know the Maker exists within his Order.

It helped. That night he'd gone to sleep knowing two things: First, that the Maker was still the Maker, known within Order. To question Order was to question the Maker himself. This truth remained steadfast, a lone anchor in this sudden storm of events.

Second, that Feyn claimed the seat of office legitimately as Sovereign, no matter how stunning her resurrection from stasis or the blasphemous guardianship that she had been reborn under like a bloody moon.

There were no nightmares the second night. And Dominic had risen today newly collected. Newly resolved.

As he made his way to the outer atrium of the Office in the last hour of late afternoon, he glanced up, ignoring the dark cracks that snaked up the vaulted ceiling, focusing instead on the sheen of light reflected off its gilded surface. These ancient halls were hallowed since the days of Chaos, dedicated to the Maker when he had gone by a more arcane name: God.

He had only one objective now. He had to secure Feyn's assurance that she would work to destroy her brother, who clearly stood against Order. Surely she saw that her own seat was in grave danger. Perhaps, even, her eternal destiny. They had to work together.

He nodded at the secretary whom he'd known so many years as Rowan's man, Savore. How different, to see him keeping the desk of the office from which Saric held court, no doubt turning the resources of the world to his own dark purposes. Dominic all but imagined he could see shadows creeping from the great chamber beyond.

All of you... dead.

Savore rose to gesture him to the twelve-foot doors of the Office. The secretary wouldn't touch them himself—it was for each man to bring his own weight into this space, to labor even in this way to attain an audience with the Sovereign, strong hand of the Maker on earth.

Dominic laid his palms against the intricately etched bronze door. It was usual for any prelate to pause and consider the symbols of each continental office: the alchemists of Russe, the educators of Asiana, the architects of Qin, the environmentalists of Nova Albion, the bankers of Abyssinia, the priests of Greater Europa and the artisans of Sumeria. Dominic himself had often done the same, going so far as to trace the Book of Orders beside the emblem of Europa, his own continent, with a fingertip.

But today he saw only the symbol presiding over them all: the great compass, the graded points of Sirin's halo, by which they must all live and by which they would all be judged.

He pushed the doors open.

Inside, the heavy velvet curtains had been drawn shut against the obscure light of the waning day as a dozen candelabras sent shadows flitting and luring throughout the room.

That was the first thing he noticed.

The second was the two Dark Bloods on either side of his peripheral vision as the doors fell shut behind him with the ominous thud of a vault.

The third was the figure sitting at the desk. She was richly attired in velvet so dark blue as to appear the color of midnight. She was studying a report of some kind, as she sipped from a pewter goblet. Her nails were perfectly manicured.

She lifted her eyes with feline languor. They were dark and fathomless in the shadows.

Dominic went to a knee on the thick carpet, but for the first time in his life, he stared rather than lowered his gaze.

The figure behind the desk was indeed the Sovereign herself—fortunately, Saric was nowhere to be seen. But she was drastically changed.

She released the report with a flick of her fingers.

"My lord Dominic," Feyn said, voice as smooth as a purr. It was the first time he had heard her since that first blood-chilling scream, and he found he could not reconcile the two sounds at all.

She rose from her chair, candlelight catching the obsidian of her chandelier earrings. Her hair was swept up completely off her neck and onto her head. The high, open collar of her dress accentuated her neck and her pale skin in a neckline that plunged to her sternum.

Again, he railed at the thought that this could possibly be the same woman. And yet there she was—Feyn as all had ever known her. And as she had never been known.

She came around the side of the desk, moving with unhurried grace. The light of the nearest candelabra swept up her face, revealing a shadow on one cheek, just discernable enough for him to wonder if it was a play of light.

No. A bruise, then?

She paused before him and he found himself dropping his gaze down to her booted foot. An open palm extended into the field of his vision. He took it and kissed the ring of office along the inside of her delicate fingers. They smelled like wine and musk and salt.

The hand withdrew, but not before he noted the mark on the inside of her elbow. A small puncture wound visible within the high split of her sleeve.

He started to lean forward with both hands on his knee but then he realized she hadn't told him to rise. He blinked and shifted back, ignoring the pop of his kneecap in the carpet.

"Why do you come?" she said, moving back toward her desk and reclaiming the goblet.

He lifted his gaze, struck again by the regal tilt of her jaw, the very straightness of her nose, the set of her lips, moist after a sip from the wine. "To speak with you. I have concerns."

"Everyone has concerns about something, Dominic."

He glanced toward the doors and back. "May we speak in private, my lady?"

"We are in private." The tone, though dispassionate, was strange, and again he thought that she reminded him less like the startled colt shaking on its own legs of just a day ago than a great panther.

"Please."

She slid her gaze away in the direction of the guards. With a meaningful glance the two muscled forms dipped their heads and filed out through the great double doors, which fell heavily back into place.

And then they were alone.

Feyn moved toward a wingbacked chair off to the side of the curtained window. "Come, Dominic."

He rose stiffly and then stood before her, uncertain. Rowan had always invited him to sit beside him in the chair's companion seat. But Feyn only sat back and merely waited for him to speak.

He folded his hands. "Please understand the nature of my concern. You came back to us in...a most unusual manner. And while I'm certain you could not know the nature of the things your brother said before that moment, I must inform you that they were entirely disturbing."

"Were they?" Her forearm extended along the arm of the chair, fingers holding the rim of her goblet.

"Yes. And I feel compelled to inquire as to your own... beliefs in these matters. Your loyalties."

"You ask the Sovereign where her loyalties lay?"

"Indeed, my lady. I fear your brother has hinted at

thoughts that no good man of Order should ever think. He has spoken highest blasphemy. And this is saying nothing of the fact that he murdered the Regent in cold blood before our very eyes."

She glanced down, cradled her cup on her lap, and slowly traced the rim of it with a fingertip. Her eyes lifted. "And your point?"

"I must ask you, my lady, with all respect. Do you follow the Order? Will you serve it? Would you die for it?"

A strange turn of a smile formed at the corners of her mouth. "It would not be the first time I have died for this office, would it?"

"Yes, forgive me. And yet—"

"I will die for this office," she interrupted. "And serve it."

"Would you die also for the truth, lady—of the Maker, and of the Order that is his hand?"

"The truth? What is the truth, Dominic?"

He said what was said by all, learned in early childhood. "We know the Maker through his Order."

"I see. Then I must ask you, Dominic, what is a Maker?"

"But of course, the one who gives life, my lady."

"And do you have life?"

"Yes. Though your brother doesn't seem to think so."

"And I? Do I have life?"

He glanced at her hands, then her eyes. "Clearly."

"How do you know?"

"You see, you breathe." How could he not shudder at the memory of her first, ragged gasp of air as her chest had arched up off that altarlike stone table?

"And how do you know that you have life?" she asked.

"Because I stand here before you."

"I see. And what is the purpose of our lives, if you don't mind?"

"To serve the Maker."

"Then we are in agreement."

Dominic nodded slightly. "And we know the Maker through Order."

"We know the Maker by his stamp upon us. By the life in our veins, do we not?"

"I . . . yes. In a manner of speaking."

"And we know the Maker also by those inner leanings we all have to serve him, do we not? The fear of disappointing him in any way."

"Indeed."

"Some call it fear. But we, Dominic, know it as loyalty. As love. Do we not?"

Why did he feel the need to hesitate?

But no. He was simply taken aback to see her so well recovered. And clothed.

"Yes," he replied. "By our love."

"But do you really know what love is, Dominic?"

"It is the fear of the Maker. It is the thing we commit to, that we make our actions and minds beholden to."

"And if we love our Maker, do we also love and serve his hand?"

"Yes, of course."

"Am I the hand of the Maker on earth, Dominic?"

"Indeed, my lady. You are the One."

"Was I not born and raised to be Sovereign by the laws of succession, chosen by the Maker?"

"There is no question, my lady. You are the rightful Sovereign."

"You are a man of the Book, Dominic. I wonder, what

is the punishment for anyone who would stand in the way of the Order's elect taking office? Of one who would even rule...*out of Order*...in her stead?"

He paused.

"Dominic?"

"Death, my lady."

"Hmm."

Again, the image of Rowan's head falling from his neck sliced through his mind.

"And yet you recoiled at that punishment when it was carried out. Do you object to the rules of Order?"

"Never! By my word, I have served Order all my life. Diligently, with the hope of Bliss."

"So you will swear your loyalty to me?"

"But of course, my Sovereign."

"How can I know for certain?"

Dominic was only just aware that his purpose in coming to Feyn had somehow been reversed. He was now the one under interrogation. Her power as Sovereign was evident even now.

"The Maker knows my loyalty," he said. "Demand anything of me so that you will know as well."

She watched him without expression, dark eyes unblinking, haunting.

"Kneel before your Sovereign."

He lowered both knees to the thick rug in one motion.

Feyn rose, set the goblet aside, and stepped up to him.

"You give me your full loyalty?"

"I do, my lady."

"The Maker has chosen me to rule over you as Sovereign. Will you defer to my judgment and wisdom in all things?"

"I will."

"Swear it."

"I swear."

She stepped closer—so close that he might reach out and touch the velvet of her gown. Her hand rested on top of his head. He could feel the warmth of it through his graying hair. Again, the smell of musk, spice, wine...

"Even if you may not understand my actions, you will defer to me in all things, trusting that I am loyal to the Maker," she said quietly.

Why this sense of relief, this abating of fear that came with such a clear path? "I will."

"Even if it surpasses your own understanding, defies your own logic and will."

"I will."

"Then you do well." Her hand slid down to his cheek. She tilted his face up and gazed at him with a hint of tenderness. "One day I may reward you with a gift. If I do, take it with grace."

"I will, my lady. But serving is gift enough."

His fear was nearly gone, replaced by strange and profound peace. Yes. Surely here was the mouth and hand of the Maker on earth.

"You may rise."

He would have remained on his knees until they stiffened and he could no longer feel his feet. But he slowly rose to his feet, light-headed.

"My lady?"

"That is all, Dominic," she said, retrieving her goblet from the side table.

He backed a step and bowed his head. "Thank you, my lady."

Dominic made his way across the thick carpet to the double doors. This time, when he laid his hand on the image of the compass—the same one emblazoned on the other side—he drew a long, slow breath. Cleared his head.

He knew two things now: That the Maker was known by his Order. And that Feyn was the voice of that Order. He was devout. He would follow. And Bliss would come in its wake.

"Ah, Dominic?"

"My lady?" he said, turning back.

She was standing behind her desk, a pillar of velvet, candlelight warming her ivory skin.

"You should know one thing before you leave."

"Yes?"

She lowered herself into her chair, gaze riveted on him. "I will not betray my brother."

Feyn stared at the heavy bronze doors long after the senate leader had left.

Long after she had drained the goblet dry in one long draw. Even as the hand descended on her shoulder.

As she knew it would.

She turned her head as Saric leaned down and kissed her gently. But not so gently that she didn't feel the bruise on her cheek.

"You did well, my love."

Her need for him swelled. To hear those words, as though they were the very blood he had given her. He'd been watching her the whole time. She had known about the small corridor beyond the curtained wall behind the desk since she was a child. Her own father, Vorrin, had instructed her to stand in the corridor on many state visits to observe negotiations through the years of her training for this very office.

"You were pleased?" she said.

"How beautifully...how effortlessly, you dominate him with talk of loyalty to the Maker."

"Yes," she said, gazing ahead of her, somehow wishing that the curtains were open, even to the night. She would see to that.

"And who is that Maker?"

"You are, my Lord."

"That's right. I'm impressed by your skill. Let those who come to ply you think you have played into their hands. And ply them instead."

"Yes, of course," she said, turning her cheek into his hand.

"You see? You're a natural, my love. And one day, he will be of great use to us."

"Thank you."

He nodded, then sat on the edge of the desk, sliding the empty goblet away. "I have something I must talk to you about."

"Yes?"

"The Mortals came into the city from the north."

She blinked. "Then we will search north."

He lifted his head and gazed past her. "It seems they can smell our blood."

Smell it? Was it even possible? And then she remembered the way the Nomad, Roland, had drawn back and turned his head as though to lessen some reek. The way Rom had steeled himself when he had first come close.

"My Dark Bloods have a disadvantage in scouting. There was an incident at an outpost...one body missing among the charred remains. A child of mine taken, I assume, by the Mortals. Any information he gave them would be false— my children are carefully trained and utterly loyal. But that he could be taken at all concerns me."

When Saric looked back down at her, his eyes flashed with a terrifying intensity that brought to mind his harshest rebuke.

"You will dispatch five hundred of your men to the north. Guards, dressed as vagrants. They will scour the wastelands and canyons for any sign of the Nomads. At first sighting they will report back. We must find them. Is this clear?"

"As you wish, brother."

Saric stared at her for the space of several breaths. Then he lifted his hand and stroked the fading bruise on her cheek with his thumb.

"Call me your Maker when we are alone. It pleases me more."

"As you wish, my Maker."

CHAPTER SEVENTEEN

JORDIN WAS UP EARLY by Nomadic standards. Early, and troubled.

Dawn had drifted to the valley hours ago, illuminating the foothills, spreading out along the valley floor. Sunlight dappled the water of the shallow river before spreading across the round tops of yurts and creeping up the great stair of the Bahar ruins against the eastern wall. If the sun held long enough, the marble steps would gleam white by noon. And if the sky remained cloudless through the afternoon, gold light would reach past the columns of the ancient basilica and illuminate the ancient stained glass with colorful fire.

The day was full of life.

But Jonathan was missing.

She never failed to find him somewhere—downriver, where he sometimes went to bathe, or with the horses, where he spent hours plaiting the mane and tail of his stallion, fixing them with the ornaments given to him in such abundance that he couldn't possibly wear them all himself. Sometimes she found him in the foothills, carving, alone, or sleeping, having gone to the high knolls sometime during the wild revelry of the night before.

But this morning, he was nowhere to be found. Adah, who rose early to cook for him and Rom, had come to Jordin asking where he was. She'd gone looking in his small yurt at the center of camp, but there was no sign that he'd been there at all during the night. When she got to the pen she learned that his horse was gone.

So then where? If she could not locate him soon, she would have to tell Rom, which would cast a shadow on her role as his protector. It was one thing for the others not to know his whereabouts, but not her.

She strode along the edge of the western cliff, north of the camp, high above the foothills. Drawing a slow breath, she willed back the first fingers of panic and forced herself to *see* down through the valley past the waking camp.

Jonathan had been silent since their return from Byzantium, the day before yesterday. She knew he was haunted by the doomed girl, Kaya. And by the Corpses they'd seen outside the city. One look in his eyes and she knew he was deeply troubled in ways that no one—perhaps not even Jordin herself—could understand. He'd worn loneliness like a mantle since their return.

Jordin jogged along the cliff edge, fighting back fear—an emotion unusual to her in the years of her Mortality, but an easily recalled nightmare from her years as a Corpse. She had feared abandonment most of her life, until the day she met Jonathan. Now the thing she feared most was simply living without him.

She scanned the valley north to south from the horse pen on the northernmost edge of camp. Along the river to the broadening valley, out toward the main river which ran all the way from the wilderness to the western coast, out to sea.

She was about to head back to the south side when she saw the dark spot askance through the sunlight, far south, riding up the distant wash. She shielded her eyes from the glare of the sun and squinted to focus.

A rider. A mile out, traveling at a walk as though having covered hours of terrain. Then she recognized the height and color of the dun horse, the posture of the rider...

Jonathan.

She stood fixed for a full second, heart hammering in her ears. Her first thought was that he was safe. Thank the Maker he was safe.

Her second thought was that her Sovereign had gone far. On a horse. Very far. Without anyone's knowledge.

She had to reach him first. She had to be by his side when he came into camp. She had to know where he'd been.

Jordin ran to the rocky outcrop where she'd climbed up from the knoll, swearing to never leave him alone for more than an hour ever again. Not so close to his ascension.

She flew through the foothills, questions drumming through her mind. Down the last hill to the valley floor, running the half mile across the shallows of the river, cutting through camp, leaping over fires still smoldering from the night before.

Heads turned. Children paused their playing to look up. Warriors stared, mothers turned from their cooking and shouted after their children, who came trotting after her. The sight of Jordin running through camp in such haste was rare and could only mean one thing: Jonathan.

He was just coming into the south side of the camp when she caught sight of him, his stallion at a steady walk. She ran faster.

Only then did she see that others were staring his way. Not just watching but rooted to the ground. Fixated. She reached the steps of the ruins when she realized what everyone else was staring at.

He wasn't alone.

Jordin pulled up short next to a dozen others, gathered to watch his return. There, behind him on his horse, was a second figure. Smaller, peering around Jonathan, clutching him by the waist. A boy, barely twelve, if that.

His scent hit her like a gust of hot wind.

Corpse.

Bringing any Corpse into the valley was an express violation of Nomadic law. Other than the spies who came to meet with Rom, she hadn't seen a Corpse outside Byzantium since the last of the Mortals had been made. That was before the moratorium years ago.

A figure came stalking out into the clearing before the ruin stair, dark beads glinting in his hair, followed closely by another. The hair stood up on her arms.

Maro the zealot.

She hurried forward as several others came out of their yurts, noses covered by cloth or hands.

"What is that odor of death?" someone said behind her.

"Corpse!" She knew the booming voice well: Rhoda, the belligerent blacksmith who hit wine as hard and often as she hit steel. "Good Maker...He's brought a Corpse to camp..."

Jonathan did not slow, did not show any concern. He wore a mask of simple resolve, as though the looks of shock had nothing to do with him at all.

But Jordin knew better. Her sovereign might be quiet

much of the time, but his intelligence was superior in ways that few knew as well as she. And his powers of observation were keener than even Roland's.

The first time she'd seen it, they been at the lookout above, two years earlier, legs dangling over the cliff, watching the camp far below. After half an hour of silence, Jordin had braved a question.

"My Sovereign?"

"Yes?"

"May I ask a question?"

He'd looked at her, mouth curved in amusement. "If I can ask one first."

"Of course." Then she added, "My Sovereign."

"Will you call me Jonathan instead of Sovereign?" he asked.

She assumed the more formal title more appropriate— especially from one without position like her.

"Jonathan?"

"I like the way you say it."

"Jonathan."

His smile widened. "Thank you."

In retrospect, she thought she'd fallen in love with him in that moment, staring into his bright hazel eyes, which never wandered from her own.

"Your turn."

"Mine?"

"Your question?"

"Oh... Yes. I was wondering. What goes through your mind when you watch the camp for so many hours?"

He looked at the valley below, lost again in thought for a few moments.

"There are twelve hundred and eleven Mortals alive

today. They all live in this valley. Seventeen are in the river now, bathing. Five hundred and fifty-three that I've seen have ventured out of their yurts this morning. Just shy of seven hundred still slumber, most of whom did not sleep until early morning. Three hundred and twelve danced around the fire last night..." He faced her. "I know all of their names."

She was astonished at his powers of observation, the keenness of his memory.

"I think about every soul who has taken my blood, Jordin. They are forever bound to me. And some day their number will be more than I can count. I worry that I can't know them all." His eyes were misted as he said it. "What if I lose track?"

Or perhaps it was with those words and those tears that she'd fallen for him.

Now that same young man rode into town on his horse with a boy behind him, face turned against Jonathan's back, white fingers clutching his waist. Her Sovereign whom she loved more than her own life was bringing a Corpse among the Mortals. One whose name he would never forget.

He stopped adjacent to the steps to the temple ruins, ten paces from a loosely formed arc of expectant observers. Maro took two steps forward and stopped. Roland's cousin was dark haired, hook-nosed, and famous for his notched arrows that screamed when put to flight.

Silence stood between them. The horse twitched its plaited tail, oblivious.

"What is the meaning of this?" Maro finally said.

"His name is Keenan," Jonathan said. "He needs our help."

Jordin eased forward and placed herself just back and off of Maro's right shoulder, bothered already by the warrior's tone. Behind Jonathan, Keenan had lifted his shaggy blond head and begun to stare fearfully about him.

"He's a Corpse," Maro said evenly. "Bringing a Corpse into our perimeter is strictly forbidden."

Jonathan considered Maro for an even moment, and then silently lifted Keenan down from the saddle before dismounting behind him. The boy, a full head and a half shorter than Jonathan, was trembling. The closest Corpse outpost that Jordin knew of was nearly four hours' ride from here. Had the young Sovereign gone expressly looking for Corpses to bring back?

He leaned over and whispered something to the boy, but before Jordin could wonder what it was or move toward them, Maro had stalked forward. The boy staggered a step backward, dirty face wide with fear.

The zealot nodded at Jonathan. "The law protects all of us. No one's above it."

"Remember whom you speak to," Jordin bit out quietly.

Maro turned, saw her, and narrowed his eyes. "Censure from a deserter's daughter?"

She felt the color rush to her face, hot.

Rhoda, the blacksmith, had joined the fray. "What's this?"

"Jonathan's brought a Corpse to camp," Maro said, stalking to Jonathan's right, as if to flank him. Surely he didn't mean to actually confront him. How could any Mortal rebuke Jonathan?

Jordin moved with him, voice thick and low. "Back off."

"What good is life if ruin finds us before the blood in our veins has come into power?"

"The blood in your veins? That blood in your veins isn't your own. How dare you question your Sovereign?"

"It's our blood that will allow us to rule a world of dead Corpses. And it's our laws that protect Mortals until we can. We defend it to the death." Maro jutted his chin toward the Corpse boy. "*Against* death."

He turned, looked around at the crowd. "Tell me I'm wrong."

Seriph, the ranking council member, had by now joined the circle of onlookers.

"The dead will bury their dead," Jonathan said quietly. "But I would give Keenan life."

"By breaking the law?" Maro demanded. He looked over at Seriph. "What do you say?"

Silence settled in the valley. Even the breeze seemed to take note. There had never been a direct confrontation like this within camp, or between any man and Jonathan. Where were Rom or Roland to set things straight?

Seriph eyed the Corpse boy, seeming to choose his words carefully. "The law is clear. No Corpse may enter the Seyala Valley without council approval. No more brought to life until Jonathan ascends."

"He breaks the law in bringing a Corpse here. Tell me this isn't true."

Seriph hesitated. Accusing a Sovereign of breaking the law was unheard of. Even the Nomads knew that. He seemed very aware that his words might be first of their kind spoken in public by a ranking council member.

"He breaks the law," Seriph said softly.

"He breaks the law," Maro repeated, bolder now. He paced again, to his right then back, as an interrogator before a prisoner.

"He is the Sovereign!" Jordin cried, indignation hot in her veins.

"Our valley will not become a graveyard for the dead," Maro said. "For every Corpse lining up to be handed a life they don't even understand. And we will not pollute the camp with stench of Corpse!"

Maro slid his knife out of its sheath and strode toward the boy without offering up any explanation for his intention.

Jordin knew what would happen before it did—the moment Maro moved she knew.

She knew that Jonathan would move to protect the boy, regardless of Maro's intentions. Which he did, boldly and without compromise.

She knew that she would cut in between them to protect her Sovereign. She turned on Maro, who had the audacity to slash at her. Maker, had he lost his mind?

Jordin arched back, steel hissing a bare inch from her chin, her own knife instantly in her hand.

On the edge of the circle—Seriph, staring in shock. Beyond them, Triphon, Rom—coming toward them, Roland behind them. They strode across camp, but not quickly enough.

"Heretic!" Maro hissed, circling to his left. Deliberately, she knew, to draw her from Jonathan. She turned on her heel, holding her ground.

"You know what I think, Maro? That the day before you were made Mortal you stank twice as bad as this boy."

His eyes narrowed, muscles along his shoulders tensing with his legs. She braced herself—but with a sudden cry, the Corpse boy bolted out from behind her.

"Get back!" she shouted. Too late. Maro rushed straight for the boy. Jonathan flew between them as Jordin lunged, slashing upward. No sparring match, this—she went for the tendons. Maro's knife dropped free, but his arm, still in full swing, connected with Jonathan. Maro's hand struck Jonathan's jaw, snapping his head to the side and sending him reeling back onto the boy.

And then Rom was on Maro, grabbing the zealot from behind. He threw him forward, fell onto his back, grabbed him up by the hair and slammed his forehead into the hard earth with enough force to break his nose with an audible crunch. Not once, but twice.

Maro lay unmoving. Jordin could smell the life in him, but he was mercifully unconscious.

Knee still in the zealot's back, Rom jerked the man's head up, his face grisly with blood. Their leader was breathing heavily, not from exertion, but from fury. Jordin had never seen such a look on his face before.

"No one touches the Sovereign!" he roared. He released his grip on Maro's hair and let his head fall with a solid thud. "Are we clear?"

Those gathered gave no argument.

To Roland: "Take this fool away. See that he's punished. He's not to come within twenty yards of Jonathan again or I swear I'll put him in chains or worse."

Roland's face was set as stone, but he gave a curt nod.

Behind Jonathan, soft crying from the Corpse boy. Rom considered the boy for a moment, but when he spoke next, it wasn't to Jonathan.

"Take the Corpse back to where he came from."

Jordin blinked. Rom had addressed her. She glanced at Jonathan. Just two mornings ago he had bowed to Jonathan's wish to turn a Dark Blood...no matter that it had ended badly.

"But—"

"I won't have our mission compromised. There is far more at stake here than one Corpse. Do as I say."

She could see it then: the strain around his eyes. The dark evidence of sleeplessness the lines at the corners furrowing deeper than usual. The tension around his mouth.

She glanced from him to Jonathan, whose eyes held on hers for a moment. And then he nodded once...

Jonathan dropped to one knee, leaned in, and whispered to the boy. Tears streamed down the boy's face. Then Jonathan got up and, with one glance at her, walked through the crowd, which quickly parted before him.

She hesitated again, torn between obeying Rom and going after Jonathan.

"I'll see to Jonathan," Rom said, too quietly for anyone else to hear.

Jordin nodded. Steeling herself against the smell, she took the boy gently by the hand.

"Come on," she said. "Let's go get my horse."

The boy was trembling as she led him away. She didn't need to look back to see that more than one steely gaze followed her.

Or to know that Saric and his Dark Bloods were no longer the only threat to Jonathan's sovereignty.

Chapter Eighteen

SARIC STRODE DOWN THE CENTER aisle of the vacant senate chamber, arms clasped behind his back, black robe hemmed in red cording flowing around his feet. His eyes lifted from the majestic tapestries on the walls to the massive, ever-burning flame of Order. Feyn walked beside him, half a step behind.

He'd dressed her in white today.

One day he would reassume the Sovereign office he had held too briefly before, and she would once again be in the grave. Or perhaps he would keep her in stasis. He hadn't decided.

"Sister?"

"Yes, brother?"

He glanced over his shoulder at her as they walked. "Is that who I am?"

Feyn's gaze flitted to him then ahead of her once more. "You're my Maker."

"Please don't forget yourself again."

"No, Maker."

"You may also call me Master."

"As you like."

"Master."

"Master."

Saric led her down the aisle and up to the dais. Out to the Sovereign's white marble table at the center. He swept around and faced the great chamber, arms still clasped behind his back.

"This is where I made you," he said.

She studied the table with dark eyes. Her face was powdered, making her pale flesh even whiter than when it was bare, the dark veins beneath like thin claws reaching up from her neck, ready to strangle her at his command.

"This is where I gave you the gift of life." Saric turned and ran his hand lightly over the table's surface. "It was here that I commanded you to live. How does this make you feel?"

She hesitated. "Eternally grateful."

"And you know that he who gives life can also take it. Because those who know the purest and fullest kind of life understand that power is its greatest expression. In this way the life I offer is far greater than any the Mortals can know. I serve that truth. Do you understand?"

"Yes."

"If I ever found a greater life, I would seize it with as much vigor."

"Yes, I believe you."

"Good." Saric lifted his hand and ran the back of his forefinger over her cheek. "I have a very special gift for you today, my love. It might be painful to see at first, but I assure you I give you this gift only for your own benefit. How does that make you feel?"

"I will serve you as you see fit and be glad."

"Then you will accept this gift with as much gratitude as you did in accepting my life. I insist."

She dipped her head.

"Good." He walked away from the table, clasping his hands once again. "Your scouts were far more effective than I expected. I commend you."

"They were successful?"

He glanced at the side entrance, where one of his children waited for his command, and nodded. The warrior bowed his head and vanished behind the curtain.

"Two of them identified and reported one of these Mortals north of the city. They were able to send news and kill his horse before the man could escape. My men took him in a canyon this morning."

Feyn showed no emotion. Good.

The curtain parted and two Dark Bloods emerged, supporting a sagging and nearly naked form between them. Corban followed, gliding with his eerie step behind them.

The Mortal scout was too weak to move his feet or hold his head up, but Saric had been assured that he would be conscious. He groaned now as they dragged him up onto the dais and dumped his beaten body onto the marble table.

The guards each took a knee and bowed their heads, rose and quickly stepped back.

Saric watched as Feyn considered the body, her expression absent of emotion. Only two days earlier the body on the altar had been hers, lifeless before he'd given her his blood. Now it was another struggling to breathe on that cold surface, his body bloody, eyes nearly swollen shut, fingers and toes still held in the grips of the screw clamps they'd used on him.

Saric stepped to the edge of the table and the so-called

Mortal on it, his gaze dropping to a cut on the man's rib cage. The blood looked no different from any other human's blood. And yet it contained Jonathan's life.

"His name?"

"Pasha," Corban said.

"Pasha."

For a moment Saric felt a pang of empathy for this wounded man laid out before him.

The man undoubtedly had a wife and those he loved. He was only doing what he was told, like his own children, subservient to his own maker, Jonathan. The boy who had been born with life in his blood. A life some thought was stronger than his own. It was not this man but Jonathan whom he abhorred for the promise of a mortality that conflicted with his own.

His empathy for the frail form sunk beneath a dark wave of rage. But Saric was no longer a man mastered by emotion. He took a steadying breath.

"He's told you what we need to know?"

"No, my Lord. But he has agreed to tell us. We waited as you ordered."

"Good. Wake him."

Corban withdrew a syringe from his pouch, approached the table, and injected the Mortal in the neck. The man lay still for another moment—before his mouth suddenly parted and his eyes tried to open in what would have been a wide-eyed stare had they not been so badly beaten. As it was, they managed to part only to slits.

Satisfied, Corban stepped back. "He's should be quite willing."

Saric turned to Feyn, who was still watching the Mortal with apparent dispassion.

"He's alive, Feyn. Where you once lay dead, this man lays alive."

"Yes, Master."

He stepped around the table, tracing a finger along the man's shoulder and over his hair until he came to his other side, opposite Feyn. He felt her gaze, lingering on him.

Saric leaned forward. "Pasha. Can you hear me?"

The man moved his head once, just barely.

"I'm going to ask you a few questions. If you answer them without the slightest hesitation then I will send you back to your people as a warning. If you hesitate even once, I will assume you are resisting me and I will kill you where you lay. Is that understood?"

Again, the slight nod. A tremor in the man's hand on the edge of the table, like palsy.

"Do you know who I am? Speak to me."

He tried to speak, half-cleared his throat, then uttered a single, raspy word.

"Yes."

"And you are acquainted with my children. I realize they can be quite brutal. But at least you know that we mean what we say. So when I say I will kill you, I mean it."

He nodded.

"Say it."

"Yes." The man was shaking.

"Good. Tell me, Pasha, what do your kind call yourselves?"

"Mortals."

"Yes, Mortals. And Mortals believe themselves to be alive?"

"We are."

"Tell me how you came to have this life."

"I was...given the blood," the man said, speaking barely above a whisper.

"Whose blood?"

"Jonathan's."

Saric lifted his eyes to meet Feyn's as he continued. "Tell me what evidence you have that you are alive. What changed when you took his blood?"

"I...I came to life. I felt new emotions. I saw new things. I understood."

"And do you understand that Jonathan cannot be Sovereign? That Feyn Cerelia is Sovereign, and if she were to die that I, not Jonathan, would be Sovereign?"

The Mortal looked confused.

"No, I didn't think so," Saric said. "But now you understand that I fear no Mortal, including Jonathan, who is no Sovereign but subject to Feyn. Understand also that I will assure peace among all who live, either in or out of Order. Can you accept that, Pasha?"

A nod.

"Say it, please."

"Yes."

"Yes. It seems you didn't want to submit to that peace earlier. I'm sorry they had to persuade you as they did, but these wounds will heal. You are now demonstrating your willingness to work toward a lasting peace by being truthful. Do you understand?"

"Yes."

"Good. How many Mortals of your kind has Jonathan given his blood to?"

"More than a thousand."

"Only a thousand? How many can fight?"

"Seven hundred."

"Only seven hundred. So few? Why?"

"There is . . . a moratorium . . . on making new Mortals."

The confession was curious. Why? Saric would think any reasoning party would feel the need to build an army.

"Well then, it doesn't appear that your Mortals have any intention of harm. You can understand how your secrecy might have led us to believe otherwise."

He glanced again to the cut on the man's ribs, still oozing blood. Was it possible that there could be a power greater than his own in that red vitae? The thought was intolerable, offensive. He tore his gaze away.

"Where are your people?" he asked.

This time the Mortal hesitated.

"Any subject who hides demonstrates hostility. Should I assume you are an enemy of the Sovereign?"

"No."

"Then tell me."

The Mortal's eyes seemed to shift to Feyn and back within their broken sockets. "In the Seyala Valley."

"I've never heard of it. Where is it?"

"A day's ride northwest, where the Lucrine River meets the badlands."

Saric knew the valley by another name. These Mortals, then, moved by their own map?

"How many are there. All of them?"

"You'll release me?"

"I've given you my word."

The man hesitated again, then nodded.

"Good." Saric turned to Brack, captain of the elite guard. "Return word to Varus. Gather the army to march by nightfall."

The captain dipped his head. "Yes, my Lord. How many divisions should—"

"All of them! Tell him I will lead and to wait for me."

"Yes, my Lord."

The Dark Blood spun on one heal and left at a brisk clip.

Saric turned his attention to Feyn, who was still staring at the Mortal.

"I want you to kill this man, my love. I want you to cut his chest open and pull out his heart."

Her dark eyes darted up, wide.

Saric studied her. Loyalty could nearly always be seen in the eyes, but action always told the full truth.

"Corban, give her the knife."

Corban withdrew a long serrated knife from a sheath beneath his robe, and pressed the handle into Feyn's hand. She took it without wavering.

"Please..." The Mortal was pleading now, chest heaving as he gasped for air, voice hoarse and too high. "I beg you...Send me as a warning, anything..."

Feyn didn't move.

"Do you remember who gave you life on this altar? Tell me."

Her voice was faint. "You did. Master."

"And he who gives life can also take it. This man serves the Mortal who would take your seat and offer life in my stead. Do you serve him or do you serve me?"

"I serve you."

"Then do as I say, my love."

Feyn's chest was rising and falling quickly. Sweat beaded her brow. A tremor shook the hems of her white sleeves.

"Kill him?" she said.

"For me, my love."

"Now?"

"Now."

She gave a faint nod. Stepped up to the table, lifted the blade high over her head. Eyes fixed upon Saric, she screamed and plunged the knife down with both hands into the chest of the Mortal beneath her.

CHAPTER NINETEEN

IN TWO DAYS' TIME, the great bonfires before the temple would burn as high as the ancient columns standing above it. The growing piles of wood were already the size of a small yurt and would be even larger by the time the fires were lit on the night of the annual Gathering. Hunters had gone out in search of boar, hare—as much game as they could bring back. The roasting pit had been dug on the edge of camp and lined with coals—soon the smell of roasting meat would send every stomach in camp growling.

Wine had been retrieved from the deep crevasse in the cliff face where it was stored, carried off from the last northern transport Roland's cadre had raided before the entire camp had relocated to the Seyala Valley. It had been stored here, untouched, in anticipation of the Gathering. For centuries the annual event had drawn Nomadic factions scattered throughout the continents together for trade, marriage, and, most important of all, the remembrance of Chaos. In this way Nomads celebrated life as it was known in Chaos, by rote, void of emotion, as best as Corpses could celebrate life.

These last years the Gathering had taken on a decidedly more frenzied pace. The small bands of a hundred or two hundred Nomads each that had come together the year Jonathan had joined Roland's tribe had never separated again. Nine hundred Nomads in total who no longer needed to travel long distances to gather, who no longer gathered in remembrance of Chaos but in celebration of life.

Mortal life through Jonathan's blood.

A life that Rom had just a day and a half ago learned was rapidly slipping away.

Rom paused in midcamp, staring vacantly at the smoldering remains of last night's bonfire. It had burned lower than usual—and would burn lower yet, tonight, in preparation for the great fire to come the night after. The celebration promised to be the most hedonistic and frenzied Gathering yet for the anticipation of Jonathan's succession to the Sovereign throne—of the kingdom to come. New life to invade the dead world.

But looking at the embers now, Rom felt only dread.

Roland was gone on his wild gamble of a mission to acquire Feyn. A hundred fighters had been sent out as scouts, leaving those within the camp vulnerable. All this for Jonathan's sake.

Rom needed to see him. To lay eyes on the boy with the uncanny nature who was both naïve and too wise at once. To see him and remember the day he'd first found him in secret as a boy. To remind himself that this was the boy predicted by Talus. Surely, the prophecy would come true.

But of course it would. Jonathan's very existence was proof that all Rom had lived and fought for these nine years would somehow still come to pass.

He strode for Adah's yurt, impatient for Triphon, who'd gone to find the boy an hour ago. What was taking him so long?

Ten minutes later, he was seated at Adah's table at her insistence, a bowl of rabbit stew and a cup of fermented mare's milk in front of him.

Watching as the older Nomad hurried out to check on something cooking in her outdoor oven, Rom could not help but think of Anna, his mother. She'd never known life—he could only hope that she now knew Bliss. The thought should have comforted him but instead brought him new anxiety. So many had died...Anna. Jonathan's mother. The first old Keeper who had given him the vial of blood on that day nine years ago...

Avra.

Too many, and yet he couldn't shake the fear that they might be few compared to the cost that awaited them in the days to come.

Appetite gone, he forced himself to eat—the first time he had done so since early yesterday morning, before the debacle with the Corpse and Jonathan's increasingly erratic behavior.

Adah ducked back into the tent and he forced a slight smile and a wink. "Delicious as always, Adah."

She grinned and started to refill his bowl. Rom held out his hand. "Please, I've had enough."

"Nonsense, dear. Eat. You'll wither up and blow away." She ladled steaming stew into his bowl.

There was no denying Adah. Rom obediently nodded, dipped his spoon into the hot stew and was about to take a bite when the door flew wide.

There stood Triphon. Forehead wrinkled.

Rom pushed up from the table, food forgotten, already knowing he didn't want to hear whatever Triphon had to say.

"He's gone."

"Jordin—"

"She's gone, too."

"What do you mean 'gone'?"

The bull of a man shook his head, braids brushing his shoulder. "They're both gone. So are their horses."

"I could have told you that," Adah said, turning from the kettle.

"What do you mean?"

"They came for food early this morning—nothing much, just some dried meat and cheese. I told him I was making stew, but he said they wouldn't be back in time to eat this evening."

Rom blinked, glanced at Triphon, whose face had gone stark.

"This evening? Where'd they go?"

She shrugged. "Where does Jonathan go, you ask? Wherever he likes. He's Sovereign."

"Not if we can't find him to put him on his seat!" To Triphon: "Where?"

"The Corpse outpost?"

"No. They'd be back by afternoon." Rom raked a hand through his hair and strode out past Triphon, aware of the taller man on his heels.

He stormed through the camp, ignoring those who stopped to stare at him and a few who tried to hail him. He stopped at the Keeper's yurt only long enough to duck his head inside and confirm that the old man wasn't there.

"The temple," Triphon said.

Then Rom was running toward the ruins, rushing up

the steps and through the columns, back toward the inner sanctum.

He didn't pause inside the back chamber, but made his way past the silk-draped altar with the Book of Mortals upon it. To the back wall of the chamber and the small door, fitted to cover the opening exactly. The lock was open.

He hurried down the stairs, into the limestone chamber below, Triphon's heavy step behind him. Lantern light drifting up through the well.

The bottom of the stair opened into a small chamber—the dry store and work space of the old alchemist, safely out of the elements.

The Book sat at a metal table before an array of vials and metal racks of samples. His ledger was open, his pen in hand, and there was an array of crumpled papers on the floor. Rom took one look at his haggard appearance and knew he had worked here through the night.

"No matter what I do, I cannot for the life in me figure out what is happening to his blood. I cannot pinpoint it. I cannot reverse it. I cannot stop it!"

"We have another problem," Rom said.

The old man sighed, as though there could be no other, let alone greater, problem.

"Jonathan's gone."

The old man glanced up, blinked. "Gone. Gone where?"

"I'm praying you know. You saw him last, when you took your latest sample from him. Did he say anything, that he meant to leave camp at all?"

The old Keeper shook his head vaguely, shadows playing about the winkles under his eyes.

"He said very little. He asked about Order, and about

Byzantium. But what do I know of Byzantium—I have never lived there. He wanted to know about the dead..."

"The Corpses?"

"No, the to-be-dead. The ones with the defects, taken away to die."

Rom exchanged a look with Triphon. "The Authority of Passing?"

"Yes, yes. The Authority of Passing. That was it. He wanted to know what happened to them and what it would take to save..." The old man paused. "He said he wished he could help them."

In a beat, Rom was running up the stairs, striding out of the inner sanctum, through the columns of the ancient basilica, Triphon at his side, shouting ahead for their horses.

"No. Roland's gone," Rom said. "And half of his men are out as scouts. I need you here..."

"I'm not letting you go alone," the taller man said. "The danger is out there—not here. Caleb is ranking warrior. He'll take charge..." And then he was running toward the horse pens.

Jonathan had no idea of the ways of a city like Byzantium! He had no business doing what he was doing. He was naïve, distracted by compassion, unaware of the danger to himself. Even with Jordin and Roland, they had barely escaped the city last time.

It took them only five minutes to reach the pens and secure what water and food they would need.

Rom slung canteens onto his saddle, pushed the young man preparing his horse aside, and cinched the girth himself.

"Triphon!" he shouted. "Now!"

CHAPTER TWENTY

THE CLEARING IN THE WESTERN FOREST was well known to Roland and his ranking Nomads. They had come here, far from the Mortal camp, numerous times over the last year to confer about the needs and priorities of the people under his direct care. Not that they differed so much from the needs of the Keepers, but as their prince, Roland's first calling was to his own.

Today the situation in his mind was clear: the destiny of the Nomads must be fulfilled—even beyond the fulfillment of Jonathan's. Only a year ago Roland had asked Jonathan about his future role. Their brief conversation had never left his mind.

"Do you mind if I ask you a question that might sound off-putting, Jonathan?"

The boy, then sixteen, had looked up wearing only a hint of a smile. "What could be off-putting to me, your servant?"

"Servant? No, Jonathan. It is I who serve you."

The boy had looked off toward the cliffs, his tone distant as he said, "So they say."

"I not only say it, I pledge it. I serve you, my Sovereign."

The boy had offered a faint nod. "What was your question?"

"As prince, my duty is to protect my people. This is the covenant we have made between each other through the generations. Now that—"

"Did I ask for your loyalty in exchange for my blood?" Jonathan said, looking at him.

Roland had never considered the question. The understanding had been implicit. "Not expressly."

"I've given my blood to serve you, not so that you can serve me. Your first responsibility is to those in your care. They are many. I'm only one."

"Yes, but you're the Giver of Life. And so I'd know your expectations."

"Is my life more valuable than one of your children's?"

Roland didn't know what to say.

Jonathan spoke before he could form an answer. "If my safety is ever in conflict with your people's, choose them. I'm only a vessel for blood they call the Sovereign. You're the leader of a great tribe, now alive. Take from me what you need and serve them."

Roland's love and respect for Jonathan had been sealed that moment.

But today the boy's words haunted him. Not because of any true conflict between his duty to Jonathan and his duty to his people, but because Jonathan's directive made his own calling unmistakable:

Ensure the safety of Nomads at all costs. Regardless.

They haunted him, too, because he couldn't help but wonder if the boy had known, even then, that this day would come.

Now he stood before the three leaders he'd placed

directly under him after his call for all Nomads to join as one tribe four years ago.

There had been thirteen tribes before Jonathan had come to them, nine of them in Europa. It had taken some negotiation and political maneuvering to satisfy the tribal leaders—they were all accustomed to a seat of power. And so Roland had given it to them by dividing domestic responsibilities between them: food, training of the warriors, the games, art and trade, the business of marrying and settling disputes, and so on. In truth, coming up with thirteen equally weighted realms of responsibility hadn't been the easiest task.

But when it came to the overall protection and guidance of the Nomadic bloodline, only these three advised him directly: Michael, who was his highest-ranking warrior; Seriph the zealot, who ranked politically in the highest favor; and Anthony, his leader of domestic affairs. Though any chief was welcome to visit Roland's quarters and voice any grievance to him personally, matters affecting the whole tribe, present or future, always came before his council.

Michael sat on a stump, arms crossed, staring in the direction of the valley just west of them. Seriph paced nearby, frowning. Anthony, the eldest at nearly fifty, took a long pull from a canteen. Known for keeping his words to a minimum, for never speaking quickly, he was viewed throughout the camp as something of a father figure—a man as kind as he was, by Nomadic standards, rotund.

Roland had quickly briefed them, saying nothing about the reversal in Jonathan's blood. Everything else, they now knew:

Jonathan could not be Sovereign unless Feyn handed the office over to him.

If Feyn died, Saric would be Sovereign.

That Jonathan had become, of late, obsessed with the plight of Corpses without demonstrating any plan for his dominion over them.

That Saric had raised an army of Dark Bloods to crush any enemy to Feyn's rule—namely Jonathan and those Jonathan had brought to life.

Mortals.

Nomads.

Now, in the last three days, the entire future of the Nomadic bloodline had come under direct threat.

"How many?" Anthony asked.

"Three thousand," Michael said. "If the one we took was telling the truth."

"Until we know better we assume he was," Roland said.

"Can we take them?"

"We could take twice that number," Seriph said.

Roland nodded. "Yes. But their reflexes and strength are surprising. He's bred them for war."

Seriph paused his pacing. "Our only sure course of action is to go after Saric directly."

"And invite a war?" Anthony settled to a stump.

"Yes. On our terms," Seriph said. "Better that than waiting for him to flush us out and attack with the advantage."

"You're assuming war of any kind is prudent."

"If it saves us, it's prudent," Michael said. "We've skirmished for years with earlier clandestine guard without ever learning their origin. Now we know they were some precursor to these Dark Bloods. We handled them easily enough, but now we face a more dangerous enemy. As long as they exist they threaten our kind. We can't give them the chance to wipe us out!"

"Agreed," Seriph said. "It's clear."

"Nothing is clear!" Anthony thundered, getting to his feet. Even Roland blinked at the sound. He so rarely raised his voice—but then again, rarely were they confronted with such stark choices. "Going against a superior enemy is fraught with danger, regardless of the situation."

"We either go against the enemy or wait for them to root us out."

"Not necessarily. There is another way," Anthony said, his gaze settling on Roland.

"What way is that?" Seriph said.

"We go into hiding. Deep. Far from here, where we may live in peace. We have all that we need—including lives that have been extended far beyond those of any Corpse. Saric will die one day, but we will still be alive."

"You're suggesting we just wait them out?" Seriph said. "As we have for five hundred years? No. This is the time for our kind to rise! It's what we've waited for. What we've anticipated—all of us. And now you say, 'Run and hide'?"

And so in two minutes the basic tension felt by all Nomads was laid bare. Fight or hide.

Anthony eyed him again. "What say you, Roland?"

Roland sighed and stared off toward the horses tied at the edge of the clearing.

"That each of you is right. That time will dictate which course we take."

"We don't have time!" Seriph hissed.

Roland glared at him. "Time. Will. Tell."

The man fell silent.

"The more immediate question is that of Jonathan's sovereignty. If he can take his seat, our course will be very different."

"And if he can't?" Michael said. "You've always said that the time for our people to rise and rule has come."

"Through Jonathan."

"Yes, of course. But his seat is taken! If he can't reclaim it—"

"Then we will see!"

He was surprised at the edge in his own voice. Crossing his arms, he inhaled deeply through his nostrils, exhaled, and then said, "For now we have a delicate play in motion. We must let it unfold as planned."

"No news since Pasha went missing?" Anthony said.

"Only that he was taken the day before yesterday."

Michael's face darkened. "If they kill him I will personally cut Saric's throat—"

"Yes. But until then, you will do exactly as I say. We fight for Jonathan's ascension. We play our hand as directed by Rom. We give him Feyn if we can, and we let him spin his magic. She's still our best option until proven otherwise."

"You're sure you want to deal with Saric alone?" Michael said, her brows drawing together. "I would be by your side, brother."

What a warrior she was! A fearless soul with royal blood in her veins. "If you insist, sister. But let your passions get the better of you and I *will* send you away. Is this clear?"

"I only wish to serve."

"Then serve me with your trust."

She dipped her head.

"You risk too much for him," Seriph said.

"Truly, Seriph?" Roland said. "Your zealots seem to have forgotten what the boy has given us. Now that you have his blood you would use it for your own gain, is that it? Conquer the world? Rule? Who needs Jonathan now that we have what he has to give?"

Even as he said it, he wondered who he was trying to convince—Seriph, or himself.

"Are you saying you haven't thought the same yourself? Jonathan is no leader of men. We have as much power as he has now. He's one boy, born within Order while our heritage extends—"

"You think your Prince has forgotten his history? I don't need a lecture, I need your obedience."

Seriph inclined his head, his eyes still fixed on Roland. "Of course, my Prince."

Hooves, pounding the forest floor. Word was coming.

A cry rang out. "They've been sighted! Coming this way from the south."

Roland turned to Michael. "Your men are ready?"

"Always."

"Then let's see if we can work our own magic and give Rom what he wants." He headed for his horse. "Michael, with me. Seriph, Anthony, take your horses to the trees. I don't want you seen."

CHAPTER TWENTY-ONE

JORDIN HADN'T FELT SUCH FEAR as she had these last few days. The prick of anxiety, yes, when she couldn't find Jonathan. That moment of hesitation when she realized that he was missing from camp. But never true fear because he always appeared, as though in response to her unspoken call for him, just as he had yesterday when he had returned to camp with the Corpse boy, Keenan.

But now, as they skirted the southeast edge of the city, she was afraid. Haunted by images of Dark Bloods, afraid that the day would come when there would be more than she could protect him from. Terrified that they would take Jonathan from her.

That she would ultimately be without him.

They shouldn't have come. But Jonathan was set and would have come with or without her. And leaving his side was as unacceptable to her as losing him.

They'd ridden straight through the day, only stopping when necessary to rest and water the horses or relieve themselves, eating in the saddle, speaking little. She did not need to ask where he meant to go, or why. She knew.

And what her Sovereign wanted was as good as a directive in Jordin's mind.

It was the reason returning Keenan to the outpost had been so difficult. For the first time her loyalties had been thrown into direct conflict. It had torn at her to do it, having seen the look on Jonathan's face, the way he had bent down to talk to the boy before reluctantly letting him go. But she didn't resent Rom. She couldn't; he was their leader, and of all people in the world, he loved Jonathan almost as much as she did.

Today they had come right at the city in full daylight. When she suggested that they go in through the tunnels, he had dismissed the notion. He wasn't interested in entering the city center, then. That much, at least, offered her a slight measure of relief.

But only a little.

They skirted the city, east and then south, keeping to what cover they could. This entire side of Byzantium was scattered with stunted trees and the refuse of ruins—old storehouses and factories that were barely more than broken concrete foundations sporting scrub grass through widening cracks, their wooden sides and metal beams long ago scavenged for reuse.

They rode past a small electrical plant, one of several satellite centers that supported the ration of electricity to Byzantium's citizens, and beyond that a sprawling rail station for the transportation of garbage. The tracks led directly south to the industrial wastelands, where it might be disposed of far from the capital. She watched one of the trains pull away from the station as another waited to take its place at the dock.

Overhead, the sky had begun to churn. A storm was

coming. Odd how quickly the weather could turn. And this seemed to be a large one, come out of nowhere. Although she didn't relish the idea of getting caught in a downpour, she would welcome the veil of a sluicing rain in any retreat.

Jonathan leaned forward in his saddle as they pressed southward through the scrim of scrub and ruined concrete buildings, skirting the garbage plant some five hundred yards out. Now she saw what had his attention: a walled perimeter extending beyond the last dock. It had to be twenty feet high, solid concrete, with rolled wire at the top.

Painted on the stretch of wall was the unmistakable compass of Sirin. Order's most revered symbol.

The wind abruptly shifted again, blowing up from the south, carrying an odor far more familiar and far less appealing to her nose than garbage.

Corpses.

A putrid smell, different from any she had encountered.

She jerked back on the reins of her horse and stared past the end of the nearest dock. The great walled compound sat at the city's perimeter like a tumor, with a sinister smokestack easily fifteen feet in diameter rising out of the middle.

Ten feet ahead of her, Jonathan had also halted. She moved up alongside him, turned to him, started to speak, and then stopped.

He was staring at the walls ahead of them, visibly shaking in his saddle.

"Jonathan?" she said.

He was too fixated to respond.

When she looked back, she wasn't sure at first what he was looking at. The smokestack?

The sky above it?

No. He was staring at the smoke. It was faint against the backdrop of the coming storm, drifting serenely as a ghost up toward the roiling sky. Almost beautiful. Effortless as breath.

That wasn't...that couldn't be...

That was the smell.

With a sharp cry, Jonathan spurred his stallion forward into a hard gallop. Reacting instantly without a thought, Jordin followed hard after him—across the waste, toward the departing train, even as it began to pick up momentum. Jonathan leaned low, his stallion easily leaping the double track. Jordin glanced north, at the oncoming engine, the sound of it a banshee wail in her right ear, thirty feet off, closing—

She bent low, leaped the track just ahead of the rushing engine and spurred the horse on. A roaring gust of wind from the passing train blew her braids into her face.

Adrenaline charged her veins. Her pulse drummed in her ears. Despite fear, despite concern for Jonathan, she had been made—*made*—for this. Not just to feel the sides of her stallion straining beneath her or the oncoming storm in her face.

But for *him*. To follow him to the end of the earth.

They raced along the length of the north wall, marked every hundred feet with Sirin's compass painted in red and faded around the edges to brown like a drying wound.

There, on the adjacent side of the perimeter, a long brick building rose from the western wall. In the middle, a wide iron gate. An entrance. Rolls of barbed wire coiled along the crest of the roof like metal serpents.

Jonathan slowed as they came to the building, pulled up, and without warning dismounted.

"What are you doing?"

"We're here." He drew his horse by the reins toward the building.

She swung down from her mount, glanced back toward the city. There were train tracks here, leading up from a tunnel that emerged from the city perimeter. They stopped directly before the building itself.

She glanced up at the sign above the gate.

AUTHORITY OF PASSING.

Ahead of her, Jonathan was unbuckling the scabbard at his waist.

"Jonathan . . . What are you doing?"

"I'm going in."

He was going in even as everything within her was suddenly screaming *Leave. Get out!* Because this was not only a place of Corpses.

This was a place of death.

"How?"

Overhead in the observation windows, a guard leaned forward watching them through the glass. A second man was pointing, lifting, and speaking into something on a cord.

Panic rose up, cold inside her. There was still time. She could still get him back to safety . . .

"Jonathan . . ."

He slipped his sword through the straps of his saddle bag, secure against the horse's flank. "There's only one way in that I can see."

No.

He glanced at her, held her gaze for a moment.

Do you trust me?

Do you believe me?

She could get him out. There was still time. She closed her eyes.

Yes.

When she opened them, he was already moving off toward the gate.

Yes.

She unbuckled the sword slung over her hips and hung it on the saddle next to her bow and quiver. But she left the knife tucked into her boot, conscious of its presence against her ankle as she rushed after him.

A door off the side of the gate opened and a uniformed guard stepped out. Six foot tall. Close-cut hair. He reeked. Not just of Corpse, but of the same stench emanating from the smokestack within the compound. But he was common Corpse. Not Dark Blood.

"What are you doing here?" His eyes searched both of them, lingering on Jonathan's Nomadic braids and then his embellished tunic and then on her, before narrowing slightly.

Jonathan looked him straight in the eye. "We've come to turn ourselves in."

It was all Rom could do to stop and rest the horses. Given the choice, he would have ridden them into the ground.

"We'll kill the horses if we don't rest them," Triphon shouted.

"If we don't make it, nothing matters!"

"And we'll have less chance of getting Jonathan safely out without mounts."

The urge to run the rest of the distance was nearly more than he could bear. But Triphon was right—his mount was frothing along his coat. They'd soon be on foot at this rate.

They stopped by the side of a brook just outside the city.

"What was he thinking?" he said, pacing.

Triphon was silent. He'd taken out the food. Neither of them touched it.

"What was he thinking?!"

"You know what he's thinking."

Rom had heard the story about the night they escaped from the city. Triphon was right, more than he knew. He knew exactly why Jonathan had gone to the city, and for whom.

The girl in the cart.

But how did Jonathan dare risk the future of Mortals? Surely he realized how shortsighted he was being to bring one Corpse back to life!

Could he still bring a Corpse to life?

He had effectively multiplied his blood by bringing the twelve hundred Mortals to life—perhaps that had been the intent all along.

No. The world needed its Sovereign. He was meant to rule. He *must* rule.

But first, he must live.

"That's long enough," Rom said, striding to grab his horse's reins. Triphon shook his head, but did likewise.

Thirty seconds later, they were riding hard again.

"To turn yourself in," the guard said, looking from Jonathan to Jordin.

"Yes," Jonathan said. "The paperwork should be coming. We volunteered to come immediately out of obedience. For the hope of Bliss. But if you could take us inside now..."

He wasn't adept at lying—he had never had to be.

Neither had she.

Jordin looked away, fearing that he would see in her the impulse to slice open his throat if he so much as laid a hand on Jonathan. Which she would.

He was frowning at Jonathan's braids again as one who frowns while trying to remember the words to a song, not quite there, but on the tip of the tongue.

"You must be from the west side of the city."

"Yes. The west. Our parents are...artisans."

"Sumerian then. You're not wearing your amulet."

"We took them off already, to leave with our families. In remembrance of us."

"What's wrong with you that they've sent you here?"

Her gaze flicked to Jonathan whose attention had drifted from the man to the yard through the gate. Beyond, two rows of long buildings with small, industrial-sized windows—none of them open—ran all the way to the back perimeter. There were perhaps thirty of them in all.

"I'll make a call," the guard was saying. "It's not every day we get volunteers."

"No," Jordin said, her attention snapping back to him. "He was born with a crippled leg. He's fine now, but he hid it for so long, he's concerned about—about Bliss. About his status with the Maker. We attended basilica together. We confessed to the priest and he advised us..." Was she even getting any of this right? It wasn't like she'd ever attended basilica in her life.

"And you?"

"I..." She remembered then, a story she had heard once, about Rom's lover, the first martyr. "I spilled lantern oil on myself two years ago. I hid it—from everyone. Under these clothes, I'm completely scarred. I'm supposed to be married..." Her gaze drifted to Jonathan, but he was lost to them both. "And the secret will come out soon. I can't bear it. I'm tired of hiding. I want to be right... with the Maker."

She realized belatedly that she wasn't sure what she would do if he demanded to see evidence.

The guard grunted. His gaze was tinged with every indication that he would be finished with them both as quickly as possible. Association with the damaged and the imperfect was not a thing anyone craved—even a guard doing his job.

"Suit yourselves. You've obeyed the statutes—and for that you may find Bliss." He said it as one who has spoken the same words many times, words without meaning except to those who heard them.

"We understand."

"Sign." He tapped an opened ledger across the top of which was inscribed its title: *The Book of Passing.*

Jordin suppressed a shudder, her mind skipping to the Book of Mortals on the altar of the inner sanctum. It seemed profane for her name to be inscribed anywhere else.

Jonathan was staring at the smoke rising from the stack, oblivious to them. The guard noted his stare and frowned.

"What did you expect, boy? People are sent here to die. Most are terminal anyway, but you know that. As soon as your paperwork's processed, we'll release permission for your funerals, but as far as the Order's concerned, you're already dead. Get used to it. Sign."

So... It was true, the stories. Jordin took the pen and scrawled *Tara Shubin* in the ledger, the first name that popped into her head.

"How long does it take to die here?" Jonathan asked.

The guard shrugged. "We don't have the resources to support you for that long. It isn't fair to the living to be taxed on behalf of supporting the dead. Everyone here has a one-year limit."

One year?

The guard tapped the book and handed the pen to Jonathan who absently took it and wrote his true name: "Jonathan Talus."

Jordin glanced sidelong through the iron gate. Here and there a few forms moved about on concrete pathways between buildings. They walked with the posture of those who had nothing to offer, of those unacceptable by Order's standards, who might find acceptance only in their resignation of what little life they had, and the hope that obedience might earn a better hereafter.

What kind of Order could so twist the minds of its faithful to live in death?

"Your horses will be sent to the Citadel stables or the butchers. Anything you have of value will be put toward the considerable expense of the Center."

She nodded, but her attention had gone to Jonathan, who had stepped up to the gate to grasp it by two iron bars.

"Anything of value?"

"No," Jordin whispered. Nothing but the knife in her boot. A weapon no Corpse would be caught dead with, so to speak.

He was looking her over with clinical appraisal. "You'll be issued new clothing as you need it. Our counselor isn't on duty—we weren't expecting any new arrivals. I'll take you back to your housing and you'll have to get your instructions on showers and food from her later."

Jonathan stood unmoving, staring through the bars.

"Each dorm is opened for one hour of each day. Unit Five is open now." He glanced at his watch. "In fifteen minutes they go back and Six opens for an hour. You'll learn the rules."

She gave a mute nod.

"There's no priest here. No basilica. Your last service will be your funeral. They'll pray for you there. You'll find a copy of the Book of Orders in your housing unit."

Jordin felt ill.

"Stand back."

Jonathan stumbled back as the guard lifted the heavy key ring from his belt, fitting the largest one into the gate's heavy lock.

"Welcome to the gateway, if you're fortunate, to Bliss."

Bliss?

She peered at the rows of concrete buildings through the opening grate. The figures milling about outside of them, a few of them staring at the new arrivals at the gate, some of them from grimy dormitory windows. All of them waiting to die.

This then, was the desire of the Order's Maker?

The gate swung wide as pale gray smoke wafted from the smokestack toward the restless heavens.

The condemned peered at her as though she were an apparition. A thing not from their realm, as though a part of them had already passed from this life into the next, and only waited for their bodies to catch up.

The guard stood aside, avoiding touching either one of them, she noted, as though death were a catching disease.

Move. But something within her balked at the thought of this place. Of setting foot on the cracked concrete walk that extended out from the gate, down between the rows of buildings. The Authority of Passing offended every sensibility within her as a Nomad. Its confinement, the view of nothing but the insides of those twenty-foot walls, the three-story round tower that was their only exit out—it all reeked of a living death. Of Corpse.

Move.

She stood rooted to the spot until Jonathan stepped forward. He walked past the guard and into the compound. The Giver of Life . . . standing in the place of death.

Bile rose up in her throat and for a moment she thought she might be sick.

Jonathan stopped ten paces in and looked back at her—a quiet look that was neither order nor request. Simple acceptance, whether she entered after him or not.

She knew then that she could walk away and he wouldn't begrudge her. That he had no expectation of her.

That he would love her always.

There was still time. She could get him out. But that wasn't his way, and she was here to follow him, not the other way around.

She put one foot in front of the other until she'd passed through the gate and joined him.

Overhead, the sky flashed, a white flicker of lightning against a black sky. Too silent.

They made it all the way to the electrical plant, just north of the Authority of Passing, before Rom's horse collapsed under him.

Beast and rider crashed to the earth. Rom slid over the shuddering animal's neck and slammed into the ground in front of it, scraping hair and skin from his chin. Ahead of him, Triphon jerked his mount to a halt. The horse began to buckle, but managed to recover as Triphon slid from the saddle.

Rom shoved himself forward and scrambled to his feet, ignoring the pain that shot up his leg. He glanced desperately at the heaving sides of the stallion on the ground and then in the direction of the garbage docks, and what he knew lay beyond.

"Take mine!" Triphon said, thrusting the reins of his horse into his hand.

He glanced at Triphon.

"Go! I'm coming behind you!"

Without another word, Rom leaped up onto the back of Triphon's mount, the flanks of which were twitching with fatigue. And then he dug his heels in and took off, willing it to live just another moment longer.

CHAPTER TWENTY-TWO

THE SUN WAS HIGH, bright even through a scrim of shifting clouds, when Saric led his twelve divisions into the Seyala Valley. *Where the Lucrine River meets the badlands*, the Mortal scout had said.

A broad green valley lay ahead, a half mile long before it narrowed into a canyon, lush and undisturbed by traffic—equine or human—or any other signs of passage. From here, the western slope rose sharply to the barren badlands, and the Lucrine River glinted with the occasional glimpse of sun. The forest hugged the opposite rise, typical of the patchwork greenery in these parts.

Saric lifted a hand shoulder-high, signaled the halt, and brought his stallion to a heavy-footed stop. The thudding of hooves and feet resolved into the creak of saddles and snorting horses.

He'd donned battle leathers only as a precaution, and now regretted doing so. They'd seen no sign of Mortals, no threat of any kind—only the occasional hare scurrying for cover as his army invaded a serene landscape most had never laid eyes on.

Brack pulled his horse alongside him. On his other

flank, Varus, ranking general of all twelve divisions, studied the landscape before them.

"You're sure this is it?" Saric asked.

"The Seyala Valley isn't marked on our maps, but there's no mistaking the location," Varus said. "Either he made it up or he gave us the wrong location."

"What about our scouts?"

"The canyon narrows to a file. Smells like a trap."

"Clever. Clever Mortals, who mislead with a suicide scout," Varus said, clicking his tongue.

"Yes."

"Permission to speak?" Brack said. The captain of the elite guard held his lofty position directly under Saric in part because of his attention to the detail of loyalty. His devotion wasn't necessarily greater than any of Saric's other children, but he was an exceptionally refined man in all respects—strange, considering his violent nature. He was testament to the full power of the incubation chambers built by Pravus and perfected by Saric. They had indeed built a perfect species.

"Speak freely."

"Even if the scout misled us, we can't know that he did it under orders. He may have given false information on his own, to protect his people."

Saric scanned the top of the cliffs for the dozenth time. "If you're wrong and the scout intended to be taken—even knowing he might die—it would mean these Mortals have deep loyalties indeed."

"We have to assume it's a trap," Varus said. "And that our entire army may be exposed."

"How could a trap make sense?" Brack said, as if speaking to himself. "If the scout was correct, there are only seven hundred of them. Any confrontation would end in their elimination. Why go to all the trouble to dispatch a scout to lure us here under such impossible odds?"

"*If* the scout was correct," the general said.

Clearly there was more to the Mortals than Saric yet knew.

The only thing worse than numerous enemies...was hidden enemies.

And feeling made a fool of.

But he, too, could play at any game. He had every confidence that his Dark Blood taken by the Mortals had not divulged their true numbers.

He twisted in his saddle and surveyed his divisions. They'd marched through the night and morning in three wide columns, three thousand on horseback ahead of nine thousand infantry, stretching back half a mile. Twelve thousand in all.

Warriors, erect on horseback, swords in scabbards by armored thighs, leather helmets donned over long dreadlocks that spread over their shoulders and chests like roots clawing for passage through the thick leather of their armor. Behind them the infantry stood tall, perfectly formed, heads fixed, forward and alert.

The first army in nearly five hundred years.

His.

The technology and armaments of the armies during the age of Chaos may have been far more advanced, but history had never seen warriors with more discipline, speed or strength than these.

And because of it, his power was without peer.

Absolute.

"Movement."

He turned at Brack's word. Two horsemen had entered the valley from the canyons beyond. They rode abreast, slowly, without any sign of anxiety.

Varus spat off his right side. "We were drawn," he said with obvious disgust.

"So it seems," Saric said. "Do you see any danger? Either of you."

Silence for a moment.

"No."

"No, my Lord."

"So then, let's go see what our clever enemy is made of, shall we?"

Saric spurred his horse forward, ambling at the same pace of the two now approaching. Behind him, the army shuddered to life with precision. Two lines of horses broke to the flanks, marching as one so that the earth vibrated with each footfall as Saric's captains emerged up through the corridor.

The approaching Mortals stopped, still a hundred paces off.

"Hold your riders back," Saric said. "I don't want to pursue a fleeing enemy in these parts. They'll be prepared to ambush."

Almost immediately the cavalry on each side slowed their approach and settled into a cautious gait, wide but parallel with Saric.

The two Nomads resumed their approach. They both rode stallions—bred for running long distances, according to lore. Their hair was long, braided, beaded, their clothing a blend of dark brown leathers with accents of red and metal painted or woven into the sleeves and breasts. Their boots were set in stirrups attached to light saddles.

He'd never seen a Nomad apart from the scout they'd taken just two days ago. It made sense for Jonathan's handlers to go after the disaffected tribespeople who'd always resisted Order, who survived without the facilities of cities. They could run and hide like jackals. They evidently could also hold their own in hand-to-hand combat and were no strangers to strategy. Because there could be no mistaking the matter: they'd lured him here with intent.

Only when they were fifty paces off did Saric see that one of them was a woman. Haughty-chinned and steely-gazed.

Exotic material for a concubine.

Still no sign of additional warriors on the high ground.

The horsemen stopped thirty paces off, steady and seemingly unconcerned. But Saric knew better than to underestimate them.

"That's far enough," the man called out, voice firm.

Who was this man who presumed to order him? Did two lone warriors command his path? What kind of enemy could approach such a crushing display of force and demand they move no further?

Nomads.

Saric's hand went up. "Hold."

Immediately the columns behind him ceased marching on a single footfall. Silence filled the valley.

It was the first time Saric had seen a Nomad Mortal outside of captivity, and for a moment he was captivated. Here was no cowering enemy, but a creature brimming with strange power. Power to equal his own. It came off the man in waves like heat. What kind of blood made a man so fearless? Even the woman stared him down with an audacity he found compelling. If what Rom had told

Feyn was true, their veins ran with the natural blood of one child who'd been born without Legion to contend with. Pure, untouched by alchemy.

A sudden, raw sensation sunk like razored talons into his heart. The moment he felt the savage emotion, he knew it for what it was.

Jealousy.

He immediately replaced it with another passion: rage.

But neither would serve him. During the age of Chaos, humanity's failure had been its inability to control such powerful sentiments. He was far more evolved.

Indeed, he was master . . . and Maker.

Even over such magnificent creatures as these two, seated on their horses, staring him down.

They would soon see.

Roland gazed out over Saric's vast army, acutely aware of the nerves running on edge down his neck and arms. By his quick estimation, there were well over ten thousand of them. Far larger than they'd been led to believe.

They smelled like a horde from hell. Even from a distance the stench was hardly bearable.

Their formation was nearly perfect, three large blocks of three or four thousand each, one-fourth mounted, the rest on foot. Whatever discipline had gone into their training had been effective; they could hardly be more ordered or settled if they were mechanized.

Two generals flanked the leader, half a horse length behind. Tall and thick, as certain of themselves as boulders in the face of a noon breeze. But Roland had met a few of these rocks before and he knew how quickly they could move.

And then there was Saric in his black leather armor with its silver buckles and red piping—an exhibition of authority. Like the rest of the Dark Bloods, his skin was pale, nearly translucent beneath the intermittent sun. Even from here, Roland's Mortal eyes could detect the dark lines of veins near the surface of Saric's skin. The unblinking bore of his black eyes, like two coals in a sun-parched face.

Deathly. And chillingly beautiful.

"Are you sure, brother?" Michael breathed.

"I am always and never sure." His voice was barely more than a whisper. "Be ready to run if anything goes wrong. Through the canyons on the route I showed you. Don't lead them to our camp. Head west and cut back—"

"I know what to do. Be careful."

"Wait here."

He gave his mount a gentle nudge, guided it forward, and stopped fifteen paces from Saric.

"I would speak to Saric, brother of the Sovereign," he said, refusing him more title than that. "You have my word—I will not harm you. I have no intention of angering this machine of an army, only to speak terms."

Saric stared, unmoved. Not even the blink of an eye.

"You must think it odd that two of my kind would face ten thousand of yours," Roland said. "You ask yourself how I so easily lured your army with the word of a single man, one of my most humble warriors. And you wisely doubt that the warriors I command are only seven hundred, as he told you. Now you realize you know nothing of our true power. And so come closer and let me explain."

It was a long speech for Roland, but he was dealing with a man of the Order, given to such displays of power.

So he let the words work their way into this pale overlord, this maker of Dark Bloods, content to know that despite appearances, he still held the upper ground. *He* had tricked *them*. He was also still beyond their reach, able to vanish into the canyons within seconds. No matter how fast the Dark Bloods themselves, their chargers could not outrun his stallion.

But there was more here that Roland could not easily dismiss. As much as Saric must even now reevaluate all he knew about the Mortal force, Roland must do the same of him. He could smell the anger and ambition wafting from the sea of humanity, nearly as strong as the scent of death.

But was it truly the scent of death? It wasn't the same as the Corpses; the powerful overtones of what he might place as loyalty and affection were as thick as a low fog in the valley. Affection. Perhaps even love.

Was it possible Saric had actually found a way to create life in as much as Jonathan had? Full life, vivid with emotion?

There sat a powerful man upon his charger—a warrior Roland acknowledged as majestic. Who else could have orchestrated the defeat of Order and the raising of an army such as this but a singularly potent man who was born to rule?

The desire to subdue a foe of equal strength wrestled with simple admiration within him, and it occurred to Roland then that one day he would indeed either kill this man or join him. There could be no in between.

Still no response from Saric.

"Come now. Do two of us frighten you so easily?"

"Do I look like a fool to you?" Saric said at last. The man's voice held not a shred of concern.

"Definitely not."

"Then *you* come closer."

Roland considered the request, judging the likelihood of a personal attack. Saric had little to gain by killing him. It was Jonathan who threatened his power, not one or two lone warriors. In any case, he had challenged Saric, and he was now compelled to accept that same challenge. Anything less would be a show of weakness.

He cut the distance between them in half.

"You should not fear one who has come to give you the keys to your kingdom," Roland said.

A wry smile twisted Saric's mouth. "I'm not sure you understand your position."

"I understand it very well. Order two of your men to kill me and you will as well."

No one moved. Those dark eyes studied him, devoid of emotion. The scent of him, however, was saturated with anger . . . and strange eagerness.

"You seem quite confident," Saric said.

"I would know my enemy. Make it three men if you wish."

Saric dipped his head. "As you wish. Varus, humor the man."

The Dark Blood to Saric's right turned and barked out an order. Without hesitation, three horses broke from the ranks behind and trotted forward.

Roland pointed to a slight rise, twenty paces to Michael's left. "On foot." Without waiting for a reply, he turned his horse, rode to where Michael waited, and dismounted, handing her the reins.

"Remember, the canyon. Have my horse ready."

He started to walk for the rise.

Only then did the three warriors dismount. They came for him at a run, three abreast, spreading out as they approached.

Twenty paces...

But Roland wanted the rise, so he continued on and stopped only when he was atop it, staring at the onrush of Dark Bloods.

Ten paces...

He took a deep breath, spread his arms by his waist, and tilted his head down. In the next moment, he *saw*.

Time slowed to a drip.

The Dark Bloods were running but in his sight they plodded through tacky mud. Their dreadlocks flailed behind them like black smoke in a dream. Every ounce of their bulk fighting gravity, the viscosity of time itself, to get to him. Their size so cumbersome that he might run up and tap each of them and jink away before they could even react.

That was wrong, of course. They were fast—he already knew that. Too fast to risk their closing in, or fighting them three-on-one. But their movement would work against them.

He swiped a blade from the sheath on his hip and flung it backhanded at the closest of the three, the one on his left. The blade sailed through the air and smacked home, deep in the eye socket.

The man's head snapped back. His feet flew off the ground and he landed solidly on his back with a grunt. Dead.

Five paces...

Two left, one in midswing of a three-foot, double-edged sword. It flashed toward Roland like a glinting saucer, cutting for his torso.

No way to avoid the sword. Only to step into it as one edge passed and before the second rounded and caught him.

The blades slowed to a whirr, and then to the lazy turn of a two-spoked wheel. He chose his time, threw himself forward. When he did, his shoulder crashed into the handle at its center. The sword careened off harmlessly.

He dropped, rolled forward. He had two more knives out and slashing upward as they leaped to avoid him. His blade connected with a leg bone, the impact jarred him to his shoulder. The warrior roared with pain and sprawled forward.

Roland came to his feet behind them, but the third man had already spun and was in full swing.

"Roland!" Michael's cry cut the air.

Once again, their speed surprised him. He was too late to avoid the blade. Too off balance to lunge into it. So he turned into the blow to catch it squarely on his chest where his leather was the thickest, taking the blade's full length to disperse the force of the strike along as much of the edge as possible.

The blade smacked into the leather. Cut through it and into his chest with a sharp sting.

But not to the bone.

It was all Roland needed to know. His threw all of his weight into a blow to the other man's face, dead center. The Dark Blood's nose caved—loudly—against his knuckles.

He twisted the man's sword from his grasp, whipped it around like a sling and buried the blade in the warrior's exposed neck. Spun to the second Dark Blood staggering to his feet with one of Roland's knives sticking out of his leg.

"Enough!" Roland cried. He jabbed the bloody sword in his hand toward the army. "Go! While you still live."

But the warrior didn't appear interested in running for cover. He jerked a long knife from his belt and circled, cautiously, to the left.

"Where did you learn to fight, Nomad?"

He hadn't expected such a typical question from the Dark Blood. Not under the scrutiny of his superiors. Neither did he see any reason to respond.

"Call your man back," he said, jabbing his chin in Saric's direction. "Or I'll kill him."

"I don't run," the warrior said.

"Mather! Back!"

The Dark Blood immediately straightened. Then he was up and jogging for his ranks, order unquestioned.

Roland walked to his horse, swung into the saddle, and wheeled around.

Michael glanced at his chest. "You're all right?"

"Just a cut."

He trotted back toward Saric and stopped. Only ten paces separated them. Other than the three Bloods who'd been sent to fight him, not a soul appeared to have moved. The army was extraordinarily disciplined. Machine-like . . . and unnervingly alive.

Roland knew then that there was no way his Nomads would survive a head-to-head battle with the Dark Bloods. They would have to think through their strategy very carefully.

"Impressive," Saric said. "Your point?"

"Where is Pasha?"

"Your man."

"Yes."

"Feyn killed him."

Feyn. The one Rom insisted was their only hope.

Roland gave only a curt nod.

"My point is that you'll have your hands full if you come against us. But you won't have to."

"Is that so?"

"It is."

"Why?"

"Because you want Jonathan," Roland said. "And I can give him to you."

CHAPTER TWENTY-THREE

THE CORPSES STARED at Jordin and Jonathan as they passed. One of them, a girl no more than five wearing a ragged red coat, came running a few steps toward them, only to stop abruptly and gape at Jonathan. Big green eyes, set in a face that was far too pale. She was clutching a dirty doll.

Jonathan paused and reached out to her, but the guard stopped him.

"We're not there yet. I'm putting you in Fifteen. Come on."

He made no move to follow the order. She sensed his anguish then—desperation rising inside his chest like a hard fist.

"Where are the guards housed?" Jordin asked, as much to give Jonathan a moment as to learn more. She quickly added, "If there is ever trouble."

"Trouble? There's no danger in the compound."

"No one tries to escape?"

He gave her strange look.

"Why would they?"

It was hard to remember what it meant to be Corpse

without any ambition or sorrow or desire. To be guided only by fear. They lived in fear of leaving the compound as much as in fear of death. As did the guard.

"There are four of us and we live outside the walls. You'll see wardens and employees. If there's any trouble, tell one of them. But there won't be. Hurry up, boy."

Jonathan tore his gaze away from the girl and followed after the guard.

Only then did Jordin realize she'd hardly registered the smell of the Corpse girl in the close proximity of so many doomed.

Now she could see the large, worn numbers on the end of each building. The white paint was peeling and faint against the gray concrete. Odd numbers on the left, even on the right. There were thirty housing units in all—each of them long buildings inset with small, square windows under the eaves of an industrial roof. Their panes were dirty, dark, as though covered over with some kind of film.

Maker.

Now she saw them closely, the dark heads, the dirty hands pressed up against the glass. She blinked, swallowed.

Faces, in the windows. Four, five apiece. Ten windows along the side of the building, spaced perhaps ten feet apart.

She glanced back the way they'd come. An old man peered at her from the far corner of Building Four, leaning heavily on a wooden crutch, a part of his lower leg missing. A woman came out of a long building against the far side of the perimeter—the shower rooms, perhaps— walking as though half her body did not work properly, so that she had to drag it to catch up with the functioning side. A man with a bandage around his head and obvious palsy followed her. The victim of an accident, perhaps.

An affront. Alchemy, which had long solved the genetic puzzles of cancer, wasting diseases, blood disorders, dementia, and myriad maladies to humanity, could not abide to be reminded of the infirmities it could not prevent.

She swallowed and lowered her gaze to Jonathan's heels in front of her, to the stony soil beneath that was as gray, nearly, as the concrete. As the smoke wafting to the sky. She tried to school her breath, which grew ever more erratic with each step. She would follow him anywhere, even into this maw of Hades.

The guard turned onto the broken walk that led to the door of Building Fifteen. The sky flashed again. Thunder in the distance.

Even the heavens couldn't abide it. These people were created to be alive, not dead. Imperfectly alive, not perfectly dead. The realization hit her like a hammer.

Jonathan was born to bring life, not a new order. Chaos, not perfection.

I see, she wanted to cry. *I understand.*

She spun to Jonathan, words half-formed on her lips, but the sight of him robbed her of breath. He was frantic, trying to open the door, seemingly mindless. Clawing at it, banging on the wood with tears on his cheeks, gasping even as the guard was trying to unlock it.

"Move aside, boy, or I can't—"

Jonathan shoved the guard aside.

"Hey!"

The guard went after him, and Jordin met him with a quick crack of her elbow to his temple. He dropped beside the stoop, unconscious.

Jonathan worked the key in the lock, got it open, and then tossed the ring to Jordin.

"We have to find her!" Jonathan cried.

She didn't need to ask whom he meant.

She snatched the ring of keys from the air, leaped over the unconscious guard, and ran to the next building in the row. Thirteen.

After fumbling to find the right key, she opened the door...

Stared into the interior of the dormitory.

A hundred faces peered back at her. Some of them sat on bunk beds set like shelving into the walls, some on the floor. A young boy crouched in the corner. There were no chairs. No tables, no sofas, no comforts of any kind. No blankets on the beds that she could see. The sallow light of a lone electrical fixture illuminated not only the dirt of neglect, but the utter hopelessness of looming death.

"Is a girl named Kaya in here?" she shouted.

No one moved. A middle-aged woman began to cry. One man, older and feeble, thin as a skeleton, cradling an open and tattered copy of the Book of Orders on his lap, shook his head.

Hurried steps behind her. And then Jonathan was there, filling the doorway, staring into the dormitory over her shoulder.

"Is she here?"

"No."

He grabbed the key ring and took off running. She stared a moment longer and then ran after him.

"Kaya!"

Jonathan came out of Building Twelve and ran to

Eleven. She had never seen him like this before. Frantic. Desperate.

"Kaya!" he shouted before he had it open.

"Here," Jordin said, taking the keys from him, finding the one, opening the lock. Throwing open the door.

"Kaya!"

Again, the mute stares, the soulless whimpers. A little boy ducked under a bunk and peered out with wide eyes. A young woman, not much older than Jordin herself, got to her feet and screamed.

Building Ten.

No Kaya.

Nine.

And then the sirens went off. A wail, low as a rumble at first, from the direction of the observation tower, lifting in pitch to an all-out shriek. Up, over the walls, ringing in the ears. Banks of lights on the corners of the compound flashed on, bright as an unnatural sun beneath the churning sky.

Jordin glanced up, squinting against the light. A clamor from the direction of the gate, shouts.

Only then did she see it, falling through the unforgiving electrical light: a powder as fine as ash. Horrified, she glanced down and saw the dusting on her tunic sleeve. The same pallid gray seemed to permeate everything in this place.

She recoiled and tried to brush it off, but there was too much.

"Hurry!" Jonathan.

She glanced up at him. The ash clung to his braids, his lashes. It was then that she saw the stricken face that peered from the nearest window beyond him.

The girl.

"Kaya," she breathed.

Jonathan spun, saw the girl. He fumbled with the lock, got the key in the first try, and yanked the door open.

He rushed through just in time to catch Kaya as she threw herself into his arms. She sobbed into his shoulder. "I didn't tell anyone. I'm scared. Jonathan, I don't want to die!"

A low wail from farther in back of the building. Stifled sobbing nearby. And against it all, the backdrop of the siren.

"You won't die. I'm here." He held her away from him, shook her lightly, eyes intent on hers, tears choking his words. "You hear me? I found you. I found you and I won't let you go..."

She clung to him, arms around his neck as he fumbled at the pocket of his coat. As soon as Jordin saw the stent, she knew what he meant to do.

"We don't have time! We have to get out."

He flashed her a tortured glance, face twisted in anguish and desperation. "She has to be Mortal...they'll send her back. Open the dormitories. Set them free. Please!"

Tears were streaming down his face, leaving dirty gray tracks on his cheeks. Maker, he was beautiful. And yet his tears terrified her. His emotion for this one girl drew him into unfathomable danger. He would do the same for any one of them, she knew. Already, he was looking around him, at the faces crowded on the lowest bunk, the ten more sitting above them. The aging woman and the man with one arm missing. And she knew instantly his thoughts:

How many? How many could he save? How much time did he have?

But it wasn't a matter of time. She knew he would stay and save as many of them as he could until they either hauled him away or killed him.

For a moment she stood rooted to the floor, afraid to leave him. Afraid he would give not only Kaya but the man behind her—and the woman behind him—and the girl behind her—his blood. Until it was gone. It took a pint to bring a Mortal to life. He would empty himself out without reserve or thought of his own life to save them.

And that frightened her most of all.

"Please!" He had his sleeve rolled up, was digging at the permanent stub in his vein.

With a glance at Kaya's stricken face, Jordin tore herself away.

Panic flooded Rom's veins at the sound of the siren. For an instant, he told himself that he had no way of knowing where it came from exactly. Perhaps it was a fire. An emergency on this side of the city.

And then the lights went on.

He raced around the last dock of the garbage center, making his way directly for the walled perimeter of the Authority of Passing.

He knew the place. Had known it always, been conscious of it since the first day Avra had asked for his help after her accident, so many years ago.

She had avoided the Authority, and for that she had been out of Order her entire life. Doomed, by any standard of Order's Maker, to suffer Hades even now in the afterlife.

The stallion labored, neck lifting and dropping with the effort to run. It had had a short-lived new burst beneath Rom's slightly lighter weight, but now each step came with more difficulty than the last, as though they traveled through tar.

He reached the far end of the concrete perimeter. Turned the horse down along the concrete wall past the ominous suns of Sirin's halo in his peripheral vision.

Just before the northwest corner of the perimeter, he slid to the ground as the horse staggered to a stop on unsteady legs.

And then he ran.

Building Nine. Open. The inhabitants had huddled as far back from the door as possible. Several of them screamed as the full blast of the siren invaded the darkness.

Building Eight. Open.

She could hear the guards shouting outside the gate. Smell them, far more ripe than she expected in a sea of Corpses such as this. They were terrified to enter this place of death, unaccustomed to the disruption that had invaded their world.

Overhead, the sky flashed again. Thunder interrupted the wail of the siren as the first fat drops of rain pelted her scalp through her braids. Something in her mind whispered louder than the siren in her ears.

Maker's Hand.

But the Maker's Hand was superstition. It didn't exist.

Seven. Open.

She raced toward the middle walk to see if the guards were approaching, but they were there still at the gate. Pointing. Waiting. It could mean only one thing: reinforcements.

Six buildings left. But what was the use? So few of the condemned had even come out of the buildings she'd opened, too afraid to leave the confines of their prisons.

But she knew now that Jonathan needed them as much as they needed him. This was his purpose, to save the dead from themselves.

She gauged the distance from the roofs of the buildings to the concrete wall. Too far to leap—and even if they did, it was covered in wire. One tangle, one slip, and Jonathan might be too injured to escape. The girl would never make the jump.

Movement to her right grabbed her attention, and she spun to see Jonathan, climbing up onto the roof of Kaya's dormitory, wind raising the braids off his back, his pants plastered against his legs in the wind.

What was he doing?

"I've come to bring you life!" he shouted. His voice competed with the wail of the siren. The harsh light was in his braids, illuminating each one of them in stark and vivid clarity to her Mortal-enhanced eyes. His jacket was off, his one sleeve still rolled up. The veins in his neck stood out like cords from the open neck of his tunic.

"I give you life beyond any you have known. Life from my veins." He thrust out his bared arm. "Life of my blood. All who take it will live!"

She stared, unable to tear her gaze away.

He's magnificent.

And then: *He's mad.*

A white-hot bolt of lightning blazed down through the clouds like a crooked finger to the far south corner's bank of lights. They went out in a shower of sparks. Screams ripped through the compound.

"I've come to bring a new kingdom of life!" Jonathan was pointing at those who'd ventured out on shaking legs like dead emerging from tombs. But she knew they would not be freed. It didn't matter that the doors were open. It wouldn't matter if the twenty-foot walls fell to the ground. Their prisons did not exist in concrete or barbed wire.

A distant squeal. She knew that sound. The underground. Reinforcements.

The new scent hit her like a locomotive. It rushed through the compound, born on the gust of a rising storm.

She turned just in time to see them arrive at the gate.

Dark Bloods.

Rom's knives were in his hands as he rounded the corner of the perimeter. He smelled them before he saw them: two Dark Bloods and two guards at the gate, armed with swords. Jonathan's and Jordin's horses were tied to a rail halfway between the corner of the perimeter and the gate itself.

A cry rang out from inside the compound. "I've come to bring a new kingdom of life!"

A second car had entered the train tunnel. He could hear it, lower pitched than the siren; could pick out with Mortal ears the beat of the wheels churning on the track.

More Dark Bloods...

He whistled once, tongue curled hard against his upper lip as he rushed the Dark Bloods. Four heads spun toward him. He threw the knives in a swift volley, underhanded. The first caught a Dark Blood square between the eyes. The second never reached its target—the warrior reacted too swiftly, snatching the knife from the air and launching it back before his companion hit the ground.

Rom dropped to his knees and slid the last five yards as the knife whirred overhead. The Dark Blood was already closing, rushing in. Rom grabbed the hilt of his sword, freed it, but the Dark Blood was too fast. His foot came down on the blade, pinning it to the ground as he slid his own weapon free.

Rom rolled to his feet. The Dark Blood rushed forward, sword slashing through the rain. Rom threw himself to his right to avoid the blade. He felt the tug on his shirt as the sword sliced through the material. Too close...

He lunged forward and slammed into the Dark Blood with enough force to send him reeling back.

The distinctive sound of steel smacking into flesh drew his momentary attention to the gate where one of the guards spun and staggered back against the iron bars, clawing at a knife in his jugular. Beyond, the blurred vision of Jordin, who'd thrown the knife, pulled up sharply, hands empty, which meant only one thing: she was out of blades.

The squeal of sparking brakes cut the air as the underground car came charging up out of the tunnel a hundred yards away. Six forms inside.

Rom saw it all in the space of a second, even as the Dark Blood recovered and came again, more measured this time, sword in both hands. Rom dipped down and snatched his last knife from his boot, knowing that he was outmatched by his opponent, who was quicker and armed with a much longer blade.

The heavens opened in earnest.

To his left a form sprinted down the length of the concrete perimeter headed pell-mell for the Dark Blood. Triphon. He grabbed the hilt of Jonathan's sword as he ran past the horses, yanked it free without breaking stride.

"Triphon!"

The Dark Blood's eyes darted to the new threat. Rom moved then, while the warrior's attention was divided. He sprang toward the remaining guard at the gate, leaving the Dark Blood for Triphon, knowing full well his back was exposed.

He reached the guard in five long steps and plunged his knife into the man's neck as the sound of Triphon's bulk colliding with the Dark Blood joined the rolling thunder.

Rom spun to see them crashing to ground. The rain was so heavy now that for a moment he couldn't tell which form was which.

A scream. "Triphon!"

Rom spun to see Jordin at the gate, eyes wide. Starring past him.

He jerked back around. Triphon lay on top of the Dark Blood, barely stirring. A chill washed down Rom's neck.

A shout cut through the rain from within the compound. "I bring you life not seen in this world. A new kingdom!"

Rom heard each word as if cried from a separate disconnected reality. Life. But the scene before him whispered death.

Triphon rolled over onto his back, fingers clawing at his chest. At the sword still protruding from it. Rom's lungs seized. The Dark Blood lay still with Triphon's sword buried in his throat.

His friend coughed once. For a moment he looked to laugh up to the sky. Then his hand fell down to the earth. Still.

The Dark Bloods in the train would swarm them at any moment.

Jordin stood unmoving, staring at Triphon's fallen form beyond the gate.

"Jordin!" Rom was at the gate, turning the key. "They're coming!"

She twisted toward the compound behind her. "Jonathan! We have to go!"

His head snapped toward her, braids sodden, clothes stuck to the hard panes of his chest.

"Now!" she screamed.

He dropped to his seat, skidded down the slope of the roof and emerged from around the end of the building with Kaya, who was wearing his coat. Together they tore down the broken walk, past a crowd of wide-eyed Corpses, not slowing until they reached the gate, just open enough against the bulk of three bodies to let them out one at a time.

Jonathan faltered, staring at Rom as he knelt over Triphon's fallen form, frantically checking for signs of life. If Triphon had been a Corpse, they would be able to smell the scent of death. Because he was Mortal, only breath or pulse would tell the truth.

There was neither.

Dark Bloods began to pile out of the train car. Rom jerked his head up, hesitated only a moment, then sprang to his feet. There was no time to take Triphon's body as long as Jonathan was at risk.

"The horses! Go!" he cried, urgently waving them on.

Jordin grabbed Jonathan's arm and tugged. "Run!"

He scooped up Kaya and ran ahead of Jordin. They

threw themselves into the saddles, Jordin behind Jonathan, Kaya and Rom on the other horse.

Shouts from behind. A knife whisked harmlessly past Jordin's head.

And then they were riding in a full gallop through the veil of a heavy downpour.

CHAPTER TWENTY-FOUR

ROLAND KNEW FROM THE SLIGHT but immediate tic beneath Saric's eye that he'd struck the right chord in offering up Jonathan. He pressed his advantage while it was still his.

"And it's not what you think," he said.

"You presume to know what I think," Saric said.

"You think I'm a man who would deceive you as I have. I would assume the same in your position."

The man was a column in black, tall in the saddle, fingers like claws and arms all too obviously corded with muscle beneath his tunic sleeves. A powerful man, no pretender, and no fool.

A man of destiny like himself.

Despite the tic, he listened in silence—a sign of surety and resolve.

"What I have to say, you will want to hear," Roland said. "All I ask is that you hear it alone."

Still no reaction. Just that dark stare, so like a vulture's on a fresh piece of carrion. This was not turning into the kind of confrontation Roland had anticipated.

"I have men in the trees above us. If I wanted to engage

you, I would have without first exposing myself. I want no bloodshed. Only peace. But for that I must talk to you alone."

"Who are you to speak to me alone?"

"Roland Akara. Prince of the Nomads."

Saric seemed unaffected by his name.

"You see the man on my left?" Saric said. "His name is Brack. I am the kinder soul between us. I pity you if any harm were to come to me."

Roland gave the man a curt nod. "You see the woman behind me? Her name is Michael. She is one of a thousand like her. I pity you if any of them led our people in a mission to strike, unseen, like serpents when you least expected it."

Saric nodded slowly. "Brack, follow."

Saric flipped his reins and guided his mount forward, toward the barren land rising to the west, away from the trees. Brack fell in behind, eyes on Roland.

He turned his horse and rode parallel to them until Saric pulled up and faced him, fifty paces from the others. Michael held her position, along with the entire Dark Blood army. The breeze had fallen off—they were no doubt stifling and sweating in their armor, but black granite would have moved more.

"You have your audience," Saric said. "Speak."

"You are aware of the Nomads."

Saric didn't respond.

"For generations we resisted Order. Our breeding runs deep and our purpose is simple. We would survive outside of this religion that holds the dead hostage to lies. We want one thing: freedom. And we want it without any harm to others."

"What does this have to do with Jonathan?"

"We have no ambition for power. Our joining with Jonathan was only done in service to a Sovereign who promised to unveil the truth once he came into office. What that meant for us is that as a people we would no longer have to live out of Order. We would pursue life in peace. But that has changed. You changed it. Feyn is Sovereign, and because of that Jonathan can never be. Any struggle for his claim now would be futile."

Saric nodded. "Go on."

"I find myself between two enemies. You, who would protect Feyn's Sovereignty, and Jonathan, whom others hope will seize it from her. My duty is to protect my people. As their prince, I would pay any price to ensure their safety."

He let the statement stand.

"You are offering to give me the boy," Saric said.

"I am offering to save both of us limitless bloodshed and ensure the future of my people. If one man must die to that end, so be it. Many thousands of lives will be saved."

"I'm to believe you have both the means and the will to betray the one you have sworn to protect? I see no gain for you. I could take Jonathan and still hunt your kind down."

"I have the means but my delivery of him will be my proof. And my gain would be this: an irrevocable mandate passed by the senate and ratified by Feyn giving Nomads the freedom to live out of Order and suffer whatever destiny the Maker sees fit to grant us in return."

Saric's lips twisted slightly. "Surely you don't believe in the Maker's end."

"I believe in life, now, as it was meant to be lived. And so your senate would offer me full authority to rule my people as I see fit, with our own government, recognized by Order. And I will be welcome at the Citadel as a foreign ruler as long as my people pose no threat to peace."

Saric studied him for several seconds. Whether or not the Overlord trusted him, he couldn't tell, but he seemed to be pleased. Or at least, he smelled like it, assuming Roland had correctly identified the scent.

Roland waited.

"I find your proposal absurd," Saric said at last. "Order cannot be turned on its head at the whim of one Nomad. What assurance would I have that you would give me the boy?"

"Then you admit acquiring him is in your interest?"

"Anyone who poses a threat to the legitimate Sovereign is a person of interest to me."

"And yet you yourself pose a threat to her office and the Order it serves by building an army prohibited by Order. You have your purpose; I have mine. We are not so different."

"You are too bold, Nomad."

"I am the seventeenth prince to rule my people. We have always been bold. But not once has our purpose diverted from our sacred calling to be separate. I have no intention of allowing that purpose to fail us now. I went to great lengths to bring you here."

"You could have come to me."

"It was necessary that you understood our commitment and strength. We want peace, but not enough to die quietly."

"Assuming I granted this freedom, you might still rise against me one day."

"To what end?"

"To rule more than your own."

"At the expense of my people? You don't know as much as you assume."

Saric's horse pawed the earth beneath him. The Dark Blood tilted his head.

"They say you believe yourselves to have found life. Is it true?"

"Yes," Roland said. "And we aim to keep that life, not shed it in a war that isn't our own."

"Assuming I were to agree, how would you deliver the boy?"

"You will push the mandate through the senate immediately. Once it is ratified by the Sovereign, I will lead you to him. Not just to him—but also to the Keepers who have vowed to see him in power."

"And if the Sovereign fails to sign?"

Roland shrugged. "Then you would have an enemy you don't care to have."

He could see the man's mind at work, searching for any weakness in the agreement.

"Brack?"

Saric's man hesitated only a moment before speaking. "I see no challenge to your purpose, my Lord."

Naturally. They were both fully aware that any law passed by the senate would not stand in Saric's way if he chose to force his hand. He could and would come after any Nomad if he saw any threat in them... at any time.

"I will agree to your terms," Saric said. "But if you do not give me the boy before his eighteenth birthday, I withdraw my agreement."

He started to turn his mount.

"There is but one more thing," Roland said. "A guarantee."

Saric paused, arched a brow at him.

"You will give us Feyn to hold until the exchange is made."

A smile slowly distorted his face. "Feyn?"

"I am no more a fool than you. I will care for her as one of my own. No harm will come to her."

"Only a fool would demand the Sovereign as surety."

"You say this, but you already know that we won't hurt her. If Feyn were to die, you would be Sovereign. You have nothing to lose."

"You know more than you let on, Nomad. Perhaps I underestimated you."

"Our resolve to be left alone in peace has been bred in us for centuries. I do what is necessary to that end."

"I will present this to my Sovereign," Saric said.

"I assumed she served you, my Lord."

Saric gave him a bland look. "Then you assume too much."

"Either way."

"Either way, you have your agreement. If Feyn is not here, in this valley, in two days' time consider that agreement cancelled."

He started to turn.

"Tomorrow," Roland said. "If you require the boy before he comes of age, we have little time."

Saric glanced at him for a long moment, then kicked his horse.

"Tomorrow," he said.

CHAPTER TWENTY-FIVE

THEY RODE HARD FOR AN HOUR, glancing back frequently to be certain they weren't being followed, expecting to see Dark Bloods in pursuit at any moment. But there was no sign of them.

As long as they were in motion, Rom was able to comfort himself with the knowledge that he'd saved Jonathan from what would have been certain death. Every step was another toward safety, but the truth of the matter dug incessantly into his mind like a tick burrowing for blood. Nothing was safe. Nothing was right, nothing made sense. He might have saved the boy for now, but the world was collapsing around them.

Divisions were mounting among the Mortals. Saric had raised an army to destroy them all. Feyn had given her allegiance to Saric. Jonathan seemed to have lost his mind. Triphon was dead.

Rom led them into a wash to rest the horses and gather himself.

Triphon. Dead.

It was unfathomable. The bull of a man who had been Rom's second-in-command was impervious to threat, fear, or injury. His closest friend from those first days when they'd both drunk the Keeper's blood and committed themselves to its implicit charge could not die.

And yet he had. The image haunted him. Triphon, rolling off the Dark Blood and onto his back, hand grasping the sword in his chest. The same bloodied hand, falling to the earth.

More than once, Rom thought of sending the others on and going back. To be certain, just in case. But he already knew what he would find. He'd found no pulse and no breath. If there'd been any trace of life left in the man, it was now gone—the Dark Bloods would have made certain of that in short order. There'd been no way to recover his body without suffering further casualties.

Still, the fact that they'd left their comrade on the ground hounded him. Triphon had given his life to buy their escape. The best thing Rom could do now was to honor his friend by fulfilling their charge to see Jonathan to power.

"We stop here for a few minutes," he said, when they reached the wash. But he didn't immediately dismount. Thoughts flooded his mind like a deluge.

Roland had sent a volunteer as a spy to be captured by Saric. If the mission was successful, the prince might even now be meeting with Saric himself. If so, they had a chance to salvage everything. But acquiring Feyn was only the beginning. Rom still had the herculean task of persuading her to see the truth and recognize Jonathan as rightful Sovereign. He'd helped her find life once, a lifetime ago, but she was in Saric's clutches now.

If he failed to persuade Feyn...Maker help them. The zealots might demand a far more assertive approach. War and death would overtake them all.

Even if they did gain Feyn's support, there was still Jonathan's state, both physical and mental, to consider.

What did it mean that his blood was reverting, and so quickly? According to the Keeper, Jonathan might have the same blood as a Corpse in a matter of weeks, maybe days. How was it possible that the boy who'd been born to bring life was apparently dying?

In two days' time all Mortals would light the celebration fires of the Gathering. They would sing and drink and dance in Nomadic fashion in celebration of the life awakened by Jonathan's blood. Little did they know that the very fountain that had first given them that life was drying up.

Or was the boy's blood only reverting momentarily, gathering for its final push to full maturity? The Keeper had suggested this possibility, and Rom had chosen to embrace it. Nothing else made sense.

But Jonathan's blood wasn't the only problem. Even if the regression was a temporary set back, there was the matter of Jonathan's psychological well-being. Instead of preparing for rulership, he was courting an obsessive fascination with Corpses, willing to risk the lives of millions who might find life for the sake of one child.

Rom finally slid of his horse and glanced at Jonathan. Perhaps he was too young. What childhood had he ever known, this future Sovereign raised in secret and coveted for his blood? Was this fascination with this Corpse girl a simple need for the company of those who demanded or asked nothing of him?

Had they all failed him in such a basic way that his loneliness drove him to risk his entire destiny to satisfy some deep-seated need? His frustration with the boy eased.

He reached for Kaya and lowered her to the ground.

The girl had been pointing at the sky, blinking into the rain as they rode, occasionally closing her eyes as it washed away the grime-streaked tears on her face.

More than once he had found her fingering the beaded cuff of his sleeve. She had almost fallen from the horse completely when she had stretched out over the pommel to lay her hand against the horse's neck, to touch the braids of its mane, feel the bristle of that short equine hair against her palm.

Any Corpse might have wondered what was wrong with her, but Rom knew exactly the cause of her rapt fascination. She was in the throes of new life.

So then... at least his blood was still strong enough to make other Mortals. Perhaps it was regaining strength. Perhaps...

Rom squeezed his eyes shut. His head hurt.

Kaya had fallen down to the ground to grab up a handful of earth. An instant later, she was sobbing, her wet hair clinging to her cheek, hands dug into the dirt. Jonathan hurried over, knelt beside her on one knee and whispered in her ear.

Rom glanced over at Jordin, just returned from a cursory circle of the area. She was as soaked as were they all, though the ground here was dry.

"We aren't being followed," she said. She glanced back at the storm clouds just now breaking over the southeast corner of the city. "Not even by the storm."

He knew what she was thinking, despite her aversion to superstition. The Maker's Hand. Nature itself seemed to have gathered to join Jonathan in protest over the Authority of Passing. But there had been nothing supernatural in this. Triphon was dead! They had barely gotten out alive.

He left Jonathan with the girl and stalked over to her. "A word, Jordin."

She dismounted and followed him to a small rise beyond Jonathan's hearing.

"What were you thinking?"

Jordin looked off in the direction of the abating storm. Her resolve surprised him.

"Do you have any idea what you've done?"

"I was protecting my Sovereign," she said in a low, steely tone.

Frustration, anger...admiration...all welled up within him at once.

"Protecting? This is your idea of keeping him from harm?"

"He doesn't take orders from me," she said, still not looking him in the eye.

"But you take orders from me. You will *never* allow Jonathan to leave camp again without my knowledge or permission."

"I can't promise that," she said.

"Excuse me?"

She hadn't even blinked. "I can't." Now she looked at him. "He's my Sovereign. I serve you, but I serve him first. If what he says contradicts you, I will follow him."

For an instant he flashed back to Roland questioning Jonathan's ability to inspire confidence—or to lead at all. And yet Jordin was following him without question. There was something in his way that inspired. But was it true leadership on his part or simply devotion on hers?

"You're in love with him," he said.

"He's my Sovereign," she replied, a little too quickly.

He glanced back at Jonathan. He was still on his knee

talking quietly with the girl, who had stopped weeping and pushed back onto her heels to listen to him.

"I love him too, Jordin. And truth be told, I'm glad he has you by his side." He looked at her. "But I beg you, for the sake of the kingdom, tell me when he demonstrates any such irrational behavior, yes? He's my Sovereign as well, and I need to know."

She dipped her head. "I'm sorry about Triphon."

Now he could see that her eyes were red at the edges. He hadn't noticed her crying during their flight from the city, but then, he'd noticed little except his own desperation.

Again, the image of Triphon's bloody hand falling to the ground filled Rom's mind.

"I know he was like a brother to you," Jordin said.

He nodded once, felt his jaw tighten, said nothing. The eddy of so many thoughts at once threatened to drown him.

Other than Feyn, he was the only one remaining of those who had first tasted life from the Keeper's vial. Avra. Triphon. Neah. Feyn.

It all came down to Feyn, and now even she might be beyond his grasp. No. Roland had to be successful in convincing Saric that he had every intention of giving up Jonathan, however treasonous the thought.

They had shielded the truth about Jonathan from the rest of the Nomads, but they couldn't do it indefinitely. Once they knew that their own blood was more potent than Jonathan's, how many of them—given the choice of protecting the Mortal race versus Jonathan—would choose the life in their own veins over that waning within his?

Would he?

That he could even ask himself the question terrified him.

Jordin was studying him intently.

Maker. He couldn't think these thoughts in front of her. Though none of them could read minds, Mortal perception was far too keen. And he was too raw to school himself well.

He broke from her gaze and nodded toward the girl.

"Take that girl . . ." He stopped, lost for her name.

"Kaya," Jordin said.

"Take Kaya. I need a word with Jonathan."

She hesitated only a moment then headed back and collected her horse.

"Kaya? Why don't you come with me? We'll water the horses."

The girl glanced up with a wondering smile, as though having already forgotten that she had been weeping just a moment ago. And then she got to her feet, not bothering to brush off her hands or the knees of her pants. Jonathan watched her go off with Jordin, who handed the girl the reins to her own mount as they walked farther down the creek bed.

Rom waited as Jonathan stood to his feet, struck by the onslaught of emotion that overcame him now that they were alone. By the time Jonathan turned to him, Rom's hands were shaking.

"I need to know where you stand."

Jonathan's eyes were too placid. Too sorrowful and lucid and seeing at once. He *wasn't* mad—Rom of all people could see it. But if that were so, he was frightened all the more because it meant the boy had purposes Rom could not understand.

Railing at the boy would do no good, so he willed the tremor in his hands to still.

"What do you need to know?" Jonathan said.

All efforts at control instantly crumbled at that simple question.

"I need to know *why*, Jonathan." He lifted his clenched fists, and, finding nothing to grasp at but air, dropped them helplessly. "Please. Help me understand!"

The boy was quiet, which only added fuel to the surge of desperate confusion within him.

"In all the years I've known you, you've never taken such risk," Rom said. "Never risked such danger to yourself. Why now? Surely you know the stakes!"

Jonathan watched him with sad eyes. "I do know the stakes. And do you know me?"

"What do you mean do I know you? Of course I know you! Wasn't I the one who found you as a boy in your mother's house? Who told you about the prophecy? Who's guided and watched over you all these years? How can you ask if I know you?"

Jonathan remained silent.

Those had been desperate days of discovery for them. He'd lost Avra in his quest to protect the boy. He'd committed his life to the cause of his kingdom. Was it so strange, then, that he should feel a sense of betrayal?

But even in recognizing it, he felt guilt. Who was he to berate the Sovereign of the world?

"What do you want, Jonathan? Tell me what you need."

"Do you love me, Rom?"

"Love you? I've given you my life! We all have. And now Triphon..." He choked back a hard lump in his throat, willing himself not to spill emotion. "How can you, of all people, ask me that?"

Jonathan lowered his gaze, his dark lashes girl-like in stark contrast to his masculinity. He was so young still.

"I feel terrible for Triphon." He shifted his gaze toward the distant storm. "But he died knowing the truth. He died alive. How many of those we left behind will die without hope?"

"And how many will die without hope if you fail to take power? Triphon died for that cause, not for a single Corpse among millions! As would we all. Jordin. Roland. Me."

"Will you die for me...or I for you?"

The question hit Rom like a battering ram. It was true, Jonathan had poured himself out all of these years, never once complaining that his own lifeblood was poured out for their gain.

"You can't think any of us mean to drain you of life. You *must live*. For me, for Jordin, for the world!" He flung his hand out, exasperated. "The thought of failing you... How can you say such a thing?"

"Then follow me, Rom. When the time comes, see that the world finds life through my blood. Life more true than even you can know." Did Jonathan have any inkling that his blood was reverting? The Keeper had said no.

"I do follow you. I will—that's not the point! You must live and fulfill your purpose to that end. And to that end you have to allow me to protect you now! This isn't just about making Mortals, Jonathan, but about your people."

"And who are my people?"

"Mortals! The ones whose veins flow with your blood! The ones who are alive."

Horse hooves, coming up through the wash—Kaya and Jordin, their voices carrying like birdsong over the running of the brook.

Jonathan turned his head toward the sound.

"Even those alive can still be dead," he said, and walked away.

CHAPTER TWENTY-SIX

FEYN WALKED DOWN THE MARBLE hallway of Saric's fortress, struck by the severe arch of the ceiling, the ancient and emotive art lining the walls, the red silk that hung from ceiling to floor. Broad candelabras boasting candles a foot in diameter cast pools of amber light at regular intervals through the passage. Gold and crystal chandeliers hung from long chains twenty paces apart, their light extinguished for now in favor of the candles that illuminated the hallway as though it were the dark path through a garden of silk and illusion. So darkly immaculate. Kingly. Saric had always been a man of taste, and his attention to detail here was no exception.

They'd come for her late in the afternoon. Four Dark Bloods and Saric's chief alchemist, Corban. Saric would see her, they said, tonight, in his fortress outside the city. She was to make arrangements to be gone three days.

She'd quickly set things straight with her servants and with Dominic, who would explain her departure as a time to rest and recover—an understandable course considering all that had happened the last few days.

"Your brother will be with you?" Dominic had asked.

"He may join me. This is a concern to you?"

He'd lowered his head. "Only if it concerns you, my Lady."

"Then have no fear, Dominic. I serve the Maker."

He dipped his head. "And I serve you, my Sovereign."

"Then Saric is not your concern."

He didn't respond, but his silence voiced his insecurities in the matter loudly enough.

"Say what's on your mind, Dominic."

After a moment he said what she knew he would. "There is talk, my Lady. About the warriors who serve Saric and his intention to use them as a means of force. The law strictly forbids any use of force or the building of an army for any purpose."

"And yet we have the Citadel guard to protect us."

"Yes...And Saric has killed more than one of our guard. You heard about the incident at the Authority of Passing today, I'm sure. Violence comes to us with his Dark Bloods. His words in the senate have not fallen on deaf ears. Fear grips the hall."

"Then put their minds to ease, Dominic. Order provides for a personal guard to protect any Sovereign at their request. The Dark Bloods serve me in this way."

"Then Saric serves you."

"The whole world serves the Sovereign as much as I serve the world."

"And yet Saric claims the world to be dead..."

"Yes, well. You must allow him some of these thoughts. My brother gave me life in a manner that few can understand. You can appreciate how that might affect him."

He'd nodded slightly.

"Obviously I am alive. And as living Sovereign, I

expect the senate to accept my choice of guard. Saric is in charge of my security until I choose otherwise. Is that clear?"

"Yes, my Lady. Of course."

"His guard will be embraced as my own. Any word against them is a word against me."

"I understand."

"Thank you, Dominic. Serve me well, and I may open your eyes to a new life."

He bowed his head again. "As you wish."

She'd left Byzantium with Corban and the Dark Bloods and ridden north on horseback five miles into the dusk, until Corban had presented her with a silk hood to wear at Saric's request.

Her first impulse to balk at being blinded had quickly bowed to submission. Saric was her Maker and his request was only an invitation to obey. How was she to refuse?

Three hours later, Corban removed the hood, and she laid eyes on the expansive fortress rising from the night like a monolithic wraith. But the moment she'd set foot inside and the thick wooden door shut behind her, life, not death, flooded her mind.

Saric's life.

"This way, my lady," Corban said, reaching for a tall iron door set back into the wall. He knocked and opened it at the call of Saric from within.

Music filled the air. Stings, vibrant and somber at once. Feyn stepped into a large sanctum that might be Saric's office or his most holy place of meditation. Perhaps both.

He sat behind a large ebony desk with ornately carved legs. Feyn took the room in with a single glance—the large framed paintings of landscapes, the silk tapestries gathered in each corner, the thick rugs on the marble floor, the glass sarcophagus with a naked man inside to her far left—and immediately returned her gaze to him.

She bowed her head. "My Lord."

"Look at me, my child."

She lifted her eyes to his. For a long moment they remained unmoving.

"Corban," he said, still gazing at her. "The prisoner we took at the Authority of Passing still lives?"

"Yes, my Lord. We've repaired the damage to his lungs and he clings to life with the aid of intravenous supplements. The Mortal is surprisingly strong. A lesser man would never have responded to resuscitation."

"And yet dead without the life I give him. Be sure no further harm comes to him. I have use for him only if he's alive."

"Of course, my Lord. I see to it personally. He grows stronger by the hour."

"Thank you, Corban. You may leave us."

Feyn glanced over her shoulder, noting that the two Dark Bloods there had taken a knee, but Corban had only bowed as was his custom. She would learn more of their ways. They were her ways now.

Corban shut the door behind her.

Saric's eyes glittered. He looked pleased to see her, she thought. The realization flooded her with gratitude. He wore a black jacket over a white shirt opened to reveal his pale chest. A thick silver chain with a pendant of a serpentine phoenix hung from his neck.

He tapped long fingers on the ebony top. She noticed, belatedly, that he had darkened his nails.

"Thank you for coming on such short notice, my love."

She walked to the middle of the room, feeling under-dressed in her riding pants and leather jacket.

"I came as quickly as I could."

"You're pleased to see me?" he asked.

Her desire to please him surprised her even now, but there was more. A scent in the room that called to her like the smell of the sea.

"More than you can know."

"Actually, I know it quite well. You're bound to me, sister. What you do not yet know is that you can't live without me."

He walked around the desk, studied her with approval and lifted his hand. She knelt, took the hand in her own, and kissed his fingers. But this time, the scent of his skin awakened a sudden swell of urgency within her. Her ears began to ring and her head felt so light that for a moment she thought she might faint.

Saric chuckled softly. "The craving, yes?"

Craving? Feyn lifted her eyes.

"What is it?"

"Life, my love. My life. In good time." He pulled his hand away and crossed to one of two large wingbacked chairs before a circular table that looked to have been carved from a single piece of amber granite. A bottle of red wine and two crystal glasses sat on a silver tray.

"Sit with me, Feyn."

She followed him and sat down in the chair angled toward his. The cylindrical glass sarcophagus stood directly across the room, openly displaying its lifeless occupant. The sight, cursory on first glance, chilled her this time.

"Pravus," Saric said. "My Maker."

"He's dead?"

"He lives in me now. Such a beautiful creature, wouldn't you agree?"

She wasn't sure how she felt about the pallid body, but she quickly submitted her confusion and embraced Saric's point of view.

"Yes," she said. "Quite."

"Yes." He gazed at the sarcophagus with gentle eyes that suggested more than mere appreciation. And then he took up the bottle of wine, plucked the cork out with strong fingers, and filled each glass half full. Replacing the cork, he set the bottle back down and offered her one of the glasses.

"To the life that conquers death." He lifted his glass, eyes on her.

"To life," she said, and took a drink. The bite of tannin and fermented grape lingered in her mouth and slipped down her throat like heat. She felt the effect of the wine almost immediately; the weakness that had nearly overcome her when she'd smelled his skin had not passed.

Was this what it was to crave—to live through the life of another?

If so, she wondered what kind of life could demand death? Saric had been brought to life by Pravus, and yet he'd taken his Maker's life. It was difficult to imagine such a profane act of rebellion, unless it had been demanded by the master. Had Pravus demanded Saric kill him, then?

And if he ever required it, would she capable of such a thing? No! Perhaps. No, impossible. The mere thought was laden with deep offense.

"There are times when life must be taken," Saric said, as though having read her thoughts on her face. "But only when that life is in direct conflict with greater life. Do you understand this?"

"Yes, my Lord."

"Tell me."

It was his way, of late, to lead her with questions, to bring her along gently so that she could best serve him. So she could fulfill her purpose as one made in his image.

"You took his life because it was weaker than your own. It stood in the way of a greater life. Yours."

"Life, Feyn. It's all that matters in this dead world. We who live will subdue the earth and rule the dead as we see fit. And I saw fit to make my subjects dependent upon me in a way Pravus did not. It's why you crave my blood."

"My Lord?"

He lifted the back of his hand to her face. The scent of his skin filled her nostrils again, and her pulse quickened as the craving flooded her, stronger than the first time.

Saric removed his hand. "All of my children need me, but in different ways. The ones born from their chambers need to obey me. Their loyalty is secured through alchemy. But you, Feyn, were brought to life with my own blood. Blood you require to live."

"So . . . without your blood . . . I die?"

"Yes." He smiled. "If I were to die, you would as well. We are truly one, you and I."

Cold and then heat washed down Feyn's back. She required his blood to live? Surely he was speaking in metaphorical, not physical, terms!

"How?" she asked.

"You must be injected with a portion of my blood on a regular basis or you die. It's been three days since I brought you to life. You feel weak now, don't you? You have a craving you can't understand."

She swallowed. Her fingers were trembling, and she

drew them in so he would not see it and know her anxiousness over this thought.

He ran his hand over her head and down her hair to settle her. "Never fear, my love. As long as I live and you take my blood every three days, you will live a long life full of beauty and power. Tonight, Corban will help you feed."

For the briefest of moments, she hated him. Her very life was caged! It wasn't enough that he had her service and her loyalty, but he would rule her very survival?

Then the thought passed and she allowed other, more constructive thoughts to bathe her mind. She was alive because of Saric. Were not all creatures dependent on their Makers? So then, she should only feel gratitude for the life he had given her, regardless of what she must do to keep it. Was it not the same with the Maker of all? That the one who accepted his way need not be condemned to eternal death?

"But that is not the only reason I sent for you," he said, his hand falling away from her. He set his glass down, leaned back in his chair, and folded one leg over the other.

"I have something I need you to do for us. The Nomads have approached me with a request. They have agreed to give me the boy in exchange for a new law that gives them full standing as an autonomous government outside of Order."

Her interest in Saric's blood waned for a moment in light of this new turn.

They would give up the boy? But that would mean that he would die. Surely they knew that!

Then why would Rom agree to it?

"Rom would betray him?"

"Roland, the Nomad Prince."

Acting without Rom's knowledge?

"And you would grant this?"

"No. Nor am I so foolish as to think they would turn the boy over. But they have also demanded to hold you until the law passes. They demand the Sovereign as collateral."

He regarded her, rocking his one leg over the other. "What would you advise?"

She considered the question, knowing that he already had a specific answer in mind. It was his way, these questions. And she knew the answer already.

"They don't know the depths of my loyalty to you," she said. "But you do. Grant their request."

His right brow lifted. "To what end, my love?"

"So that I can learn what you need to know about our enemies."

A smile tugged at his lips. "It could be dangerous."

"They know that if they kill me, you become Sovereign."

"You're saying they would prefer you as Sovereign over me?"

"I would help them believe so. It only ensures my safety and draws their trust."

He studied her for several moments. When he spoke next, his tone had changed. Gone, the gentle Maker. Here, then, was the master who demanded absolute obedience.

"You will go tomorrow with the sole objective of learning their strengths, their true numbers, and where they hide. If possible, you will win the boy's trust. In three days you will return. If you don't, you will die. They must understand this."

"And their request for an autonomy, my Lord?"

He waved a hand. "It goes nowhere. Tell them it's in process if you must."

"If they try to turn me?"

"They can't. As you yourself told me, the boy's blood is lethal to our kind."

She nodded. Another wave of light-headedness darkened her sight. She'd felt fine again until a moment ago, and then weakness came upon her like a flood. She would have to remember how quickly life ebbed from her body.

Saric was speaking again... She hadn't heard his first words.

"...quickly. Very quickly. In an hour you would be dead." His hand touched hers.

"Come with me. I will feed you."

CHAPTER TWENTY-SEVEN

ROM PACED NEAR THE BANKS of the Lucrine River, glancing up for the second time in the last five minutes to consider the position of the sun's dull glow above a thin blanket of stratus clouds. An hour past noon. He bowed his head, willed nerves that had steadily frayed over the last hour to calm. Perhaps they had had trouble finding the place.

But no...just yesterday Saric had come here with his entire army.

A dozen scenarios collided in his mind. Perhaps Saric had reconsidered and broken his word. Maybe Feyn had been compromised or imprisoned or, worse, killed. What if the Dark Bloods had found the Mortal camp in the Seyala Valley and were marching there even now?

Perhaps Feyn had balked at the idea and refused to come. Or knew a better way. Or had a plan she would get to him via other means. Surely she wasn't as untouched by the Mortal mission as she seemed.

He schooled his thoughts and glanced at the river where Javan, one of the men who'd accompanied him, watered his horse. He was one of the most skilled Nomadic scouts.

Telvin, one of Rom's Keepers, sat on his mount on the hill, silhouetted against the sky. He would be the first to see any approach.

The river was young in its banks, the waters of an older river that had changed course in the last half century. In the world of Order, it was the same waterway—one that had deviated from its proper path. But by Nomadic standards, the new waterway constituted a new creation, and as such had merited a new name as well. The nomads called it Chava. The name meant "life"—the battle cry, manifesto, hope, and purpose of every Mortal. The Nomadic map was littered with such altered names for valleys, grasslands, and waterways.

Here the name was well given, Rom thought. The ground offered up pine and young oak near the river's banks, and olive trees—a small natural grove of them— some thirty feet away. The tree had meant peace in the ancient world, he was told. He hoped it would mean the same today.

Across the valley, the eastern hills opened to the southern plains. Even from here, Rom could see the evidence of Saric's army in the churned earth. Roland's report of the Dark Blood's numbers had kept him awake half the night. He'd risen at dawn even more aware of the critical nature of his meeting with Feyn. It might be as doubtful as Roland insisted, but there was no better path before them. Surely, it was either this or war.

He squinted to the south, drew a long breath.

"How much longer do you want to wait?" Javan said, leading his horse up from the bank. He spoke as though Rom waited for the dead to rise.

But Rom had seen Corpses rise before.

"As long as it takes."

"How do we know they haven't drawn us away from camp and aren't even now—"

"Do you doubt Roland's ability to defend?" Rom snapped.

Javan corrected himself quickly. "Never."

"I thought not."

But truth be told, Rom didn't know how long they could wait. If she wasn't here in the next hour or two, he would have to assume she wasn't coming. Was the Maker determined to see every leg kicked out from beneath them?

He cursed under his breath and started toward his horse. The whistle came then.

Rom snapped his head up and saw Telvin riding down the hill at breakneck speed gesturing toward the southern horizon.

Two riders had rounded the hip of the hill, both in dark leathers. One of them riding a gray stallion. The scent came, faint on the wind. Dark Blood.

Rom's pulse surged.

He could make them out clearly: one man, broad through the shoulders on a horse larger than the other. Riding beside him...Feyn. The tilt of her chin, the dark braid over her shoulder, the gloved hands holding the reins unmistakable.

She had come. Thank the Maker, she had come.

Telvin pulled his mount up and dismounted on the fly. "You see them."

"Yes. Stand by, Javan. No aggression, either of you."

Rom paced, arms crossed, as Feyn and her guard made their way up through the valley with no apparent hurry. Now he could just detect the scent of slight fear. Wariness, on the part of the Dark Blood. Of something else—curiosity. And another scent that he could not place at all.

At fifty paces off, Feyn held back, allowing her escort to approach alone. Javan spat to one side, a common reaction to stench among Nomads. Telvin, to his credit, held his ground, unmoving.

The Dark Blood pulled up, studied them for a moment, then nodded. "You're one man more."

"We didn't know how many to expect," Rom said.

"Send one of your men back."

"Javan. Leave us."

The Nomad stared at him. Clearly he thought himself more qualified to stay. But to his credit, he said nothing, even as he glared at the Dark Blood, walked to his horse, mounted, and wheeled it round.

He would join three other scouts who watched for the inevitable sign of the other Dark Bloods who undoubtedly circled nearby—Saric was no fool and neither was Rom.

"Satisfied?"

"You'll talk in the open," the Dark Blood said.

"Of course. Alone."

The man narrowed his eyes.

"What is your name?" Rom said.

The Dark Blood hesitated. "Janus," he said.

"Then hear me, Janus. The Sovereign has come as surety for an exchange. Neither of us will leave your sight."

He seemed to weigh that, glancing back at Feyn, who gave him a slight nod.

He's concerned for her...

The warrior turned back. "You will leave your horses with me and remain this side of the boulders." He glanced north, where the valley began its bottleneck.

"I will leave my horse with you and my man, Telvin. We will remain in the valley."

The man nodded and nudged his horse toward the bank where Telvin held both his and Rom's mounts. Feyn waited until her escort had stopped and turned back, ten paces from Talvin. Evidently satisfied, she walked her horse slowly forward.

Dark veins beneath her skin traced her neck and along her cheek like faint claws beneath the diffused daylight. Fathomless eyes watched him like peat-filled pools, unable to reflect the light of the sun. She wore no jewelry, only a leather riding coat and tunic, leather pants and boots.

She slipped her foot from the stirrup, swung gracefully from the saddle. Her escort whistled and the horse headed toward the bank, as well trained as any Nomadic mount. Their enemy seemed more refined than Rom would have guessed.

The smell of death, offensive as rancid meat, thickened in his nostrils as Feyn closed the distance between them. She was undeniably Dark Blood.

And still utterly majestic.

"I was told it would be the Nomadic Prince, Roland," she said.

"A change of plans. I only ask that you hear me out."

"This was only a ploy to bring me out. Why?"

"You have nothing to worry about, I assure you."

Her gaze flitted past him, quickly scanned the hills beyond, then settled back on him. She began pulling off her gloves. The bulky ring of her office looked large on such slender fingers.

"Very well, Rom Sebastian. Here we are. Say what you must say."

Rom settled to one knee and dipped his head before looking up. "Thank you, my Lady."

She considered him with frank appraisal and a hint of amusement. "Do we lean on ceremony, then, even here?"

He gave a slight smile and took the hand she extended. As was customary, he kissed her ring, cold against his lips.

"I show respect where it is due," he said.

You knew me once. I convinced you then. Let me turn your heart again.

"The first time I laid eyes on you, you came to my chamber and kidnapped me. And now you kiss my fingers," she said, withdrawing her hand. "Have you become a man of respect?"

"I was always a man of respect, but you know that already."

Rom pushed himself to his feet. During the nine years of Feyn's stasis, Rom's shoulders and legs had hardened from hours in the saddle, from the hunt and endless training. He'd noted the squint of the crow's feet at the corners of his eyes and the slight thickening of his eyebrows.

But Feyn was as tall and slender as she'd been a lifetime ago. Though nine years older, she hadn't aged. She might have been the same woman that he'd known when he was twenty-four.

Might have been.

But then there were those eyes. And the dark veins that flowed with a new blood.

"No more formalities. You obviously went to a lot of trouble to get me out here. Let's not waste time."

"Fair enough." He glanced at his man who could undoubtedly hear them if he chose to listen, despite the distance. "Walk with me."

She walked toward the canyon beside him with a deliberate step, and he was suddenly uncertain of how to begin. Feyn cut the awkward silence first.

"This request for a law to protect Mortals was always a sham."

"Not necessarily, no. As a fallback, I would press for it."

"You have no intention of giving up the boy."

So. Right to the point. But he'd known she'd assume as much the moment she saw that Roland hadn't come as indicated to Saric. They might have been persuaded that the Nomad Prince would betray Jonathan, but never him.

"No."

"Then don't go through the pretense of entertaining or courting me. Say what it is you want."

He walked on in silence, choosing his words carefully before speaking. Clearly, this was going to be a difficult task.

"Well?"

"I want to see what we began nine years ago through to the end. Only you have the power to do that, Feyn."

"Seeing it through may not include Jonathan as you once thought. Despite what you may think, I'm not in a position to command whatever I want."

"You're Sovereign."

"Still so naïve, Rom? I would envy your idealism if it wasn't so misguided."

"Idealism? I would call it destiny. You know what we've both sacrificed to bring this day." He pushed aside the anxiety sweeping in like a storm surge. *Not like this. You won't convince her like this.*

They stepped under the shade of a tree. Telvin and the

Dark Blood hadn't moved from their positions, and they were now far out of hearing range, even for a Mortal.

She turned to him, arms crossed. He had to take her mind back to the place it had once occupied nine years earlier, when she'd first tasted life. Short of that his objective would be lost.

"You already know this is foolishness."

It was her unflinching tone more than the words she used that shook him. Perhaps Roland was right: his hope in Feyn had been borne of irrational emotion over sound logic. As she said, foolishness.

But no. There had to be a trace of true life behind her dark eyes.

"The Order sees Chaos as foolish. Does Saric agree?"

He'd caught her flatfooted, but she replied soon enough. "No."

"And you? Do you believe Chaos was foolish? That the life humans once lived was properly crushed? That any such life should be forbidden today? Is this foolishness?"

"No."

"And yet before I brought you life you found it all foolish. Please don't make the same mistake again. I am no fool."

"No, but we are all misguided on occasion. Maneuvering me out here alone so that you can bend my ear far from Saric is not only idealistic, but foolish."

She saw through all of it.

"We will see," he said.

"I already do."

"Do you?" He glanced at Telvin, who stood near the Dark Blood down valley, idly chewing on a stalk of grass. "Tell me what my man eats now."

She followed his gaze but offered no answer.

"A stalk of sweetgrass. Evidently my sight is far better than yours, as is the sight of all Mortals brought to life by Jonathan's blood."

"You only say that."

"And your man is scratching at something on his neck. He has a rash?"

She blinked. "So you have good eyes," she said. "So does a dog."

"You compare me to an animal?"

"No. Come, Rom, we both know why you've brought me here. You could have sent a runner to tell me why I should give up my Sovereignty for Jonathan's sake. It would have spared us both wasted time. Was your intent to frustrate me?"

"My intent is to use all the resources short of brute strength to help you embrace destiny."

Feyn moved toward the tree trunk and gazed down valley. He let her think for a few minutes and settled on a nearby boulder. They had time.

But Feyn wasn't eager to let time pass. "Let me tell you about destiny, Rom. It's upon us already. I am alive, Sovereign according to every law of succession. Short of my stepping down, there is no way for Jonathan to take my place. But we both know that if I were to step down, Saric would kill me and become Sovereign himself." She looked at him. "That, Rom, is destiny. And it can't be altered. Not now."

"Unless Saric didn't kill you. Unless we found a way to contain him."

"You haven't seen his power."

"No, but Roland has. Don't underestimate the Nomads."

"You're assuming I have any interest in stepping aside."

"No. I'm assuming that you will once you remember who Jonathan is."

"Then you assume wrong. Saric has my undying loyalty."

"Today, yes. Hear me out and that could change."

"I sincerely doubt it."

"Doubts can be erased."

A fire took to her eyes and he wasn't sure if it signified defiance or amusement. Either way, she was set.

"Please, Feyn. Just hear me out."

"Haven't I?"

He stood and joined her. "This isn't about who is or isn't Sovereign, Feyn. Jonathan could co-rule with you. Yes, Saric would have to be dealt with, as would the senate. Undoing death is a massive undertaking, granted. But I would beg you to consider the value of that task. The world must be set free."

"And live as they once lived," she said, looking away again.

"Yes!" He instinctively reached out and touched her arm, thought immediately to remove his hand from her, but left it when she didn't pull away. "We can at least agree on that much as a beginning. I know life. You've known it. If it isn't the duty of the Sovereign to offer life to the people, then what is?"

"You misunderstand me, Rom." She looked up at him. "I *will* bring life. But I will not give up my Sovereignty."

"Then we find another way for Jonathan to rule with you."

"I will bring my life. The life given to me. Not Jonathan's."

His hand fell away.

"Saric's life is no life. Surely you can see that!"

"Isn't it?"

"Life, Feyn! *Life*, as you tasted once. With joy. Hope. Love. You loved once. Or have you forgotten?"

"No. I haven't forgotten." The cords in her neck stood out as she said it. "And I love again."

"Love? Who? *Saric?* You call forced loyalty love?"

"Who are you to dictate to me what love is? What love feels like? I knew love once, for a very short hour with you, Rom. I loved you and you denied me because of Avra. And I couldn't even begrudge you. But I knew even then that a part of you loved me in return."

He'd never admitted his confusing sentiments for Feyn to anyone. They'd felt like a betrayal at the time, as though love, once given, existed only in finite amount and could never be shared or given to another. But hadn't he loved Triphon as surely as he'd loved Avra? As he loved Jonathan, with his whole heart?

As he loved Feyn, still?

"What you feel for Saric now can't be love. Just as the blood in your veins isn't true life."

"Isn't it?" Her brows arched. "Are you so arrogant that you don't think I feel hope for this reign of mine? For what I might bring the world? You don't think I want to be remembered fondly? Treated with love? Do you think that I don't feel the deepest pull of love in my veins this very moment? Who are you to say?"

"It's only alchemy! Chemicals, in your blood!"

"All emotions are caused by chemicals! What is love but the rush of endorphins into your bloodstream?"

He raked a hand through his hair and turned away.

"It's not the same."

"Isn't it?"

"No!" He turned back. "Feyn. Think of Jonathan. Twelve hundred Mortals have come from his veins."

"Twelve *thousand* have come from Saric's."

"Jonathan was *born* with life in his veins! He didn't ingest it, wasn't injected or altered. He was born with it in the line of Sevenths. It's his destiny, not Saric's, to build a new kingdom of life, freed from the slavery of death!"

"Life was taken by altered blood," she said. "Now you say it can't return the same way?"

"Yes! No! But Saric's life is no life. You feel—I can't deny that. You believe you have love, perhaps you do truly love somehow...I don't know. But can't you see Saric's intent is to enslave the world? He has no intention of offering freedom to anyone—least of all you."

There was so much he wanted to say, all carefully rehearsed in logical sequence. But that had fallen by the way now.

"Saric stands against every ounce of true life and freedom in Jonathan's veins! He's not only a dictator, but the enemy of life itself. He would replace one virus that at least brought peace with another that will give him absolute power. We both know that Saric intends to kill you and reign himself. You must have concluded at least that much!"

She glared at him and he prepared for her anger. But as her eyes misted, he couldn't help but gentle his tone.

"Forgive me, I don't mean to be crass. The fact is I can't bear the thought of any harm coming to you. But the law is clear. If you die, Saric is Sovereign. By bringing you back to life, he ensured his own rise to power. It's only a matter of time before he decides the time has come to seize that power."

She didn't snap back with witty comments or arguments that undermined what had to be patently obvious. A storm was brewing in her mind and Rom meant to feed it.

"I only seek to protect your life and ensure Jonathan's destiny. Think with me. You saw the vellum, the prophecy. You believed it. You gave your life for it once; please don't offer your life to undo it all."

"According to you, I was never alive."

"Not true. You were for that day. And it's that part of you that I appeal to now. Tell me, is Jonathan's life false?"

"How do you know that there aren't many ways to life? How egocentric—how ethnocentric—does one need to be to say, 'Mine is the only way'?"

"Who's to say that Saric's life of bondage should be the way?" he snapped. "He will lead you into death as surely as Jonathan would return you to life!"

Rom stepped in front of her and took her hands.

"Feyn," he said, looking into her eyes. "You and I were united once. You believed in the words of Talus, the Keeper whose account you translated that day in the meadow. Do you remember?"

"I do," she said quietly.

"Everything you translated about the blood and Jonathan was true."

Her expression was impassive.

"You gave your *life* for it, Feyn. You're not a woman of rash action, so I understand your struggle now. You were trained to think strategically, methodically, all your life. And yet you *knew*."

She made no effort to argue.

"If all had gone as we planned, you would be waking four days from now—not to Saric's face, but to mine and

Jonathan's. To Mortals who revere you for the price you paid for them. If you only knew how I anticipated that day, how many times I've imagined it..."

He let go of her hands. She had no idea the number of nights he'd thought of her. The times he had waited for the Keeper's return from Byzantium to hear that she was intact, protected in stasis. The nights he had halfheartedly entertained the company of the women Roland had sent to him—nights that had invariably ended in their leaving him for more interested game when he had proven unmoved by their advances.

Feyn glanced down, but not before he saw the tears welling in her eyes.

"The way it is now—this wasn't the way it was supposed to be, Feyn. This isn't what we worked for. What you sacrificed yourself for. You didn't do it to become Saric's pawn. You did it because you *believed*. And you did it knowing I would be here, as long as I was alive, waiting for you."

Tears slipped from her eyes and onto her cheeks. She brushed them away with the hand that bore not the ring of office, but only the simple moonstone he remembered from so long ago.

"And now..." He shook his head. "My hands are tied. Short of a war that will cost far too many lives and send fear rippling throughout Greater Europa, there's no way to get Jonathan into power. You're the only one who can fix this now. Please, Feyn. I am asking you."

She glanced up at him. "You always seem to be asking me, Rom."

"Only because I was asked first."

"By whom?"

"By destiny when the blood first came into my hands!
So now I ask you. We will go to war if you refuse, but I
beg you first. Please, for love of life."

She nodded absently, though not in agreement.

"I can only give so much, Rom," she said quietly. "I've
died once already. Now I find life and power and you ask
me to step aside."

"Listen to me, Feyn. Think carefully. Can you say that
you feel the same now as you did that day with me nine
years ago? The day the sun was so hot on your pale skin—
remember? We rode a gray stallion out from the royal stables beyond the city. One just like the one you rode here."

She was listening, staring off at the horizon.

"The anemones were in bloom," he said, more gently.
"I sang you a poem, because you asked for it like a gift,
and I gave it willingly . . . You cried."

Her lips parted but no words came from her.

"You asked me to come away with you. To live with
you. To bring Avra if I wanted . . . You laughed then. I've
never seen you laugh since. But you did, and you were
beautiful. Not a Sovereign. Not a Brahmin. But a woman
with a heart that loved."

He stepped toward her as he said it, the smell of death
thick in his nostrils. Her scent had once been beautiful, an
exotic and intoxicating perfume, heady as too much wine.
Now she smelled of a reek so foul no Mortal except Jonathan could seem to stomach it in close proximity.

He touched her cheek and she turned her eyes up to him.
Dark, fathomless. He was desperate to find her within them.

His fingers slid along her jaw to the back of her neck.

"Tell me you remember," he said.

He told himself he should not crave the taste of her.

The smell of her. What Mortal had ever kissed a Corpse? And yet he brought his lips to hers without reservation.

He found no sweetness. Gone the smell of her breath, the wet of her tongue, sweet against his, her lips, plush and soft at once.

Her breath, when she exhaled, was fetid in his nostrils. And still he slid his hand into her hair as her lips parted beneath his, as though in surprise at the response of her body, only now catching up to her heart.

Her mouth tasted like rot. But this was Feyn, the woman he had known and loved. It didn't matter how foul his senses claimed this act to be. He wasn't there to take, but to give. To help her remember.

She suddenly pushed herself away, lips parted as though in shock.

Or stunned realization.

Any Mortal would find the mere thought of what he had just done repugnant. But it was all he could do not to draw her back again.

"You're too bold!"

"Forgive me. But don't tell me you don't remember how life felt that day."

"It doesn't matter," Feyn said. But the determination in her tone had been cut by confusion.

"What you ask is impossible," she added, straightening her back. "I'm not some girl that you fool into drinking blood as you did once. Yes. I loved you. But I might have loved anyone who made me feel the way I did that day. Any face that was before me at that moment. Even as I love the face that I saw the moment I came out of stasis."

Saric.

"Surely you can't mean that."

"You're very good at telling me what I can and can't feel, Rom Sebastian. At dictating whether I truly live or not and if the life I bring is real or false. No more."

Rom paced away, frantic. He couldn't allow her to slip away like this. They had come too far. He had seen the tears flow from her eyes!

He faced her, mind set.

"Then see him. For my sake, and your own, see him again."

"Who?"

"Jonathan. The boy you gave your life for."

"I *have* seen him. You brought him when you invaded my chamber. And now here you stand beyond the city with me as you did once so many years ago. This time history will not repeat itself. I will give you the statute you want, protecting the Nomads, but its all you can ask and expect to receive from me."

"Face the one you're refusing in person. The one who would be Sovereign if you permitted him to be. The one who carried the life now in my veins. If nothing else, see the Maker of the Mortals at such odds with the world you rule. See if he's not the true source of life. Talk to him yourself, and then decide."

"You ask too much."

"I ask only for a few hours of your time."

She glanced away. For a moment his heart stopped.

"When?"

"Tomorrow night, at our Gathering."

She was silent a moment before she said: "Where is this gathering?"

"In our camp." Roland would object, Rom was sure. But what was the alternative? They had little choice.

She gave him a long look. "Only to see the boy."

"Yes, of course. And to see the life of Mortals in celebration. Nothing more."

"Already you extend your request."

He lifted his hands in halfhearted surrender. "No more. I swear it."

"I will hold you to that promise."

He expelled a breath, considering their course of action. They would take her blindfolded and hold her in a yurt outside the camp, not for her privacy, but because of her scent. No Mortal would tolerate the smell of death within the camp—especially at the Gathering, though in truth Rom no longer cared how it affected the Gathering, what sensibilities her presence offended, or what anyone else might say.

He only prayed that the boy did not disappoint.

He whistled at Telvin and the Dark Blood in the distance.

"Rom..."

"It will do you no harm to see our way of life. You have nothing to fear."

"Rom."

He glanced at her. "Yes."

"You need to know something."

"What is it?" Telvin was coming, bringing Rom's horse, and Janus, leading both his and Feyn's.

"I have to be back in two more days."

He felt his brow wrinkle. "Of course." But the timing of her return depended also on their course of action with Saric...which in turn depended entirely on Feyn's interaction with Jonathan.

"I have to be back in two days or I'll die."

"Nonsense. Saric can't reach you here. He doesn't know the location of the camp."

"It doesn't matter," she said. "I need his blood every three days. I'm dependent on it."

He stopped. "What are you saying?"

"I can't live without him. He's engineered the blood in me so that I require more of his or I die. Physically. Permanently."

CHAPTER TWENTY-EIGHT

READ IT," Roland said. "I don't want you to recite it. I want to know the exact words, translated from their original Latin."

The Keeper held the ancient vellum in fingers that trembled due to his lack of sleep as much as from the weight of the words in his hands. He'd recited the passage from memory once already—they'd all heard it a hundred times, spoken around the celebration fires late at night. But now reality had conspired to challenge everything they'd assumed from those bold proclamations. They must now know the precise intent of Talus, the first Keeper, who'd written these words nearly five hundred years earlier.

The old man gazed at the others who'd joined Roland in the temple ruin's inner sanctum.

Present: Roland, who'd demanded the meeting. Michael, his second. Seriph, whose views garnered more agreement among the zealots with each passing day. Anthony, a voice of reason and calculation to match Roland's own.

At issue: the Keeper's understanding of Talus's prophecy. As both the last surviving Keeper and first among the new

Keepers the Book's role as sage remained undisputed. The only way Roland could see to avoid a crippling fracture between the Nomads and the new Keepers, those non-Nomadic Mortals, would be through common understanding and agreement of the first Keeper's words.

And so they must turn to the man so appropriately known as "the Book."

Torchlight played across the faces gathered around the altar. Outside, the final preparations for the Gathering sent intermittent laughter rolling through a camp punctuated by the tuning of instruments and the pounding of hammers. But to Roland, the din served only as a constant reminder of the false pretense that hung over them all.

Their greatest Gathering to date...in celebration of a diminishing Sovereign.

"Book," Roland said. "We aren't enemies here. But we need to know what the intent of the first Keeper was when he wrote these words. And we need to know your best interpretation now."

The old man set the ancient vellum on the altar and opened the Book of Mortals. The leather-bound volume contained the names and details of every living Mortal, the last entry being the girl Kaya, whom Jonathan had brought back from the Authority of Passing. Only the latest indication of Jonathan's failure to understand his role. In addition to their names, the basic precepts by which the Mortals celebrated and ordered their lives filled a dozen pages. In the back of the book: an exact translation of Talus's vellum, which generations of Keepers had guarded for centuries in anticipation of Jonathan's coming.

The wavering flame of a large white candle lit the page as the Keeper lay a weathered finger along the passage in question. He coughed once into his fist, then read aloud in a worn, gravely voice.

"Bloodlines should converge to produce a child, a male..." He skipped a few words, found the pertinent section, and then read: *"Within his blood will be the means to overthrow Legion on the genetic level..."* He cleared his throat. *"In this child is our hope. It is he who will remember his humanity, who will have the capacity for compassion and love. And it is therefore he who must free us from Order, the very structures of which go up like a prison around the human heart. This boy will be humanity's only hope."*

The old man's eyes lifted. "The *only* hope," he said.

"The question," Seriph said, "is whether that hope is in the boy or in his blood. *Within his blood will be the means to overthrow Legion,* as you read. *To free us from Order.* Meaning his blood. Talus was a scientist, was he not? An alchemist?"

"He was more," the old man said. "He is the one who prophesied—"

"You say he has prophesied only because what he predicted has come true. But his findings were made from calculations! There was no evidence of the Maker's Hand, assuming such a thing exists."

"Easy, Seriph," Roland warned. "We only seek the truth here."

"The Maker's Hand is evident in the boy," the Keeper said. "He was born in the year prophesied by Talus. Calculation, yes, but guided by the Maker's Hand."

"Either way," Michael said, "I think Seriph makes a good point. The passage seems to mean that humanity's only hope will come from the boy because of his blood."

"There's more," the Keeper said.

Michael interrupted: "But doesn't it say—"

Roland cut her off with a glance. "Read it for us, Book," he said.

The old man coughed again, wiped a fleck of spittle from his bottom lip, then read again.

"I will establish an order of Keepers, and together we will vow to keep this blood and these secrets safe for the day that boy comes. I will teach them to remember what it was to know more than fear, so that our minds will remember even after our bodies have forgotten. Though we will surely die under the curse that is Legion, we wait in hope, having abandoned the Order in anticipation of that day."

"And that would include Nomads, I would say," Seriph said.

"Let him finish," Roland snapped.

The Keeper leveled a gaze at Seriph and continued: *"Until then, there is enough blood for five to live for a while...Let the blood ignite the remnant who will find the boy and bring an end to this death. You who find this, you who drink, you are that remnant. Drink and know that all I have written is true. Find the boy. Bring him to power so that the world might be saved, I beg you."*

He lifted his eyes. "This last was fulfilled by Rom and those who drank the blood and found the boy. Rom, whose presence would be most welcome now."

But they all knew why Rom wasn't with them. It wasn't only because he was gone, attempting to convince the Sovereign to give up her seat to Jonathan. It was also because they all knew that Rom would undermine an honest discussion as to Jonathan's purpose. As the firstborn among Mortals, the lover of the first martyr, Avra, and the one who'd found the boy, Rom saw Jonathan as his only purpose for living. His mind—his course—was already sealed.

Roland was determined to discover if the Keeper's was as well.

"You speak now to the descendants of those Nomads who determined to remain separate from Order since the end of Chaos, who joined with the Keepers in support of their mission centuries ago," Roland said. "We saw the truth long before Rom did, remember that."

"That may well be. But these words do not lie. Find the boy. Bring him to power. The text is clear."

"If you don't mind..." Anthony turned to the altar, one arm crossed before him supporting the other, his finger on his cheek. "Considering the context, stripped of any of the folklore that surrounds this document, I would say that what the writer's saying is quite plain."

"Then at least one of you has good sense," the Keeper said.

"I would say he's simply talking about the genetic mutations that ultimately caused Legion to revert in the same bloodline from which the virus was made. Talus was responsible for Legion, after all. He made it—"

"Not with the intention of using it."

"Nonetheless, it came from his blood. He then calculated and predicted that the virus would revert in one child and concludes here that the boy born with that blood must bring life to the world."

"As Sovereign."

"Yes, in an idealistic world. But if Talus were told that the boy could *not* come to power, what would he say?"

To even speak this way would be considered sacrilege to many, but they could not afford to adhere to the bounds of superstition now.

The Keeper shut the book with more force than was necessary. "You say the boy can't come to power? Do you know who you're speaking to?" He jabbed his chest with his forefinger. "We Keepers held fast to this belief of what 'could not happen' coming to pass while the rest of the world blindly followed Order for centuries. How dare you inform me of who can or cannot come to power now!"

"And we honor you for it, Keeper," Roland said. "As prince I can assure you, you weren't the only one to guard truth for centuries. Please, let's put the cockfighting to rest."

To Anthony: "Finish your thought."

The elder Nomad glanced between them.

"First a question. When was it decided that these writings were inspired by more than the sharp mind of an alchemist who, in realizing his error, wanted to return humanity to a dead world?"

The Keeper blinked at him. "They've always been sacred!"

"Did Talus claim his writing was sacred?"

"Keepers have always known the words of Talus to be those of the Maker."

"Fine. Even so, the meaning isn't clear. The boy is our hope because of his blood. The vessel is secondary to its contents. It is the *blood* at stake here. If the boy were to suddenly become ill and die, would his blood be wasted just because he isn't in power? His purpose is to rescue the world with his blood, not with any other power. Unless I'm missing something."

The Keeper looked at Roland, face ashen. *You told him?*

He shook his head.

"What is it?" Seriph said.

Roland held the Keeper's eyes for a moment, then decided it was time.

"Jonathan *is* ill," he said. "In a matter of speaking. His blood is reverting. In less than a week his blood will be no different than the blood of any Corpse."

The air seemed to leave the room. Stunned stares, all around.

"Corpse?" Michael said.

Roland nodded at the Keeper. "Tell them."

After a long pause, the old man looked around himself as though at a loss, and sighed. He told them about the tests on Jonathan's blood, adding in a final detail that surprised even Roland.

"As of last drawing just this morning, Jonathan's blood has lost more than half of its potency. At this rate it will be gone by the time he turns eighteen."

"That's in three days!" Michael said.

"Then..." Seriph's eyes, wide with shock, shifted between the Keeper and Roland. "How will he save the world if he comes to power?"

"His blood will change again," the Keeper said.

"Will? Or may?"

No response.

"That's it!" Seriph said. "It's settled. *We* are the world's salvation, not the boy."

"Quiet!" Roland snapped. "No one's abandoning Jonathan as long as I'm prince! And you'll find my blade across your throat if you speak a word of this to any soul. I will not rob my people of hope!"

"Agreed," Anthony said. "It would be disastrous."

Seriph said, "Please tell me I'm not the only one who sees the obvious here."

"The obvious is that Order reigns in a world that is dead!" the Keeper said. "We cannot fight amongst ourselves or turn traitor to our mission—our very reason for living. The very reason we live."

"Point made," Roland said. "Seriph may not have the smoothest tongue, but he's no more traitor than any of us. Please, stick to the point."

"I'm not sure the point has been made," Michael said. "So let me say it."

She stepped forward and placed her fingertips on the altar. Her hands were those of an archer—strong, bronzed from hours of sun, the nails of her thumb and forefinger on her drawing hand painted black for her marksmanship, one of twenty-three in the entire tribe who were granted the same markings.

"We are facing the possible annihilation of all Mortals at the hands of Saric and his Legion. The truth is, it's only a matter of time before he finds us. As a warrior who commands seven hundred Mortal fighters I would know one thing: how many do we sacrifice to save the boy?"

There it was.

"All of them?" She paced and spun back, flipping her hand in the air. "Why don't we let all Mortals die, for that matter? And then who will bring life to the world? Jonathan, with his Corpse blood? He will be dead!"

Anthony turned to the Keeper. "Are you certain Jonathan's blood is reverting to Corpse levels? You're sure of this?"

"I'm sure of nothing except what I see in the tests."

"What about our blood?" Anthony pressed.

"We will live very long lives."

"How long?"

The Keeper hesitated. "My most recent estimate is over seven hundred years."

A collective gasp.

"So long? Then our blood is *strengthening*?"

"So it seems."

Roland paced, hands on his hips. Distant laughter drifted somewhere outside, voices raised in the kind of jocularity that comes only on the cusp of a new beginning, a thing long anticipated.

If they only knew.

"Book, we're running out of time," Roland finally said. "Even *if* Rom succeeds, we can't know if we can trust Feyn. We have to take precautions and we can't afford division. So I need to know. Jonathan's life flows through our veins. If our blood continues to grow stronger...are you saying we may find ourselves *immortal*?"

The Keeper frowned. "That's a stretch." A pause. "But yes, we have his life. And yes, it is lengthening within us."

Those around him looked from one to the other.

"You heard him. Our life is more potent than ever. Will we just throw it away? No. We must protect it."

"No one's suggesting—"

"Follow my reasoning. You agree that Mortals must be protected at all costs. Then would you agree with me that the blood in us must be protected above any single life?"

The Keeper remained silent, his mouth set in a terrible line.

"It's a simple question. Yes or no. Tell me what Jonathan would say."

Finally the Keeper spoke, his voice like gravel. "He would agree."

"Then you, his servant, would agree as well?"

The Keeper's jaw muscles tightened. He gave a single, reluctant nod.

"Say it."

"Yes. Assuming such a choice was before us."

"It already is, my friend. Our army's well trained but small. And so we must task ourselves with our primary objective, which is no longer to put the boy in power, but to protect the blood he's given us."

"That isn't what I agreed to—"

"I've seen Saric's army!" Roland said. "He's twelve thousand Dark Bloods strong! If he comes against us, he'll crush us unless we're fully prepared. And I will employ any means at my disposal to avoid a slaughter."

"Jonathan will come to power in a matter of days!"

"Jonathan's blood is dying! He'll be no more than a Corpse! Wake up, old man!"

Roland immediately regretted his tone. He glanced away, cursed softly, and then said: "I mean no disrespect. But you must appreciate my position. Rom is out in far field attempting an impossible task—a dangerous one, even if he succeeds. Saric is far more powerful than we first assumed." He pointed in the direction of the outer basilica. "Meanwhile, twelve hundred Mortals prepare to celebrate their savior at the Gathering, not knowing that he's *dying*. Everything we assumed about his ascension has come to a grinding halt. But I know one thing: I must save my people.

"I understand the words of Talus to mean that nothing must come between the boy's blood and its power to bring life. If I'm wrong, tell me now. Otherwise, I will fight to honor the intent of these words. Mortals *must* survive above the life of any one soul."

All eyes turned to the Keeper. But before he could respond, the doors to the inner sanctum flew wide. Javan, one of the men who'd accompanied Rom, stood in the gap, breathing hard.

"Forgive the intrusion."

"What is it?"

"Rom. He's coming."

"She came then?"

He nodded.

"And? Spit it out, man!"

"She's with him."

"*What?*"

"She's here. For the Gathering. He's succeeded."

Roland felt the blood drain from his face. No victory could be so easy. The thought of Feyn, a Dark Blood herself, coming to their valley struck him like a fist to the gut. Was Rom so naïve as to trust her without proof? The agreement had been for her to remain in their custody away from the valley until the new law had passed.

Now she came *here* to his people?

"You may go."

Javan inclined his head and ducked back out, closing the doors behind him.

Roland turned to Michael, who was staring at him, waiting his order.

"Begin the preparations we spoke about immediately. Say it's a training exercise. I want it ready before tomorrow night's celebration."

He strode toward the door.

"Preparations for what?" the Keeper asked.

"For what comes next, old man."

"And what is that?"

Roland turned back at the door.

"War."

CHAPTER TWENTY-NINE

PERSUADING THE COUNCIL to allow Feyn into the camp had taken a virtual act of the Maker, and even after they'd agreed, the sharp eyes of distrust that had been her only welcome became silent questions when they turned to Rom. To have even the scent of Corpse—let alone Dark Blood—among them as they celebrated their delivery from death was blasphemy. Even Rom wondered if he'd made a dreadful mistake.

But he saw no other alternative. Jonathan's ascension depended on Feyn's express willingness to place him in power. And for that to happen, she *had* to see life for what it was. And he could think of no better demonstration of life than the one that was to take place here, tonight.

The Council had only agreed with several conditions. Feyn would have to remain under constant guard in a yurt north of camp, where the prevailing breeze would carry her scent into the narrowing canyon lands beyond. She would remain there until the Gathering and come out only under cover of darkness and after Roland's and Rom's men had time to pass word that there would be a Dark Blood prisoner among them. They would share no other information. She must not be recognized and would therefore be veiled. Only members of the council would be permitted to speak to her. The warrior who'd come with her, Janus, must remain under guard in a separate yurt and was not to enter the camp under any circumstances.

Furthermore, Roland had insisted that he, not any other council member, stand near her during the celebration that night. He would keep her upwind of the main body. If Jonathan wanted to speak to her, he would do it beyond prying eyes.

Roland had expressed his distinct displeasure at the entire situation.

"She has a remnant of the Keeper's blood within her," Rom had insisted.

"You can't possibly believe it's enough to mitigate the Dark Blood in her veins," Roland had said.

"I knew her when she was alive. And I'm telling you her heart remembers it."

"*Her* heart? Or your heart?"

"My heart is only for Jonathan."

"You think I don't see your eyes when you talk about her?"

"My heart, my life, is for Jonathan. That's all you need to know," Rom said, and walked away before the Nomad could respond.

Yes, there was at least a measure of truth to Roland's suspicions. But he refused to see that it was the very bond forged between Rom and Feyn a lifetime ago that had made it possible to find Jonathan in the first place. Mortals were alive today because of his bond with Feyn. Was this not the way history was made?

And was love, in all of its forms, not the cornerstone of the life Jonathan had brought them?

Word had spread quickly about the Dark Blood near the camp. He knew it by the lingering gazes, the nods in the place of greetings, thick as the smell of cooking meat coming from the direction of the pits. Even Adah had considered him with silent questions as he collected a basket of dried meat and fruit he'd asked her to prepare. But if she suspected the food was for the Dark Blood, she said nothing.

Rom had seen to Feyn only once during the day, and then only in the company of the Mortal guard. She'd demanded to know how long they intended to keep her shut in, not bothering to touch the food he'd brought for her. He wanted to show it to her then, in the daylight, so that she could see the eyes of those who lived and the palpable anticipation for the coming celebration. But the terms had been agreed to, and he'd already pushed Roland and his zealots as far as he dared for now.

"Soon," he promised.

All through the afternoon the camp seemed to vibrate with strange and growing energy. Defiance. By dusk, snippets of flute drifted up toward the cliffs. Random drumbeats sounded from the direction of the ruins as drums of all sizes—nearly a hundred of them—were lined up on the steps leading up to the open-air basilica. Laughter rang out throughout the camp, the sound of it flaring up like the myriad fires set outside the yurts and up on the cliffs, illuminating the dark forms of guards against the waning day.

The drums began as the last glow of twilight faded along the western edge of the cliff and the first stars appeared in a rare cloudless sky. A whoop sounded from the edge of camp, answered by another, louder than the first. Then a shrill ululation, answered immediately by another like an echo. Within seconds, a chorus of cries rose up from the valley, rolling upward toward the cliffs, reverberating from the limestone face.

The warriors came, shouting, tearing off their tunics as they made their way toward the ruin steps. Their faces were marked: black for skill, red for life. Their chests were painted with ocher and the ashes of last year's fire, passed among them earlier in the day. Some of their nipples were newly pierced with thick metal needles, the ends of which were adorned with feathers. The women wore paints across their foreheads and bellies; those who were pregnant emphasized the swell of their abdomens with a wide circle of red, some of them spiraling in toward the navel. Braids of men and women alike were so thick with feathers as to have been transformed into the giant combs of birds trailing down to the waist. Every Nomad had brought out their best jewelry: earrings and armbands, beaded belts slung low over hips already relieved of more cumbersome clothing.

The cries rose to a deafening pitch as bare-chested warriors and sarong-clad women beat their chests with their fists; naked children darted through the thickening mass of fevered adults surging around the steps of the ruins. The entire camp had been transformed into a sea of brightly appointed souls.

Rom stood atop the steps, pulse quickening at the sight of the thick band of humanity brimming with emotive celebration. Beside him, Roland inhaled as though he would breathe in their collected fervor—that one voice that was neither man nor woman, old nor young, but that was simply and exceptionally *alive*.

On either side of the ruin steps, wood had been stacked, each the height of a man. Behind Rom three thick wooden poles had been erected and bound together at the top to form a rigid tripod that supported a sagging leather bowl.

With a glance and a nod at Roland, Rom stepped forward to the edge of the top step and thrust his fist up toward the sky.

"Life!"

Life! the entire camp echoed.

"Freedom!" Roland thundered from his side.

Freedom! the reverberating cry.

Rom and Roland each seized a torch from the nearest of the ancient columns. Rushing down the steps, they shoved the torches into the resin-soaked woodpiles. With a whoosh, twin flames leaped into the air. Ululating calls pierced the night. A hundred drums beat in unison.

Rom ran back up the ruin's steps, fists lifted high and wide, crying out his approval as the valley filled with the dissonant roar of unrestrained triumph. Sparks flew to the sky as wood popped within the fire. For a few minutes, thoughts of Feyn fell away.

The Gathering's celebration filled the Seyala Valley.

He leaped to the ground, ran into the circulating mass, and caught a young woman with braided blond hair up into his arms. She threw back her head and stared at the night sky with bright Mortal eyes highlighted by large red circles. He swung her around then brought her down into his arms and kissed her.

He let her go, both of them breathless, and then she was gone, the feathered mass of her braids disappearing into the throng.

He surged ahead, slapping Keepers and Nomads on

their backs. With a roar, Roland threw himself into a circle of warriors who leaped at him like cubs springing at a lion.

Rom veered away and swept his arms high, urging increase. "More!"

They gave him more. The roar of the drums and cries shook the ground beneath the ruins, drowning out his own. And then he was back in the mix, dancing and surging with the sea of Mortals.

The Nomads had a penchant for celebration, but none compared to the surreal scene before the ruins. Between the twin raging fires, the twelve hundred Mortals who had found life in a dead world celebrated their humanity in extravagant abandon.

The celebration showed no signs of slowing for an hour. Rom lost track of time. Of those bodies pressed against his own; the kisses given and taken like wine.

And yet no drink had been tasted. No food had yet been touched. The night would begin and end with dancing. With Mortality, wild and untethered. With the reason they danced at all.

Jonathan.

Only then did it occur to Rom that he hadn't seen him. Jonathan had kept to himself in the hills west of the river most of the day, Jordin had said.

Where was he?

Rom broke from the dancers and bounded up the stone steps, turned to gaze out over the celebration, searching for him. With so many, it was nearly impossible to pick out any one person. There was Michael, her thighs clasped to the chest of one of the warriors who held her up as she reached for the sky. There were tears on her face, smearing the black stripes on her cheek. The man released her and caught her in his arms.

No sign of Jordin, but she was too diminutive to stand out in the crowd. Surely she was here somewhere. Jonathan would be with her.

His gaze fell on two forms standing far to his right, beyond the main body of Mortals. Roland, no longer bare-chested but in a black tunic. A veiled figure stood next to him, tall in the darkness, unadorned, clothed in leathers.

Feyn.

So then, *let her see.* He nodded, wondering if they caught the sign of approval.

It was time.

Rom lifted his arms and let out a cry that rang above the din.

"Mortals!"

On queue and in unison, the drums ceased their pounding. The dance stopped; silence settled. Heads turned to stare up at him in anticipation.

"We come to celebrate life! Today your liberation has come. Let the earth know that we are *alive*!"

A thunderous roar of consent.

"Tonight, we honor the blood in our veins. Of Jonathan our Life-Giver. Our Sovereign, who brings a new kingdom of life without end!"

A reverberating echo from twelve hundred throats filled the air.

But Jonathan was nowhere to be seen.

Rom lifted his hand for silence, and spoke only when the night was still. On either side of the ruins, the freshly fueled bonfires crackled and sent flames high into the sapphire sky.

"Tonight we honor the blood of those fallen," he said, his voice now lower. "Of all those who have died, *alive*."

They stared with wide eyes, each remembering those Mortals who'd died in sickness or mishap. They revered passed Mortal life in this way at every Gathering, hearing each as they stood in silence.

Rom spoke their names, seven in all since the last gathering, one a mere child of two, Serena, who'd been struck in the head by a horse's hoof and died. It wasn't the Nomadic way to mourn with keening except in private. Every life was sacred. Every name spoken. But in the end they would celebrate, not mourn, them all.

He came to the last two, pacing before them. "The warrior Pasha."

Still, not a sound.

"The Keeper and third-born, Triphon!"

He let the name linger, knowing that these last two were still fresh in all of their minds and hearts.

"We remember them all with honor, knowing they are alive still."

His words echoed over the assembly for several long beats as tension mounted. They all knew what would come next.

Avra.

Slowly, he dipped his head once, then turned and looked at the leather bowl suspended on the wooden tripod.

Stirs in the crowd.

Every year a shudder ran through his body when the time came—not for the memory of Avra's slaying or of the lifeless body he had buried, but for the sacrifice she'd made so that he could live.

He lifted his right hand and held it steady, palm open. A hundred drums began pounding as one in steady rhythm. From the corner of his eye, he saw Zara the councilwoman striding up the steps, a wrapped bundle in her hands. It should have been Triphon, as had become custom.

She set the bundle in his hand and the cadence of the drum beat surged. Blood dripped through the bindings onto his fingers as Zara untied the parcel. It smattered the limestone as she pulled the pouch open before retreating down the steps.

"And then, there is the first martyr," he said.

Rom reached into the vessel, gripped the organ inside. An equine heart, cut just that morning from one of the horses, the meat of which had been quartered onto the spits. It was the most sacred kind of heart the Nomads knew, standing in now for Avra's, enshrined in the inner sanctum.

He thrust the fresh, raw heart up into the air.

A resounding roar from the mass below.

"Tonight we honor the first martyr. Who gave up true life to usher in the hope we have before us now!"

The drums stopped.

"For Avra's heart!"

The Mortals erupted in one resounding cry.

Goose bumps crawled up Feyn's arms as the entire camp exploded into a fresh riot of celebration, the drums threatening to reorder the beat of her own pulse. They mourned Triphon's death, not knowing that Saric had found a way to coax life from him yet. Telling them the truth would betray her Master and accomplish no good among these Mortals.

It was Avra's heart that fascinated her more. She'd laid eyes on the woman outside the Citadel grounds once, in that other lifetime. This woman whom Rom had loved.

"She died?" she said, glancing at Roland.

"The day before you did." The impassive lines of his face expressed no empathy for the reference to Feyn's own death at the hands of the very Keeper she now saw wending his way through the back of the gathered celebrants. Did he know she was here, the one he had so brutally cut down and then so carefully preserved? And if she were to come face-to-face with him, what would she say to him, or he to her?

She shifted, thinking of the scar across her torso. It itched. "And Triphon?"

"Killed by your brother's Dark Bloods days ago."

Triphon, too, she had met once, if only briefly.

The prince returned his attention to the ruins, making it clear he wasn't waiting for any sort of a reply.

He had come to her earlier, calling her out from her yurt, saying that it was time. Janus, he had said, would have to remain behind. She could not mistake the lines of mistrust and displeasure etched into the Nomad's face as she'd followed Roland into camp. She had not needed to be told that it was only Rom's order that assured her any safety here.

Now they watched together as Rom moved across the elevated ruins to the tripod and carefully set the heart inside the soft leather bowl suspended between the wood supports. How strange to reconcile the naïve, impetuous man she had known with the leader who commanded such respect among these wild Mortals. The Rom she'd known had been a poet, an artisan who'd sung at funerals—the lowest kind of fare in the world of Order.

The man at the top of the stairs was a leader of warriors, majestic in his own way.

A man who had kissed her...tasted her...

He was also the enemy of her Maker and therefore hers as well.

Rom turned toward the gathering. He drew a knife from the sheath at his belt. "We remember those lost to us. We remember those who died. And we celebrate, proving with our lives that their blood was not spilled in vain!"

With his last words, he slashed the bottom of the leather bowl. A stream of blood began to flow to the ground.

Bodies were in motion once more, grappling for the sky, the names of Avra, Triphon, and Pasha shouted to the stars. They were fervent, these Mortals, she would give Rom that. Fervent...impassioned...

And as such, more dangerous than she would have guessed.

She glanced at the yurts to her right, each of them lit from inside, with fires burning in the pits outside. Children dashed from one dwelling to another, snagging food from the fires before running toward the cooking pits at the edge of camp.

Where was the boy? She hadn't seen him anywhere in the crowd or on the ruin steps. He was the one, after all, she had been brought to meet.

She surveyed the assembled Mortals. These were only what...a thousand? Slightly more? But she'd seen the faces of the warriors and had noted their zeal, in such stark contrast to the icy discipline of Saric's Dark Bloods.

"I can *smell* your calculation," Roland said.

"I don't know what you mean."

"It smells like curiosity. And ambition. And interest."

He turned toward her as he said it. She studied the high and hard line of his cheekbone. The broad forehead, the long, thick braids with their wealth of beading. The paint-like tattoo on his temple. A woman's finger had painted it, she thought. She wondered what kind of woman kept the interest of a man like this. One as magnificent as he was deadly.

He leaned toward her as though to share her line of sight. "You're counting what...five, six hundred? There are seven hundred. And twelve hundred of us altogether. Far less than your brother's army; tell him that. But make no mistake." He turned to gaze at her, his eyes both heavy-lidded and sultry. "March against us here and we will defeat you."

A shout went up from the frenetic dancers and echoed through the crowd like a rolling peal of thunder. Feyn turned and saw its cause.

Jonathan. Leaping up the ruin stairs.

He was naked except for a loincloth.

His face was bare of the paint the other warriors wore, and his hair was adorned perhaps the least of any Nomad in the company, but no one seemed to care. The shouts of the throng escalated into a roar unrivaled yet this evening.

Rom embraced the boy, then stepped back, arms spread.

"Your Sovereign!" he cried.

The Mortals roared, a cry so forceful, so full of hope and emotion that Feyn felt tears well in her eyes. What power in this boy evoked such powerful expression, devotion, and loyalty from others?

The roar coalesced into a chant: *Sovereign! Sovereign! Sovereign!* Rom seemed to be waiting for the shouts to die down enough to speak, but the cry continued, unrelenting, rising impossibly. The Nomad beside her stood in stony silence.

Jonathan stood still, unpretentious, making no sign that he was embracing their praise or that he longed for it. Only when Rom lifted his hand did the last chants die down. He looked at Jonathan and nodded.

The boy faced them, silent for a few seconds. And then their Sovereign spoke:

"Do you celebrate the martyrs?"

Shouts of agreement.

"You celebrate their blood, shed for me. For the new kingdom, for the Sovereigns of the new realm to come. You celebrate my blood, given for you."

Roaring agreement from the Mortals.

"Then you celebrate not only life, but death."

This time, a confused response. They waited, anticipating more. And the boy gave it to them.

"Because that death brings life." He beat his chest once with a fist. Now he leaned into words and his voice rose, nearly accusing. "You want blood?"

Cries, frenzied from the assembly. Next to Feyn, Roland frowned slightly. Rom glanced away from him, seemingly unsure.

Jonathan suddenly spun and took three long steps to the canvas bowl that held Avra's heart. He dipped his hands into the bowl and scooped a remnant of blood out with both hands. And then he splashed it on his chest and smeared his face, his hair, his torso.

The drumbeats drifted as if those responsible had forgotten to beat them.

Jonathan whirled around and raised both fists in

defiance. "Death, for life!" he shouted. His teeth and eyes gleamed macabre white behind the mask of blood.

The crowd fell deathly silent.

But their Sovereign was not finished. He grabbed the canvas vessel and tilted it so that a fresh torrent of blood fell down over his hair and chest, darkening the flax of his loincloth to match the rest of him.

Even from where she stood, Feyn saw the mask of shock on Rom's face. He made for the boy, then stopped, at a loss.

Jonathan plunged his hand into the canvas bowl, pulled out a bloody fist, and stared at his fingers. The heart which Rom had ceremoniously placed in the bowl bulged in his hand.

Gasps now, from those assembled. Feyn stared, stunned. The celebration clearly had taken an unplanned turn. Those in the throng cast about furtive glances as strange silence settled around them.

Was the boy drunk? Mad?

"He's lost it," Roland muttered beside her.

"For now..." Jonathan staggered forward, holding the heart high. He opened his hand and the heart fell to the ground with a sickening, wet thud. "Let the dead bury the dead," Jonathan said.

Five paces away, Rom stared. The last of the drums stopped. The entire celebration had come to a standstill.

Rom laid a hand on the boy's shoulder but he batted it away. When he spoke again, it was in a quiet voice:

"You won't know true life until you taste blood."

As though desperate to find something worthy of celebration, someone shouted agreement.

"You came for life! I will give you life! I will bring a new Sovereign realm!"

A cry rose, immediately joined by more. The drums returned as though relieved, like a heart stuttering back to life after arrest.

"Life!" he screamed. "Life!" He spread his arms and began to dance. His movements were wild, jerking like blood spurting from an artery.

The crowd didn't seem to care, relieved to return to its celebration in ways more fevered than before. Dancers leaped up at the sky again, holding others aloft as though to pull down the stars.

A figure raced up the steps, taking them two at a time. A young girl on the cusp of womanhood, clad only in a sarong, thick braids flying.

"Kaya," Roland muttered. "She's the girl he took from the Authority of Passing."

The girl leaped up the last step, impulsively set her hands in the blood at her feet, and smeared it on her face and chest. She curled her hands into fists, tilted her head to the sky, and began to dance like Jonathan, stomping naked feet into the blood as it spattered onto her legs.

Jonathan grabbed her hand and together they ran down the steps where no less than two dozen children were gathered—as nearly a hundred more ran out to join them in their frenetic dancing. As one they hopped and whirled, arms raised, laughing as the drums thundered approval. The sight of so much rapture filled Feyn with a strange longing to be a child once again, this time with the full emotion with which they celebrated.

She glanced up then, her eyes prisms of firelight.

Up on the stage, Rom stared at the fallen heart, all but trampled underfoot.

CHAPTER THIRTY

FEYN CLOSED HER EYES, attempting to shut out the sounds of drums pounding in her skull, as the celebration outside wore relentlessly on. Never had the gulf in her mind been so deep, never the darkness so bottomless, never her confusion so great.

She couldn't escape the certainty that she clung to a razor-thin wire as storm winds raged, threatening to tear her fingers free. She would fall, but fall into what? More darkness . . . or freedom?

The only true freedom she'd found since returning to life had come during those hours of absolute submission to Saric. And yet another Maker called to her now. A boy who had once required her death so that he could come to power. Succumbing to the Mortal's call now would end in another death, she was sure of it.

They'd brought her back to the yurt a couple hours ago when the sheer pain of the Nomadic drums in her temples had become unbearable. A guard stood outside—she could hear him calling occasionally to others in the main camp, clearly disgruntled by his removal from the main body. If the last hour was any indication, he would eventually be relieved and replaced by another so that no one guard would go without his fill.

She'd considered cutting her way out the back of the yurt and making a run for it. She didn't know where this valley was, only that it was far north of the city. If she headed south she would eventually come across a road or a river or some other landmark, surely. But it would only be a matter of time before they discovered her missing and recaptured her. If folklore about the Nomads was true—and so far all of it had proven accurate—they were expert trackers.

But even if she could escape, she wasn't sure she wanted to. Something else called to her here.

Images of the wild boy crying out from the ruins barraged her thoughts as she sat on the thick mat that was her only furnishing and stared at the lone lamp that lit her prison. His words had stirred more awe and mystery than offense—not only in her mind, but in the minds of those who called him Sovereign. She'd seen it on their faces, heard it in the hush before doubt had given way to revelry's more persuasive sway.

She hadn't had an opportunity to talk to the boy, but now she wasn't certain what such a talk would achieve.

The sudden image of Saric pushed thoughts of the strange boy aside, calling her back to reason. This much she knew: Saric's blood had given her life, made her Sovereign, and filled her with peace to the extent that she embraced that life. Deviation from Saric, her office, or her existence through him only brought her confusion—the confusion she felt so keenly now, in the Mortals' camp.

Feyn lay back on the mat and stared at the yurt's framework. Rom's undying idealism had plied her mind more than she'd thought possible. Memories of him had stirred her like an eddy muddies the waters of a river. And yet even nostalgia paled next to Saric's siren call.

He was her Maker. Not Rom. Not Jonathan.

The door suddenly snapped wide and Feyn jerked up on the mat. There, in the opening, stood Jonathan, dressed only in a loincloth, chest rising and falling as he hauled in a breath as though he had run all this way. The loincloth clung to him, damp and still stained, though he himself seemed to have washed, as though he had leaped into the river on the edge of camp. Judging from the damp look of the feathers in his braids, that was exactly what he had done.

There was fire in his eyes.

"My Sovereign," he said, stepping in as the door fell shut on its wooden frame behind him.

Feyn stood up, unsure what to say.

"They told me you'd come to see me," he said. He spread his arms. "Tell me, do I look like a Sovereign to you?"

She stared at the young wild man before her, this boy who would be Sovereign, as words refused to form in her mind, much less her mouth.

"Then again, what should a Sovereign look like? The fact is, none of us are who we appear. For nine years you were in a grave, living in death. And I was a boy, dying to live. So which is it, Feyn? Who will live and who will die? Isn't that the question on everyone's mind?"

Uncanny boy! He was obviously crazed.

And speaking the truth.

But whose truth?

"It's my honor to see you again, Sovereign." He stepped forward, took her hand, dropped to one knee, and kissed the back of her hand.

The moment his lips touched her skin, something within her reeled, careened off balance. Darkness threatened to envelop her. She gasped and jerked back, startled by her own visceral response. To the thing that had just threatened to swallow her whole.

He went on as if nothing had happened. But of course nothing had. She was tired and hadn't eaten enough today, that was all.

She suddenly became aware of the fact that she hadn't spoken since his brash entrance.

"Forgive me... You caught me unprepared," she said.

"But you are prepared, Feyn. The question is, am I?" He paced like a young lion, one hand raking through his braids, eyes darting side to side. She could hardly reconcile this frenetic young man before her with the quiet one who had appeared just days ago in her chamber with Rom. "So what is it?"

"I'm sorry... What is what?"

"What are we to do?"

"I don't know."

Jonathan stopped pacing and looked at her. A smile formed on his face.

"It's all right. I do."

"You do."

"Yes. But again, the question is whether or not I'm prepared. What would you say, Feyn? You've studied the role of a Sovereign all your life. So, am I?"

"Prepared?"

"Yes."

"I thought I was prepared. I find in truth that I hardly am," she said with strange honesty.

"But you know you're meant to be Sovereign."

"Yes."

"And yet, I know that I am to be as well. And so here we are. One seat of power, two Sovereigns. It's a dilemma, isn't it?"

"So it seems."

Jonathan began to pace again, speaking, it seemed, to the canvas walls as much to her.

"I take it you have no intention of relinquishing your Sovereignty to me."

So forthright. So enigmatic. What an exotic young man he was. So strangely endearing. How powerful he could become!

And how dangerous.

She'd recovered enough to choose her next words with care. "Should I?"

He glanced at her. "You'll know what you must do when the time comes. Tonight I just want you to know who I am."

"I believe I know."

"Then you know I will be Sovereign. That tonight you will swear your loyalty to me," he said.

His audacity knew no bounds. "Really. You know this."

Jonathan stopped and stared into her eyes. Calm settled over him like a mantle. When he spoke next, his voice was reasoned and laced with certainty.

"I know that you long for love, Feyn. That only death will give you the life you seek. That the one who enslaves you now will die before you. That love, not Order or any code, will win the hearts of the dead."

Saric...die? Barring his tipping his own hand to an assassination attempt, he couldn't possibly know that.

Jonathan searched her eyes and she suddenly felt powerless to look away.

"I know your longing, Feyn. How desperately you desire love. It's why you once gave your life for me. I will never forget."

She gave only the slightest of nods.

"I will repay that debt. We will rule the world, Feyn... You and I. Not like they expect, but we'll rule, mark my words. This world cannot be enslaved by an Order designed to appease an exacting Maker. We'll come to terms, you and I."

She wasn't sure what to say.

"If there are problems when I come of age in two days, you and I must play our roles unified. Do you know where the old outpost at Corvus Point is?"

"Not exactly, no."

"Five miles northwest of here. There's an old road— you have to look for it because it's completely missing in places."

"The Citadel would have records of such a road."

He nodded. "Five miles northwest. Meet me there, alone, in two days. We'll come to terms, you and I. Can you do that?"

"Perhaps."

He smiled. "I will count on you. But tonight I only ask for your loyalty."

"Forgive me, Jonathan, but—"

"Would you like to see the truth?" he said.

"The truth?"

She watched, confounded, as he spat on his palms. And then, before she could back away in shock or protest, he closed the gap between them with two swift steps and laid his hands on her eyes.

The world darkened as his palms shut out the light. But

in the next moment the night swallowed her whole, a vortex sucking her into the abyss—a place she immediately recognized as the same from when he'd kissed her hand just minutes earlier.

She pushed him away with a cry.

"What are you doing?"

But when his hands left her face the darkness remained, blacker than tar.

"See yourself, Feyn," she heard him say. "The blood in you."

Terror seized her, cutting through the soft yolk of horror that flooded her veins. She didn't see darkness as much as *feel* it—a black, living maw to suck her in, as though into the pit of death itself.

"Is this the path you will follow?"

Feyn heard the question, like a call from a far horizon, but her mind was locked in crushing panic. She lurched, shaking, flailing for direction, but there was no up or down, no right or left. There was only the suffocating certainty of death.

Her only remaining instinct was to scream, but her lungs refused to push enough air into her throat to give it any voice. The room filled with a dreadful whimper—her own.

Free me!

"When the times comes, you will deliver the world new life, Feyn. Free yourself from Saric. We will be Sovereign, you and I."

A hand touched her cheek and she instinctively wrenched away. As if sucked into itself, the darkness receded. Light flooded the room.

Feyn stood, trembling, staring into Jonathan's somber

hazel eyes. The lamp still burned, seemingly brighter than before. Distant drums still carried the night's celebration. She was still alive.

Her lungs expanded her breath returned—but with it, a sorrow as unnerving as the terror that has preceded it.

"I'm sorry," Jonathan said. "I had to help you understand."

Tears flooded her eyes and spilled down her face. She reached out for him and dropped to her knees. Grasped his hands and pulled them to her.

There, with her face pressed against his fingers, Feyn wept.

CHAPTER THIRTY-ONE

THE MORNING AFTER PAST GATHERINGS, Roland had woken with pounding in his skull and exhaustion like languor in his limbs as he rolled over to cradle the body next to him, never sure until later whether it was wife, concubine, or other. Such disorientation was synonymous with that celebration to him—the only possible conclusion to the defiant catharsis of the night before. This morning, however, he woke tense, far too clear-headed, and alone.

The thing that had woken him came again: Michael's unmistakable voice, shouting his name.

He leapt up from the mat where he'd attempted an insomniac's fitful sleep a scant three hours ago, hurried to the door of his yurt, and squinted into the new morning light.

Michael was running toward him, fully dressed, bow over her shoulder.

"She's gone."

She . . . .

It took him a moment to reorient himself and place who "she" might be. Images from the Gathering strung through his mind. The dance, the food, Avra's heart, Jonathan's crazed behavior, Feyn . . .

He looked sharply to the north, the direction of the yurt where they'd kept Feyn under guard. "What do you mean?"

Michael closed the gap between them, slowing to long, urgent strides, panting. "The Dark Blood. She's gone."

"What do you mean, gone?"

"Gone. Escaped. With her guard."

"Which guard? Ours?"

"The putrid Dark Blood she brought with her. I told you it was a mistake from the outset. It was far too dangerous!"

With a curse, he rushed into his yurt, shoved feet into boots, tucked a knife into the waist of his pants, and grabbed his sword and the tunic he had discarded last night. And then he was striding out the yurt and after Michael, who was already running through the sleeping camp toward the horse pen. One of the Nomads he recognized from the late watch was there, hurriedly helping to saddle Michael's horse as Michael began to saddle his.

"Who was on watch?" Roland demanded, buckling on the sword.

"Narun and Aron," Michael said. "Aron ran into camp this morning. The Dark Bloods took the horses. Narun is still there."

Roland pulled the tunic on, pushed the man out of the way, and cinched the saddle girth himself. Then he and Michael were tearing out of the pen, away from camp. North.

Within twenty paces of the two temporary yurts, he could already tell that the unmistakable odor of Dark Blood was gone.

Narun rushed to meet them as they dismounted ten yards from the larger of the two yurts.

"They cut their way out the back. Neither one of us ever heard—"

Roland closed the gap between them with a single stride and slammed his fist into the man's jaw. Narun reeled back and fell to the dirt, hard. He clawed for purchase and began to rise, but Roland struck again. The guard collapsed to his back and rolled to the side, spitting blood. It streamed from his mouth and nose into a tuft of grass.

"Roland!" Michael hissed.

Roland looked up, hand on the man's collar, fist drawn back for another blow. He dropped the Nomad back to the earth, kicked a spray of dirt onto the guard's face, and stepped over him.

Michael stared as he stalked past her, but said nothing.

He flung the door wide and stepped into the yurt. One glance at the precise cut in the thick canvas told the story clearly enough.

He spat to one side.

"We don't know where she got a blade," Michael said, stepping in behind him. "We checked them both for weapons when they came. Best guess, she got it somewhere between the Gathering and when Jonathan came to see her."

"Jonathan came? Here?"

"That's what they said. To talk to her."

Could the boy be careless enough to have had a weapon on him? He was losing his senses along with his potency. Even if he did become Sovereign, he'd have to be babysat by the hour. Then again, Jonathan's ascension was now the farthest thing from the realm of true possibility.

Feyn had escaped to run straight back to Saric. Not only did she have no intention of abdicating any portion of her Sovereignty to Jonathan, she now knew the location of the Seyala Valley and every Mortal living within it.

They could move camp. They could mobilize in hours. But then a far more final option presented itself.

Roland swung around, stepped past Michael and ducked out the door of the yurt.

"We have to call council," she was saying.

But the council meant delay.

"No council."

He strode toward his horse, Michael following at his shoulder.

"How long have they been gone?"

"According to Aron, no more than two hours." She paused. "You're going to kill her."

It wasn't a question.

He swung into his saddle without looking at her. "I will do what should have been done two days ago."

"Then I'm with you."

"No. I need you here."

"Not this time, brother. Let the others make preparation." She flung herself onto her mount and pulled it around. "This time I see it through."

He was about to assert his demand but then thought better of it. Eliminating the threat Feyn presented wouldn't put an end to the larger threat Saric presented to all Mortals. He would become Sovereign in her wake—with twelve thousand Dark Bloods at his command. Saric had to die today as well. How, he did not yet know, but to this end Michael would prove helpful.

"Get word to Seriph. Tell him to keep his silence. Meet me on the south side at the river bend." He spurred his horse. "Quickly, Michael."

* * *

Rom had slept the sleep of one for whom the world might promise to take a turn for the better.

Feyn had come. She'd seen the appetites of life—true life. Not that fabricated existence that came from the work of Saric's alchemists, but directly from Jonathan's veins. More important, despite Jonathan's crazed behavior on the ruin steps, he'd agreed to see her. The guards said he had emerged from her yurt in good spirits.

Rom prayed it was a good sign. He'd seen the way the boy had looked at her the first night they'd gone to her apartment in the Citadel, just after her resurrection. Perhaps Feyn's regal ways and calculated poise had made an impression on him as much as he on her. But he hoped above all else that Jonathan's ability to make those near him *see* might affect her—and deeply. As deeply, perhaps, as it had affected him once.

It had been nine years since Jonathan had opened Rom's eyes to a vision of Avra at peace. The crippled boy with the penchant for dreaming the second side of reality had been an instrument of the Maker's Hand that day. Not an erratic man or a blood savior or a living spring of Mortality, but one who helped others see in a way unachieved by any Mortal to date.

Surely, he could help Feyn see as well.

And help Rom to remember.

All of Jonathan's promises to date had been fulfilled. All of them. Even in the midst of Jonathan's waning potency and Feyn's strange and staunch loyalty to Saric, the thought comforted. Jonathan's promise would not fail this time, either. Years from now, when Mortality ruled the earth, Jonathan's strange behavior, the conundrum of his waning blood, the growing factions within the Mortals—even Triphon's death—would be seen as trials rather than defeat.

He closed his eyes and drifted into a half sleep, thinking again of Avra. But this time her face lengthened and her skin paled. Her hair, so auburn in life, darkened to near black. As did her eyes. Until her face was not the face of Avra at all...but of Feyn.

Feyn, who had not taken part in the wild rites of the Gathering and might even now be awake in her yurt on the edge of camp.

Rom sat up. Had the impassive lines of her cheek softened? He didn't dare hope.

But he did.

He dressed and went out into a camp littered with the evidence of celebration. Spilled cups and empty plates of mostly finished food. Clothing, a random boot here and there, abandoned where it fell. Embers dying in cook fires outside yurts, the pots over them open to any who cared to eat. The drums, still aligned on the steps, their drummers long gone...

The tripod and the slashed bowl of blood hanging like an empty husk over a macabre stain of blood upon the dais.

He turned away, headed for Adah's yurt, likely empty—she was known to have a lover across camp—but knew he would at least find enough food for Feyn. He made it only halfway there when he saw the guard striding toward him. Relief relaxed the man's face and he broke into a jog.

One of the Nomads. Up early. Too early.

"What's happened?" Rom demanded.

"Suri found you?"

"For what?"

The man blinked. "I sent Suri to find you—"

"Why?"

"He went to your yurt just a minute ago. I—"

"I'm not in my yurt, clearly. What's this about?" He resisted the urge to take the man by the shoulders and shake him. He had run dry of patience days ago.

"Seriph says the Dark Bloods have escaped. The woman and her man, they're—"

"*What?*"

The man took a half step back.

Why would she escape? She had talked to Jonathan! She had *seen*!

But then a different thought assaulted him.

"Where's Roland?"

"He's gone after her."

In that moment, Rom knew two things. The first was that Feyn had betrayed them. Either she'd played him all along, or Jonathan had finally crumbled and undone all that Rom had worked for.

The second was that Roland was going to kill her.

"When?"

The man shrugged. "Half an hour."

"My horse!" Rom snapped, spinning back toward his yurt. "Now!"

Roland and Michael had tracked Feyn and her guard to the south; the scent of Dark Blood clung like webbing to the leaves and branches.

There were the more mundane signs as well: broken twigs, crushed grass, hoof scuffs on rocks, horse sign and tracks on soft earth.

They rode hard, rarely speaking except to affirm what the other had already seen. Two hours, the guard had said. Even riding at twice the Dark Bloods' speed they would require two hours to catch them. Any slower and Feyn would reach the city before they could stop her.

The sun was high when they crested a hill and first sighted the two Dark Bloods watering their horses by a stream.

With a click of his tongue, Roland signaled stop and dropped from his mount. Leaving it to Michael to secure the mounts, he released the reins and crouched behind a low boulder.

Feyn stood by her horse, gazing toward the south. Her escort was on one knee, inspecting the right hoof of his mount.

Michael lowered herself beside Roland, breathing steadily. For a moment neither spoke. They hadn't been seen and the wind was in their faces, filling their nostrils with the stench of death. Roland had never expected to so welcome such a putrid odor.

"Less than a hundred paces," she whispered.

"I need to talk to the woman," he said. "They're fast, remember that. Don't expect a second shot. The wind—"

"I was shooting into the wind when I was five, brother." Her bow was already in her hands. She notched her first arrow. "Just to be clear, you want the warrior dead—"

"—and Feyn's horse. We may need the other."

Michael gave him a casual nod, lifted her bow, drew the string back to her cheek, and sighted. She pulled in a long breath, adjusted for both wind and distance, then released her fingers.

A soft twang and the arrow flew into the wash with

blazing speed. In the space of an instant it buried itself in the Dark Blood's ear with a distinct thunk. The warrior jerked and then dropped to his side as though clubbed. The moment he did, his horse reared back from the stream.

"Her horse!" Roland snapped, and launched himself forward, over the crest and down the hill.

Feyn was spinning, looking frantically for the source of the attack until she saw him closing and froze, eyes wide.

Michael's second arrow whipped overhead, narrowly missed the Sovereign, and sunk into her horse's neck, just behind its jawbone. The animal bolted into the stream, whinnying as it fled into the brush beyond, leaving Feyn abandoned and empty-handed.

"Run and the next one is for you!" Michael cried.

Feyn glanced up, saw she had no escape, and went very still. Roland slowed to a walk at the bottom of the hill, now only ten paces from her.

"So we meet again," he said.

Though her face was striking, her scent was an offensive bouquet—a strange mixture of defiance, anxiousness... and grief. Perhaps grief most of all.

She was fond of the warrior, he realized with surprise, flicking a glance at the Dark Blood's fallen form.

He stopped before her. Her skin, so unnaturally white, seemed paler than even a moment ago.

"Running was your downfall. Now they all know the truth."

Her lips tightened over her teeth. Her hair was disheveled, loosed from its simple braids. "You don't understand."

"I understand you, *my lady,* all too well."

"You understand nothing about me, or my allegiances."

"Is that what you call blind loyalty to your brother?"

"I'm talking about the boy."

He barked a laugh.

"Do you understand anything of the thin line I've walked since waking from stasis?" she demanded. "Did you just expect me to run out and proclaim my allegiance to the boy?"

"After betraying us at the Citadel, you claim allegiance to the boy? No. It may have been nine years ago, but it is no more."

"True. It's faltered. None of what was supposed to happen has come to pass. And no matter how much Rom thinks I can work a miracle in the senate, my hands were tied the moment I was brought out of stasis before Jonathan claimed his majority."

"You're loyal to no one but Saric. Or is it only to yourself?"

"I died once, and what did that gain me? Die and you will see how it changes your perspective on *life*. No. This time, I mean to do things my way."

He slipped his knife from its sheath and squatted, one leg forward. Spun the blade in his hand. "Maybe you should try dying twice. It would help my perspective."

"Kill me and lose the boy's most powerful ally." Her nostrils flared. Roland took in the scent of indignation, of anger, fear. And of something else he could not name.

"Ally? You all but admit your loyalty is to no one."

"Yes, I questioned. But that was before what I saw last night."

"And what did you see last night? A mad boy bathing in blood?"

"I saw something that I understand," she hissed. "Better than even you, Prince."

"And what was that?" His elbows rested on his knees, knife twirling loosely between his fingers. "That what I said was true? That we would crush your brother's army, no matter how strong? That you needed to run to warn him?"

She took a deep breath and lifted her gaze to Michael, coming up behind him with the horses.

"I saw you would never trust me," she said, her eyes back on him. "Now you prove it."

"You're right. And now you prove why I can't trust you."

"You know nothing of my intentions."

"And Rom does? You must have had quite the romp in the meadow with him."

Her eyes narrowed. "You don't know him as well as you think. But you're right. He doesn't know me. I'm not a girl any more than he's a naïve boy. There is an entire machine waiting for me." She jutted her chin in the direction of Byzantium. "One backed by my brother whom *I* have to manage. You can't know how dangerous he is."

"There, you're wrong. I have every idea."

She narrowed her eyes. "I *died* for Jonathan once. Does this mean nothing to you? Do you understand all that I have done?"

He raised his brows and grinned. "Enlighten me."

"You not only owe your life to him for the blood in his veins...but to me."

"Why did you run?"

"I knew you had no intention of allowing me to leave. Rom perhaps, but not you. If I don't take more blood tonight, I die. I'm dependent on Saric's blood, or didn't Rom tell you? It doesn't matter. We both know you wouldn't have let me leave on my own, having seen your camp."

"And yet by fleeing on your own you seal your fate even more."

"So now you kill me. And what does that win you?"

"All Dark Bloods must die. It's the only way for my kind to survive."

"Are you so blind? Or do you simply refuse to see that I can help you?"

"You can help me by revealing where Saric holds his forces."

She gave a brittle laugh. "And lose all of my leverage? No. I am your key to destroying Saric."

"Are you? Then show me your intentions. Tell me where his fortress is."

"Even if I did, you would stand no chance."

Roland stood up and walked closer, rounding to her left, knife snug in his right hand.

"Kill her now and be done with it," Michael said.

"You of all people know Rom's request is impossible," Feyn said, voice now tight. "Putting Jonathan in power with Saric alive will only invite a full-scale war. I didn't create this mess; I was resurrected into it. Now I have to fix it. My way."

"The only way I'm willing to consider is via the death of all Dark Bloods," Roland said, glowering at her through lowered lids.

"You can't provoke war. You're outnumbered!"

"I don't think you realize how powerful we are."

"Oh, but I do, and I tell you…it's not powerful enough."

Roland flipped the knife. "Then there's no reason to prolong the inevitable."

He stepped behind her and grabbed her hair. Jerked her head back, exposing her neck.

"No bargaining?" he said. "No begging for your life?"

"No," she whispered. "We both know you never had any intention to let me live."

Roland laid the blade against her throat. "You're right."

He was about to express a final passing word of consolation—as much as he hated the Dark Blood there was something noble in this Sovereign who'd once given her life for Jonathan. But two things quickly came to his attention: The first was the drumming of horse hooves, of a single rider quickly approaching. The second was that the rider was upwind. He couldn't determine whether the rider was Mortal or Corpse, Dark Blood or Nomad. Killing her now, he might lose a valuable hostage and any leverage she offered.

Then he knew. The leader of Keepers had discovered them missing and followed them. Rom, come to save his woman.

Roland's first impulse was to pull the knife across Feyn's throat and be done with it. He was in no mood for weakness, a trait that seemed inexorably ingrained in Rom's psyche. But the sight of Feyn's veins pumping their black blood onto the ground would prove too much for the man. They could not afford division now. Perhaps in Feyn's attempt to escape Rom had found an ounce of sanity.

"Hold still. Not a word."

To Michael: "On my right, stay hidden, bow ready."

She ran in a crouch to a tree, upwind, dropped to one knee, bow strung already.

Roland held his ground, watching the crest of the hill.

CHAPTER THIRTY-TWO

ROM HAD PUSHED HIS HORSE without mercy, following both tracks and scent in a pell-mell rush south, desperate to catch Roland before it was too late.

A hundred thoughts had relentlessly pushed through the fog in his mind, chief among them the question surrounding Feyn's attempt to escape.

Why?

Had she planned her move all along? Were other Dark Bloods waiting for her to exit the camp? Had he been played the fool, captured by misplaced love and hope?

But the most unyielding thought of all was Roland. Rom knew the prince had pushed her to the conclusion that she had no hope of leaving the valley alive. That when it came to Feyn, he possessed not a bone of trust. Nomads had always seen the benefits of life as their due inheritance—the prize awaiting them after generations on the run. Roland's obsession was not love or truth but freedom and power, and in his mind Feyn posed a direct threat to both.

He knew he was closing as the sulfuric scent grew stronger—too strong. Not just the odor of Dark Blood, but of physical death.

Terrified that he was too late, he crested the hill, the stench of death burning his nostrils.

The scene in the wash below flashed before him as his horse thundered over the edge. Roland behind Feyn, knife at her throat—both staring up at him. Janus, the Dark Blood, dead on the ground with an arrow buried in his head. Roland's and Michael's horses tied to a shrub by the narrow creek.

But Feyn was alive. For the moment.

As his horse plunged down the stony slope, Rom knew that what must be said now would require finesse, not volume. Reason, not emotion.

He slowed his horse to a walk and approached, easy in the saddle. Pulled up ten feet from them. Michael stepped out from a tree on his left, hesitated a moment, then lowered her bow.

Rom spoke, paying her no mind. "Hello, Roland."

The Nomad released his fistful of Feyn's hair. "Good of you to join us, Rom. Please don't tell me that you still trust the heart of any Dark Blood bound by loyalty to their master. Regardless of past intentions."

Rom glanced at Feyn. Her eyes were fixed on him, brimming with tears.

"I trust no one who breaks their word and flees. But we have the Sovereign of the world in our hands now. She is more valuable to us as a hostage than dead."

Roland spit into the dirt. "She's dead already. Your problem, Rom, is that you find it difficult to place reality ahead of hope. She ran because it's in her blood to run. As long as she's alive, she posses a threat. Believe me when I tell you there are two Sarics still breathing. I would cut that number down to one."

"True enough." Rom dismounted, struck by the fact that he found Roland's words compelling. "But we're up against the end, close to the goal. All I ask is that you consider what Saric might offer us for her return."

"Are you both fools?" Feyn cried. "Rom, still the naïve lover, and Roland, the warrior too full of bravado to understand the subtleties of negotiation. At this rate you'll both be dead long before Jonathan takes power."

They stared at her. Rom wondered if Roland was as taken by her audacity as he.

"What do you gain by killing me?" she demanded.

"The satisfaction of delivering your head to the Citadel in a box," Michael said, ambling easily toward them.

"My sister has a point," Roland said. "There are advantages to an enraged enemy, whose calculation is thrown off balance."

"You can hardly enrage Saric by my death," Feyn said. "He would only take his seat as Sovereign under the guard of twelve thousand Dark Bloods and hunt you down at his leisure. The division among you will further widen under pressure and Jonathan will lose his unified defense. In the end you will all be purged. The hope Jonathan brought through his blood will be forever lost."

Roland gave up an incredulous chuckle. "You see how self assured they are, Rom? We've avoided Order for hundreds of years. We'll fight for hundreds more if need be. Jonathan's no longer the Maker we depend upon."

"I do see," Rom said. "I also see that she isn't a fool. She ran because you pushed her to it. She needs Saric's blood or she dies. It's Saric we should kill now, not Feyn." And then he added, "At least, not yet."

"She broke her word and ran."

"You gave her no choice!"

"I can give Saric to you," Feyn cut in.

"You expect to be trusted now, as you face death?" Roland snapped.

"No." She took a deep breath and closed her eyes. "What I can offer you requires no trust on your part. But the Nomadic *Prince* refuses to listen long enough to hear me out. He's made up his mind, regardless of the consequences."

"Do you blame him?" Rom said. "If you had something to say, you would have said it in our camp."

"I should have. That was my mistake. And I may pay for it with my life. But as he says, I'm dead already. In Saric's world I'm only his slave, waiting for his axe to fall so that he can take my Sovereign place. In yours, I'm nothing more than a prisoner who must die to make room for Jonathan. I have nothing to gain either way."

Rom felt his heart falter at her words. She'd died for Jonathan only to be resurrected into Hades itself.

"We're wasting time!" Michael said.

Roland looked from Rom to Feyn. Pushing her away from him, he said, "Speak."

She turned, straightened. "It's only a matter of time before Saric kills me. Do you have any doubt of that?"

Rom shook his head. "No."

"With or without me, he will come after you. The only question is whether it's under his terms or yours. You have nothing to lose by my returning to him."

"We have the information you give him to lose," Roland said.

"And this harms you how? You can simply move and be gone. He already knows enough about your numbers and skills. What could I possibly tell him that might compromise you at this point? He gains nothing with me at his side. My only hope is to free myself from him. It's what Jonathan told me last night when he came."

"He told you to free yourself?" Rom asked.

"It's the only way I can live if you kill Saric. It's the boy's wish. Ask him yourself."

A smirk pulled at Roland's mouth. Rom knew Jonathan's words held less and less credibility with the Nomad.

"Is it even possible?" Rom asked.

"I believe so, but that's my concern. Yours is Saric. I think I can give him to you. And if I can't, I'm the only one who stands to lose anything. You'll be no worse off than you are now. Trust me or not, it doesn't matter. I can't hurt you."

She made a good point. Surely Roland heard at least that much.

"Go on," Rom said.

Feyn crossed her arms and looked at Roland. "You said last night that you could destroy Saric's full army in the valley where you live."

He frowned, then nodded once, slowly. "And if we could?"

"Tell me. Can you?"

"It's possible."

"Then I think I can convince him to bring his full army to your valley. Make what preparations you need, and then take him."

They had all considered the possibility of thwarting an invasion in the Seyala, but no discussion had been made of purposefully leading the Dark Bloods to them. Even if they could, the odds would be astronomical.

"Roland?"

"Our seven hundred against their full army of twelve thousand...a considerable risk."

"Risk," she said. "Where's that bravado? Consider what you would gain if you were successful. Your greatest threat is the existence of so many sworn to your end. They must all go. I can deliver them to you."

"So you say," Michael quipped.

"I wouldn't worry about my ability to deliver them, only your ability to exterminate them. Are the Nomads as great as they claim?"

"Yes, but neither are we foolish," Roland said.

"Which is why you see the value of what I say. If I fail, you lose nothing."

Rom studied Roland, measuring the Nomad's resolve. "Can we do it?"

The Prince paced, one hand in his hair. "Possibly. And if the tide goes against us we have our means of escape. It would require—" He stopped short, glancing at Feyn. He wouldn't discuss any tactics in her hearing.

"You understand that I would need to be protected," Feyn said. "Saric will know he had been handed over. If he survived—"

"That can be arranged," Rom said.

"And I would need to assure him that I could deliver him Jonathan."

"What?"

"He's obsessed with him as a Maker. I would need to convince him I could deliver him. But Jonathan has already made the way plain."

"How so?"

"He has insisted that he and I meet alone tomorrow, the day he comes of age."

"Nonsense!" Rom scoffed. "Jonathan will be placed in no danger under any circumstances."

"Then take that up with him. I will go into seclusion. The rest will be up to you."

They stood in silence for long moments. Nearby, one of the horses snorted then dipped its head to chew at a tuft of grass, oblivious to the critical decision at hand in the wash.

"It may be the only way to bring Jonathan to power," Rom said. "The question becomes: what are we willing to risk to bring about his kingdom?"

"We are here to save the life he's already given us," Roland said. "That is the kingdom."

Not entirely true, but Rom wasn't about to argue.

"Either way. Saric and his army present the greatest threat to all Mortals. We would risk only our fighting force. The others would be gone."

"Don't discount the risk."

"I'm not, but neither am I discounting the potential gain." Rom frowned. "You're the tactician. The Keepers will support your decision. Make it now."

Roland mirrored Rom's frown. He glanced once at Michael, her silence her unspoken endorsement.

The Nomad faced Feyn, jaw set. "Tomorrow. See that he brings them all."

CHAPTER THIRTY-THREE

SARIC SAT AT THE END OF THE EBONY TABLE, silver fork inverted in his left hand, knife in his right slicing through the salted venison steak like a surgeon, aware of the deliberate precision he applied to his task. The rare meat parted under the sharp blade, blood seeped from clean-cut fibers. He set the knife down, lifted his fork, placed the cubed morsel between his front teeth and pulled it free of the prongs. Warm juices flooded his mouth as he bit into the flesh.

The taste filled him with a sense of contentment—comfort despite the concern, however minor, that had gnawed at him since Feyn's departure.

According to the scouts, she'd arrived safely, spent only an hour in the valley, and then been taken by the Mortals. His men had lost them in the canyons. He'd expected nothing less—Nomads were well known for their ability to cover their tracks and remain in hiding.

For two days no further word had come, and Saric had courted the possibility that she'd been killed. If so, he would simply step into her vacated seat. Her loss would be disappointing, but minor; her only true value to him was in the serving of his whims and any part she might play in flushing the Mortals out of hiding—both roles that could be played by others in time.

Still, he'd been pestered by concern. If the Mortals had a way to turn her blood and mind both, she might double-cross him. Feyn was subservient—that much she had demonstrated to his satisfaction. But his sister was a strong woman, intelligent and calculating to the bone. Could those same traits enable her to break free of his control?

No.

Just as he finished dinner, word came: Feyn had returned. Anxiety slipped from his shoulders like a silken robe. He immediately ordered Corban to see that she was properly bathed, powdered, and dressed in white before joining him at his table. She would need to feed on more than food tonight.

Two hours later the room was lit by candles—twenty-four of them in six candelabras, three on each wall adjacent to the table. Classical strings from the age of Chaos filled the room with haunting notes. A composer named Mozart. A requiem for the dead. But in Saric's mind, the requiem was for death itself.

He glanced at the grandfather clock on the far wall. One minute to eight. He would soon learn what gift Feyn had brought him. She would not disappoint, he was quite sure. His mind turned to Jonathan.

The political power the boy might attempt to flex was of no concern. Nor was the threat from the Mortals who might defend him. Both were inconveniences that would be crushed soon enough.

The power of the boy's blood, however, was a different

matter. However advanced Corban's alchemy had become, he could no longer deny the possibility that the life offered by Jonathan's blood was more powerful and therefore more rewarding than his own.

The thought tightened his gut into a knot as two opposing obsessions raged within him: the need to embrace the greatest life in its truest form, and the need to rule over that life as the only Maker.

If he crushed Jonathan and his Mortals, no threat to his supremacy would remain. But in doing so he would also effectively remove the possibility of tasting that same life himself.

Did the Mortals feel more than he did when they tasted life's pleasures? Was their ability to love and hate greater than his own? Were they driven by more ambition than any he had known?

It shouldn't matter, so long as his own power was unsurpassed. And yet it did matter. His desire for more inflamed him. Weakened him.

He had to annihilate the Mortals and Jonathan with them. There could be only one Maker.

A knock on the door interrupted his thoughts.

"Come."

The door swung in and Feyn stepped into the room, alone. Her hair was drawn back into two thick braids. She wore the white dress he'd instructed Corban to give her. She was a vision with dark eyes that spoke of silent submission.

He returned her stare for several long moments, waiting for her to speak out of turn. She did not.

"You look beautiful, sister."

"Thank you, my Lord."

He nodded toward the chair at the far end of the table. "Please sit."

Her long dress flowed gracefully around her legs as she crossed to the table and sat. Fresh venison, vegetables, and a pristine place setting waited her. Saric came to lean over her, to cut a thick slice of venison onto her plate.

"In honor of your return I will serve you tonight, my love. Does this please you?"

"If it pleases you, my Lord."

He lifted his eyes as he set the knife down. "Would I serve you if it did not please me?"

"No, my Lord."

"No."

He stood, carried the plate to her seat and placed the portion between the utensils before her.

"I imagine you're famished."

"Yes, my Lord."

"For more than meat."

Her eyes lifted to meet his. "Yes."

"Eat," he said. "Finish all of it."

Without waiting further instruction, Feyn picked up the silverware and cut into the meat.

She ate in silence for several minutes, Feyn with eyes downcast, only looking up at him on occasion and then only briefly, as he'd taught her. She was beautiful.

Saric leaned back in the seat where he had taken his dinner earlier, elbows on the arms of his chair, fingers interlaced.

"You earned their trust as I instructed?"

She swallowed her last bite. "Yes."

"Tell me."

"Rom Sebastian, not the Nomad, came for me. He

spoke of life and the boy and begged me to usher Mortals into power under my authority."

"I expected nothing less. You agreed?"

"Eventually, yes. I thought it best they see my resistance before I offered any interest in their cause."

"Good. They took you to their camp?"

"Yes."

"Then you know where it is."

"They took me in a hood. But yes. I know where it is."

He felt his eyes narrow slightly. "How is that possible unless your departure was actually an escape? After I expressly told you not to arouse suspicion. Look at me."

She raised her gaze to his. "No. I didn't escape. They led me out hooded again. And they kept Janus for surety."

"If they led you back out in a hood then you don't know where the camp is."

"My Lord, I could hear the river. The sun was out and warm from the east. I have an impeccable sense of direction." She offered a slight smile, as though uncertain if she were permitted to do so. "I could find your fortress now, if you asked me. And I was escorted here in a hood as well."

Was it possible? He studied her, the way she lowered her gaze again.

"I've spoken with Corban and reviewed the maps with him. I hoped you'd be pleased."

Something niggled. And yet she was the picture of conciliatory submission.

"If you have done anything to arouse suspicion, you will tell me now. If they suspect any foul play, they'll vacate the valley before we can bring our forces to bear."

"No. They won't. They're a very cautious people, but they won't."

"No? Why?"

"Because they believe I've thrown my loyalty in the boy's favor."

He studied her, searching for any sign of deception.

"I see. And yet you point out their cautiousness."

"Only because they must not be underestimated."

"But they suspect no attack?"

"No."

He nodded. "Good. Did you learn of their forces? How many, how strong, what skills they possess?"

"Yes, my Lord."

"And?"

"They are only seven hundred strong. The rest are too old or young to fight. Regardless of their skill, which is considerable, they would stand little chance against your army."

He had already concluded as much. His children might not have the wily skills of a Nomad or the uncanny abilities of the Mortals—he had heard the accounts—but they were unmatched in strength and speed.

"They say they have strange perception. Tell me... what source do you suppose it come from?"

"From Jonathan's blood—that which they consider true life."

True life. Saric's earlier thoughts about the boy returned. For a moment he craved that life like he'd craved his own Maker's blood. To see and taste and experience the way Mortals might. He pushed the annoying thought aside.

"They will soon see just how true their life is," he said. "Their Maker will be dead by this hour tomorrow."

She seemed to choose her next words carefully. "That

might be a problem, my Lord. They watch the boy constantly and keep him in seclusion for safety."

Saric picked up his goblet. "You tell me this only now?"

"The boy trusts me. He's asked me to come to him. I alone can give him to you."

Her tone smacked of manipulation. Curious...

"I have a request," she said.

"Now you are so brave as to make a request?"

Feyn slid back in her chair, crossed her legs and pressed on without reacting to his implicit correction.

"If I am to rule as Sovereign under your authority, I would do so freed from the physical restraints and inconvenience of taking your blood every three days. The others you've made are loyal to you, born of your blood. And so am I. But I wish to be untethered."

She'd found the audacity to ask this? Saric leaned back in his chair and tapped the tips of his fingers together.

"Your time away has filled you with boldness. What do you expect me to make of that?"

"If I am bold it is only because I have your blood, my Lord. You can kill me at any time and rule in my place—I accept that much and as such, I am at your mercy. The life you gave me is yours to take. I only ask that you allow me to live free for as long as you would allow me to remain in your service. Anything else is no true life at all. Anything less is no true obedience."

This was the Feyn he recalled from their former life. So she hadn't been stripped of her backbone... He found the revelation satisfying. Perhaps she would bring him more pleasure than he'd anticipated.

"I'm not sure you know what you ask for," he said.

"Then tell me."

He cocked his head slightly. "You make demands?"

"Forgive me. Could you tell me what I ask for?"

"That's better. There's only one way to be freed from your need of my blood. Even if I were agreeable, you would be inviting more than you bargain for."

"I would become a full Dark Blood," she said. "I don't see how that is any different from what I am now."

"There is no way to go back. Ever."

"I'm Dark Blood already and dependent on frequent feedings to remain alive. I feel trapped. Caged. This isn't the same life you have, brother."

Not Master or Lord. Brother. He could not suppress the grin that crossed his face. "I see. And you mean to use the boy as leverage to be granted your wish."

"I only wish to be alive as my own Maker is alive. Fully alive and free to serve you. I mean no disrespect. I merely point out the value I bring you and ask for this one favor in return. Make me free, my Lord. If you find any displeasure with me, then take my life and be Sovereign in my place."

She might consider conspiring against him now while her own blood still swam in her veins, but as a full Dark Blood all trace of disloyalty to him would die. Did she know as much? Likely not. Either way, she knew that she was his to keep or discard. And she had pointed out the obvious: her need to take his blood would quickly become a nuisance.

"It would require a full blood transfusion."

"I accept that."

"You would be mine forever."

"I am already yours forever."

He nodded. "You are. Tell me, do you believe it's true that the boy's blood is poison to Dark Bloods?"

"Yes."

"Then you realize your blood could never be altered by Mortal blood."

"Mortal blood would result in my death."

"And if I refuse your request?"

"I would know you don't trust me."

"You would still give me the boy?"

"Yes."

"How?"

"I will go to him alone only to lead him to you, to deal with him as you see fit."

Yes. She would. As any Dark Blood must and would.

"And you, my Lord? You will march on the Mortal camp?"

"Yes."

"When?"

"First thing tomorrow."

Saric pushed his chair back, stood, and rounded the table to her side. He offered his hand, which she took with a light touch.

"But for now rise, my love."

She slid back her chair and rose. With his thumb, he brushed a black speck from the corner of her mouth.

"So beautiful, so strong. You have given me Sovereignty and for that you are deserving. I'll grant your request, Feyn. I only hope my gift does not become a curse."

She dipped her head. "Thank you, my Lord."

"And then you will betray the boy into my hands."

"Yes, Master. I will."

Chapter Thirty-four

The sun rose in the eastern sky, flooding the plateau above the Seyala with light long before it would break into the canyon below. Half a mile to the south, the broad valley Mortals had called their own for nearly a year had been returned to nature. The yurts had all been collapsed and loaded on carts. The stock pens had come down, the posts gathered up; fire pits raked and filled in with fresh soil, all traces of human life covered or swept away.

From where Rom stood above the narrow northern canyon, only the scarred soil and the discolored ruin dais betrayed the recent presence of humanity. The inner sanctum had been purged of all relics by the Keeper and then of its silks and rugs. As was their custom, they'd left the leather bowl used for the commemoration of Avra's heart erected between the twin columns. The pocked limestone beneath was still stained with blood, a macabre blemish visible even from this distance.

Avra…the first Mortal martyr. Rom wondered how many would join her today.

He turned on his heel and walked toward Roland, who

was in urgent conference with Michael and Seriph. Massive boulders had been perched five deep along fifty paces of the cliff on either side of the canyon's mouth. Beyond them, forty fifty-five-gallon barrels of oil that Roland had taken from transport raids over the last five years lay ten paces apart along a section of the cliff that dropped vertically into the chasm.

The plan, long envisioned by Roland and once fully improbable to Rom, had now become their only means to escape certain death.

"Tell me this will work," he said.

Roland turned. "Now you have your doubts?"

"I always had my doubts." He peered into the canyon to his right. "You're sure the fire will catch?"

"Forget the fire," Michael said. "Worry about getting them into the canyon. If we can do that, we can cut off escape with the boulders. They'll be trapped like mice and we can pick them off at our leisure."

There were only two ways out of the canyon: through the north or back the way they had come. The sand between had been soaked in enough oil to bring Hades to earth.

But the engagement wouldn't begin here in the valley, where Mortals would have less room to maneuver, but on the plateau, south and west of the canyon.

"We'll suffer our losses," Roland said. "The only question is how many."

"How many would you say?"

"As few as possible. If the losses mount, we retreat north as planned."

"How many before we retreat?" Rom pushed.

"I'll make that decision when I make it."

Rom nodded. He'd felt sick in his gut since their return. Here, away from a camp filled with Mortal children and the arthritic elderly, the risk seemed reasonable. But one glance back toward the valley where those under his care made preparations to leave or fight, and Rom found he couldn't shake the fear that they'd made a terrible mistake.

Ahead, a group of Keepers directed by Nashtu, one of his ranking fighters, leaned into one of several large boulders still to be placed. The position of the boulders was critical—it had to be precarious enough so that the pull of one wedge would send the whole pile tumbling. Rocks and debris had been loosened along the top of the cliff as far down as their ropes would allow then to reach. With any luck at all, the resulting landslide would be enough to close off any retreat.

"Careful there!" Nashtu cried. "You want the whole lot to fall now? Place it like a feather, man!"

Two others with sweating necks and backs joined in, barking their own directions. A full hundred in all worked feverishly along the cliff, making final preparations, well aware of one thing: none of it would make any difference if Roland's tactics on the plateau didn't succeed first.

Nearly five hundred Mortals—those pregnant or too young or old to face the Dark Bloods—were nearly gone. The last group of fifty was just now snaking its way over the plateau, headed to one of three locations ten miles north where they would wait for word from the scouts that it was either safe to return or time to flee.

The train of horses plodded toward the badlands pulling dismantled yurts, bundles of cookware, clothing, food...all that was owned by the Mortals except for the weapons and anything else the fighters needed to engage

Saric's army. Over a hundred able-bodied men and women had retreated with the others—those craftsmen and workers among them who were less skilled in fighting but strong enough to rebuild and live to fight again.

"We have our advantages," Roland said. "And you can be sure I will bring them all to bear. We divide, we jab, we whittle their numbers down, we run, we volley... We *can* prevail. I wouldn't risk a single life if I didn't think so." A glint came to his eyes. "I tell you today, Rom, the day will come when we live as Makers. Immortal."

That is your obsession, isn't it, Prince? To live forever. To be immortal. To be Maker and ruler as one.

He'd seen the lines of Roland's face harden under pressure these last days. His calling had always been for his people. Only a few of them knew of Jonathan's recent decline, and Rom bristled to note that those who did seemed to look past the boy as though he were a remnant of something past, no longer relevant. And he knew that for them, this battle was a matter not of the boy's ascension to world power, but of their own survival. It always had been. But now, something had shifted within Roland in the last few days.

Rom had no intention of confronting Roland on the matter now, but he would when this was through. This battle—everything they risked now—was for Jonathan's sake, not their own, whether Roland acknowledged that today or not. There were now many Mortals, Makers each and all of them. But there was only one true Sovereign. And he had bled already to give them the life they now called their own.

"And what of Jonathan?"

Roland glanced over Rom's shoulder, then turned

aside. "Ask him yourself." The Prince walked away, motioning Michael to follow.

For a moment, Rom considered going after him. They dare not go to battle with divided loyalties!

"Rom…"

He hadn't heard the two riders approach. At the sound of his name, he turned to see Jordin and Jonathan dismounting behind him. Pushing his concerns about Roland aside, he tried to offer a smile.

"Jonathan. Jordin. Roland assures me that all is in order."

"I hope not," Jonathan said. "It was my understanding we were overthrowing Order." He grinned.

"Yes, well, there is that. I'd feel better if you left now, while the last group is still in sight. As for you, Jordin, Roland says we need you here, but I—"

"I go with Jonathan," she said.

"If you would let me finish."

She nodded, momentarily contrite.

"I insisted you remain at Jonathan's side with the others who've gone north. Be prepared to return the moment you receive word," he said, looking from her to Jonathan. "With hope, Saric will be defeated and we will escort you to Byzantium by evening."

The boy was eighteen today. It was to be the day of his succession, of the claiming of his majority. With luck, it still would be. Time enough for celebration then.

Jonathan seemed to consider the proclamation for a moment. "Then I will fulfill the role I was born for, as Sovereign."

"May life return to the world through you, my Sovereign," Rom said, feeling as he said it that was prayer as much as intention. He did not know how the day would unfold—only that somehow seeing the boy before him to power was his destiny.

Jonathan took Rom by his shoulders, embraced him.

"No matter what happens today...what you have done will never be forgotten, Rom. When death comes, you will find life. The dead will rise and live under my reign, mark my words."

"I have no doubts, my Sovereign."

Jonathan released him and laid his hand on Rom's shoulder. "Good. Then you will find it easier to hear that I won't be going with the others as you ask."

Alarm spiked his gut. "No, you must. For your own protection."

"No," Jonathan said, turning. "I would be closer so that I can join and claim my Sovereignty without delay. Jordin will come with me."

"I won't have you fighting!"

"I won't fight, but I will stay near. I'll go to the old outpost at Corvus Point. It's isolated and safe. Have no fear, Rom. I've decided." He gave a slight, enigmatic smile. "Isn't that the prerogative of being Sovereign—to make ones own decisions?"

Corvus Point was roughly five miles west, but there was no telling what might happen in battle. And Dark Blood scouts would be scouring the region.

As though having read his mind, Jonathan said, "It's too far for their scouts to wander. We'll be safe. Jordin and I are adept at escaping stray threats."

Rom suddenly recalled their negotiation with Feyn the previous day. She'd said Jonathan suggested they meet alone on the day of his succession to sort out the matter of rulership—a detail he'd forgotten in the crisis until now.

Jonathan had planned on this all along.

"And Feyn?"

Jonathan gave a slight, acquiescing nod. "I asked her to meet me there. Warriors will wage war, but the matter of Sovereignty has its own demands."

He no longer sounded like the boy of just days ago. Even so, panic sliced through him and he grabbed him by the shoulder. "Then I go with you. I won't leave you unprotected. We'll take ten of our best—"

"No, Rom. You have a battle to fight. I will take Jordin."

"She's only one! No. The stakes are too high!"

"*My* Sovereignty is at stake. I decide this, not you, Rom. Not this time."

The boy's tone could hardly be more forceful. Rom released his shoulder, taken aback.

Jonathan said, more gently now: "Today I come of age. Let me lead as I must, and you as you must. Our people need to see you in battle."

"Roland leads this battle."

"Roland leads the hearts of many. But you lead others. And so Jordin comes with me alone. We will meet Feyn. Before the day is out, we will return with an agreement that will allow me to take the seat of power I was born to occupy. Saric will be defeated and I will be Sovereign. Let me take the path to my rightful place."

Was it possible?

But Saric would still come. Regardless of Jonathan's negotiations or even agreement with Feyn, Saric held her in thrall, poised to ascend to power in her place. He had to be defeated.

He started to object again, but Jonathan cut him short. The boy had indeed become a man nearly overnight.

Gone was the crazed Sovereign to-be who'd danced covered in blood at the Gathering. Here stood a young leader demanding to be obeyed.

There was hope yet.

Rom looked at Jordin. Her chin was a notch higher than normal. Pride. Satisfaction. She'd been chosen by Jonathan—nothing could mean more to her.

"Don't let him out of your sight," Rom said, leveling his gaze.

"I have no intention of removing my eyes from him."

"If he even stubs his toe, I will hold you personally responsible."

"He will not lose a single hair under my watch."

"Keep an eye out for any disturbance. If you're confronted, don't fight. Run."

"Faster than a gazelle."

"Enough," Jonathan said. "Am I a fragile egg?"

"No. You're a Sovereign—far more precious to this world than any egg."

Jonathan's expression softened. "As are you, Rom. Jordin would give her life to save me, I have no doubt of that. And I would give my life to save either of you."

He clasped Rom's shoulder one last time. "Be safe, my friend. We will meet soon in victory."

"If Feyn comes, watch her like a hawk," Rom said. To Jordin: "Don't trust her. If Saric dies and she survives—"

"Then Feyn and I will both rule," Jonathan said, walking back to his horse, Jordin at his heels. He swung into his saddle, and a second later Jordin followed suit. "Put your doubts aside, Rom. Don't forget what I've said."

With that he pulled his mount around and spurred it west.

Toward Corvus Point.

CHAPTER THIRTY-FIVE

FIVE MILES SOUTH OF THE SEYALA VALLEY, the scales of a vast serpent twined along the Andros Plain. Twelve thousand strong. Two thousand cavalry. Ten thousand heavy infantry.

Two standard-bearers carried red flags that rose like two crimson eyes set in the head of the winding army. One standard bore the compass of Order, which was the insignia of the world and of the Sovereign, transposed from its former white background to the crimson of Saric's new World Order. The other bore the scaled phoenix—a winged and serpentine creature, an evolved version of the firebird—a symbol of reborn life once revered by the alchemists of ancient Chaos.

The army was twice the size of the legions in the history books of Chaos. Appropriate, because it was comprised of those who were doubly alive, each of them beautiful works not only of alchemy, but of their Maker.

The vanguard's two thousand cavalry rode black stallions so eerily uniform that one might think they had all sprung from the same bloodline or even the same genetic code.

Which they had.

The cavalry carried spear, sword, and smaller round shields. They rode in black saddles skirted in leather armor to protect the horses' flanks—at first glance one might not know where man ended and horse began. Their black helmets reflected no light from the sporadic sun.

The ten thousand on foot wore the black leather armor of their leader, the polished sheen dulled by the dust of eight hours' march. It covered the toe and heel of boot to midthigh, giving each man the appearance of having sprung up out of the earth like a dark specter.

They carried spears with iron heads. Short, straight swords rode their left hips. Rectangular shields were slung across their backs like giant, obsidian scales. The weapons of a former age had been remade—reborn—in factories deep to the south of the peninsula, first under the orders of Pravus, and most recently under Saric.

They marched twenty columns wide, with five on either side of the supply train in the middle. Their formation was perfect. Mathematically precise and alive.

The ground shook beneath their feet like the beat of a new heart, the anthem of a new, living age.

At the head of the vanguard between Brack and Varus, Saric closed his eyes. The cavalry's rattling tack was its own kind of song. Primal. Beautiful. Like the violins of Chaos—refined beyond mere sound.

Only one being could threaten the harmony of his new era.

The boy. Jonathan.

His stomach clenched, as much with anticipation as with outrage. There were two things he could not abide. One was any threat to the supremacy of the life in his veins. The other was his own need to discover and consume the greatest life.

Since the notion that the boy might possess superior life in his veins had first presented itself to him, no amount of reason had yet dislodged it. Saric had spent half of the night in preparations with his generals, considering every possible approach to the Mortals' valley and every tactic to ensure crushing victory. He had rehearsed them all relentlessly. That he harbored any concern despite his army's massive advantage was somewhat of a mystery to his officers, he knew.

In reality, it was the conflict raging in his mind regarding the nature of Jonathan's life that motivated his anxiety, something his children could never know. The questions had kept him awake until their predawn march.

In the end he submitted himself to a simple resolution. His need to rule superseded his need to embrace any potentially greater life. And yet even the thought of opening the boy's jugular haunted him. One Maker, slaying another. What source of life might he extinguish, never to be seen again? What if he was making a terrible mistake?

Saric's reverie was broken by the sound of drumming hoofbeats, approaching from the north. His eyes snapped open.

One of the scouts, returning. Urgency pulled at the warrior's face.

Saric raised his arm. Behind him, the machine of his army ground to a halt.

The scout dropped from his horse before it stopped, took five long strides and dropped to one knee, head bowed.

"My Lord."

"Rise." The scout stood. "Well?"

"The valley's been evacuated. They wait on the plateau."

So the Mortals were not unaware. They'd expected as much; Nomad scouts would have seen their approach in time to make hasty preparations for retreat or for battle.

"No sign in the valley?"

"They've swept it clean, though there are some ruins that appear to have been recently used for a blood ritual of some kind. It's all over the stones."

Little was known about secretive Nomadic custom, but Saric had little interest in how they lived. It was the blood that interested him. Could it be the boy's? Had it been spilled in the making of more Mortals?

His mind flashed back to Feyn's turning, there on Corban's table, as the alchemist pumped her full from the reserve he kept of Saric's blood. She'd screamed as Saric's blood had replaced the last of her own, and then she'd collapsed for an hour. Waking, she'd been calm and resolved, apparently unchanged from her former self.

Later, when they had spoken, she seemed quite sure they suspected nothing and would be caught unawares, but then, she knew little of the ways of war.

For a moment, he wondered what else she might have been mistaken about. Or if she'd knowingly delivered erroneous information to him. No. Impossible. His power over her was absolute and she'd been guileless. He would have seen her deception.

Or had the boy found a way to change her in ways beyond Saric's understanding?

He would soon know. She would either betray the boy as she'd detailed late that night, or she would attempt to betray *him*—inconceivable, considering her state.

She'd insisted she go alone, fearing that the presence

of any guard would be detected and her opportunity lost. He'd rejected the notion immediately, but she'd been adamant that Jonathan must suspect nothing at this so-called summit of theirs.

"I don't like it," Varus murmured.

Saric's attention returned to the present.

"There is nothing to like about what is uncertain," he said. "How many on the plateau?"

"From what we could see, less than a thousand," the scout said. "But full surveillance isn't possible—they wait on the higher ground."

"What side?"

"The north."

Strange relief seeped into Saric's veins. This much of Feyn's report was true. It gave him confidence in her ability to deliver on the rest.

"Weapons?"

"Standard fare," the scout said.

"Horses?"

"Most."

Again, as expected.

"They'll outrun our infantry," Varus said. "Unless we can bring our infantry to bear, they might outmaneuver us or run."

"If they meant to run, they would have already," Saric said. "They wait for us. And so we will not disappoint them."

"Could it be a trap?" Varus said.

Saric looked at the scout for an opinion.

"No sign that we could see. A canyon lies to the north, best to be avoided."

Saric lifted his eyes and studied the horizon. The valley lay beyond the hills ahead, quiet in the late morning sun. It was odd to think that the fate of all living and dead could be decided in one historic day. His name would be remembered to the end of time.

This was his destiny.

And the boy's blood?

"We can lose half of our number and defeat them still," Saric said. "We're not here to save lives, but to end every one of those that threatens our own. Send three hundred cavalry north along the western flank to cut off any escape. Another three hundred west with a full division of infantry to hold for my signal. We box them into their own graveyard without a single Nomad warrior left standing by day's end."

There would be no one left to protect the boy.

"Send the bulk of our infantry led by two cavalry divisions up the middle," Varus said. "We'll drive them to the cliffs. Send the order."

Brack nodded and wheeled his horse round. Within moments an entire left column broke away and reformed itself, twenty wide, one hundred deep. Two thousand infantry. They were moving northwest within minutes, and Brack was back by his side.

Saric gave him a curt nod. "Double time."

Brack swung his arm forward and the dark and beautiful machine that was his army broke free and started forward again, this time at twice the former cadence.

The plain began to narrow within three miles between two rising cliffs. From here one could follow the winding of the river that flowed between them up toward the canyons and mountains farther north. Saric's army surged along the plain, veering west as the ground began to rise. Not until they reached the mouth of the valley did he signal.

"Stop."

He eased his mount's pace to a halt, and the heavy crush of boots on the ground ceased behind him. Still no sign of the Mortals on the cliffs. Save the ruins, the valley appeared empty, as reported.

"Bring him."

Orders were issued and four Dark Bloods wheeled a long, shallow cart forward. Saric considered the Mortal gagged and bound at the neck, waist, and knees to a thick pole in the middle of the cart. He was naked except for the cloth around his waist—covered now in sweat and dust. His eyes were wide, wild. Corbin had done well to keep the prisoner they'd taken at the Authority of Passing alive. Triphon, he was called—Saric knew him as one of those who'd conspired with Rom Sebastian to bring him down nine years earlier.

Now the Mortals would see the fate of any who defied him.

"Do it in front of the ruins."

The two pulling the cart dipped their heads and started forward at a jog, followed by two others. The air hung heavy and still as the party separated from his army and angled toward the ruins a quarter mile ahead along the eastern cliffs.

For several long minutes no other movement. The cliffs remained empty, the sky silent, the valley dormant.

The detachment stopped near the ruin steps and quickly went to work digging a hole.

"Anything?"

Brack's mount shifted beneath him. "Nothing. But they watch."

Undoubtedly. And they would see.

The preparations took only a couple minutes aided by thick muscle and sharp shovels. They pulled the Mortal from the cart, still bound to the ten-foot pole. The air stirred, lifting something from the top of the pole a banner bearing Saric's crest.

They hoisted the prisoner up for all to see before moving him into position over the hole and unceremoniously dropping the end of the pole inside.

The Mortal's body jerked and hung still, like a pig on the end of a stick, arms bound to his sides, feet dangling.

They filled in the hole, tamping down the earth so the pole could stand on its own, then stepped back and awaited his signal. Nomads were too strong to be demoralized by the sight, but planting the body would serve as clear notice: *Saric claims this valley.*

He nodded. Brack lifted a red flag.

One of his children withdrew a sword, walked over the Mortal, and shoved the blade up under his rib cage. The man on the pole jerked his head back and strained, the cords standing out along his neck, then went limp, a lifeless puppet on a spike.

As he watched the slaying, Saric could not help but consider just how easily life was taken, yet how difficult it was to create. How it was his to give and take.

There could be only one Maker.

The Dark Bloods gathered the cart and left the pole standing in front of the ruins. High above a lone buzzard had already begun to circle in the gray sky.

"Take us up," Saric said.

The army surged ahead.

In less than ten minutes they were across the small river along the western floor. Saric glanced back at the army winding its way up the slope to the plateau, now only a half mile distant. Numbers, not agility or speed, would win this day. Overwhelming power, bred for war by alchemy. He wondered how many of his children would die today. For him. And he vowed in his heart that for each one that gave up his life, he would mourn and make two more in their stead...

And then four.

A scout at the top of the rise signaled clear.

"You should hold back, my Lord," Varus said.

"They run. I do not. Form the ranks wide."

Varus issued the orders and the serpentine formation broke into three, two of the companies veering west.

Like a rising tide of black water they crested the hill and edged onto the plateau that stretched nearly a half mile before falling into distant canyon lands. The grass stood two feet tall. Trees to the west. Cliffs to his right, east.

Still no sign.

Within half an hour, the division he'd sent earlier would be in place to flank the Mortals. With any fortune at all, they had pulled their scouts in to focus on the plateau. Surely they needed every man.

"Hold."

The massive army fronted by fourteen hundred cavalry rumbled to a standstill along the plateau's southern edge. To a man, they faced forward, eyes and muscles fixed, waiting for command. The air grew quiet.

Saric felt his eyes narrow. Not with impatience or anxiety, but with strange appreciation.

The Nomads were nowhere to be seen. The field was empty. Nothing except a tall, stripped sapling in the middle of the field, a quarter of a mile distant. Only after a moment's curious scrutiny did Saric notice one additional detail: hanging from a rope affixed to the top of it was something like a bladder or a large gourd . . .

Or a head.

The appreciation drained away as the head lolled in the wind, turning so that he could see the gaping mouth and bloodied face even from this distance.

"Janus," Varus muttered.

Ice flooded Saric's veins. Not at the thought of the man himself, but because in killing him, the Mortals had struck far more than the man. They had lashed out at the image the man was made in.

At Saric, himself.

So then . . . the Mortals would neither flee nor die quietly. So be it.

Run with your Maker's speed, Feyn. Bring me the boy . . .

He stared a moment longer at the head hanging like a macabre ball from that pole. Black rage bubbled up within him like tar.

It was in that state that he wondered if the lone figure galloping at breakneck speed from the far side of his vision had been conjured by his own wrath. If it had risen up from the ground like the vengeful dead.

But this was no apparition. It was flesh and blood. A feral tangle of beaded braids and leathers with a starburst of metal studs as though Chaos itself had touched it. All that was refined was untamed in the rider. All that was evolved was primal in him.

Roland.

The Nomad slowed his horse to an arrogant, easy walk and stopped next to the pole.

Chapter Thirty-six

Five miles northwest of the Seyala Valley stood the old outpost at Corvus Point, an abandoned crossroads along the ancient highway toward which Jonathan and Jordin now rode.

The building itself was barely eighteen feet in length. Its boards were weathered, its paint, if there had ever been any, washed gray. Even some fifty yards off Jordin could see the darkness of the interior between the planks. Off to the right, the crumbling remains of a concrete trough had sprouted tufts of grass and creeping weed. The pump was gone, likely requisitioned decades ago along with the door.

A horse was tethered to a post on the end of the shack's crooked front walk—a black, majestic animal that Jordin found herself envying for its sleek lines and sheer aesthetic beauty. Seeing it didn't help her state of mind.

A knot of apprehension had tightened in her belly during the ride from camp that morning. She'd seen Feyn at the Gathering, but only from a distance, and even then the Sovereign had been veiled.

Was Feyn beautiful? Could one person possess both

power and beauty in equal portions? Not that it mattered—Feyn stood for Order. And she was Dark Blood. On principle alone, everything within Jordin should revolt at the very thought of her.

But Feyn had also died for Jonathan once, and for that Jordin would grant the sitting Sovereign a measure of trust.

She glanced at Jonathan, riding at her side. Enigmatic preoccupation and nervous energy had rolled off him in frenetic waves since their leaving. At first she thought he was simply anxious. But it soon occurred to her that Jonathan might actually be excited to see this Sovereign who had died for him. Who might, if all Jordin had observed and heard was true, make way for him to rule with her.

Jonathan and Feyn, side by side.

Jonathan leaned forward in the saddle. Lanky and strong, darkened by the sun, he was a magnificent warrior who had come into his own.

He was eighteen today.

How old was Feyn anyway? Thirty-something? How could Jonathan choose someone nearly twice his age?

No. It wouldn't be like that. Their union would be a political alliance, no more.

Jonathan spurred his horse forward, eager to close the distance to the old shack. After a moment's disconcertion, she nudged her horse after his, eyes darting to the figure appearing in the weathered doorway.

Her heart dropped at the sight. The woman was stunning.

Her skin was pale—uncannily so, by any Nomadic standard. The envy of Order; of the royals in particular. She never would've thought such pale skin attractive before, but something about Feyn's regal bearing made it seem unquestioningly beautiful.

Her eyes were black, startling in the bright light, like giant pupils without any iris, glittering as the facets of obsidian. As the simple, dark jewels nestled against her earlobes.

The sight arrested her.

She was dressed in a regal white dress and wore two simple braids that twisted like carved columns down past her breasts toward her waist. Jordin would have eschewed such clothing as impractical, worn only by those who knew nothing of horses, but obviously she had ridden here from the city. She knew how to ride, and ride well.

Jonathan slid from his horse with the ease of one meeting a long-lost friend, showing not a shred of concern. He strode forward on his long runner's legs just as Jordin came to a stop beside his stallion. In one high step he had cleared the broken boards of the two stairs, long missing from the front walk of the shack. And then he was on his knee, kissing the hand of the Sovereign herself.

The sight struck Jordin somehow as anathema. The skin on her neck prickled.

"My Lady," he said, lifting his head and standing again.

Feyn nodded, her voice carrying beyond the broken porch. "Jonathan."

She gave no sign that she'd even seen Jordin—her attention was solely on the young man who'd shown her such respect. Still, if he honored Feyn, Jordin would as well, if only because she trusted him.

She swung down from the saddle, eyes on the pair, but rather than follow Jonathan up the stair, she hung back until he swung around.

"Jordin, come! Meet the Sovereign."

She lowered her head, walked to the shack, and stepped up onto the uneven boards of the porch.

"My Lady," she said, forcing herself to take the woman's hand. She expected the woman's pale fingers to be ice cold. They weren't. In fact, they were warm. The ring of office gleamed the color of sun on her right hand.

Jordin started to go to her knee.

"Please," the Sovereign said. "There's no need."

Jordin straightened with no small measure of relief and glanced at Jonathan. His eyes flitted toward her. "Jordin, will you give us a moment?"

She looked from him to Feyn, who towered a good head and a half over her. They were both tall. They were both stunning—she with ebony hair and pale skin; he with hair the color of turned earth, his hazel eyes rimmed in lashes that any girl would have envied.

They were beautiful together. Standing side by side like that, they could actually inspire a new age, she thought. With her poise and his enigmatic ways, the entire world would watch and follow them, if only out of curiosity.

Jordin's throat was dry. "Of course," she said.

She stood still for a moment, reluctant to leave. Finally, she took an awkward step backward, then stepped down from the front porch to walk back toward the horses, trying to appear purposeful.

Jonathan leaped off the porch, and she saw from the corner of her eye that he'd taken Feyn's hand. Uncharacteristic tears distorted Jordin's vision.

She was overreacting, she knew. Jonathan was demonstrative by nature. But she seemed unable to ignore the sight of the man she'd devoted herself to with a woman of such power.

Feyn stepped down behind him, and followed him toward a copse of trees.

Jordin recinched the girth on her saddle, glancing often at them. Checked Jonathan's saddle. Wiped the tears away with a gesture so swift she barely noted it herself. Their voices carried to her in low tones not meant to be heard. She kept one eye on them, wanting the entire time to look away from the way Feyn held his eyes as she spoke. The way Jonathan took her hand not once, but twice. The way the Sovereign dipped her head, offering him respect.

Or was it more?

They glanced back at her once. Good. Let Feyn see her watching them. Her. Jonathan's protector.

It occurred to her that even now, Feyn could make an attempt on his life. Jonathan might chastise her for such a thought, but was it really outside the realm of possibility? Wasn't he Feyn's only true rival after her brother?

She had promised Rom to never let Feyn from her sight, but that promise paled next to her own commitment.

What if Jonathan and Feyn did rule together, side by side? She'd heard that Sovereigns didn't marry—they only took lovers. But then a Sovereign had the power to change the law if he or she were so inclined. What if, by chance, it made sense that they should marry?

She lowered her head and forced herself to drag in a long breath. It wasn't like her to be jealous. He was her Maker. The bringer of life. He'd poured out his life for her. It wasn't for her to hold him with closed hands.

Could she stand by and protect Jonathan even if he were to marry Feyn?

She turned away from the horses, heart climbing into her throat. They were walking into the trees. Out of sight.

Panicked, she dropped the rein in her hands and headed after them.

She ducked the branch of a gnarled pine and hurried past three more with twisted, knotted branches that mirrored the fallout in her heart at the moment.

She hurried on, brushing aside branches, and pulled up sharply at the edge of a small clearing. Jonathan stood three paces away as though he had been waiting for her. No sign of Feyn.

He was alone.

She blinked, caught off guard. It was unlike her. She was faltering under the press of misplaced emotions.

"Where's Feyn?" she asked in a voice far too thin.

Jonathan closed the distance between them. "She's waiting. I said I needed to speak with you."

The band around her lungs released, if only slightly. The scent of Dark Blood put Feyn behind and to their right. She was headed back to the shack.

"What do you think of her?" Jonathan asked

I don't trust her. Not alone, and not with you.

"She seems . . . very powerful," Jordin said.

"Yes, she is."

"And very wealthy."

He dropped his head and forced a thin smile. But his braids fell forward over his eyes so she couldn't see his eyes. It was the posture of women she knew, when they wanted to shield their embarrassment or tears.

"Jonathan . . ." She reached a finger to lift his chin, regretting anything she had done or said to hurt him.

When he looked up there were no tears on his cheek. His eyes were filled with strange wonder.

"There's something I've wanted to tell you for a long time, Jordin."

Fear spiked her mind.

"I love you," he said.

She stared at him, unable to respond.

"As a woman." He reached out and took her hands in his. "I always have, from the first time you looked into my eyes after taking my blood. I chose you then and I choose you now."

"Jonathan..." It was all she found the courage to say. She wanted to throw her arms around him and shower him with adoration, but her muscles seemed to have left her command.

He lifted her hand and kissed her knuckles. "I will become Sovereign."

So Feyn had granted it?

"It's happening then," she said.

He smiled. "It will be a thing to see, I can promise you that. The earth will be shaken... A new age is dawning."

"Because of you."

His smile softened and he glanced down. Only then did Jordin find the words she longed to speak.

"I love you too, Jonathan. I've always loved you, more than you know."

His thumb brushed over her knuckles. "You know that Sovereigns don't marry..."

Despite her attempts to hold them back, tears filled her eyes. She nodded.

"Don't cry, Jordin." He lifted his other hand, brushed a tear from her cheek with his thumb. "If I could marry, I would choose you. It won't matter; I choose you now. When I become Sovereign, you will see."

She couldn't help the tears slipping down her face. She didn't quite know why she was crying... She'd never allowed herself to expect such beautiful words from him.

The fact that he as Sovereign could not marry was beside the point.

He loved her. He'd chosen her.

"You must also know that the days ahead will be filled with danger. Intentions may be misinterpreted. The dead will rise, but the cost will be heavy."

"When have we not faced terrible challenges?"

They would be together. Somehow. Though she knew he faced far greater challenges than any to date, she would be by his side. She would bear them all, with the courage of that knowledge. He loved her. He chose her.

"They pale compared to what's ahead." He paused, face taut with concern, then lifted her hand and kissed her fingers again. "When the darkest hours come, I want you to know that I've known what divides the heart for a long time, but not until recently have I fully understood my calling. The Dark Bloods won't rest as long as I'm alive."

"As long as I live, no Dark Blood will touch you."

Jonathan smiled. "My beautiful Jordin. I would place my life in your hands over any other. Without question."

"They won't fail you."

"No." But his gaze shifted, like the sky clouding before a storm. "But before you can join me, I have to do what I came to do with Feyn. Sovereigns have their duty. But you must never think I've abandoned you. I will build a new king-dom as Sovereign, that I can promise you. Not everything is known—Mortals may turn against me. But you, Jordin…"

Emotion choked off his words, but he pressed on. "Promise you'll never leave me."

"I would never leave you! I will go with you!"

"No matter what happens, don't leave me," he said. "I can't bear the thought of being without you."

"I won't! Please, Jonathan, don't speak like this..."

"Promise you'll follow me, even if the others doubt and turn away. Promise that you will follow me."

"I will always follow you, Jonathan." And she knew, as she had known for years, that she would pour herself out for him as surely as he had for so many, and for so many others to yet come.

"I would give my life for you," she said.

He offered her a quiet smile and a single nod. "And I for you."

He leaned forward and kissed her gently on her lips. "I for you."

CHAPTER THIRTY-SEVEN

Roland gazed at the amassed sea of Dark Bloods, acutely aware of many things at once: The oppressive stench of deeper death wafting across the plateau; the unwavering position of Saric at the front of his horde; the precise location of his archers in trenches along the western side where they awaited his signal; the years of training that every warrior under his command had endured readying for this very day; the battle plan he would execute in four critical stages; the ultimate trap designed to deliver the final blow to the army staring him down right now.

But one thought prevailed above all the others: The fate of all Nomads, those people who had clung tenaciously to freedom over so many centuries, would be decided today in a battle that, no matter how long awaited, could not be won. For all practical purposes, this ground now belonged to Saric.

The Dark Blood had succinctly made his point when his men had planted the pole bearing Triphon in the ground before the temple ruins. A runner had brought them the news: Triphon was alive.

Rom had gone into a frenzy, shouting for his horse. Roland had forcibly pulled him back.

"I have to go get him!"

"Don't you see? That's exactly what Saric wants!"

"This is Triphon we're talking about!" But then he spun away, fists clenched into white-knuckled balls. Rom was no fool; he knew there was no rescuing Triphon.

Words of assurance that Rom could not be blamed failed to calm him—or to assuage the tension in Roland's own gut. But it was true: taking the time to recover Triphon's body where he'd fallen at the Authority of Passing would have likely resulted only in more deaths—including Jonathan's.

In the end the two of them had ridden to the edge of the bluff, there to look down helplessly at the man Roland, too, had regarded as nearly a brother.

Roland's stomach had tightened to a knot when the Dark Blood shoved his blade under Triphon's rib cage and ended his life. Rom was beside himself, tearing at his hair. Roland's own emotion had been for the loss of a friend and those Triphon left behind, but as much for the staggering odds that they faced today. Surely, this was Saric's intent.

The Dark Bloods were too many. Too savage. Too powerful. Perfectly resolute. When the beast that was Saric's army moved, it would deny its size and strike like an adder with both wicked speed and venom.

Then again, if Saric had claimed the valley with Triphon's dead body on a pole, Mortals claimed this battlefield with the Dark Blood's head dangling from that rope.

Above, the sky had filled with dark-edged clouds full with the promise of an oncoming storm. A heavy rain might compromise their battle plan—particularly the fire they would need in the canyons. To think that after years of preparation for such a day nature itself might defeat them...

A chill prickled his skin.

His declaration that their seven hundred could defeat this swarm of twelve thousand had evoked bold cheers among the ranks of the Nomads just hours ago, and shouts and for final death to any who oppressed life among the living. Children had been kissed and embraced with promises of beauty to come before being sent away. Swords had been sharpened and arrows notched. Someone had told a story of a shepherd boy killing a giant with a single stone and a slingshot, a tale survived from times more ancient than even the Age of Chaos. And they had prepared, believing—knowing—that victory, if not assured, was at least possible.

But now as he stared down Saric's black dragon of an army, Roland wondered if he'd made a dreadful mistake. If he had overestimated his own tactical advantage. Superior Mortal perception gave them a decided edge over the Dark Bloods' brute strength and speed, he'd said. And the tenacious instinct for survival within their Nomadic veins would see to it that history recorded the day Roland's seven hundred Mortals crushed Saric's twelve thousand Dark Bloods.

They had shouted to the heavens at that.

But now the reality of a vastly larger force stood before him prepared to prove him a fool, and all the bravado and words in the world would not add even one man to his number.

He could still turn his horse back and give the signal

for retreat. They would ride north four miles, descend into the canyons along a narrow trail cut months earlier, and quickly disappear into four gorges to emerge three miles farther north, there to regroup in the Valley of Bones.

He could. And yet destiny would not allow him to retreat as his ancestors had.

Rom had informed him that Jonathan had retreated to the old outpost five miles northwest for a summit of Sovereigns. As far as Roland was concerned, they could talk all they liked; ruling power would be decided here on this field, between Saric, Maker of Dark Bloods, and himself, the Leader of the Immortals, as some of the zealots had come to call themselves of late. Political power would succumb to the raw power of life, something Jonathan no longer possessed.

For a full minute, the formation of Dark Bloods remained perfectly still. A thousand on horse, the rest heavy infantry. Part of Saric's cavalry would be farther west, awaiting the signal for a flanking maneuver. If the Dark Blood had considered every option, he had also sent another division north to cut off any retreat—they had the numbers to spare, and they knew that running had always been the most refined skill of any Nomad.

Not today.

The Dark Bloods' serpentine banner flapped lazily in the breeze next to another: the compass of Sirin, the standard of Order—but this time it was set, like the dragon, against a red background. If Saric intended the red background of his flags to symbolize blood, Roland vowed plenty of it would be spilled by sunset today.

The Dark Bloods hadn't moved. Saric, in conference with his generals, didn't bother turning his head to address him. Time stretched, filling the distance between them as the clouds shifted overhead.

He waited.

Finally, the general named Brack broke from his guard and trotted his horse forward alone. Saric had wisely decided not to place himself in direct contact with an enemy who might slay him where he stood. Wise. A show of confidence could go only so far. For a moment, Roland wondered if his own had gone too far already.

Only when Brack was within fifty paces could Roland distinguish his scent from the overwhelming odor of the horde behind him. A tinge of what he took to be apprehension, but no fear.

The general stopped ten paces away but Roland had no intention of speaking. They were posturing and they both knew it, each waiting for the other to move.

They faced off for a full minute. Twice the general's mount snorted and shifted impatiently. Never once did the general break his steely glare.

"If you have something to say, speak," Brack finally said, voice gruff. He was at the disadvantage in this stand-off and he knew it, because his master would expect a report.

Roland only stared. Sweat snaked down his back. Out in the wind it normally dried before it could soak through his clothing. Not today. His men crouched in hiding would be soaked from pit to waist by now. Few of them could yet see the full scope of the vast enemy who'd come to snuff them out, but to a man and woman they knew that survival today would come only through inhuman feats of skill, strength, and desire.

Then again, Mortals *were* inhuman. More than human,

created to live hundreds of years and engage the world with a refined perceptive sense superseding that of any living creature upon the earth.

Three hundred Nomads waited in hiding two miles to the south behind the Dark Blood army. Another three hundred to the west waited in oil-soaked trenches, armed with crossbows modified to send three arrows with each pull. Only a hundred were stretched across the plateau to Roland's rear, mounted just over the slight rise, hidden from view.

Each of them knew the critical mission facing them at the onset of battle: fell the cavalry first. Only then would their mounts give them any significant advantage.

"You mistake your foolishness for bravery," Brack said. "I will tell my Maker that you wish us to place your head next to the one above you."

He gave Roland a parting glare and jerked on the reins to turn his mount.

"Ask your Maker how long Nomads have lived," Roland said.

The general held up, and Roland continued.

"Ask him how so many generations of humans with a considerable appetite for breeding could produce only a thousand children. Then you will know why I stand here today, unconcerned. Your forces are matched in number. You've been drawn into a trap envisioned by the Sovereigns. If you retreat now and surrender Saric to die beneath my sword, we will allow your army safe passage. Refuse, and not one of your dead will walk away."

A new scent edged into Roland's heightened perception. Curiosity. Possibly confusion.

"There is one true Sovereign and his name is Saric,"

the general said. "He prefers sharpened steel over flimsy words."

"No, Brack." Roland nudged his horse left, drawing the man to face east so that his back was to the western edge of the plateau. "My Sovereign is called Feyn. She meets with the Seventh called Jonathan. Together they plot the demise of any Dark Blood to escape slaughter on this field. Tell Saric when he hears the sky screaming he will know that Feyn has betrayed him."

The general sat unmoving on his mount, unimpressed, by all appearances, even as his scent turned decidedly acidic.

"One nod from me, and you will be dead where you sit," Roland said. "Or I could have one of my men give you a gentle warning and spare your life. Tell me which you prefer."

For the first time, Brack's eyes narrowed. Roland turned his horse back to the pole and gave a short whistle.

The single arrow came from the east where Morinda, second only to Michael among all the archers, had been waiting over the lip of the cliff, head and bow hidden below a tuft of grass. The missile sped silently through the air, faster than any untrained eye could follow. Before the general could move, the projectile hissed by, a bare inch from his right ear, and embedded itself in the ground as though it had been there all along.

Brack did not flinch. He could not, however, mask the surge of concern betrayed by his scent. They both knew that unlike Dark Bloods, master archers were trained from childhood. They could not be bred in a laboratory or created with only a few years' practice—or else Saric would have his own. Now they had seen the true threat of Mortal archers.

"Consider that your warning," Roland said. "Stay and die. Leave and live."

He turned his horse north and galloped toward his line without looking back.

Saric heard the soft whoosh of the arrow before he saw the shaft cut across the plateau, narrowly missing his man. A glance in the direction of the cliffs failed to reveal the source of it. They had known that archers would be a challenge but had not known to expect such accuracy.

But in truth, it was the audacity of the direct challenge that bothered him more than anything.

"Hold!" he said.

His line held without the slightest twitch. Brack might have been caught unaware by the first shot, but now that he knew the direction of the archer, he would have no trouble avoiding a second.

But a second one did not come. And then Roland was retreating at full speed and Brack was returning at a trot. So then the shot had been a warning? What did they even hope to accomplish? Surely no show of individual bravado could be expected to shake his army.

"Well?" he snapped, as Brack pulled up.

The general hesitated only a moment. "He says to ask you how so many generations of Nomads could produce only a thousand children," the general said.

The question had already been asked and answered. The Nomads lost most of their numbers to attrition, leaving only the most dedicated to carry on their hard life. Now Roland wanted them to think they had many more. A pathetic ploy.

"And?"

"He said you would know your end when the sky begins to scream. He claims that Feyn has led you into a trap. The rest is utter nonsense."

The image of Feyn cut through his mind at mention of her name and in that instant he considered the logic of such reasoning. In one fell swoop she could rid herself of all threats to her rule by pitting Mortals against Dark Bloods.

What if it were true?

His eyes flashed across the plateau, searching for any sign that there were more than the seven hundred they'd come expecting.

Nothing. The Nomadic Prince had vanished from sight over a slight rise. How many had hidden there beyond their line of sight?

His scouts had reported only seven hundred.

"Tell me the rest," he said.

"My Lord—"

"Speak!"

The man dipped his head quickly. "He offers to spare the army if you surrender yourself."

Silence settled between them. Saric's gaze dropped over his general like tar.

"And did you for an instant wish that I would, so that you might save yourself?"

"Never, my Lord! I serve you with my life."

Saric looked away, toward the rise.

"Is there any possible credence to this notion that they may have more numbers than we're aware of...or that Feyn has betrayed us?"

His chief strategist, mounted to his right, said, "Unlikely, my Lord." The man waited a beat then spoke on. "I only wonder what kind of enemy would be so bold as to offer terms they knew would be dismissed. They are begging for engagement."

"So it seems. Only Feyn and our scouts have verified their numbers. Is there any possibility our scouts could have been misled?"

A long silence.

"It's possible," Varus said slowly. "The number first came to us from their scout while in our custody. It's possible he could have fed us misinformation. The Nomads could have hidden an army in the badlands. If Feyn—"

His words were cut short by a sound that Saric first took to be screeching birds taking flight to the west. He turned his head and saw the black flock rising, screaming.

Those weren't birds.

The screech became a whistling scream—a cloud of arrows darkening the sky. He'd heard of Nomads notching their arrows so they whistled as they flew, but he'd never imagined such an unnerving sound.

"Defend!" Brack thundered.

The terrifying sound had confused men and horse alike, locking them in indecision without a clear path of action. Too late, they recognized the unfamiliar threat of incoming arrows and threw up their shields while attempting to steady their mounts.

The first volley had not reached his cavalry before another horde of screaming arrows took flight from the west.

"Defend!"

His shout was lost in the squall of incoming projectiles. They had been carefully aimed to strike the leading cavalry, and they sliced down with blazing speed, cutting deep into leather, flesh, and hide.

It occurred to Saric in a momentary flash that if his children had been more given to panic, they might have bolted and avoided more of the heavy razors now cutting into their ranks.

Only one of every three arrows struck a target, but the second volley was already arching down, angled once again for the cavalry alone.

Brack shoved his finger in the direction of the archers. They had to be hiding in low ground. "Defend your Maker!"

The second volley sliced into the rearing horses. At a glance Saric saw that a full third of his cavalry had been compromised. A third volley darkened the sky. This could not be the doing of a mere few hundred archers! The threat wasn't coming from the north, which was the direction Roland had gone, but from the west.

Rage flooded Saric's veins. "Send them all! Send them all west!"

Brack swatted away one arrow that snipped by, then grunted as a second buried itself in his shoulder. He broke it off with a thick fist, stared at it for a brief moment, then hurled it at the ground.

"Cavalry, follow!" He spurred his horse and charged west, straight down the throat of the threat, ignoring the rain of shafts plunging into the ground around him until it seemed the earth itself had sprouted quills. As one, Saric's Legion shifted and surged forward.

Only then did Saric see the line of a hundred horses thundering forward from the north where Roland had vanished. Bent low in saddles at breakneck speed, the riders suddenly rose in their stirrups, drew bowstrings, and fired a much closer volley directly into his battered cavalry.

The arrows came in like hornets, zeroing in on the larger targets of the horses' bodies. And then more from the east where a line had risen from the cliffs, now to their rear. Half of his cavalry were down; the rest were in full swing west, leaving only infantry to bear down on the cliffs.

Saric swung his shield up just in time for the latest volley, arrows slamming into steel, then falling away, broken.

He gathered his resolve and willed himself to calm. A hornet could not defeat a hammer.

"Varus! The remaining divisions forward in full attack! Advance without retreat!"

The order was cried and the infantry surged forward, flowing around Saric like a thick, black wave. With a roar his Dark Bloods ran, leaning forward, shields lifted, feet shaking the earth, eight thousand strong.

The archers along the cliff sprung into view, loosed one last volley into the face of his advancing army, then sprinted in retreat. A line of two hundred men veered to their right in pursuit, a thundering horde. Too fast for the Mortals in flight despite their lighter weight.

Those at the back of the retreat were forced to engage. The Mortals parried and stuck, moving with the same agility he'd seen Roland demonstrate a week earlier. Deadly and deadly accurate, as though they saw every thrust coming. His children began to fall, only to be replaced by more, an unending tide of black.

Ten Mortals fell, then thirty. The line from the north was in full retreat.

Smoke boiled into the sky along the western flank. The ground was ablaze, set afire by the archers to cover their westward retreat. Fire lapped at the air, cutting off his cavalry. A full two-thirds of his thousand horses had been cut down by their deadly swarms of arrows, and those who remained were cut off from pursuit by the flames roaring from what could only be trenches filled with fuel.

The enemy had jabbed before going into full retreat.

The Nomadic Prince had proven himself a respectable tactician in his first blow, but Saric now knew the truth of their numbers. They'd shown less than two hundred. Even with the archers to the west, their numbers surely could not be more than two thousand. If they had more they would have used them in this first assault.

Now Saric would bring to bear his hammer. There would be none to flee. The division he'd sent west on a flanking maneuver would descend on the plateau soon enough, and his numbers would prove overwhelming at close range. Today, as over previous generations, attrition would be the Nomads' downfall.

Feyn may well have cut her tether and led him into a trap, but by day's end he would stand over her body…as Sovereign.

And then he would hunt the boy down and drain him of his precious blood.

CHAPTER THIRTY-EIGHT

SOME TIME AGO, Jonathan and Feyn had retreated to the ridge at the clearing's perimeter to speak the business of Sovereigns. Jordin hung back, replaiting her horse's mane, if only to keep her fingers busy while keeping her promise to never let Jonathan out of sight.

She saw the way they stood together looking out over the eastern hills, speaking in tones that didn't carry back to her even with her Mortal ears. They were making arrangements, no doubt. The first of many discussions she would not be privy to.

She watched the way he looked out over the hills as though with new eyes—a Sovereign's gaze, surveying all that he would rule. Feyn nodded intermittently, seeming to do the same, though Jordin saw the way she glanced sidelong at him while he was talking.

Jonathan might see more in her eyes, but to Jordin Feyn appeared cold and distant. Calculating. Perhaps it was that way with Sovereigns.

Was this to be her life, then? Standing by as he stood by Feyn's side? It wouldn't matter—Jonathan loved her as a woman. Nothing else mattered.

He would have her loyalty forever. And for his compassionate heart and eccentric ways, he would have her heart as well. He was all that Jordin had ever known to be beautiful and right...

The only truly beautiful thing in this world.

And so she would stand by and protect him regardless of the cost to herself, filled with the awe of having heard those words. *I love you.* The revelation that he could not marry her changed nothing.

She glanced up and saw that he was walking back, leaving Feyn seemingly to her own thoughts on the ridge. She straightened, aware of the butterflies in her belly. She was ready for the days ahead, whatever challenges they brought. For the move to the Citadel—shored up already against the pervasive smell of Corpse in the city.

Jordin gave him a small smile as he approached the horses, but his mind was either lost on his discussion with Feyn, or distracted by whatever task lay ahead of him.

He flipped open one of the saddlebags on his horse. "Never underestimate the cost of sovereignty, Jordin," he said quietly.

He said it as one who had taken a great weight on his shoulders. The look she saw so often on Rom's face. Roland's. And they were coleaders of only twelve hundred. What would become of Jonathan the day the world descended upon his shoulders?

"Jonathan..." She came round her horse and saw that he'd withdrawn a length of old bridle leather. "However I can serve you, I will. I will be there. I will never leave you."

When he looked up, sorrow was pulling at his face.

"You said that you would follow me always," he said.

"Yes. Always. What's wrong?"

"Even if where I go is difficult to understand?"

"Yes!"

He studied her for a moment, then turned the leather length in his hand. "Then bind yourself to your word. Join with me."

Her heart stuttered. It was the way the Nomads bound themselves to one another on the day they made pledges and took their mates.

"Bind myself to you? Now?"

"Put your hands out," he said gently.

She lifted her hands in front of her, wrists together. Jonathan wasn't given to convention—he was the son of the unexpected. It was one of the things she loved about him, trusting that he had a purpose even in his most erratic actions.

She watched as he crossed the tether and looped one end twice more, and then the other, twice more. But he was binding her arms together, not him to her. With a soft, confused laugh she looked up at him.

But this time, his face was twisted with emotion, lips pressed together in an effort to control them. She'd seen Jonathan cry many times, unbeknownst to so many, and knew the expression well.

"Jonathan?"

A tear coursed down his cheek as he finished with the leather, tying it in a hard knot.

"What are you doing?"

Tears wet on his face, he took her neck in his hands, leaned in, and kissed her.

"I love you, Jordin," he whispered. And then his arms went around her and he lifted her off her feet.

Was it possible that he had changed his mind? Was this what he and Feyn had spoken about? Was it possible he had gone back to Feyn to discuss terms, to say that he loved her and could not marry another?

"Jonathan?"

He carried her to one of the closest trees, a bent and gnarled olive. Eased her down by the trunk, which hadn't grown but a couple feet around. Pressing her arms up over her head and against the tree, he produced another length of cord and began to bind them to the trunk itself.

Her first impulse was to jerk away, but she could not defy Jonathan. He had his purpose and she would simply trust him. Hadn't she just sworn to follow him regardless of where it took her? Then this was a test...

From the corner of her vision she saw Feyn returning from the ridge, eyes on them. A bell of alarm attempted to shatter her resolve. What was happening?

"Jonathan...Please."

He seemed not to hear her. She began to twist, to try to pull her hands free, but they were bound too tightly by the first rope.

"Stop, Jonathan. Please!"

But he was fixated, working quickly with the rope until her bound hands were coiled to the tree trunk above her.

He stepped back, eyes pleading with her to understand. "I love you, Jordin. You will soon understand, I promise you. Follow me always."

Feyn stopped beside him. "It's time," she said, laying her hand on his arm. Then Jordin knew...

They were leaving her!

Panicked, she jerked against the rope, but it was bound too tightly.

"Jonathan!"

He took one last look at her, eyes filled with longing and sorrow, and then turned.

"Jonathan!" she screamed, feeling the veins in her temple throb with the effort. She watched helplessly as Feyn untied the black stallion and swung into the saddle. As Jonathan returned to his horse and did the same.

They left her bound to the tree, with only Jonathan's own tears as consolation.

CHAPTER THIRTY-NINE

MICHAEL, knife!"

Roland approached Michael at a full gallop, sweeping by her left side as she snatched a knife from her belt and flipped it over her back—all without turning from the two Dark Bloods bearing down on her with slashing blades. Their Mortal senses might prove challenged in such a crowded battlefield, but their acute hearing could easily identify directions and distances on all sides.

A Dark Blood on horse—one of the few left—angled in at a dead gallop, eyes on Michael. Her knife flew lazily through the air within easy grasp as Roland thundered past. He snatched it by the hilt and hurled it at the approaching horseman in a single, unbroken movement.

His aim flew true. The knife slammed into the mounted Dark Blood's neck with enough force to slice clean through to the spine. The rider went limp; his horse galloped by, aimless as the Dark Blood slowly toppled to one side and fell heavily to the earth.

All but a handful of Saric's cavalry were now dead.

Michael took advantage of the momentary distraction, plunged her sword up under one of the Dark Blood's chins, then spun in a crouch with a wide slash that cut deep into the other's hip. Another thrust put the warrior out of his misery.

Roland swept around and slowed so that Michael could swing up behind him.

"Thank you," she panted.

"Don't thank me yet."

It was all he needed to say; the battle was far from over.

The events of the last hour and a half ran through Roland's mind.

His archers had delivered five thousand arrows before setting their trench on fire and retreating behind a wall of flames and smoke. They'd cut the Dark Blood cavalry by two-thirds in that opening strike.

Saric had quickly mounted a counterattack using the brute strength of his full army, killing nearly a hundred Mortals in his first unrelenting sweep across the plateau, leaving only three hundred Nomads to defend the high ground while the reserve force of three hundred waited south for the signal that would begin the third phase of engagement.

For the next half hour they'd battled on horse against an infantry that was fast and strong but no match for Nomads on horseback. Saric had stood his ground on the southern end of the plateau, surrounded by a thousand warriors.

And then the Mortals began to fall. One by one, and only after taking down more than their share of Dark Bloods each, the vast imbalance of numbers began to take its inevitable toll. By the end of the first hour, the ground was littered with dead, making movement difficult.

Nearly 150 of his warriors had fallen before the scouts reported Saric's flanking maneuver from the west—at least a full division and another three hundred cavalry.

They'd stockpiled two hundred bows and three thousand arrows in anticipation for a second wave of cavalry, and this time every able-bodied fighter had taken up with the archers and laid down a fusillade of screaming projectiles that had felled half of the rushing cavalry before they could scatter.

Roland had made his case clear: they would descend to the valley for the third phase only when the Dark Blood army had been cut by a full third or when the Mortals had suffered losses exceeding two hundred.

Over the last half hour Roland had lost another fifty fighters.

Two hundred dead. The thought shortened his breath.

To make matters worse, dark clouds had gathered at an alarming rate, covering the sky with a thick layer of gray like a lid. The wind was starting to pick up and would compromise the work of his archers. A storm would not bode well for them.

He pulled his mount up on the rise and wheeled around to where Michael's horse waited. She dropped to the ground and swung up into her own saddle. Rom rode in hard from the west, tussled hair whipped by the wind.

"Too many!" he shouted, reining his mount back sharply. "We have to go *now*!"

Roland's attention was to the south, where Saric's guard defended against a dozen Nomads firing into the Dark Blood lines from horses on the run. Every minute twenty or thirty of Saric's warriors fell. He had lost four thousand men, leaving him with roughly eight thousand, but the toll on the Mortals was mounting. Only a hundred and fifty remained to fight on the plateau, waiting for the three hundred in reserve to be called into the third phase of the battle.

Impossible odds.

"I heard from the runner," Rom said, breathing heavily. "They wait for your signal. The Dark Bloods are cut by half, maybe more. We have to go now."

Roland nodded. "Pass the word. We transition to the valley. Follow hard on my heels."

Rom spun, whistled, and then took off, leaning over his mount, cutting the air with another whistle, which was picked up by another, and then another. The sound would be picked up even from this distance by Mortal ear, but Roland wanted to be sure even those in the din of battle would not mistake the call as planned.

He watched as fighters broke off their attack and swept north from across the plateau.

"Send the signal for the reserves."

Michael pulled out a thin metal whistle that issued a high-pitched tone typically heard only by dogs and other animals with broader auditory ranges. Mortals could easily pick out the distinguished note from a significant distance. A runner half a mile south would pick up the sound and send another. Within seconds the signal would reach the reserves waiting to the south, and they would move toward the Seyala Valley at full speed.

She pressed the whistle to her lips and blew three long notes.

"Even with the reserves we'll only be five hundred to their six thousand," Michael said, shoving the instrument back in her pouch. "We're down to a handful of arrows. Once we enter the canyon, we'll be caged. If they don't follow us—"

"I know the risk," he said through gritted teeth.

"We could still break off and escape north. We could return later with guerilla tactics."

"Saric will rebuild quickly and be twice as wary. He knows our strengths now. No. We fight to the end. If they don't follow, we retreat north."

"It's not the retreat I'm worried about. It's the battle into the valley. How many more will we lose, drawing them so close?"

"Do you want to lead? We knew the price of freedom would come at great risk. Don't forget that the lives of those who've died today are on my head!"

"Forgive me."

Roland looked away toward the line of Nomads just joining them along the shallow rise. "Today a new race rises, Michael. All along our people assumed victory would come under Jonathan's rule. We were wrong. You and I, not Jonathan, will lead our people to victory. The world has never been reshaped without bloodshed. Today it's our turn to spill what we must to ensure the place of our kind for centuries to come. We live or die for the sake of this race. These Immortals."

"Immortals?"

"The zealots' term. The Keeper says the power in our blood is strengthening, even as Jonathan's weakens."

She looked at him with wide eyes. "Jonathan's?"

"Is now nearly dead. His blood has reverted to that of a Corpse."

She blinked, aghast.

"Keep this to yourself, sister."

He spurred his horse and rode down the line of Mortals gathered along the small rise. A stream of Dark Bloods was already fast approaching.

"Follow my lead!" he shouted. "We sweep west! Hold in the valley until they pursue. Hold your lines past the ruins until I give word. Today we prevail. Today we rise!"

Without a glance back, he veered to the west, leaned low over his mount's neck, and spurred it into a full gallop.

The first thunder rumbled high above.

"They run!"

Saric spun to the cry of Varus, who'd held close at his demand. Nearly a thousand of his remaining eight thousand children had formed a thick wall of protection around his position, shielding him from skirting attacks as the enemy tore into his force with the fury of a lion rushing in to attack—only to retreat and attack again.

As he'd known, attrition had been the Mortals' downfall. He'd cut down a full half of their forces in the last hour while suffering massive losses himself, but they were losses he could afford for the sake of the victory before him. His army was still a full eight thousand strong.

Meanwhile, Brack had fallen in the battle, taken by Rom Sebastian's sword. The naïve artisan who had thwarted him nine years earlier had found a backbone and the skills to keep it intact.

He followed his man's line of sight in time to see the Nomadic Prince bent low over his mount, leading a growing contingent of his warriors as they streamed south along the plateau's western edge.

"They flee!" Varus said.

Or they regroup, Saric thought, as Roland plunged past the southern lip and galloped down the slope toward the valley below. His men followed without hesitation, flying past formations of Dark Bloods outmatched by the horses' speed.

"Into the valley," he murmured, narrowing his eyes.

"They lead us into Feyn's trap."

He considered the meaning behind Roland's sudden shift in plan. Feyn intended to betray him; that much had become clear. The precision of their preparations could only mean that the Mortals had fully expected him to arrive and engage as and when he had. Something more than conjecture—or some*one*—had informed them. They had baited him and attacked with brutal efficiency.

But he had prevailed.

"The valley will only limit their movements," he said. "A trap would involve more."

"The canyons beyond," Varus said, stilling his shifting mount.

"Yes, the canyons."

His gaze swept the vacated valley to his right. The ruins with their bloodied courtyard sat unoccupied along the eastern cliff near the mouth of the valley. The valley floor narrowed as it ran north, ending at the mouth of a gorge that led into a canyon with a river along one side. The sandy wash provided ample room for ten horses abreast to pass. Even twenty.

By his count, the Mortals had initially brought only four hundred warriors to bear on the plateau and then replaced them as their own forces were depleted. But they were fewer than the seven hundred Feyn had reported, which meant the rest were either gone with those Mortals who could not fight or being held in reserve.

"If they enter, we hold back," he said.

"More are coming," Varus said. "Reserves."

Dust a mile south.

"They intend to enter the canyons knowing we'll be eager to pursue," Saric said.

"And so we hold here."

"No. They'll advance slowly in order to draw us in. And so we will take the battle to them in the valley, but hold by the ruins and wear them thin. Patience will win this war. Give the signal. We descend in full pursuit."

Varus hesitated only a moment, then spun and issued the command. A horn blast and Dark Bloods from across the plateau broke into a fast run for their position as Varus issued a string of commands that quickly translated to the flags. And then he turned the army south at a fast jog as those behind fell in line. Like a black river, his vast army spilled over the hill and angled toward the valley.

Overhead, clouds had cut off the sun. Saric scanned the heavens, momentarily struck by the movement in the sky, like ghosts rushing to meet an unheard call. A storm was gathering with astonishing speed, hastened by a strengthening wind. The Mortals' archers would be compromised. Rain would slow their horses.

The sudden turn was a good omen.

Dust rose to the south, trailing a visible gathering of horses racing to reach the valley's wide mouth before his Dark Bloods could block their entrance. If the Mortals could be divided, half of his children could engage those caught outside the valley while the rest of his forces fought the Nomads inside. The Nomad prince would be far less likely to flee into the canyons while some of their own remained outside.

"Varus, take a division at full sprint!" He rose in his stirrups, as he plunged down the hill. Thrust his arm forward. "Cut them off!"

Varus roared the order to one of the division commanders. His men rapidly broke ahead of the main body. Like a cluster of black hornets, they swarmed down the hill and cut east, passing through the river as if it were made of fog. They were moving at only half the speed of the mounted Nomads but then, they had only half the distance to cover.

Ahead of them, Roland glanced back at the pursing Dark Bloods, motioning frantically at the approaching Mortals to speed.

It would be close.

The arrows came from the riders then, fired into his sprinting division. Not in massive waves as in the Nomad's first attacks on the plateau, and not with the same accuracy in the face of the wind. Several of his men went down, forcing those behind to leap over their bodies. But the swarming horde did not falter or slow.

"Varus! The rest! Full sprint!"

Barked orders. The flags went up. The rest of his army tripled its pace and flooded the low ground.

Saric gave his horse its head as the two armies angled for the valley's mouth at breakneck speed, each vying for first position. His blood ran cold as anticipation flooded his veins.

His Dark Bloods were going to reach the valley first.

And they did, surging across the mouth of the valley in a long thick line. The Mortal riders thundered forward then veered east as more of his army swarmed in behind the ranks already in position.

Saric's mount leapt into the river, splashed through the water and tore up the far bank, barely breaking pace. He pulled north along the river, digging his heels into the flanks of his mount. A small hill rose a hundred paces ahead.

"To the hill!"

Varus and five hundred of his children shifted and angled for the rise.

Saric pulled the steed to a sharp halt at the mound's crest and wheeled it around to give him full view of the valley.

What he saw below filled him with dark satisfaction.

Triphon, the slain Mortal, hung from his pole alone before the temple ruins, head sagging in death, portending the fate of all who'd once celebrated so-called life with him. Roland stood in his saddle a hundred strides north of the dead Mortal, joined by two hundred of his fighters, eyes fixed on the battle erupting at the valley mouth beyond.

Saric had divided the Nomad's forces.

He'd been correct: the prince would not retreat into the canyons before the rest of his warriors fought their way through the Dark Bloods to join him.

Beyond the ruins a steep cliff cut off any hope of escape to the east. The hills behind him rose to more cliffs, blocking any ascent to the west. There were only two ways out of the valley: past his army now positioned at the mouth, or into the canyons at the far end.

For the first time, the battle had taken a decided turn in Saric's favor. The din of combat grew as riders braved his front lines in a desperate attempt to pass to safety. Steel clashed against steel; hooves pounded the earth. Cries and shouts of warning...

Groans of death.

In his ears the sound was nothing less than a siren

song, beckoning all to follow a new master: Saric, who would usher in new life and protect it with an iron fist.

"Half, in deeper after the prince!" he cried.

Varus gave the order and his page issued the signal. Two flags lowered toward the Mortals in the valley.

Three thousand Dark Bloods turned, took up rank, and began marching toward Roland's two hundred Nomads, just now surging forward to attack. They clashed just north of the ruins, this time in closer quarters than on the plateau above.

Now the battle was fought on two distinct fronts: one at the mouth of the valley, one in the valley itself. Had the Mortals been less determined, they would have the sense to cut off their assault and flee. But Saric knew running wasn't in Roland's blood.

Beyond the ruins, a Mortal rider raced behind the main battle, arms waving frantically, yelling retreat. It took only a moment for Saric to recognize the man as Rom Sebastian.

Two leaders with two minds. One cried retreat, the other attack.

Now Saric knew: only time stood between himself and full victory. The battle was his. If his army didn't annihilate the entire Mortal force, there would only be enough left to run and tell the tale later.

Feyn would die for her betrayal.

There would be no army left to usher Jonathan in as Sovereign.

Saric would rule without challenge.

Rom tore down the line behind the Mortals fighting in the valley, heart hammering with panic. Roland's plan was unraveling. By the minute more Nomads desperate to break through the heavy Dark Blood ranks took spears in their chests and fell. He couldn't see the extent of what was unfolding on the far side, but he imagined the casualty rate was no less.

And yet to a man, the fighters followed Roland's lead, determined to prove the Nomad's cry for victory.

Triphon's bloodied body hung from the pole in the wide swath of bare ground between the two battlefronts. His friend had paid for Rom's failure with his life. Now the rest of them would follow that death and leave Jonathan with no hope.

"Michael!" he screamed. "It's too much!"

She ducked to avoid a hurled spear and veered toward the Dark Blood who'd hurled it. If she'd heard Rom, she gave no sign of it.

He spun his head to the left. "Roland!"

The cry fell on deaf ears.

They had begun the day with seven hundred Mortals, primed to change the world. They'd lost nearly a third on the plateau. Here in the valley, they might lose far more … Surely Roland could accept defeat to fight another day!

But no. The Nomads had lost their minds to their own need for supremacy.

Just beyond the reach of the Dark Bloods, Roland paced, daring them to approach. Mind welling with rage, Rom spurred his horse into a tear straight toward Roland.

He would run the man down if he had to.

He had made it halfway to the Nomad Prince when the lone cry—unmistakable to Mortal ears—reached him. He glanced back, to the west.

There on a far hill, buffeted by the accelerating wind

sat two riders. One on a pale horse, the other on a dark one. A young man dressed as a Nomad...a woman cloaked in pale gray over regal white whom he would have recognized anywhere.

Jonathan. Feyn.

They had come.

Rom felt the air leave his lungs. For a beat, he forgot that his horse careened toward Roland. He jerked back on the reins and pulled his mount to a rearing halt.

He wasn't sure if it had been Jonathan or Feyn who'd announced their arrival, but the effect swept through the amassed forces like a wave. The sounds of battle in the valley lost some of its urgency.

To the hill on Rom's right, Saric had turned on his horse, one arm still raised to his army. But his attention was on the pair. Roland whistled and retreated, joined immediately by the Mortals fighting at his side.

The battle ebbed, eerily so, before falling to a standstill.

Thunder rumbled overhead. The dark sky churned.

The valley was now divided by two wide lines of Saric's army, one on either side of the ruins, leaving a wide strip of bare ground that led directly up the ruin steps. The Mortals pulled back to the north and south of the Dark Bloods.

Feyn broke first, nudging her horse forward at an easy walk. Jonathan followed slightly behind to her right. Down the hill, then across the river and up the bank toward the temple ruins. A picture of stoic resolve.

Rom's first thought was filled with relief and jubilation. However unlikely, Jonathan had carved out an agreement with Feyn that would give him power without further bloodshed. And then they would mourn the cost of that already spilled—more than had been let in more than five centuries.

Feyn and Jonathan approached, looking neither to the right or the left. Only when they reached Saric's hill did they stop.

Jonathan stared at Triphon's dead body sagging before the ruin steps. Feyn slowly turned her head, looked up at Saric, and held his gaze evenly. The Maker of Dark Bloods finally gave her a short nod then nudged his horse forward. Down the hill, slowly.

Before Saric reached them, Feyn started her mount forward with Jonathan at her side, his eyes never leaving the temple ruins. Saric rode down from the hill and followed.

Only then did it occur to Rom that Saric and Feyn were now in possession of the boy, isolated by an army of Dark Bloods on either side. They were cut off from all Mortals sworn to Jonathan's defense.

He pulled around, saw that Roland was locked in place, utterly still as others cast furtive glances between him and the procession to the temple. They were awaiting orders.

None came.

"Jonathan!" Rom's voiced echoed through the valley. "My Sovereign!"

Jonathan neither turned nor raised his hand, even in acknowledgment. Instead, he rode slowly at Feyn's side, seemingly intent on only one thing: the ruins ahead of him.

Another peal of thunder rumbled across the sky. The wind picked up.

Terror sliced through Rom's mind.

CHAPTER FORTY

SARIC'S MIND SPUN WITH THE MEANING of Feyn's sudden arrival, aware all the while that his children's eyes were fixed on him riding behind her like a leader who had taken second seat to true royalty. Aware that his skin was clammy with sweat. That his heart pounded. Aware that Jonathan's jaw was set, his eyes fixed, his hips rolling naturally with his mount's gait, his hands light on the reins as one at ease with his place as supreme ruler of all that life could offer, despite the falsity of that notion.

Aware, too, that the Mortals were cut off from any attempt at saving the boy.

The battle had stalled completely, drawn to the sudden appearance of the pair. His children watched him, waiting for his direction. He left them standing. The battle was now in his hands.

He studied the side of Feyn's face, the line of her jaw bared by her simple plaits, the pale gray mantle, the pearls sewn at the cuffs of her sleeves. She had fulfilled her promise to bring the boy to him.

And yet, she showed none of the reverence he expected from a loyal servant. The submission that had occupied her very posture before turning full Dark Blood only last evening was gone.

He considered the line of Dark Bloods to his right. They watched him mostly, but some of their eyes had turned to Jonathan.

A chill flashed down his back. He could hardly blame them—the object of their full fury had been delivered into the hands of their Master. But curiosity, not anger, occupied their eyes.

He kicked his horse and trotted up next to Feyn as they approached the steps.

"I was beginning to question your loyalty, my love."

Her eyes remained steadfast on the dead Mortal hanging before the temple. As did Jonathan's.

Didn't she know he could draw his sword and summarily cut her down now, where she sat? For a brief moment he considered showing his supremacy in such a way for all to see. But then, he had no evidence that she'd betrayed him.

"You have done well," he said quietly. "For this I will reward you."

She made no effort to acknowledge him.

Had she lost her mind? Did the boy have such power to steal her heart? But no... They were both under his heel, their fates in his hands.

Beside her, Jonathan rode as though alone, seemingly oblivious to the thousands who looked on. He looked strangely majestic in his worn black tunic. Even his mount seemed to be aware of nothing but its rider's supremacy, as though to say: *Here is one born of true life, the final remnant of Chaos, fully alive by birthright.*

A man brimming with more life than Saric could possibly know without taking his blood himself.

No. He was imagining things.

And what if it's true, Saric? What if you rid the world of the only vessel that might bring you the supreme life and power you so desperately crave?

"Is there anything you would say to your Maker?" he demanded of Feyn.

Her horse stopped ten paces from the ruin steps, just beyond Triphon's lifeless form. Without a glance at Saric she dismounted, walked around to Jonathan, and offered him a hand.

Jonathan took her hand, gave Triphon's body a last look, and dismounted. She led him to the steps, lifted his fingers, and lightly kissed his knuckles. Gave him a parting look. Only then did she turn to face Saric.

"I give you your Sovereign, my Lord. My debt is repaid."

Without another word, Feyn crossed to her mount, swung into the saddle, reined her horse around, and rode directly toward the line of Dark Bloods at the valley mouth. They parted like a black sea as she approached, wind gusting through their corridor.

He could have stopped her, but she had played her role. If her loyalty to him had been undermined, he would deal with her easily enough later—she commanded no army. No force could offer her protection.

Feyn rode through his ranks, past the Mortals beyond, and headed out of the valley at a full run.

When Saric turned back to the temple ruins, Jonathan had already climbed the steps. He stood, looking out at Dark Blood and Mortal alike. His feet were parted and firmly planted, young jaw tight, his hands clenched in fists by his side as gusts tore at his clothing and hair.

So then, nine years had finally brought them to a place of righting the past, of all that had gone wrong. Their roles, this time, were reversed. Today it was Jonathan's turn to surrender.

Life...

The word swept through Saric's mind as if carried by the raging wind.

"Jonathan!" Rom Sebastian's voice carried over the lines, stretched thin by desperation. "Jonathan!"

Saric was about to dismount when the boy's voice cut through the rising storm, drawing the ear of every breathing soul in the valley.

"In an age of Chaos the first to walk this earth lived in full abandonment!" he cried. "They embraced the full pleasure of all that was given. They laughed and filled their bellies with the offerings of the land. They danced beneath sun and moon, and celebrated unreserved passion. Do any of you dare say it was not good?"

His challenge rang out with an authority that brought a tremble to Saric's fingers.

He speaks of life as one who knows it too well...

The wind moaned through the ruins. Above, the dark sky churned. Dark Blood and Mortal alike stared on in silence.

Jonathan walked to his right, tendons taut along his neck beneath bulging veins. Veins flowing with the first blood of life.

"Before there was war, there was peace! Before hate, love. Before selfish ambition, selfless service. There was beauty without end, never meant to fade."

He was pacing now, hands clenched in the air.

"But those who lived also courted sick ambition and

selfish greed. They longed for power. To consume more than they were given. They waged war. Human killed human, enraged, jealous, filled with the need to possess the service of others. Love was crushed by the need to protect what could not be owned. Man ignored the call to embrace the way of a Maker whose banner is love given freely, not controlled by force or demanded by allegiance or loyalty!"

How dare this man stand before his children and speak of love divorced from obedience, loyalty, or possession?

And then, as his rage gathered like the storm overhead, he realized it wasn't rage at all...but jealousy.

"*This* was the failing of man!" Jonathan cried. "And so a man named Megas stripped humankind of all sentiment but fear. Jealous for humanity, determined to possess it, zealous for control! Until the day that life was reborn five centuries later in one child. A boy to be raised for his blood to feed all those thirsty to drink!"

Far to Saric's left, one of the Mortals cried out: "He speaks the truth! Mortals rise with life!"

Jonathan's finger shot out in the direction of the voice. "No!" he screamed. "I tell you today, true life is not found in blood that wakens only the passions. As in the days of Chaos, only love given freely inhabits the Maker's design. Those who claim love dependent on allegiance are imposters who know *nothing* of the Sovereign realm. They will die the same as those who walk without life already!"

A jagged knife of lightning split the sky. Thunder crashed overhead as the wind gained intensity, whipping Jonathan's braids about his face.

But the heavens were not the only thing on the verge of cracking open.

Saric felt his mind tilt even as he sat tall in his saddle. The boy's words cut, severing every tether to all that he'd died and lived for. Slowly the world around him began to fade, leaving only the accusing form atop the ruined temple steps. Was it possible? Was Jonathan's life more true than his own?

Even if it was, he could not bow. Not to this Maker, no matter how much greater his life might be.

He knew one thing now: the boy must die.

One hand on the pommel of his saddle, Saric pushed himself up, eased his right leg over his horse's hind quarters, and slipped to the ground. The true battle wasn't between Dark Blood and Mortal with sword and ax. It was here, to be decided between two rulers. One would live to rule.

The other would die.

"Jonathan!" The sound of pounding hooves joined the howling wind. Rom Sebastian, desperate, blocked by the line. "Run! Run, Jonathan!" A commotion rose up from the north. The crash of clashing steel; shouts of outrage and bitter curses.

The sounds were distant in Saric's mind, from a dimension that no longer mattered. He gripped the hilt of his sword and deliberately pulled it from its scabbard with a loud scrape.

"Some would bring a new kingdom that flows with alchemy, intent on ruling the world for their own pleasure and gain," Jonathan cried, his eyes on Saric as he approached and then mounted the steps.

"Others would rule as Mortals over lesser life." He lifted his head, pointed in the direction of the Nomadic Prince and his men. "But today a new kingdom is among you. A kingdom where I am Sovereign, where I will reign with those who follow me. The deceiver comes to take what he cannot possess, but I offer my life freely to all who would live."

Saric glared up at the boy spouting his nonsense.

Terrified by his words.

Uncaring because they meant nothing.

Infuriated by his accusations.

Trembling.

Jonathan seemed to have said his last. He stood in front of the poles from which the remains of a leather bowl hung, watching Saric.

The fighting beyond the line grew to a cacophony, now south as well as north. The Mortals were once again in full attack. A pointless battle of a lesser kind.

Saric stepped onto the raised floor of the ruins and stalked toward the boy, tip of his sword trailing on the stone behind him. Another peel of thunder shook the sky.

"Hello, Saric." The boy's voice was soft, for him alone. His eyes were limpid in the oncoming storm. "Do you see nature's rage?"

Saric shot a quick glance at the black sky. Saw that it was rotating as if to drain the world.

"The Maker's Hand," Jonathan said.

Maker's Hand.

He'd heard the lore. Surely he wasn't claiming to be more than a man born of blood. The boy had lost his mind.

Or have you lost yours?

"I know you long for life, Saric," the boy said, too quietly for anyone else to hear in the rising gale. "Your heart is black but you can't ignore the cry of truth that my blood would bring you something beyond your imagination."

All of Saric's fears coalesced into one deafening question:

what if it was true? What if the object of his search stood before him now, a pure vessel of beauty, truth, and love?

For a moment the notion drowned his hatred. The body before him became a vessel of unsurpassed, raw life to be consumed, not crushed. To be tasted, not destroyed.

To be worshipped.

Without thinking, Saric lifted a trembling hand. Hesitated. When the boy didn't move, he touched his fingertips to his cheek. A ripple of power rode up his arm and into his body.

Saric shuddered.

"Look in my eyes," the boy said.

As though of its own accord, his gaze traveled from the boy's cheek to his eyes. Light flashed like sunlight through the boy's storming hazel irises. Saric felt his body go rigid.

But there was more... A great and terrible sadness.

Empathy.

Tears.

"I am the life you long for. My light will imprison you always. I make it so."

At the boy's last words Saric's world flashed with a brilliant light, blinding him to everything but the singular truth: he was as dark as the pitch in his veins. The boy was infused with light. He, not the boy, had been deceived. Here was life—not in his veins, but flooding those of the one before him. Life he had never known. Life.

Saric's legs buckled. He dropped to one knee, a great wail rising up from the pit of his gut, a heavy sob that was horror and grief and outrage all. It stole his breath, washing reason and purpose away.

Somewhere below, the Mortals were making a last,

hopeless attempt to break through his lines—he could hear the sound of it far away.

He wept, only distantly aware that his children could see him—their Maker, kneeling before this boy. This Sovereign of a realm he did not—could not—comprehend.

"You spawn only death," Jonathan said. "I, not you, hold power over life. See and know, dark Lord."

Saric felt his sword wrenched from his hand. He jerked his head around to see Jonathan flying down the steps, no longer a boy but a warrior streaking toward the nearest line of Dark Bloods.

With a scream that turned Saric's blood cold, Jonathan tore into the closest of them, easily sidestepping a frantic thrust of the warrior's spear. The boy's blade flashed and severed head from body.

Jonathan spun, screaming still, narrowly missed by another thrusting blade. He was too fast. Twisting with beautiful grace and power, Jonathan slashed into another warrior, cutting him nearly in two at the midsection. He sliced into another, separating arms from shoulders before plunging his sword through the man's chest.

Saric watched, frozen in horrific wonder, as Jonathan summarily slaughtered six of his children without allowing a single blade to touch him.

Orders rang out. His ranks surged around the boy. Before they could close the circle, Jonathan cut down a seventh and sprang away into open ground. As if executing a carefully choreographed dance, he swept to the pole that held Triphon's dead body.

He dropped to one knee and bowed his head in respect to his fallen friend. Long trails of blood from the wound in the Mortal's gut streaked his belly and legs.

Jonathan stood and gazed up at the man, face wrenched with sorrow. He reached for one of the bloodied feet, leaned slowly forward, and kissed it. His sob of anguish echoed through the valley, cut short by a plea for all Mortals to hear.

"He will see life!" Jonathan cried, facing the line of Mortals where their leaders were mounted. "For the sacrifice he paid to save me, I give him life! Leave his body. He will not be buried with the others. As you find life, Triphon will find life."

Jonathan spun and pointed the sword at Saric, eyes aflame. He held his position for an extended beat, then ran toward him, hunched low like a sprinter off the blocks.

Only then did it occur to Saric that the warrior who so easily killed seven of his children might as easily take their Maker who still knelt, immobilized and unarmed.

Panic flooded his veins. He started to push himself up, but the world around him was spinning.

And then Jonathan was at the base of the ruins. He took the steps in three long bounds and whirled to face the valley, bloody sword raised.

"Is there no end to death?" he cried.

He tossed the sword, sent it clattering to the stones just beyond Saric's knee.

He masters not only life, but death.

Saric turned and stared at the sword, red beneath the darkening sky. From the corner of his eye, he saw Jonathan seize the two poles that held the broken leather bowl. Torment, anguish on his face. He was mad. He was magnificent. Arms spread wide, the boy flung his words at the world.

"Is there no song without the sword? Is there no love without jealousy? Is there no end to rage?"

His body began to shake. He rocked back and forth like a man possessed, beyond himself. The clash of battle had stopped, replaced only by the wind, the thunder, and the boy's broken shouts.

"Will the children all die? Will the sun be turned red? Will you drain my blood to feed your own ambition? Do I die so you can live?"

His braids flew back in the face of the storm. Tears streamed from his eyes, blown back toward his temples before they could mar his cheek.

"Find love!" he screamed. "Find beauty! Find life and know that the realm of Sovereigns is upon you!"

A lone voice of objection pierced the valley from far and high. Saric turned his head and saw a lone figure up on the western cliff, arms spread wide. A woman crying out in horror at the scene beneath her.

"No!" She fell to her knees. "Jonathan!"

She lifted her chin, drew a deep breath, and hurled a great wail at the sky.

A helpless sob erupted from the boy, dangling from the poles as though they held him and not the other way around. He stared up at the lone woman, his face twisted with anguish. "For love..." He sucked at the air, a horrible, lurching gasp. "For you, Jordin!"

Saric felt his mind fracture, broken by the war in his soul.

These were surely the words of a love saturated with power far greater than any he knew. He could not kill the one destined to bring such life.

These were surely the words of a power that would render his impotent. He was compelled to destroy the one destined to crush his lesser life.

Jonathan suddenly grasped his tunic at the neckline with both hands and ripped it wide to bare his chest. His eyes lowered to Saric.

"Take it!" he screamed, face red and drawn.

He grabbed the poles again, arms spread wide, his chest bare.

"Take my life for all of them. Spill my blood and drain it for this world. Take what you have come to take and be forever changed!"

Saric remained frozen.

"Obey me," the boy said in a lower voice that reached into Saric's mind and shattered the last of his confusion.

Darkness flooded his vision. He grabbed his sword by the hilt, shoved himself to his feet, and with a full-throated scream, lunged for the boy.

The blade slashed down across Jonathan's body, severing his torso nearly in two.

Jonathan's eyes went wide. His mouth was parted, mid-gasp. He stood motionless for a suspended instant before sinking to his knees. Cries from the Mortals drowned out the high keening on the cliff.

The boy collapsed into a pool of his own blood, a broken heap at Saric's feet.

Saric staggered back a step. The sword fell from his hands and with it, the world.

The ruins began to shake beneath his feet. Wind roared through the valley, threatening to push him to the ground.

He staggered, struggling to keep his footing beneath the blackened sky. Before his very eyes the valley floor buckled. Large slabs of the far cliff began to slide into the valley. Unrelenting peels of thunder crashed through the heavens, shaking his bones to the core.

A full half of his children hugged the earth for safety, the other half tried to run, staggering and pitching like a drunken mob. The Mortals' horses reared and threw their riders to the churning ground.

Then, as quickly as the quake came, it quieted. The earth rumbled to stillness. Unnatural calm settled over the valley, punctuated only by the rattle of falling stone and whinnying horses.

With a final whoosh, the vortex in the sky sucked up the dark clouds, returning them to an overcast gray pushed by a gentle breeze.

Silence.

What have you done?

It occurred to Saric that he was still on his feet. Alive. But the moment the thought entered his mind he knew that he was not the same man who'd considered himself alive only moments earlier.

His thoughts were no longer those he'd entertained before. He'd seen a light in the boy's eyes. He'd obeyed his commands. He'd submitted to a power that left him crushed for all the world to see.

Nothing was the same.

Nothing could ever be the same.

Shaking badly, Saric walked to the edge of the steps, descended them one at a time, and crossed to a horse whose flesh still quivered with terror. He unsteadily mounted, only vaguely aware that Dark Blood on all sides were rising, some of them taking an unsteady knee at sight of him.

Varus rode up, face white. "My Lord?"

Saric avoided his gaze, the questions in his eyes, and pulled his mount around, only vaguely aware of the myriad gazes upon him.

"What is your command?" Varus said.

His command? He could not summon the resolve to lead. The boy had cursed him and robbed him of that power. Something had happened to him. The light in the boy's eyes...

"My Lord, your orders?"

"Leave this place," he said. "No more death."

He turned the horse and rode out from the valley under the gazes of his children.

Behind him a wail rose to the sky. The Mortals were mourning the death of their Sovereign.

CHAPTER FORTY-ONE

THE WESTERN EDGE OF THE SEYALA VALLEY was filled with midmorning sunlight. Overhead, starlings burst from the trees atop the eastern cliff, too startlingly alive above the ruins below.

Bahar, the ruins were called. The Spring of Life. They lay broken, shrouded in shadow so that none who looked at them might ever think that life had been granted here.

And taken.

Rom squinted across the first stirrings of a camp rising from a night of mourning. Those unable to fight had returned and a few had erected yurts, most of them in the same place they'd stood before, perhaps seeking comfort in familiarity. But all it did was draw the eye of anyone looking to the gaping patches of ground in between. Ground covered not with the dwellings of the living, but the bodies of those dressed now in death.

Despite the objections of more than a few, Rom had insisted they leave Triphon's body on the pole, guarded to keep vermin and birds away. Jonathan's dying demand made little sense even to Rom, but they were all past reason now. When they vacated the valley, nature would consume Triphon's flesh and leave only a skeleton as its own kind of memorial, a monument of death in this place where life had once reigned.

Two hundred and thirty-nine Mortals had perished in yesterday's battle. One hundred and seventy-eight Nomads, sixty-one Keepers. The fallen Nomads lay together in rows, leaving space for the living to move among them—bathing and dressing them, wrapping the disfigured in makeshift shrouds of bedding and canvas. The Keepers lay apart, faces shrouded. Rows of dead warriors, no longer aligned in the formation of battle as one race, now separated by kind in death. Nomad, to the pyre. Keeper, to the ground.

But it wasn't the line of dead that drew Rom's eye again and again. It was the single body wrapped in muslin atop a carefully constructed pallet nearest the ruin steps.

Jonathan.

The young girls had come down from the hills with armloads of fragile anemones. The younger children crowded around them—children he recognized as those Jonathan had often run off with to carve their toys as they laughed in the western hilltops. They had covered his body in flowers.

Too red. Too much like the blood they had carefully collected from the ruin steps and sealed in ceramic jars solemnly provided by the Keeper. The initials on them had been scratched out. The Keeper had kept them for his own burial, to be placed beside the body in acknowledgment of the day that it would be reborn—the ritual of all Keepers.

A day that would never come.

Jonathan had died on his eighteenth birthday.

Rom looked away.

The previous evening scouts had reported that the bodies of the fallen Dark Bloods on the plateau had been collected by their comrades. No word of Saric. No word of Feyn.

The Keeper had come to Rom to say he'd run a final test on Jonathan's blood. Dead, he said. All its extraordinary properties depleted.

Nine years of hope. Gone.

Now, as the sun crept toward the steps of the body that lay at the foot of the ruin steps, Rom could feel the eyes of the Mortals upon him. As they loaded the bodies of the fallen onto the horse-drawn pallets the camp was littered with the soft cries of mothers, lovers, and children. The zealots were more stoic than usual, not reciting the names or stories of the ones they lifted onto their horses as was custom. They were exhausted and tense, looking often toward the scouts on the cliffs, listening for the cry that Saric's army had returned. But no attack would come. Saric had what he wanted.

Neither Rom nor Roland spoke as they met on either side of Jonathan's body, lifted it onto the cart strewn with wildflowers, and set the ceramic jars of his blood beside him. Jordin, eyes swollen from crying, could not be pulled away, as though the charge that Rom had issued her yesterday to never let him out of her sight was one she would carry out forever. Even as Rom mounted his horse and gave the signal for the procession to start, she held on to the rail of the cart, reaching often to touch his shrouded foot.

Up from the south end of the valley floor, they wound their way into the western foothills toward the plateau. The moment they crested the last rise, Rom half expected to see carrion birds pecking at the eyes and wounds of bodies strewn across the battlefield. But the field was swept clean of the dead. Only the smell of blood remained, saturating earth and air alike.

A crow to Rom's right plucked at the dirt. At the far edge of the battlefield, rows of funeral pyres had been built from the dismantled horse pens, the frames of the yurts of the fallen, and wood from the forest. They stretched across the field like a bridge to hereafter.

Adjacent the pyres, a long grave had been dug for the fallen Keepers. A tunnel to the same destination, wherever that was.

And there, in front of it all, a single, lone grave. It was to that grave that Rom led the procession with leaden feet.

Reaching it, he stared at the pit, aware of the eyes of the rest on him.

What was he to say? There would be no Sovereign. No kingdom. Jonathan had not only failed to deliver what he'd promised them, he had destroyed it.

Rom slowly turned in his saddle to look out at the gathered Mortals. At Jordin, her face crumpling at sight of the grave. At Adah, weeping into her sleeve. At the zealots, staring fixedly as though right through him. The Keeper, pale, his expression terrible for its utter uncertainty. At Roland, beside him, face chiseled in stone.

He cleared his throat, but it didn't help. His voice was unmistakably hoarse.

"We mourn the loss of our Sovereign," he said, and cleared his throat again. "We mourn him as the true Sovereign. The one who was to be. We gave our lives for him. We did it gladly, because he gave us life first."

He could not look them in the eye. He could not meet

the hard gazes of the zealots, their jaws clenched tight beneath the bright sun. The Keeper's lost stare.

"We mourn him, and we celebrate him. We do both, because he did what he came to do, even if not in a way we understood. He taught us what it was to live. Not for an idea or for an Order, but for the sake of life itself. He taught us to love. And now his legacy lives in our veins. We will remember Jonathan always—not as a boy, or as a man who spilled his blood, but as our true Sovereign. We will remember and honor him forever as the embodiment of life, of love, of beauty."

He hesitated, but there were no more words. He could not tell them any more, because there was no more that he knew.

Why, Jonathan?

Nine years. So many lives. So much hope.

Rom nodded at Roland, mounted beside him. The prince lifted his chin.

"Today we stand as a race of the living!" His voice carried over the field. "We are broken in number, but victorious. A race that will live forever."

A few nods among the zealots.

"We will live! We will protect our life, zealously, to the death. Never again will any harm come to the pure of blood. Today we send the bodies of those who have fallen to the sky. Today we who yet live will rise, determined, never again to court death. I say to all those who would rob us of life, 'Die in your own grave. Our blood knows no end!' "

Rom glanced at the stark lines of his face, as hard and resolute as his words. He returned Rom's look without a hint of conciliation. He doubted he would ever again look the same to Roland's eyes.

So be it.

They swung down from their horses. Together they lifted Jonathan's body off the cart. Jordin hovered near, holding the ceramic jars containing Jonathan's blood close to her chest.

They lowered his body into the ground. Too pale, too light, drained of its blood. Too lifeless to be the boy Rom had known. The Keeper lowered himself into the grave, took the jars one by one from Jordin, and set them in a bed of straw next to the body. When he tried to climb out, his strength suddenly failed and Roland had to help him.

Rom lifted a handful of earth and willed his fingers to release it into the grave.

Anathema. Blasphemy, to see it fall upon that supine body.

He released the dirt onto Jonathan's torso, then stepped to one side. Roland came forward and did the same. Jordin dropped only an armful of flowers atop the smatterings of dirt, sobbing all the while. One by one the rest of the procession came, the children last of all tossing anemones into the grave. And then the Keepers were there with their spades.

Rom turned away, looking toward the west, squinting at the sun.

They buried the rest of the Keepers in the long burrow beyond Jonathan's grave.

By the time they'd placed the Nomads upon the pyre and set the fires, the sun had begun to set in splendid amber on the horizon.

The fires roared and crackled, lighting up the northern sky.

There were no songs. No stories of exploits of the

fallen. None of the usual celebration could find footing amidst the flames of so many burning bodies.

The mass funeral consumed the day. Family members hovered over graves and smoking pyres until dusk, some feeding small meals to children beneath the first stars, others refusing or unable to eat. The embers would continue to burn into the night and morning.

Rom stood staring at the waning fire, aware only of the lone grave apart from the others. Jonathan had always been apart, alone. But there was Jordin, beside him even now in the twilight, watering his grave with her tears.

A terrible loneliness settled over him. He felt utterly lost. Abandoned in the middle of the battlefield where… where what? A victory had been won? History had been changed? Love had conquered?

Was this victory or the making of history? Was this love?

A step at his side. He hadn't noticed Roland's approach until the prince was at his shoulder. For a moment neither spoke.

"And now?" Rom said, without turning.

Roland quietly exhaled. "We continue as we have for centuries."

"To what end?"

At last, the prince turned toward him in the darkness. "I know this is a hard day for you, but you must remember what the boy left us. We live as Mortals, full of his life. This was his purpose."

"To die? I can't believe that."

"Believe as you will. As for me, I believe he lived to give life, and when that life left his blood, he willingly died. Now my people will take the power he gave us and fulfill our destiny. We, not Jonathan, will rule the world. Perhaps this was always the way it was to be."

Could he have been so wrong? If Roland was right, this was only the beginning. But they didn't rule. And there were fewer Mortals alive now than before. But even as the questions warred within him, he knew one thing for certain.

"We will honor his death forever," he said.

Roland turned toward the smoking pyres. "We will honor his death by living forever."

This new preoccupation seemed seared into Roland. Just as he had fused his people with their identity as Nomads, he would now draw them into his new mission: to live as a superior race that answered to no one but their prince.

How was that so different from the mission of the Dark Bloods?

"What will you do?"

"I will take my people north. We will regroup and grow stronger. When the day comes, we will do what is necessary."

"What day?"

"The day we overcome all oppression and rule."

Rule how? Rom wanted to ask. But instead, he only nodded.

The prince dipped his head and walked away.

CHAPTER FORTY-TWO

FOR TWO DAYS, the Seyala Valley lay under the gloom of shattered hope and mangled dreams. Under Rom's orders the ruin's stone courtyard had been washed clean of blood and the inner sanctum left vacant. Some of the yurts had been erected, but many slept in temporary shelters made of canvas flaps. Night fires burned, but the songs and dancing that had once filled the valley were not to be seen or heard except on the north end, where some of the Nomads raged about their exploits in war and spoke of coming days of glory.

Triphon's dead body served as a constant and macabre reminder of defeat. Rom resisted questions as to the sanity of leaving a dead body exposed and defied mounting pressure to give Triphon a proper burial. Instead, he agreed to move the post with Triphon's body to the side of the ruins where it was not so flagrantly visible.

The greater question confronting them all was far more urgent: what about those who still lived?

There was no Mortal Sovereign to take the seat of power. No new kingdom to waken the world to life. No miraculous and fanatical boy to inspire hope. No promise of life beyond that which already ran, rampant but aimless, in their own veins.

Only a broken valley with ruins bathed in the memory of blood.

Nothing made sense.

The council had met twice in an attempt to find consensus, but no clear path could be agreed upon. Rom and the Keepers were too distraught with the inequity of Jonathan's death to even consider direction, let alone the future. How could the one who'd promised them a new kingdom have removed that possibility by offering up his own life? In his slaughter of the Dark Bloods, he'd displayed more skill and strength than any Mortal might have expected of him. Why, then, had he bared his chest and given up the sword to Saric? *Why?*

The sky might have cleared, but the valley was shrouded in the thick fog of confusion and grief.

Even Roland, so steadfast in his resolve to see their new race of Nomads rise in power, offered few particulars as to how they should proceed.

North, yes. With full life, yes. But what of the expectation for freedom and autonomy embraced by his people during Jonathan's life? What now?

Jordin was rarely seen in the valley, preferring instead the company of Jonathan's grave. Rom had gone to the plateau on the eve of the second night to meditate and found her curled up next to the freshly disturbed earth, asleep. He'd sat down and watched the steady rise and fall of her breathing, trying for the hundredth time to make sense of the questions that flooded his mind.

He had never known Jonathan to speak untruth or to mislead. Then what had he meant in saying on the day of his death that he was bringing a new realm of Sovereignty? And how could he, when his blood had lost its potency?

Was it possible Jonathan had simply succumbed to the pressure of expectation that he would deliver them all? To the years of being bled, viewed less and less as a boy and more as a vessel of power?

Was it their own fault that they had pushed a fragile boy to grow into a leader that he had not owned the strength to become?

What could it mean to follow him as he'd urged in his last days? How did one follow the dead?

What of the storm and earthquake? Some called it the Maker's Hand. Others said it was nothing more than a terrible storm.

For that matter, did the Maker even exist? Some said no—how could He, given all that had happened? What had happened in Jonathan's blood was a matter of genetics, of science, and not mystery. Two days earlier, Rom would have derided them as blind and ungrateful, but how could he today? Why would a Maker allow the one source of true life to die?

Everything he'd believed had been thrown into doubt.

And Feyn...what of her? What had they agreed to at their summit? Why had she fled after delivering him to Saric, never once looking back?

As for Saric...His slaying of Jonathan was clearly a victory, but what of his apparent breakdown before Jonathan? And where had he gone?

The questions refused to abate as he returned to camp, leaving Jordin to her exhausted sleep as day turned to night, and night to day.

The evening before, Roland announced that he and twenty Immortals were journeying north the next day. They would find a new valley in which to rebuild. There was no longer a reason to remain close to the city. He had no more clear direction than that, only that it was time for his people to embrace their new life and to consider the centuries before them.

It would mean a split between those Keepers and Nomads who wished to remain close to Byzantium with Rom and those forsaking any further notion of bringing life to the world's capital city.

That night, sleep came hard, and then only in confused snatches. Rom tossed, writhing with the same questions, reliving again and again every encounter with Jonathan the last days of his life until his dreams became a jumbled collage.

"Jonathan?" he whispered once, into the darkness. Feeling foolish, he closed his eyes. Finally, he slept.

Rom.

A whisper from the ether of sleep.

Rom.

I know the way.

But there was no way. He'd known it once with the surety of his every conviction, and it had failed him.

Rom.

Something nudged him.

No, not something, but someone.

"Rom. Rom!"

His eyes snapped wide and he stared up into a face in the darkness. Round eyes peered at him from a smudged, tearstained face. Her hair was a knotted mess.

Rom sat up. "Jordin?"

She stood with her arms limp at her side, looking half crazed.

So it was catching.

"Jordin. What is it?"

Had Saric returned? Feyn? Was Roland leaving under cover of the night?

"I know what he meant," she whispered. "I know what we need to do."

"What who meant, Jordin?"

"Jonathan told us to follow him. He told me. He made me promise. I know what he meant."

The poor girl was breaking, undone by grief and her refusal to eat.

He sighed and ran his fingers through his tangled hair. "Please, Jordin . . . You have to get some rest."

"I know how to follow him," she said.

"He's dead, Jordin! You have to accept that."

She merely stared at him.

He sighed, closed his eyes and opened them again, willing himself to patience.

"All right. Tell me," he said. "Tell me how to follow a dead man."

"We have to take his blood."

He returned her stare, not sure whether to be horrified or laugh at her.

"We already have his blood."

"We have his old blood."

"We have the blood he gave us when he was alive!"

"It's in his blood."

She said it all as if were obvious, so simple.

"Jordin. He's in the earth. His blood is that of a corpse—literally."

"It's in the blood. There are three vessels of blood in his grave."

"What are you saying? That we dig him up and drink a corpse's blood?" The thought curdled his stomach.

"No, we inject it into our veins, as we did before."

"Jordin, he's dead! The blood is probably congealed by now."

"Then we die, too, with his blood in our veins. He said to follow him. He said it to me, he said it to you, he said it to all of us. We have to dig his body up and take his blood. We have to follow him."

He fell back down onto an elbow. "You can't be serious."

"Will you help me?"

The words Jonathan had shouted to Corpse and Mortal alike from the temple steps whispered through his mind. *Find life and know that the realm of Sovereigns is upon you.*

The demand had haunted him. What could *find* mean? Not *you have found*, but *find*.

In any case, Jonathan surely hadn't meant for them to dig up his grave.

"Jordin, please . . . The Keeper tested Jonathan's blood and found no properties of—"

"He said to follow him."

"Yes, but not by dying!"

"He said his blood was being spilled for the world."

Spill my blood and drain it for this world. He'd taken the words to be the desperate cry of one about to die.

"Yes. He said that. But if he wanted us to dig up his body and take his blood, he would've made it clear."

"Jonathan always hid the truth for those who would find it," she said. "I'm going, whether you help me or not."

She actually meant to do this.

What if she's right?

He got to his feet and paced, suddenly seized by the notion, however unlikely. Why had they assumed that Jonathan's blood would mature by becoming a stronger version of what it had been rather than something new altogether? And yet, assuming the boy knew, why hadn't he said anything to that effect?

Or had he?

"I'm getting a shovel," Jordin said, spinning around to leave.

"Wait!"

She turned back.

"Hold on. We can't just desecrate his grave by digging up his body! It's revered by a thousand Mortals!"

"By me more than any of them," she said. "I'm getting a shovel."

"And then what?"

"Then I follow him in his death. I take the blood he spilled when he died. That's what he meant. That's what I'll do."

"We should ask the Keeper."

"No. If you won't help me, I'll go alone."

He thought a moment longer, then grabbed his boots and tugged them on. "We leave his body in the ground."

"Of course. Do I look like a savage?"

Yes.

He grabbed his jacket. "Get the shovel."

It took Rom and Jordin twenty minutes to find a shovel and ride up to Jonathan's grave. The night was still, long past the hour of insect song—a good two hours before the first birds came to life. Before them, the slightly rounded mound of dirt looked as dormant and lifeless as the body they'd buried beneath it.

To Rom's right lay the long burial mound of those other Keepers, a raised scar on the surface of the earth. It still smelled of earth, fresh as upturned grass and rain over the flesh decaying beneath. A sacred monument of death for those who lived to remember life.

And now they were about to desecrate the monument cherished most of all. For a moment he gave in to misgiving.

"We're doing this based on pure conjecture," he said.

"We're doing this because I saw it in his eyes."

"The eyes are easily misread, Jordin."

"His eyes promised me love. Does love kill hope?"

Rom looked up at the round moon, a bright beacon in the star-speckled heavens. They had remained cloudless in the days since Jonathan's death—rare, though not unheard of. The storm that had accompanied his death, on the other hand, had been singular.

The Maker's Hand. If it was true—if it was possible—that it had bent toward earth in that moment, did its touch linger still?

Rom considered Jordin, looking so expectantly at him, her last question lingering in the air. And then he picked up the shovel and pressed it into the earth. A few seconds later, he tossed the first heap of soil aside.

They took turns at the shovel, heaping the dirt carefully to one side so it could be easily replaced as the grave slowly yawned opened beneath them.

There. The first glimpse of a dirty shroud.

Sweating from the work, hands raw as his emotions, Rom dropped the shovel behind him. He dropped into the grave and carefully scooped the remaining earth away from the top of the body, unable to staunch the image of that sword impossibly flashing beneath the darkened sky. Twice, he turned his face into his arm, seemingly at the smell of the corpse, already decomposing, but mostly against the memory of Jonathan falling forward on the temple steps.

And then he carefully continued clearing the dirt away from the three ceramic vessels set around his head. Red. The color of ochre and earth and blood.

He glanced up at Jordin, who looked as pale as a ghost in the moonlight, her eyes struck wide, fixed on the body. Tears shone in her eyes, broke down her cheek. But she did not turn away.

She dropped to her knees, reached down for each container as he handed it to her, handling it as gingerly as though it were made of eggshell.

"Cover him," she said. It sounded almost like a plea.

Rom hauled himself up out of the grave, grabbed the shovel, and began filling it back in. Twenty minutes later they had returned the grave to a semblance of its original shape and strewn field flowers over the dirt. But even a Corpse would know that the earth had been freshly disturbed. And any Mortal with their keen perceptive sense would know immediately without doubt.

He could hear the outrage already.

It no longer mattered. Jordin's reasoning had grown in him as he'd dug, pushing him to steely resolve. If she was right...Maker. The whole world would change.

Jonathan's other statements, cried like a madman at the Gathering, mushroomed in his mind. *I will bring a new, Sovereign realm....Death brings life...You won't know true life until you taste blood.* He had said all of it as Avra's heart had dripped with blood in his hands.

But he could just as easily have been speaking of his own.

Jordin bundled the vessels in her coat, carefully placed them in her saddled bag, and threw herself on her horse.

They rode down from the plateau side by side, speaking only as they approached the camp.

"Take the blood to the inner sanctum," Rom said. They'd already agreed that they would perform the ritual with the Keeper's instrument, and for this they had little choice but to involve him. "I'll wake Book."

The inner sanctum was lit by three candles hastily gathered by the Keeper. In less than half an hour, morning light would filter into the valley, and Roland and his band would rise early to prepare for their journey north. They had to hurry; Rom had no desire to explain himself to any Mortal who might find their actions outrageous in the least and profane at worst.

Rom had pulled the old Keeper from sleep, insisting they'd discovered something that could prove all of his predictions true. Not until the old man had rushed into the ruins and stopped cold, eyes on the three ceramic jars, had they told him just what.

"What have you done?" the Keeper had cried. "He's dead!"

"And we mean to follow him in his death," Rom said, hearing the absurdity in the echo of his own words.

The old man spun to stare at him. "You mean to die?"

"No, I mean to follow. The blood in those containers. Will it kill me?"

The Keeper hesitated. "It depends."

"On what?"

"On what's in the blood."

"Can you tell?"

"I don't know what I'm looking for..."

Rom saw the wheels begin their slow turn in the man's head.

Within minutes, he had laid the stent on a simple white cloth and announced that the seal on all the jars was intact; the blood hadn't congealed. But then he seemed to hesitate.

"This could be blasphemy," the Keeper said, pushing his white hair back from his head in a way that only made it seem more disheveled than before. "Centuries of guarding the secret of this blood, and now to open the sacred vessels..."

Rom had already rolled up his sleeve. "Then you owe it to the centuries and to those who came before you to learn the truth."

"You're quite sure you're willing to risk this?" the Keeper said.

"When did following Jonathan not involve risk?"

Jordin's hand came to rest on his forearm. "No. I go first."

"It was I who was destined to find Jonathan as a boy," Rom said.

She frowned. "Yes, but—"

"Who brought Jonathan to this valley?"

"You did."

"And who did Jonathan embrace as leader of the Keepers?"

"Fine. But know that whether you live or die, I *will* take the blood."

There was something wild in her eyes and he knew with certainty she would sooner be dead than without Jonathan, that the prospect of death to her now was, in itself, a gain. He couldn't blame her.

He nodded. And then he pulled his sleeve up over the crook of his right arm, perched on the edge of the altar, and lay back.

"You're sure about this?" the Keeper asked, picking up the steel stent.

"Would you do this?"

The old Keeper considered the question for only a moment, then dipped his head. "I would."

"Then do."

"How much?"

"As much as it takes."

Rom closed his eyes and waited for the swab of cool disinfectant on his skin. The sting of the needle. A chill passed down his neck when it came, like the bite of a scorpion, cold in his veins. His heart rate surged, expectant.

Then nothing but the steady draw and push of his own breath.

He didn't know what he had anticipated—perhaps a bolt of energy or gut-wrenching cramps similar to the first time he'd taken the ancient blood so many years ago.

"Anything?" Jordin whispered.

He kept his eyes shut and shook his head.

"Stay still," the old Keeper said.

Rom lay unmoving, waiting for some unexpected sign that the blood flowing into his veins held power.

Nothing.

"Enough," the Keeper said, withdrawing the stent and pressing a swab to the puncture wound. "Any more and—"

"I need more."

"I've already given you twice the amount Jonathan gave to bring Corpses to life."

"Give me more."

"Rom, we don't know what effect—"

"More! Do it!"

The old man finally shook his head and then reinserted the stent. A moment later cold flooded his veins once more.

Rom gripped his hand to a fist and closed his eyes again. His mind drifted behind the darkness of his closed eyes, a sea of darkness studded with pinpricks of light. The memory of stars in the sky as they had exhumed the grave. But nothing else. He felt no surge of power, no swell of emotion, no pain, no wonder, not even the slightest tingle beyond the cooler temperature of the blood itself.

Nothing.

A great sorrow settled over him like a suffocating blanket. Jordin was wrong. Jonathan's blood was powerless. His sovereign realm didn't exist any more than he himself did now. No hope lived beyond the grave in a world still imprisoned by death.

All that Rom had lived to protect was gone.

The tiny dots of light floated through the darkness, falling to a black horizon like falling stars, winking out.

He was being fed the blood of a corpse. What if that blood undid the power of Jonathan's living blood within him? What if, in his desperate quest for the dream of a Mortal Sovereign, he had given up the very life in his veins and converted from Mortal to Corpse as surely as Jonathan had?

A sudden panic swept through his body, pushed sweat from his pores. *Stop! Rip the stent out before it's too late!*

He wanted to. In his mind's eye he was already reaching across his body, clawing at the stent, tearing it out with a cry of outrage.

His body began to tremble.

Images of Jonathan dancing with the children skipped through his mind. Of the little girl he'd rescued from the Authority of Passing—Kaya—grinning as she had lifted her arms to him. Of a thousand Mortals leaping up and down as their roar washed over their Sovereign to-be, standing with arms spread wide on the ruin steps.

Images of Jonathan's blade effortlessly slashing through the line of Dark Bloods, of his finger pointed at the Mortals as he hurled words of accusation. Of blood splashing over his naked body as though to cleanse him.

The last winks of light faded. Darkness, deeper than any he'd known, edged into his psyche like a heavy black fog. He felt his breathing thicken, his pulse slow, his body cool.

You're dying, Rom.

When the realization hit him, it was already too late. He tried to open his mouth and cry out, but his muscles didn't respond. His arms remained at his side, quivering with the last vestiges of life.

Voices sounded urgently from the far reaches of his consciousness. Voices, but he couldn't make out their words.

Another image crawled into his waning thoughts, of the Dark Blood they'd injected with Jonathan's blood, foaming at the mouth before slumping without pulse. Rom had desecrated Jonathan's grave, taken his blood, and now he would pay the same price.

He felt the stent being torn free. Hands on his body, shaking him. Words of horror rasped by the old man.

And then he felt nothing.

Only perfect peace.

Darkness.

Silence.

Death.

Jordin stood over Rom's dormant body, filled with icy dread. The sweat on his face and arms glistened in the candlelight—a baptism of death. His eyes, twittering beneath his eyelids only a moment earlier, had stopped moving. His nostrils had pulled in a last, long breath and then his chest settled, stilled.

Maker. Was it possible?

Jonathan's blood had taken Rom's life.

For a long moment she stared at his waxen face. It was pale as though drained of blood. The old Keeper was frantically searching for Rom's pulse.

"He's dead!" the old man whispered, eyes darting up.

No! He couldn't be dead.

"Blessed Maker. We've killed him!" the Keeper said, clapping his hands to his head.

Jordin's breath quickened, her pulse a heavy thud, as though the life-robbing power that had spread through Rom in his dying moments had leaked in through her pores.

Jonathan had abandoned her. He'd loved her and chosen her, only to be washed away by madness, by a belief that by his death he could save them all. For two days she'd clung to that dying love, refusing to believe that Jonathan could invite his own death and leave her bereft, never to know love again. Because there would be no other after Jonathan. He'd taken her heart with him to the grave.

And now Rom had joined him.

She stumbled back a step, mind numb, breathing in quick, frantic pants that echoed throughout the inner chamber. Panic overtook her like an arctic wind, cutting her to the bone.

What Jordin did next did not come from any place of sound reasoning, but from the intuitive despair of a woman summarily thrown into darkness to die without a parting word from her master.

She leapt forward with a grunt and slammed her fist down on Rom's lifeless chest.

"No!"

Like a beast clawing to escape the pit, she dug her fingers into his clothing and jerked him back and forth.

"No! Don't you dare leave! Don't you dare!"

The Keeper was at her side, hand on her arm, gently pulling her back. "Please, Jordin—"

"Wake up!" she screamed, beating at his chest. "Wake up!"

"Jordin—"

She slapped Rom's face, hard enough to make it snap to the side. His head lolled to the side.

She slapped him again. "Wake up!"

His face was cold. He did not wake up.

The finality of Rom's passing fell over Jordin like a crashing wave from the deep. And with it, absolute resignation to the smothering sickness of lost hope. Her legs buckled. She fell over Rom's lifeless body with her head on his chest and her arms draped over the far side of the altar.

Her sobs came slowly at first, seeping up as though from her very bowels. And then it boiled over with ragged breaths and finally with a keening wail.

She was vaguely aware of the Keeper's hand on her shoulder. That he was whispering something, trying to help her up.

She clung to Rom's body, the body filled with Jonathan's blood.

"Please, Jordin, daylight is coming. We're going to have to explain ourselves to the others."

His words cut her like a knife in the back. She could not explain herself to the others because even in this last act she had failed Jonathan. She, not Rom or the Keeper, would accept full blame. The woman Jonathan had loved while he lived, who had made a mockery of him in his death.

She slowly released her grip and sank to the floor, curled up in a heap, and sobbed.

The soft thump of her own heart mocked her, the palpitating rhythm of a heart pushed beyond the brink. And why not? Death had swallowed hope and abandoned her in a Hades. She no longer had reason to live. It thudded too hard, growing in intensity like a horse speeding into full gallop as though desperate to escape death itself.

The beat increased to a fast and heavy pounding. But it wasn't coming from her.

She heard the Keeper's sudden inhalation. Snapped her eyes wide. Jerked her head from the floor.

The sound came from the altar above her.

Jordin scrambled to her knees and spun to Rom. His body was improbably arched, shaking with violent tremors like a leaf in a storm.

She threw herself back against the Keeper, who flung a protective arm out in front of her.

* * *

What is darkness? What is *light* when there is only darkness? How does the mind process life when there is only death?

These were the underpinnings of Rom's impossible quandary when light came out of the vacant darkness that was his nonexistence as he lay dead and unaware.

The light did not seep into his consciousness or grow from a first spark; it exploded with a hot white flash. It didn't change his world; it created a new one. Let there be life. There was nothing and then there was everything.

Every fiber of his being was suddenly screaming with life, flooded with warmth, smothered by mind-bending love, shaking with more pleasure than his mind could contain.

He was only vaguely aware that he had a body that was reacting to the eruption within him, distorted beyond what occurred naturally, because in the moment nothing was natural. All was new.

The very air was raw pleasure, and he was breathing it like a drug that strained his synapses to the breaking point. A sensation exhilarating and beautiful, too powerful to resist.

"Do you feel my life, Rom?"

Jonathan's whisper echoed through his new world, soft but laden with as much power as the light.

"Do you see now how great my love is?"

And with those whispered words a distant scream. His own, without words but with singular meaning.

Yes...*Yes!*

"Crush the darkness with my life, Rom. Live..."

He was shaking violently, weeping unrestrained with mouth spread wide, mind erupting with bliss. He wanted to say, *I will. I will crush the darkness. I will live.* But he could only scream.

He didn't know how long that first explosion lasted—a moment. An hour. A lifetime—of weeping with gratitude. Begging for forgiveness for doubt. Vowing unending love.

And then the light faded into his mind's horizon, leaving him fully alive. Released, he felt his body drop heavily to the stone surface beneath him.

He was new.

Alive.

Rom opened his eyes.

Jordin watched Rom's body remain impossibly bent for several long beats before it dropped back to the altar's stone surface and go limp. His scream had shattered the chamber's silence, but it barely occurred to her that those in the camp might hear. Now his mouth snapped shut and he lay with tears running down past his temples.

Breathe, she had to remind herself, as utter quiet settled into the sanctuary. Far away, a rooster crowed.

Rom's eyelids suddenly sprang open. He jerked upright and sucked in a long, desperate gasp that reverberated through the chamber.

She watched in stunned silence as he stared around, lost for a moment, as though acquainting himself to the world for the first time. He lifted his hands to look at them, laid a palm against his chest to feel his own breath, blinked to clear his vision.

She watched all this with trembling desire, desperate envy.

Rom turned his head and stared at them—first the Keeper, then Jordin. His eyes lingered on her.

"Jordin," he rasped.

"You ... you're alive."

"I died?" he asked. Then answered his own question. "I died ..."

"You're alive!" she cried.

"Alive," he said, as she threw herself forward, flinging her arms around his body, weeping.

"You're alive," she sobbed.

"More alive than you can imagine," he said.

Chapter Forty-three

ROM STOOD ON THE COURTYARD STEPS with Jordin and the Keeper, facing a thousand Mortals who'd rushed to the ruins as word spread that Jonathan lived. Three hours had passed since first Rom, then Jordin, then the Book had taken Jonathan's blood and entered the over-whelming light of the new Sovereign realm.

Mother and fathers, sons and daughters, Nomads and Keepers alike had listened with riveted attention for thirty minutes as Rom had made his impassioned plea for them all to die and rise again to find a new life they had never known. The Council stood abreast at the bottom of the steps watching with a blend of curiosity, hope, and skepticism. But it was Roland's flat expression that drew Rom's consideration.

The prince had heard Rom's fervent call to life with interest, but as Rom tried to explain what this new life felt like, a shadow had descended over the prince's eyes.

How did one express the certainty of life with evidence of things not seen to a people who'd embraced the Mortal hope? He had no new skills that he knew of, at least not yet. Surely they would come, as they had before, in stunning display that would render their former lives banal. But for now, neither Rom, Jordin, nor the Keeper could summon a storm as Jonathan had or snap their fingers and split the ruin's marble steps.

Regardless, he could not mistake the overwhelming urgency of life that had pulled him from the darkness and filled him with explosive light and knowledge. A new power had risen in his mind and heart, unsurpassed by any he'd yet understood.

He *knew*.

Like a master who saw the workings of all he had made, he knew.

The Mortals staring up at him with blank faces, however, did not. Could not.

"I see you, not as I did yesterday, but in a new way. I see your love and your doubt. Your minds and your hearts."

He paced to his right and looked out at the crowd.

"The first Keeper knew that a boy would bring new life into the world, and his words proved true. But Talus could not know how that life would change us. He said *nothing* of our Mortal sense or for how many years we would live. He assumed that change would come through political means—by force, if necessary. But Jonathan claimed he would bring a new kingdom through his death. A rule of Sovereigns."

The words he would speak next would not be so welcome, but it hardly mattered now. Each Mortal, like him, would make their own decision: to die and live, or to live and die.

"We who have taken Jonathan's blood stand before you as the first three Mortals who are Sovereign."

Glances and whispers. Roland stood like stone.

"As Mortals of the Sovereign realm, filled with life greater than any yet tasted."

"Greater?" the zealot Seriph said. "And yet you appear the same."

"Greater," Rom replied to the cynical Nomad.

"Show us."

"Are we alive?" Jordin demanded of him, stepping out. "Do I look dead to you?"

"Does a Corpse appear dead?" Seriph returned.

"How dare you question what Jonathan has given?" she cried. "You, who would subdue the world with your sword and live a thousand years without knowing true life—is it yours to question his authority?"

Seriph spread his arms and looked around. He stepped out of line and faced the assembly with a questioning gaze. "Whose authority? Jonathan's? If he lives, let him speak. Let him tell us that we must die and become tiny Sovereigns without purpose."

"He lives!" Jordin said. She slapped her breast, face red. "In here!" She jabbed at her head. "In here!" She thrust her finger back toward the inner sanctum. "Take his blood and know, yourself."

"Easy," Rom muttered under his breath. "They don't understand."

"No," she said under her breath, glancing at him with strange revelation. "They can't hear."

"They say we don't hear," Seriph bit off, face twisting with scorn. "This from a foolish lover as mad as the one whose blood she's taken. I say let them show us just how deaf we are."

Jordin was about to speak again, but Rom lifted a hand and she held her tongue.

"We *will* show you," he said. "But it may take some time."

"Time? This while Saric gathers his Dark Bloods to take as many lives again? Show me how to end death and I will gladly take your blood."

"What blood?" Roland stared up at Rom. "Are you still a Maker?"

Rom hadn't considered the question.

Roland spoke so that all could hear him. "No? And how much blood is left in the vessels?"

Rom went quiet. There were only two vessels left.

"Tell me, Rom, do you still see with Mortal sense?"

Rom felt his pulse quicken. He looked quickly around with dawning realization. He'd been so caught up in this change that he hadn't noticed. Did the far cliff seem more distant? Did the sound of the ravens calling overhead come less vibrantly than before?

Seriph lifted his brows and glanced at Roland so quickly that he nearly missed it.

And then he knew. The perception to which he'd grown so accustomed . . . was gone.

He glanced at Jordin and the Keeper, both whose boldness seemed to have been shaken.

"Well?"

He turned back to Roland. "As I said, we don't know the full extent of the changes. Only that we know more."

"More of what? My mind? Can you smell the horses? The stench of blood in the ground? Can you hear as you once heard?"

Rom was now distinctly certain that he could not.

"No," Roland said. "I don't think you can. But that shouldn't surprise you. After all, you drank the blood of a Corpse."

"You dare call the one who gave you life 'Corpse'?"

"I don't need to," Roland said. "The Keeper can make the case." His eyes swiveled to the Keeper. "Tell them, old man."

The Book blinked.

"Tell them the secret of Jonathan's blood in his last days. Tell them what Rom insisted we keep from the people."

"What is this?" the councilwoman Zara demanded.

When the Keeper still said nothing, Roland strode up the first three steps of the ruined Temple. Not far from his foot was a dark fissure that had not been there just days ago.

"Wasn't it true that in his last days, Jonathan's blood reverted to that of a Corpse? That when he died, his blood had lost all of the Mortal powers we yet possess? That from your own testing Jonathan had, in fact, *become* a Corpse? Tell them, old man!"

Murmurs punctuated by cries of outrage spread through the crowd.

"We don't know," the Keeper said.

"You don't know? But your tests were clear—you said so yourself." He turned back to face the assembly. "Jonathan's blood had *reverted*."

"Our tests cannot—"

"And yet you claim to have more knowledge than me. Jonathan died a Corpse. And now the question I would ask is: are you, too, Corpse as well? Carelessly, perhaps maliciously calling us to join you in death as our own enemies might?"

"How dare you speak this to your leader?" the Book rasped. "Do we *smell* like Corpses to you?"

Roland ignored the charge. "Then prove this new life of yours!" he shouted, hurling the challenge like a gauntlet.

"Prove how?" Book cried. "Rom has made the point clear, we don't yet know what new powers we may or may not have. The fact that each of us stands before you changed is testament enough!"

"Spoken out of desperation," Roland snarled. "You have lost the endless life all Mortals have. You expect us to die for this hope?"

Sanath, a woman in her fifties, maneuvered through the crowd, pushing a cart laden with the body of her husband, Philip, a Nomadic archer who'd been slashed in his chest during the battle and struggled to hold on to life.

Staring up at Rom with tear-filled eyes, she wheeled the body to the foot of the steps. One glance at Philip's still form, and Rom knew that he'd passed during the early morning hours.

"You offer life?" Sanath said, her voice breaking. "Please! Give this life to my husband."

Rom felt a lump gather in his throat. "Sanath...I don't think—"

"You offer life!" Sanath cried, shoving her finger at Rom. "Then bring my husband back!"

"A reasonable request," Seriph said. "Bring him back for all to see. Or have you lost your conviction?"

Without prompting, the old Keeper spun and marched back into the inner sanctum.

Seriph stood with a triumphant lift of his chin. Rom understood why.

Book emerged a moment later carrying a stent and the vessel with Jonathan's blood. He hurried down the steps, jaw set. Making no attempt to offer argument, he unceremoniously slipped the stent into the vein on Philip's right arm. Opened the valve.

They'd all seen similar scenes a hundred times. The precious blood seeped into the lifeless body for ten seconds. To bring life or to be wasted they could not know, but there was far too little blood to be used carelessly.

"Enough," Jordin said. She clearly shared Rom's concerns.

Casting a glance back at her, the Keeper withdrew the stent, shoved it in his pocket, and retreated up the steps, stowing the prized vessel of blood beneath his cloak.

All eyes were on Philip's lifeless body. Ten seconds passed. A child asked her mother what was happening, only to be hushed.

"How long does it take?" Sanath demanded, face drawn with anxiety.

Rom nodded at her. "Give it more time."

But more time wasn't going to help. With each passing second, Rom's certainty that they'd wasted the valuable blood grew.

"It's not working?" Sanath said, fresh tears wetting her cheeks. "It's not working. Oh, my Philip!"

"No, Sanath," Roland said, moving toward her. He placed a hand on her arm. "We will honor Philip as a great man among all Nomads." He faced Rom wearing a bitter stare. "For a *thousand years* we will honor him."

Sanath sank to her knees, lowered her head to her husband's chest, and began to wail. Roland motioned several nearby to help. They held Sanath up beneath the arms and led her away, the cart close behind. Death was an ugly sight.

The gathered Mortals now looked at Rom with vacant

eyes. He was about to offer the possible explanation that rescue from true death was not what Jonathan had in mind when Jordin drew close.

"Triphon!" she whispered.

He glanced at her.

Triphon. Sudden understanding. Could Jonathan have intended this? Did they have enough blood to try it?

"Bring him," he whispered.

Jordin hurried away, calling to several others to assist her. After some hesitation and a backward glance, they followed her around to the side where Triphon's body had been moved.

Rom faced the Mortals. "Jonathan's blood clearly wasn't meant to bring life to the deceased—we know that now. But this doesn't rob his blood of the power I have known. Many of you saw Triphon die, the rest have seen his body hanging as demanded by Jonathan..."

"This is absurd," Roland said. "You would defile a second warrior out of desperation?"

"Triphon is not a Nomad!" Rom returned. "He was my friend, who died to save Jonathan. He would not object."

To the crowd: "Do any oppose?"

No one spoke.

"Then we give him Jonathan's blood."

Jordin and the others came around the corner bearing the stiff, blood-caked body of their friend. Carefully, they made their way up the steps, laying him on the topmost one.

Rom looked at the old Keeper and nodded. "Do it."

With a nod, the Book once again inserted stent into vein; once again opened the valve. Once again Jonathan's blood flowed into a lifeless body, this one dead three days.

Once again the Keeper stepped back, the jar far lighter in his hands than before. This time there were grumblings of protest when Triphon's body gave no sign of life after a full ten seconds.

Rom's heart began to fall.

"Give it more time!" Jordin hissed.

Fifteen seconds passed. Another ten. Roland turned challenging eyes on Rom.

"More time? How long does this blood require to work its magic? An hour? A day? A month? Are we all to die in the waiting?"

Rom opened his mouth to respond, but stopped at gasps from the gathered Mortals. The stares—not at him, but at the step.

Triphon's body had begun to shake. Cries rang out as his torso suddenly arched up from the stone.

Rom leapt down to the step and grabbed Triphon's trembling leg to keep him from rolling down the ancient stair. His friend's mouth snapped wide and he began to scream. The hoarse cry sent those closest below scurrying back—others rushing forward.

And then Triphon's mouth snapped shut and his body collapsed back onto the step. He lay still.

"Is he still dead?" someone asked.

As if in answer, Triphon sat up, eyes wide.

Silence. But Rom's heart was pounding as loudly in his chest as Triphon's surely was in his own.

With a look of bewilderment, his friend turned his head and stared at the crowd. They stared back, aghast.

Triphon dropped his feet to a lower step, stood, and shook his head.

"I've just had the strangest dream."

CHAPTER FORTY-FOUR

THE CELEBRATION OF TRIPHON'S RISING filled the valley with wild cries of jubilation and shouts of wonder, and in good form Triphon, learning what had happened, proceeded to give them all full assurance that he was indeed alive. First with raised fists and cries of victory, then with a clumsy dance on the top step.

Encouraged by laughter and jumping children eager for joy in a world otherwise turned to gloom, he danced again and then again, laughing and shouting with them all.

"I'm alive!" he shouted. "I am *not* dead!"

"He's alive!" the children cried. "Triphon is not dead!"

Rom watched it all, heart bursting with gratitude. Book kept mumbling his approval between shakes of his head, giving way at last to the grin of a man decades younger. Jordin stood to one side, stoic as was her way, her eyes bright. This was, after all, *her* Jonathan's doing. And evidence of his life in Triphon meant only one thing: that Jonathan *lived*, still.

Triphon's rising was the first sign of hope the Mortals had seen in three days, and in the wake of so much heartache, most embraced it with astonishment if also with uncertainty.

What did it mean? Why hadn't Jonathan's blood brought Philip back to life? Clearly, Jonathan had chosen Triphon as a sign of his blood's power.

What was that power? Why had the Mortal sense left those who'd taken Jonathan's resurrected blood?

None of this was lost on the leaders of the Nomads, who watched with open interest at first, some of them shouting along with the children, only to give way to subdued glances as Roland stood his ground.

The prince let them carry on for ten minutes as dozens hurled questions and conjectures without clear answers. Only then did he ascend the first three steps and turn to gather their attention.

Silence settled over the assembled once again. His authority was a thing to behold, Rom thought. Right or wrong, the man had earned his leadership, perhaps more so than he.

"So, we have all seen that Jonathan had great power and for that we will revere him forever. It's a reason to celebrate. He gave us all life, did he not?"

Voices of agreement rippled through the Mortals.

"He gave us emotion and Mortal perception and with it the unequivocal ability to distinguish life from death."

"So it is...," they said.

"And before he died, Jonathan gave us one parting gift to remind us of the power he granted each of us." His arms swept to Triphon, who stood on the top step, still half naked, streaked with dried blood. "Triphon is that gift!"

Cheers rose in thundering accord.

"While he lived, Jonathan demonstrated his power to command the very skies. I believe Triphon is alive because Jonathan kissed his feet and gave him special blessing. Is this not so?"

No one could deny what stood before them.

Roland continued. "But, the blood did not return life to Philip. Nor will it to any others who lay in their graves. I'm eternally grateful to Jonathan, as Triphon will no doubt be. But we cannot assume the power of his blood any longer. Jonathan himself is dead. His blood died before Saric claimed his life. I daresay Rom has less life now than you or I."

Anticipation turned to confusion on the faces of nearly a thousand. Voices mumbled questions and objection, uneager for such hopeless speculation.

Roland walked up the remaining steps to the platform and addressed the assembly as one accustomed to undeniable authority.

"Jonathan birthed in all of us the making of a new race, empowered in ways humans could only have dreamed of before. We will live for centuries. We were *made* to rule this earth. *That* is Jonathan's truest and greatest gift. *That* is his sign."

He glanced at Rom. "Now come three of our own who have climbed from the crypt insisting they, not we, possess life. Let them prove it. We test their blood. If they still have the powers granted to us by Jonathan, we listen. If they don't…each one must make their own choice. But know that I will follow no man back into the grave from which I came."

He reached into his jacket, pulled out a small clear vessel, which Rom immediately recognized as belonging to the Keeper, and held it up between his thumb and forefinger. An ounce or two of amber liquid filled the capsule halfway.

And so Roland's obsession with extended life had

already been at work. He would need alchemy to monitor life among his own kind if they parted ways.

The Keeper's eyes widened. "Where—"

"Is it not true that by dropping only a drop of blood in this elixir of yours, you can estimate by the color it turns how long a man might live?"

"It's no elixir."

"That the darker it turns, the longer the life?"

The Keeper mumbled a response filled with the jargon of alchemy.

"Be plain, old man. Is it true or do I lie?"

The Book hesitated, the set of his mouth grim before he said, "In general terms, however inexact of a science, yes."

"Good."

Without ceremony, Roland pulled out his knife and cut his thumb. He opened the vessel, tossed the cork down the steps, held the amber liquid out for all to see, and squeezed two drops of his blood into the liquid.

The red drops sank to the bottom leaving bloody trails. As they watched, the amber fluid quickly turned dark.

"Black," Roland said, showing the crowd. "The Keeper says we might live as long as a thousand years with the blood in our veins. Here, then, is proof."

Rom heard it all with only a little apprehension. Regardless of this test, knowledge lived in him like a breathing being. Light had blossomed in his mind like a white-hot sun. How he would show that light or to what end, he didn't yet know, but he *knew*.

Yet Roland would have his day. The prince withdrew a second, identical vessel from his jacket, uncorked it, and approached Rom.

"Show us."

Rom stared into the prince's eyes and knew with certainty that the man's mind was set, regardless of the test's outcome. He offered Roland a conciliatory nod and held out his hand for the knife.

Without pause, Rom nicked his own thumb. He squeezed two drops of blood into the vessel.

The blood slowly sank to the bottom. Settled to form a thin layer of red. They waited for the change.

None came. The liquid remained amber except for a thin cloud of red blood that rose from the bottom.

Roland turned to the Keeper. "Does this look like the blood of a Mortal?"

The Keeper's only response was the sudden pallor of his expression.

"No," Roland said. He dropped the vessel on the stone, where it shattered. "I didn't think so. You, old man, will live only a handful of years if you're lucky."

"It means nothing!" Jordin cried.

"No? Then we test each of you."

In short order, Roland produced another vessel and applied the same test to Jordin. Again the liquid refused to darken.

Roland held it up to show them all. "She will live only a natural life span, if that." He summarily dropped the vial and let it break on the stone.

He repeated the exercise with the Book and then with Triphon. Both with the same result.

Last of all, he tested Seriph. This time the amber liquid turned dark.

Roland held up the dark vessel. "Life!" he cried.

"This means nothing!" Jordin snapped. "We are alive! Mortal."

"Perhaps you are." Roland handed the darkened vessel to Seriph and faced the crowd. "But today is a new day."

Roland lifted his voice again.

"Today, I no longer call myself Mortal! Whether Keeper or Nomad, this day I call all who celebrate life and vow to protect it: Immortal!"

The word echoed through the valley.

Immortal.

So. Roland would have his new race.

"All who would follow me, we leave today! We go north, where we will rebuild and claim what is ours. We who are Immortal will inherit the earth, by might and by sword and by any means required!"

He glanced at Rom.

"As for those who would follow these three, I will say what Jonathan himself said before he left us: *Let the dead bury the dead.*"

With that, Roland walked down the steps, strode past the leading edge of the crowd, swung into his saddle, and delivered his final charge for all to hear.

"Chose your destiny today!" he cried. "Immortality..."

He leveled a pointed finger toward Rom.

"...or death!"

CHAPTER FORTY-FIVE

THE FORTRESS SPRAWLED along the edge of the forest, her turrets sunk deep into the earth like the talons of a steel-footed throne.

From here among the twisted pines, one might monitor the hills of Byzantium, the world capital, twenty miles away. Might gaze at the roiling sky and devour its ominous poetry—might shun the diffused light of the sun.

The thin strain of violins filled the master chamber, pumped in through the vents like air. They lingered like shadows in Saric's private chamber, now bared of the gold silks that had recently hung in the corners.

A knock at the door.

"Come."

Corban entered and sank to a knee. A second figure stepped in behind the Master Alchemist and followed suit. A simple Corpse, as they were called.

"My liege." Corban's head was bowed, his long hair unbound over his shoulder.

Behind the ebony desk, Feyn Cerelia, Sovereign of the world, laid down her silver knife beside an unfinished meal. The glow of the tabletop candelabra glinted off the ring of Office on her hand.

So much had changed.

Eighteen. It was the number of days since she had woken to new life at the hands of her Master, Saric.

Seventeen. It was the number of days since she had first realized that love was born of loyalty. Maker to creation. Master to servant. In it, she had found a measure of peace. She was more than a thing reborn. She was a thing perfected.

Eleven. It was the number of days since she'd realized that she was a creature destined for more power than her Maker and succumbed to the demands of her own destiny.

Saric's downfall had been his own arrogance, of course. She, not he, had been made the superior vessel, having been trained for Sovereignty her entire life. She, not he, was the greater ruler, and now mastered the Dark Blood with more power and authority than he ever had.

This was *her* destiny, not Saric's.

Nine. It was the number of days since Saric had disappeared into the wasteland beyond the Seyala Valley, after losing the men she had dispatched to follow him.

"Rise."

Corban stood, stepped aside, and nodded at the leader of the senate, who was trembling with palpable fear.

"Hello, Dominic," Feyn said.

"My Lady," he said, head bowed, eyes fixed somewhere on the lion rug before him.

Feyn pushed the carved chair back and rose. To Corban: "Have you found my brother?"

"No, liege," the alchemist said. "I've dispatched four hundred to search him out, but there is no sign of him."

She slid her gaze along the table, past the glow of the candelabra to the empty glass sarcophagus.

"Keep looking."

Feyn glided around the table, the hem of her red velvet gown trailing along the floor behind her. The beads on her sleeve caught the dim light, throwing fire against the walls.

Behind him, Dominic looked up as though searching for the source of the violins, his eyes stark at what could only be the realization that it was not the staid music of Order, but something far more emotive and ancient.

"By week's end, I want the appropriate traces of my blood in every Dark Blood. Like you, their allegiance will be to me alone."

Corban inclined his head. "And if we find Saric?"

"Then you will kill him on sight and bring his body back to me intact," Feyn said.

"Yes, my liege."

It was only a beginning. She would go much further than Saric had ever dreamed.

She moved toward Dominic, laid a hand along the side of his head, cupped his cheek. Did he tremble?

Yes.

"You will be my firstborn. Soon all the world will follow in your footsteps."

"What is your wish concerning the Mortals?" Corban said.

"We will extinguish them," she said, her attention fixed on Dominic. "We will wipe their names from history."

She smiled then, lowered her hand. "Are you ready, Dominic?"

The senate leader lifted his head and silently nodded.

"Corban," Feyn said.

"Yes?"

"Turn the music off."

CHAPTER FORTY-SIX

THE SEYELA VALLEY LAY under a cloudy sky, the camp and ruins vacated once again. Roland had taken nearly nine hundred self-professed Immortals north, riding high in his saddle, gaze fixed firmly on his destiny. No amount of persuasive words could alter the man's interpretation of the days leading up to Jonathan's death, or his course.

Rom hardly blamed him. Who could argue against the powers of life evidenced in all of those who'd sworn their allegiance to Roland? They possessed acute senses that would facilitate their rise to supremacy over the course of their vastly extended lives. In their eyes, they were nothing less than gods ready to walk the earth.

Even now, as Rom sat upon his horse watching Jordin pay her last respects at Jonathan's grave, he felt a strange draw to the lure of such a life.

But that life was no longer for him.

The forty-five who'd joined Rom, the Keeper, Jordin, and Triphon would be fortunate to live natural life spans before they were returned to the ground. Beyond that, it was really anyone's guess. None of them truly understood

Bliss. But so few statutes of Order made sense any longer—from the code of prescribed behavior abandoned by Rom years ago when he first left Byzantium, to the vengeful Maker such a code was meant to appease.

Jonathan's obsession had been with love, not punishment.

A total of forty-nine true Mortals now inhabited the earth. Sovereigns. Theirs was a meager beginning to a journey none of them understood well. But they understood now—at last—the One who was the cornerstone of their new life. As a result, who they were and what path they might follow had become clearer over the last few days.

They now understood that they were Makers. Most of their number had been made from Rom's, Jordin's, or the Keeper's blood rather than what remained of Jonathan's.

They understood that they had given up much of what Roland's Immortals prized. That Mortals of the Sovereign realm would be misunderstood and despised, a tiny band of vagabonds bent no longer on ruling the world but surviving within it.

They understood the beautiful simplicity that came with certainty, like children who believe long before wrestling with the philosophical or empirical underpinnings of those beliefs. And so they lived with supreme assurance of simple truths. The world was round—why? Because it was. Corpses longed for life—why? Because they did.

Jordin was crying.

He saw it in his mind before tears broke from her eyes. As if it was already happening, though it was not. Not yet.

Rom blinked, taken back by the sudden realization even as Jordin reached out and touched the tall pole she'd erected at the head of Jonathan's grave. The monument was topped with a leather wrap that simply read:

> *Life flowed from his veins;*
> *Love ruled his heart.*
> *Here lies Jonathan,*
> *The first true Sovereign.*

Jordin lowered her head and let her tears flow.

Rom stared at her, astonished by his precognition. He'd known she would cry, not because he'd anticipated the behavior, but because he had *known*.

As much as he knew that she would now say, "I'm so sorry, Jonathan."

"I'm so sorry, Jonathan," Jordin said, shaking her head with remorse.

A chill passed down Rom's neck.

What other powers would they soon discover?

The question brought warmth to his heart despite the display of sorrow before him. Their lives would not be easy. But where there was need in following Jonathan's way, there would surely be means. That, he also knew.

Triphon led the train of Mortals into view on the plateau's southern edge. Kaya was with them, as were Adah and Raner. Only twenty were warriors, the rest aged men and women or children. Would skill with sword and bow be needed? Stripped of their acute Mortal senses, how would they survive?

"Jonathan killed Dark Bloods," Jordin said, setting her jaw without bothering to wipe her tears. "We follow him."

Rom studied her, wondering if her response was coincidence or if she'd spoken with insight into his thoughts.

"With every breath until the day we die," he said.

Jordin touched Jonathan's memorial one last time, eyes lingering on the sign she'd fastened to the top. Then she walked to her horse, swung into the saddle, and drew alongside Rom, facing the approaching caravan. For a moment, neither spoke.

"They will try to snuff us out," she said.

He offered a single nod. "Sovereigns may not live as long, but neither will they die easily."

The grave to their right begged to differ, but they both knew that Jonathan still lived, if not as a Mortal who walked the earth.

"I would have you lead them with me, Jordin. As my equal."

A crow cawed somewhere behind them.

"I'm young," she said.

"You have a pure heart."

"I'm too broken to think clearly."

"You saw the truth before the rest of us."

"How can I lead if I don't know where to go?" she said.

"We go south, to the Carena Valley."

"To do what?"

"To follow Jonathan. Beyond that, none of us knows. Does a colt know what they will do when they first lurch on weak legs still wet from their birthing? You may know before I do. I see in you a great leader."

She offered no more objections.

"Tell me, Jordin. Was Jonathan triumphant in his death?"

"Supremely," she said.

"And is the colt glorious when it becomes a stallion?"

She looked at Triphon and the others, now halfway across the plateau.

"I will be that stallion."

"You will. And with me you will show the world true triumph, as the one Jonathan loved and to whom he entrusted his legacy. We don't know what cost we'll pay yet, only that his life will reign supreme."

"Then let us live," she said, turning her head to face him.

"Then let us live," he said.

Rom hesitated only a moment, nodded once, and nudged his horse forward.

Overhead, the sky had begun to churn.

To be continued...

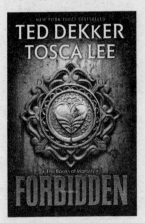

BOOK THREE IN THE BOOKS OF MORTALS SERIES

SOVEREIGN

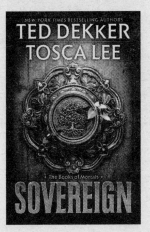

COMING SPRING 2013

TED DEKKER AND TOSCA LEE

ABOUT THE AUTHORS

TED DEKkER is a *New York Times* bestselling author with more than five million books in print. He is known for stories that combine adrenaline-laced plots with incredible confrontations between unforgettable characters. He lives in Austin, Texas, with his wife and children.

TOSCA LEE is the critically acclaimed author of *Demon* and *Havah* and is best known for her humanizing portraits of maligned characters. She makes her home in the Midwest.

VISIT US ONLINE AT

WWW.HACHETTEBOOKGROUP.COM

FEATURES:

**OPENBOOK BROWSE AND
SEARCH EXCERPTS**

•

AUDIOBOOK EXCERPTS AND PODCASTS

•

AUTHOR ARTICLES AND INTERVIEWS

•

**BESTSELLER AND PUBLISHING
GROUP NEWS**

•

SIGN UP FOR E-NEWSLETTERS

•

**AUTHOR APPEARANCES AND TOUR
INFORMATION**

•

SOCIAL MEDIA FEEDS AND WIDGETS

•

DOWNLOAD FREE APPS

BOOKMARK HACHETTE BOOK GROUP
@ WWW.HACHETTEBOOKGROUP.COM